JURY DUTY

JURY DUTY

a novel
by

LAURA
VAN WORMER

CROWN PUBLISHERS, INC.
New York

Copyright © 1995 by Laura Van Wormer

Published by Crown Publishers, Inc., 201 East 50th Street, New York, New York 10022. Member of the Crown Publishing Group.

Random House, Inc. New York, Toronto, London, Sydney, Auckland

CROWN is a trademark of Crown Publishers, Inc.

Manufactured in the U.S.A.

BOOK DESIGN BY DEBORAH KERNER

Library of Congress Cataloging-in-Publication Data

Van Wormer, Laura
Jury duty : a novel / by Laura Van Wormer.
p.   cm.
I. Title.
PS3572.A42285J87   1996
813´.54—dc20   95-22002
                                                                           CIP

ISBN 0-517-70065-4

10 9 8 7 6 5 4 3 2 1

First Edition

For

CAROLYN

and the rest of the jury

ELAINE LUCASH, BRIAN SWORD, JIM MARTIN, NORA LANE,
JEAN JAWOREK, BETTY WILEY, STEPHANIE GODLIS, MAUREEN GRAHAM,
JANE FISHBIN, DARYL H. MILES, MOSES CARDONA, AND KAREN ANDERSON

I

COURTHOUSE

I

A PERSON had to be pretty desperate to *want* to go on jury duty, Libby Winslow decided, but given the state of her life, it seemed like the best game in town.

She moved to stand in front of the full-length mirror. Okay now, what was a juror supposed to look like?

Well, this prospective juror was five foot seven, had hazel eyes and long light-brown hair, streaked with blond. She was wearing beige stirrup pants, brown flats, an Irish knit sweater, a suede jacket, and gold earrings, bracelets, and ring.

Hmmm. She looked more like an escapee from an advertisement in a Condé Nast magazine than a New York City juror. She was just too damn Waspy looking, a minority currently representing something under three percent of the city's population. But what did they expect from a woman from Greatfield, Ohio, where two hundred and fifty years of hot suns and freezing winters had bleached everyone to the colors of the corn, hay, oats, and winter wheat they grew?

Libby grabbed the leather bag she had packed the night before, said good-bye to her cats, and hit the elevators. Her apartment building was only two years old, a vaguely attractive colossus located in what Libby had come to call the Grand Canyon of the Upper East Side. It was a part of town that had a lot of these enormous new residential buildings, which threw great looming shadows during the day and created strange echoes at night. But hey, they had a pool in their building, a gym, a combination garden and sun deck on the roof, and another gorgeous garden below for Libby to look out on from her study window.

"Good morning, Miss Winslow," the morning concierge said. Libby had only asked him a hundred times to call her Libby, which only made him smile as he continued to call her Miss Winslow. "Where are you off to this morning?"

Living in this building was very much like living in a small town, and since Libby was leaving at a time when she was always upstairs writing, this drew attention.

"I've got jury duty."

"Well, he's guilty," he told her.

"What?" the doorman, Mike, asked, coming into the lobby.

"Miss Winslow's going on jury duty."

"Oh," Mike said, nodding. He looked at Libby. "Guilty!" And he slashed a finger across his throat.

Libby laughed, shaking her head, and took the short walk up to the Lexington Avenue subway station. It was rush hour; the subway plat-form was packed. It had been a long time since Libby had faced rush hour, and she let one train pull out without her, but made herself push her way into the crush of people on the next. She had to if she was to get to the courthouse on time. The notice said to be there at nine. And so there she stood, packed into the middle of the car with nothing to hold on to, but unable to fall down anywhere even if she wanted to.

Ah, the intimacy of New York.

"Looking good," a weirdo at her side said in a raspy voice.

That's the point, isn't it? she thought. If she had learned only one thing from her mother, it was how a woman could hide almost anything behind looking good, including heartache, depression, and anxiety.

"Smell good, too," the weirdo rasped.

Libby looked up into the face of a huge man standing in front of her. "I believe he must be talking to you," she said, making people laugh.

William Klein stood up and put on his jacket, eyes running over the desks that surrounded his at Connors, Morganstern. He had been work-ing since five-thirty this Tuesday morning; the trading room had started filling at seven, was packed by eight-fifteen, and now it was twenty min-utes to nine.

"I can't believe you're going to fucking jury duty!" Jerry yelled across the trading desk at him. "Nobody goes to fucking jury duty."

"Well, I'm going," William told him, sliding on his jacket.

Each desk had eight to twelve people, thirty phone lines, twenty-four to thirty monitors, and a squawk box. Multiply that by the nine other trading desks William could see around him, plus the twenty other trading desks elsewhere on this floor, and one had the dizzying view of life at Connors, Morganstern. Even at midnight, when the floor was largely empty and the phones were quiet, traders in Tokyo would be yelling over the squawk boxes.

"Just make sure to hang him," Rick, a trader, instructed.

"They don't hang them anymore," said Sheila, a visitor from high-yield.

"Really?" Rick said, surprised.

William knew better than to say anything, but this he could not let pass. "You don't know that we don't hang people in New York State?"

Rick shrugged. "No wonder it's such a pisshole."

"That's why they all come here," Jerry explained over the noise.

"That's why all *who* comes here?" William said.

"You know who," Jerry said, snapping up the phone. "Connors, Morganstern."

"I didn't know we were allowed to go to jury duty," Analiese, a trainee, said to nobody in particular.

William turned to Rick. "When you voted for Pataki, which I know you must have, you thought he was going to bring back hanging?"

Rick made a face. "Who's says I'm registered to vote, asshole? That's how they get you for jury duty, dumkopf." He paused, squinting at him. "How the hell did you *get* this way, Klein, anyway?"

"Get *what* way?"

Analiese was persistent. "But who said you were allowed to go to jury duty, William?"

"The Constitution of the United States of America. Oh, forget it!" William said in disgust, waving them off. Anything would be better than this.

"Melissa, we *want* you to go on jury duty," the account executive assured her.

"Then let me out of here!" she cried in mock desperation, trying to leave their department meeting. "They're going to put *me* in jail if I don't show up this time."

Everybody laughed, including the division president. "Go!" he instructed. "And God be with you, Melissa Grant, we love this cat food campaign!"

Melissa Grant, twenty-nine, current wunderkind of S. Wiley Kearnan, advertising agency, smiled at the boss and ran down the hall as best she could in a short skirt and high heels.

Hers was a comparatively new office, because Melissa was still comparatively new, here at S. Wiley Kearnan for only four months. The name of the game, it was said, was to keep moving—because the accounts kept moving, too. Gone were the days of long-term client-agency relationships, and Melissa's specialty in life seemed to be maintaining excellent short-term ones. And not just in business.

"Melissa," her secretary, Bonnie, said, "I put a sheet of names and numbers in your briefcase, plus all the backup material on the Norquist account." She cocked her head to the side. "You don't suppose there'd be a VCR you could use there? I seem to remember a VCR at jury duty. Maybe they'd let you run some videos."

"I'll just take the written presentation, thank you," Melissa said, whipping on her coat. "And thanks for getting the phone numbers. I'll get back as soon as I can."

"Car number sixty-three is waiting for you downstairs," Bonnie called.

"Thanks!" Melissa said, running out.

"Melissa!" someone said in the hall.

"Don't even look at me!" she instructed. "I'm late for jury duty."

The City Hall/Brooklyn Bridge station was the last stop on the express line before the train crossed the East River into Brooklyn. Libby piled out with everyone else. Outside, above ground, it was a cool fall day, actually rather lovely. Her jury duty notice said to report to the Supreme Court of the State of New York, 100 Centre Street, Room 1517.

As she approached the building, Libby noticed with satisfaction that this courthouse at least looked like one. The last time, she had been summoned to 111 Centre Street, a tacky, 1960s boxlike structure across the street. This building was much older, built in the 1930s (part of a WPA project, she bet), and had a certain granite panache. It was not nearly as grand as the New York State Supreme Court down the street, the gorgeous old landmark with all the pillars and steps that was always used in TV dramas, but it was nice to feel as though she was serving in a real institution this time.

She followed the signs that directed jurors to the south entrance of the building, skipped up the stairs past the throngs of people milling around on the landing, only to be stopped by a guard just inside the door.

The throngs of people, it turned out, was the line she had to wait in to go through the metal detectors.

She glanced at her watch. Eight fifty-seven. So much for being on time.

Sighing, Libby went back outside, across the landing, down the stairs to the sidewalk and got on the end of the line. After fifteen minutes, she began to wonder if maybe some of the people waiting in line shouldn't be going on trial instead of jury duty. It was a pretty tough-looking bunch.

"Whooz yo pah-role offser?" the man in front of her asked. He had three gold earrings in one ear, a bandanna pulled tightly over his skull, and one of his eyes was swollen shut.

Libby had no trouble understanding him because she had taught in a Cleveland inner-city school for four years right after college.

"Some asshole," his companion replied. He looked relatively normal, except that he only had four upper teeth left in front. It made him look a little like a shark. "Got this fuckin' drug thing, man."

"Hey," the pirate said, "thaz where I'ms goin' at."

"Yo, fuck!" Four-Teeth-Left said, slapping his friend five.

"Please remove everything from your pockets and put the contents in the tray before going through the metal detector," a guard called in the lobby. "Please remove all jewelry, watches included. Yes, sir, tokens, too."

Suddenly there was skirmish on the other side of the metal detectors. "He fuckin' stole my money outta dat thing!" yelled a man (who looked as though he, too, might be going to that same drug class as Pirate and Four-Teeth-Left).

"Don't even try it!" barked a purple-faced man. "I'll mop the god-damn floor with your lying mouth!"

Charming place, this courthouse. And the Manhattan courts, Libby knew, were supposed to be elite compared to the ones in Brooklyn, Queens, or the Bronx. But she still felt a sense of excitement tingling in her spine. She always got this feeling when she was experiencing something new. It was like an internal alarm for a writer: *Something's happening, Lib! There's material here!*

When she reached the long table alongside the metal detector, she handed her briefcase to the guard and took off her earrings, ring, and bracelets and placed them in a gray plastic tray. She dove into the pockets of her jacket and came up with a subway token and a nickel and put those in the container as well. The pirate ahead of her was having a little trouble getting through the metal detector. "Hate to tell ya," the guard said, "but if those studs in your ear are setting this thing off, they aren't real gold." Eventually the pirate was cleared and Libby was waved through the detector.

No alarm. She was fine.

Her briefcase was not, however. Her laptop computer had been handed over to a police officer, who now walked over to yet another table to raise the lid of it and turn it on. He glanced over at Libby and smiled. "Have to make sure it's really a computer." He turned it off and closed the lid again.

"What else could it be?" Libby asked.

He shrugged, smiling still. "We don't like to give anyone ideas." He handed her the computer back, giving her a wink. "Even you."

"Ma'am, you'll have to check these over there," the guard at the first table called to her, holding up the pair of scissors she had brought. Jury duty, she had thought, would be a good time to update her scrapbook. Might as well have a memory book of a career that seemed to be inexplicably going to hell of late.

"I can't bring my scissors?" she asked.

"No, ma'am, not these kind," the guard explained. "You'll have to get the rounded ones. The kind kids use."

"Will you hurry up!" a woman yelled from behind Libby. "We got places to be!"

"Yeah, yeah, keep your shirt on!" the guard yelled back good-naturedly.

Libby's head was spinning with all the strange sights and sounds as she dutifully checked her lethal scissors and got a receipt. Then she moved with a mob into one of the elevator banks. People crowded in around her and she wondered if she should be worrying about tuberculosis.

The elevator stopped on nearly every floor, 3, 4, 5, 7, 8, 9, 11, 12, 14, prompting so many sighs and groans that Libby really was getting nervous about TB. Finally they reached 15 and everybody left piled out. She followed the crowd around the corner to Room 1517, the central jury

room, passing through a cloud of cigarette smoke billowing from another room on the way. She went in through the double doors of 1517
and found herself in an enormous auditorium with at least five hundred
people in seats, waiting.

A nice-looking gray-haired man was calling out names. Libby went up
to him and handed him her jury card, received a juror's packet, and then
made for a raised desk area on the far side of the room. It must have
served as a makeshift judge's bench at one time. Two other women were
up there, papers spread out on the desk area. Libby took the last empty
chair. The clerk continued to call names—including Libby's, now that
he had her card to read her name from—and when he was finished, explained that some jurors were here for the first time today, while others
were in the middle of their jury duty service, and on and on he talked;
Libby started reading *The New York Times.*

The clerk then played a video that he said would explain all about
jury duty. When Libby heard Jane Alexander's voice on the tape, she
didn't even look up; one more jury duty term and she'd know this thing
by heart. About fifteen years ago the chairman of the National Endow-
ment had made this tape for the Justice Department and good ol' Jane
had been talking day in and day out ever since, still looking younger
than springtime.

Once the Jane Alexander video was over, the phone in the jury room
rang. The clerk picked it up and listened, then hung up and announced
that he would be drawing names for a jury panel. He rotated a lottery
bin, stopped it, and started pulling out cards and calling names. People
yelled, "Here!," packed up their belongings, and disappeared through a
door by the clerk's counter. Both women sitting on the old judge's bench
with Libby left for this panel. Libby happily spread her stuff out, thinking she had more space here to spread out on than she did at home in
her study.

William Seymour Klein had no sooner sat down in the central jury room
than he was called for a jury panel. William gathered up his things and
moved to the room across the hall, glad to be doing something—anything, frankly—where no one could get at him for a while.

Between work and Betsy, he thought he might have a nervous breakdown. At least with work, though, he made a hell of a lot of money to
compensate for anything he didn't like about Connors, Morganstern.

That, however, didn't mean he wanted to spend all of that money on Betsy—she who had moved in temporarily and never left! Fourteen months it had been now. And had he said anything? No, of course not, because he didn't know what to say. "Listen, you conniver," he could imagine himself saying, "I know we started off great, but dating for two months is no grounds for moving in!"

Granted, in her defense, Betsy was very pretty, used to be sexually available at all times, was a knockout cook, and had reorganized and redecorated his two-bedroom apartment on Gramercy Park so that it finally looked like a home. The fact remained, however, that they had been dating for only two months when Betsy had to leave her roommate's apartment and move into her own place, and asked if she couldn't stay at William's for the week he would be away at a conference in London. When he came home, she was still there, planning to leave in just a day or two, but then they had sex that night and somehow her apartment never came up again and she simply never left.

It was when he got the bills for the furniture she had bought for the living room that he first panicked, about a year ago. But when he said to her that she should at least talk to him about things like that before she went ahead and bought them, she interrupted and said, "But William, you won't ever talk about furniture! You know you won't. It's just easier if I do it for you."

"And give me the bills to pay," he couldn't help adding.

"You have *tons* of money!" she said. "And you always give away so much of it, you might as well spend a little making a home for yourself."

"Okay, ladies and gentlemen," a court officer announced, snapping William back into the present, "follow me, I'm taking you to court. Please make sure to bring all your belongings." William and the others stood up, ready to follow.

When Libby reached the book page of the *Times*, she felt depression starting to pull at her again. A little over a year ago she had been on top of the world, living with Hal and looking forward to the publication of her third novel. Then came her explosive breakup with Hal, which had not only been incredibly painful but had become an enormously expensive undertaking when it came to breaking up their household. Then when her novel came out, things started out well, but then—nothing. Sales not only ground to a halt, but unsold books were now starting to return to the publisher in droves from bookstores around the country—and no one seemed to know why.

And *then*, as if to make sure to finish her off once and for all, a few days after her publisher had announced she was going to appear on "The Oprah Winfrey Show" (this was often a miracle for authors and publishers alike, because an appearance with Oprah could sell tens of thousands of books virtually overnight), Barbie, her book publicist, called to say, "I'm so sorry, Libby, but 'Oprah' is definitely off. The New Age thing didn't work."

"*New Age?*" Libby had asked, confused. There was nothing New Age about her novels that she knew of, except that they took place in present-day settings.

"It was the only angle I could come up with," Barbie explained. "Anyway, they didn't get the New Age handle, either. I guess they must have read it."

Becoming a novelist was the most wonderful thing that had ever happened to Libby, but now that things were not going well, she realized it could end up being the cruelest thing as well. She had a book that bookstores were returning to the publisher's warehouse, and an agent she could strangle, mainly because last year he had begged her to turn down Haverhill's initial offer on her next book, explaining that after *When Smiles Meet* was a hit they would pay a lot more. And so, going against her conservative instincts about money (i.e., nothing beat cash in the bank), Libby had essentially agreed to go a year without income, and now that she needed a new contract and an advance, Haverhill had withdrawn its offer, wanting to "wait and see."

Libby had always known the Oprah Winfrey thing was too good to be true. She just wasn't the type miracles happened to. She was, however, the type who was accustomed to years of hard work paying off. And therein lay her heartache.

"I'm so sorry I'm late!" Melissa Grant puffed at 10:33 A.M., exactly one hour and thirty-three minutes late, extending her jury card to the gray-haired clerk. "I got here as soon as humanly possible."

"Gee, I never heard that before," the clerk joked. "Okay, fill out your name and address on the card first—here. And who knows? You may get lucky. We're going to be calling another jury pool in about five minutes."

Melissa filled out her card and took a seat. Five minutes later she was indeed "lucky" and was called for the next jury pool. She looked at the clerk out of the corner of her eye as she passed by. He held up his hands in defense and said, "It was the luck of the draw, I swear!"

As Melissa walked across the hall, she wondered what she would do if she was actually picked for a jury. She had this cat food campaign to execute, the Norquist account to finish, and her boss wanted a brainstorm to lure some AT&T business their way. She hadn't had a decent night's sleep in weeks or a date in months, so when she was not completely stressed out, she only felt desperately lonely. And so she would work harder. Jury duty, in other words, could be a mildly dangerous thing if she had to stay long. It could give her time to think.

Libby had never won a contest, a door prize, or a lottery in her life, so why she thought she might get picked for a jury panel was beyond her. About three-quarters of the people in the big room seemed to have been chosen, and Libby was left to herself high atop the old judge's bench on the far side of the room. The clerk retired to his office somewhere down the hall, and before Libby quite realized what was happening, all late-comers to the jury room were making a beeline to her, assuming that *she* was the person in charge.

"My grandfather speak no English," a young Chinese boy said to her, thrusting a jury summons at her. Behind him stood an ancient old man, stooped over a cane, encouraging his grandson in a series of small wails.

"I'm sorry," Libby said, "I don't work for the courts. The clerk is around the corner in his office."

"What? Who?" the boy said, looking confused.

"I couldn't help it!" a woman cried, dashing across the room and flinging her jury duty notice at Libby. "I'm in a divorce proceeding and I was too upset to come."

"Hey! Get in line!" someone cried.

Libby looked around for assistance. Someone started shouting at her in Spanish, another in God only knew what language, and everybody was clearly scared and upset about having to have anything to do with jury duty. She tried putting on her blue-and-white badge from the packet that said NEW YORK JUROR on it, but all that did was provoke gales of laughter from jurors around the room.

A handsome man in a flannel shirt and blue jeans called to Libby, "Tell them whatever they want costs one hundred dollars up front—in cash."

More gales of laughter. Feeling increasingly sympathetic toward this panicked little crowd in front of her, Libby got up, threw her shoulders back, and stepped down from the judge's bench. "Come this way," she said to them authoritatively, and she led the whole crew through the doorway and down a hall to the door that said CLERK'S OFFICE. She knocked and poked her head in. "Excuse me."

The clerks were sipping coffee, pouring over computer printouts, writing lists, and making phone calls.

"Yeah?" the gray-haired one called.

"I've got some people here to see you," she said.

"Who are you?"

"An upstanding citizen," she said, stepping forward to open the door all the way and wave the group in. "Talk to him. Over there. That's right, big boss. Yes, he in charge, el Presidente. You're welcome. Bye-bye."

When Libby returned to the jury room, she received scattered applause. She smiled, returned to the judge's bench to gather up her things, and moved down into a normal seat. A moment later, a shadow fell across her paper and she looked up.

It was the man who had suggested she charge one hundred dollars. Boy, he was good-looking. Brown hair, nicely cut, twinkling blue eyes, a charismatic, weathered, outdoorsy face—late thirties, maybe forty— nice teeth in a nice smile. Like the Marlboro Man. "I'm going downstairs to the cafeteria to get a cup of coffee," he said. "May I bring you one?"

Libby smiled. "I don't think we're supposed to eat or drink anything in here."

"We can outside," he said. "In the hall."

"Well, okay," she said, reaching for money in her bag. "It's really awfully nice of you."

"No, let me," he said, covering her hand to stop her from bringing out money. His touch was gentle; his hand large, fingernails clean and neat. Left hand and no wedding band. "It's the least I can do for all your hard work this morning."

She watched him walk across the jury room to the exit, noticing that several other women and one or two men did as well. His flannel shirt was L.L. Bean or something similar, his blue jeans were standard Levi's, and his boots were dark Timberlands. It was an outfit that would work well back in Greatfield.

A few minutes later, another shadow fell across Libby's newspaper.

"Excuse me," a woman said. She was black, in her twenties, nice-looking, rather chic. Libby wished she could get away with wearing a colorful outfit like this woman had on and not feel too conspicuous. "I hate to bother you," the woman said, "but are you related to Elizabeth Winslow, the writer? I heard the clerk call you Cornelia Winslow, but—" She held up a battered paperback copy of Libby's first book, and opened it to the back inside cover. There was a picture of Libby, overly made-up, looking a kazillion years old instead of the mere twenty-eight she had been at the time.

Libby had to laugh, pleased. It didn't happen often, but when she was recognized there was no feeling like it. "Cornelia was my grandmother's name and I was named after her," she explained. "Elizabeth's my middle name. For obvious reasons, I guess, my publisher preferred I use Elizabeth. But you can call me Libby."

"So you are her—she," the woman said, excited. "Would you—?" She held the book out to her. "It's my mom's copy. She loaned it to me, said I'd love it. And I do—and here you are!"

Libby signed the inside cover of the book, writing something nice, while the woman, whose name was Celia, told her how much she liked her writing. "It must be so wonderful to be a writer!" she exclaimed when Libby handed the book back to her.

"Well, that's what we like people to think," Libby said. "No, you're right," she added quickly with a smile. "I've been very, very fortunate. I love writing."

Celia went away then, and Libby returned her attention to her newspaper. She wasn't reading it, though, she was thinking.

If ever there was a time she needed something to happen in her life, it was now. But what the hell could happen to her while hiding out on jury duty?

2

PSSST, HEY. I've got our coffee. Let's go outside."

Libby looked up. The Marlboro Man was back with the coffee.

Just then the jury room phone started ringing and the gray-haired clerk came running in.

"Another panel," the Marlboro Man groaned, and he sat down next to Libby, holding the brown paper bag in his hands.

"Okay, jurors, listen up!" the clerk called in the microphone as he started rotating the lottery bin. "We need another panel. When you hear your name, call 'Here!' loud enough so I can hear it, and move to the room on the other side of the hall. Make sure you take all your belongings because you will not be coming back. Okay, Rafael Ramirez!"

"Here!" cried a man, jumping up.

"Myriah Goldberg!"

"Here," a woman said not very enthusiastically.

"Myriah Goldberg!" the clerk called again.

"HERE!" screamed the woman. People laughed.

"Cor—" The clerk squinted at the card. "Cornelia Winslow!"

"Here!" she said.

The Marlboro Man looked at Libby with a forlorn smile. "Well, I guess I get two cups of coffee. Unless I get called, too."

No such luck. Libby waited until the clerk had finished calling names. The Marlboro Man's was evidently not among them. "I'm really sorry you have to go," he told her as she gathered up her things and stood up. "For all of ten minutes I was going to like being on jury duty."

"Me, too," she told him. "Bye."

Libby followed the other people into a waiting room. In a few minutes the group was led down the hall to wait outside a courtroom on the same floor.

"I don't care if I have to say I'm a mass murderer," one woman declared, "I'm not letting them put me on another goddamn jury!"

Libby looked at her.

"Five times!" she told Libby. "Five times I've been on a jury! It's like they see *juror* written all over my face."

The officer of the court told them they could go in. The courtroom was not overly large. The judge sat up front; IN GOD WE TRUST was on the wall behind him. There was the jury box, the prosecution and defense tables, a court stenographer, and a gate that separated them from the gallery, where the jurors now found places to sit.

The judge asked them to rise and raise their right hand. He swore them to something—what, Libby wasn't sure; she wasn't paying attention because she had spotted the stooped-over old Chinese man with his young grandson. Now, how were they going to use him on a jury? she wondered. Not a word of English.

Oh, this was ridiculous. Why didn't they let the poor old man go home?

When they sat down again, the judge announced that this was a rape case.

Libby looked at the defendant. Although rather clean-cut, he was still creepy-looking. He was a scowling, dark-skinned man with a scar running from behind his ear all the way down to his chin.

The juror cards were put into a lottery bin again and one of the officers of the court began selecting cards and calling names. Libby was called, and she filed up to the jury box and sat in chair #9, in the second row, feeling unexpectedly nervous. She tried not to look at the defendant and tried not to be irritated by the defendant's interpreter, who rattled off a Spanish translation after anyone said anything. While she believed in the American judicial system with all her heart, she also believed she might well go crazy if she had to sit on a trial with this screaming translator.

"Mr. Clark is number eleven?" the prosecutor asked the court officer while writing something down on a legal pad.

"*Es Señor Clark numero once?*" the interpreter shouted at her client.

"Yes," the officer said.

"*Si!*" the translator shouted.

The judge wanted to ask the prospective jurors some general questions that could save some time. What did they do for a living? One by one, they answered. When they got to Libby, the interpreter announced with great flair to her client, "*Novelista!*"

In what part of Manhattan did they live? Did they know any policemen or attorneys? How many of them were married? (A show of hands.) Had any of them been the victim of a crime? (A show of hands.)

And then the defense attorney got up to ask them some questions. She was a woman—wise move, Libby thought, a woman defending a rapist—who clattered over to the jury box in very high heels. She wanted to make sure, she told them, that her defendant got a fair trial. This was the United States of America, she said, where a defendant did not have to prove his innocence. Under the eyes of the law he *was* innocent. It was only if the prosecutor could prove his case beyond a reasonable doubt that her defendant could be considered guilty.

She began with the juror in seat #1, asking about earlier answers given to the judge, or about other things, slowly making her way across the jury box. One guy, when asked whether he thought he could be a fair and impartial juror, clutched his head and started to wail that he had REAL PROBLEMS, HEAD problems, he couldn't THINK, he couldn't LIVE! ("Thank you," the lawyer said politely, moving on.) Another admitted that her brother was a criminal lawyer in Virginia. The next woman, the one Libby had met out in the hall, wanted to know how the hell could anyone be an impartial juror if they had already served on five goddamn juries?

The judge interrupted to announce that profanity was not allowed in his courtroom.

Another prospective juror swore he only spoke Turkish, but since he said this in English, Libby thought he was pushing his luck. Evidently the judge did, too, since he then announced there was a penalty for lying during jury selection.

"Well, I speak some English, but not goodly," the juror admitted.

On and on the questions went, time starting to drag, the interpreter all the while half-screaming translations in Spanish at the horrible-looking defendant.

Finally the defense attorney reached Libby.

"Miss Winslow," she said, looking down at her pad to review her notes, "you write novels."

"Yes."

"What kind of novels—novels about crime, murder, rape?"

"No. They're contemporary. Sometimes there is white-collar crime, but that's it."

"Generally do they have happy endings?"

Libby nodded. "Yes."

"You also raised your hand when asked if you had ever been the victim of a crime."

"Yes," Libby said.

"What was your experience?"

"My car got broken into a couple of times, and then—well . . ." She hesitated. "Well, I don't know if you could call this a crime, although the police were involved."

"What happened?"

Everyone's ears had perked up now and Libby felt like an idiot. But she was under oath. "Well, um, my ex-boyfriend stole my cat."

The laughter was spontaneous.

The interpreter shrieked this translation with glee.

"I see," the defense attorney said, trying not to laugh. "Did you get it back?"

"Yes. The police got it for me. Him. The cat, I mean."

"And did you press charges?" At this, the lawyer tried valiantly to suppress a laugh, but was not altogether successful.

"No," Libby said, smiling.

The defense attorney met Libby's eye, as if searching for something hidden in her. Then suddenly she smiled and nodded. "Very good, Miss Winslow, thank you," and she moved on.

If the defense attorney liked Libby, the male prosecutor hated her. "Miss Winslow," he bellowed when he got to her, "you are a novelist by profession!"

(*"Eres una novelista professional!"* screeched the interpreter.)

"Yes." Libby's hands were instantly clammy. Everybody was looking at her now as though she were the defendant.

"Your job is to create a false reality that seems real to the reader, is that correct?"

Libby couldn't help but smile. "I'm just a writer, not a witch."

Everybody laughed again.

The prosecutor glared at her. "Miss Winslow, do you have any idea of the seriousness of the crime in this case?"

"Yes," she said, meaning it.

Silence throughout the courtroom.

"And so we are to assume that despite your full-time occupation of making up stories, that you can listen to the facts in this case, and consider the facts, and only the facts, and refrain from making up a story of your own about what you guess really happened?"

"I'm not going to make up what happened," Libby said. "But I would weigh the plausibility of the facts presented. That's one skill a novelist has that would probably make for a pretty good juror." She looked at the judge for a sign of support.

The interpreter was shouting all this at her client in Spanish.

The judge was looking a little distressed. "Miss Batista," he murmured to the translator, "could you please lower your voice just a little?"

"Señorita Batista—" the interpreter started to tell her client. Then she covered her mouth and said, a little less loudly, "Yes, Your Honor."

"Thank you." The judge turned back to the prosecutor. "You may continue, Mr. Roscoe."

"Miss Winslow, isn't it true that your full-time occupation is to blur the line between fantasy and reality?"

"Mr. Roscoe," the judge sighed. "Since Miss Winslow herself is not on trial here, and since she does not appear to be a raving lunatic—"

Laughter erupted yet again.

"—you will please confine your inquiry to her ability to serve as a juror."

"Yes, Your Honor," the prosecutor said.

When the prosecutor finished his questioning and the lawyers conferred with the judge, they announced which jurors could leave and which had been chosen to serve on this case. Hardly surprised, Libby learned she had not been chosen. Actually, only two of the twelve were selected, one of whom bitterly hissed as Libby stepped down out of the box, "My *sixth* goddamn jury. Can you believe it?"

William had been sitting in the courtroom gallery for over two hours now, listening as lawyers interviewed what seemed like every prospective juror in town except him. It was a drug case. Another panel of jurors were brought in and jammed into the gallery. Behind William a woman started making a hell of a racket with her newspaper. Finally a guard sauntered over and whispered, "You will stop making noise with that newspaper or I will take it from you."

The woman scowled and literally threw the newspaper down on the floor, making William turn around. She made a face at him. She was about fifty years old, overly made-up, had a scarf wrapped around her head, and was wearing Lina Wertmuller glasses. When William turned back around, he heard the woman let out an exaggerated sigh. And then there were bumping noises. He turned around again. The woman was trying to lie sideways over the bench to take a nap, but couldn't do it because of the seat dividers, and so was beating the divider with the heel of her boot. The guard came back.

"If you do not sit up and behave, the judge will cite you for contempt of court."

The Lina-Wertmuller-Glasses Lady made a slightly obscene noise, but did start to behave. She was also called for the next jury panel. When the defense attorney asked her what she did for a living, she straightened her glasses and said, "Soycial soyvices counseleh for the City of New Yawk."

William blurted, "Of course!" and everyone burst out laughing.

A few minutes later, the lawyers approached the bench to discuss something with the judge in hushed whispers. When they were done, the judge announced that the defendant had changed his mind about going to trial and was pleading guilty, and so all the jurors were dismissed and could return to the central jury room.

"Melissa Grant!" the officer of the court read off the card from the lottery bin.

Melissa dutifully rose from the bench in the gallery, picked up her briefcase and coat, and made her way up to the jury box. In a few minutes the box had been filled and the questioning by the defense attorney had begun. It was a stabbing case.

"And what kind of work do you do, Ms. Grant?"

"Advertising—I'm a creative director."

"And you work at?"

"S. Wiley Kearnan on Seventh Avenue," she said. She felt inexplicably nervous, as if they were going to catch her at something.

The defense attorney cocked his head. "Is that a trace of a Southern accent I hear?"

"Well, Southern California," Melissa told him.

People laughed.

"How long have you lived in Manhattan?"

"Almost two years."

"And how long have you worked at the ad agency?"

"This one, about four months. I worked at another agency before that."

"And where did you go to school?"

"UCLA." Pause. "University of California at Los Angeles."

"Now, Ms. Grant," the lawyer said, "when the judge asked how many of you had ever been the victim of a crime, you raised your hand."

"Yes."

"What kind of crime was that?"

"I was robbed," Melissa answered.

"Could you tell us about it?"

"Well, I was here in New York—before I moved here—and I was staying in a hotel. One afternoon the doorman was in the street trying to flag a cab for me, and a man came up to me with a knife. He wanted my purse. I gave it to him."

"He threatened you with a knife?"

"Yes. A switchblade."

"And you gave him the bag?"

"Yes."

"And did you call the police?"

"Yes."

"And did they catch the thief?"

"No."

"Did you get your bag back?"

"No."

They might as well have dismissed her as soon as she mentioned the knife, but they went through the whole charade of both sides thoroughly questioning Melissa, as if the defense would ever let her sit on the jury.

Still, when she was excused, Melissa was relieved.

Everyone in the central jury room was excused for lunch until two. Libby left the courthouse and spent most of the time wandering around Mott Street, wondering where the heck she was. She had no sense of direction, and certainly not here where on one block was a courthouse, the next Chinatown, and the next Little Italy. She got a bite to eat, found the courthouse again, went through the metal detector, and returned to the central jury room to settle in and read a book.

"Hi," a deep voice said minutes later.

She looked up. It was the Marlboro Man.

"Do you mind if I sit?" he asked.

"No, not at all," she said, moving her stuff to make room for him. It was nice to have a rapport with someone in this dismal place.

"So they didn't pick you for a jury?" he asked her.

"Hardly," she said, rolling her eyes. "When I told them I was a novelist, the prosecutor tried to prove I couldn't tell the difference between fantasy and reality."

He smiled, eyes crinkling at the corners. "Can you?"

"Well, sometimes." She smiled.

"So what does a novelist do all day?" he asked her. "I mean, do you just sit there?"

"A lot of the time. The first six months of a book I'm usually doing research at the library, though, talking to people, traveling, things like that, making notes, gathering materials, and then, when I start writing,

I'm afraid that is pretty much what I do—just sit in my study and write and rewrite and rewrite for months until I get it right."

"You must get very lonely," he said.

"When I finish a book, yes," she acknowledged. "It's like coming to after months of living in a dream world."

His eyebrows went up. "Did you just finish a book?"

She felt a vague chill. A perfect stranger could sense her loneliness and vulnerability, two things she had vowed her entire life never to show—and almost never did. And yet this man could smell it.

"No," she said, a little more sharply than she had intended. "In fact, I'm in the middle of one." She smiled slightly. "I'm afraid it's not going very well. In fact, I'm thinking maybe I should just toss it and start all over again." She wasn't exaggerating. The novel was taking on all the anger, bitterness, and futility about life she had been feeling since breaking up with Hal.

The jury room phone rang and the clerk came out. "Ladies and gentlemen," he said into the microphone, "we have a very large panel to call right now."

Groans around the jury room.

"If I call your name, please answer back, take all your belongings, and go into the room directly across the hall."

About the tenth name called was Alexander McCalley. "Here!" the Marlboro Man said, getting up. He turned to look down at Libby and gave a sad smile. "This is the kind of luck I really don't want to have right now. Look, my name's Alex."

"Libby," she said, shaking his hand.

"Well, Libby, see you." And he was gone. And then he was back. "I thought your name was Cornelia."

William was positive the woman across the aisle from him in the jury room was Elizabeth Winslow, the writer. He knew it because one of her books had been sitting facedown on the shelf of Betsy's night table for about three months and he had once actually picked it up to see who the pretty woman was on the back.

And now here she was. He wondered how he could approach her. "Excuse me," he imagined saying, "but every time I have sex with my girlfriend, I see your face looking up at me from the back cover of one of your books."

She got up at one point, stretched, and walked out into the hall. For a writer she certainly had nice legs and a terrific derriere, he thought. Didn't writers have to sit all the time? He got up quickly, fumbling in his briefcase for his address book, and went out to the hall. With any luck she'd be using the only pay phone there and he would have to wait around to use it.

No such luck. She wasn't at the phone. He came back down the hall and saw her approaching the jury room from the other direction. She was almost as tall as he was. But she had on heels. So she was about five-seven, he guessed, to his five-eight-and-a-half.

They hit the jury room doors at the same time. He smiled and quickly reached to open the door for her, but someone on the inside pushed out first and the door smashed into his hand. "Ow!"

Whoever it was on the other side tried again and really gave the door a shove, and this time the door slammed him in the shoulder. He felt Elizabeth Winslow's hand on his arm, pulling him back out of harm's way. "Careful," she said, and then she was gone, past him, into the jury room.

Great move, Klein. Nice going.

At four-thirty, the clerk announced that they were all dismissed for the day and were to report back by nine-thirty the next morning for roll call.

William considered saying something to Elizabeth Winslow, but when she breezed past him, a slight frown on her face, he decided against it.

Time to go back to the office, anyway.

"Mom!" Peter, her ten-year-old, yelled from the kitchen. "It's for you!"

"All right, sweetie, you don't have to scream," Jill said from the laundry room. "Katie," she said to her seven-year-old, "when all the clothes are in, lower the lid and push the button." She went into the kitchen, pushing the hair off her forehead with the back of her wrist. "Petey, help your sister." She picked up the phone. "Hello?"

"Mrs. Tompkins?"

"Yes."

"It's Kathryn Schnagel, Mrs. Tompkins, from the DA's office."

Jill's heart sped up. "Yes, Kathryn."

"Mr. MacDonald asked me to call and tell you that jury selection for the trial will be starting tomorrow, and that the trial might begin as soon as Monday." Pause. "As you know, we'll be counting on you."

Already? It was here already? After all these months? After all the delays? "Yes, I'll be there," Jill said. "I just have to see about a baby-sitter."

"Mr. MacDonald also wanted me to remind you how very important it is for you to be present at as much of the trial as possible."

"Yes, yes, I know. As I said, I just have to see about the baby-sitter."

When Jill got off the phone, she stood there a moment. She could see Katie and Peter wrestling over the clothes in the laundry room; she could hear them arguing; she was also having a very hard time breathing. As if she had forgotten how. It was a horrible, hollow feeling.

"Mommy!" Katie wailed. "He stole my underpants!"

"Give them back, Peter," Jill said automatically.

"Ooh, with little frills!" Peter teased, putting them on his head like a hat.

Katie screamed at the top of her lungs.

Monday. Monday she would have to go to New York. Monday she would have to deal with Sissy's murder all over again.

3

LIBBY awakened Wednesday morning before her alarm went off because Sneakers, her young cat, was on her neck, and Missy Mouse, her old cat, was on a burrowing mission beneath the sheets. It was chilly this morning and Libby had opened windows all over the apartment, except those in her bedroom, because the noise from the street would have kept her awake all night.

Well, clearly she had opened too many. It was freezing!

She got up, closed the windows, turned on the radiators, turned on the humidifiers ("Ooh-la-la, kitty climate control," she told the cats), and jumped into the shower.

Ahhh. This was one of the major reasons she had moved into a new building. Unlimited hot water in the morning. And water pressure.

Sneakers, a black cat who got his name from having white feet, got in between the shower curtain and the liner and started swatting at Libby through the plastic, while Missy Mouse, a rather severely overweight tiger, plucked something out of Libby's makeup basket by the sink, dropped it on the floor, and started playing hockey.

This cat thing, Libby just didn't know. When she moved into this apartment, it had just seemed so empty. And lonely. And so Libby had wandered over to the ASPCA to see about getting a small dog. As she entered the ASPCA, however, the cat room had been first, and volunteers had just wheeled a cage of new kittens into the room, drawing a crowd and heartfelt ooh's and ahhh's. Libby thought she'd just peek at them—they were adorable little gray pieces of fluff, weighing all of an ounce or two—when she heard a stifled sob. Turning around, she saw an elderly woman, dressed in a volunteer's jacket, weeping quietly into a tissue.

"Are you all right?" Libby murmured, going over to her. "Can I help?"

The woman took a deep breath and held it, chin trembling. "Not unless you can save that poor cat up there."

Up there was Missy Mouse, on the top row of cages, first on the left. She was very fat, no doubt about it. And seemed to be very pleased about it, too.

"Her owner died and the family brought her in," the volunteer said, "but no one wants her. They see the kittens and it's all over."

"Oh, surely some family would want a grown cat," Libby said. "With small children and all."

"But not this one," the volunteer said, weeping again. "They're putting her to sleep tomorrow."

And so Missy Mouse had come home with her to live.

Then, in September, Libby had been out in the Hamptons when a hurricane came blowing through. Sitting in front of the fireplace of her rented cottage, reading by candlelight, she had heard this wretched sound—like a sickly baby or something. It turned out to be Sneakers, a torn-up, emaciated, black soaking little thing, huddled against the back door. At this point Libby knew enough about cats to know he might have rabies or cat leukemia, and so she locked him in the bathroom, where, after choking down food and milk, he collapsed on a warm bed of old towels.

In the morning, after the storm, Libby brought him to the animal shelter, but they couldn't take him because hundreds of animals had gotten lost in the storm. She then took him to a vet, where she received a checklist about what, according to the preliminary exam, was wrong with him: He was malnourished; had infected bites and cuts; had worms; had fleas; needed to be fix; and needed a battery of shots and antibiotics and medical care for about ten days.

"We take American Express," the receptionist said brightly.

What else could Libby do but pay up?

"What's his name?" the receptionist asked, filling out the forms.

"I don't know," Libby said, "he's a stray."

Stray, the receptionist wrote on the form.

Libby felt a twinge in her heart. "Oh, come on, you can't call the poor thing Stray."

"You'll have to name him, then," the receptionist said, twiddling her pen.

"Well . . . Sneakers, I guess, because of his white feet."

"Sneakers!" she said happily, writing it in.

The vet poked her head around the corner, smiling, holding Sneakers in her arms. "Now that you've named him, I'm afraid he thinks he belongs to you."

The little cat was looking at Libby, purring.

And so Sneakers came back to New York, where he drove Missy Mouse crazy, regularly pulled over the ficus tree, climbed between the shower curtain and liner, and, when he could, took the elevator to parts unknown in the building.

At any rate, it was time for the woman with cats to report to her second day of jury duty.

No doubt about it, the novelty had definitely worn off. Libby felt inexplicably fatigued sitting around in the central jury room today. She remembered this feeling well from her days trying to teach at Logan High School in Cleveland. There was the same lack of fresh air; the same institutional paint; the same lousy lighting; even the same awful plumbing. Someone had flushed one of the johns in the ladies' room adjoining the jury room two hours ago, and it was *still* flushing, making it sound as though they were sitting around the launching pad of the space shuttle. Even a walk was out of the question since the gray-haired clerk had announced, "Don't go far or get too comfortable this morning, because we've got some very big panels being called today."

At around ten-thirty Alex McCalley came bounding into the central jury room and looked around. When he saw Libby, his eyes lit up and he waved. He went up to the desk to talk to the clerk and hand him his jury card, then came over to Libby to sit down. "They finally finished jury selection on the case we were on," he explained. "God, I'm so glad you're here. I was hoping you would be."

Libby smiled. "What kind of case was it?"

"A slashing," he answered. "Look, before anything else happens—"

"Jurors, hello!" the clerk called over the microphone. "Settle down, please, we've got two very large panels to call. If you're talking, you won't be able to hear your name." He looked at them. "SO BE QUIET." He smiled and then proceeded to draw names for the first panel.

"This place sure is jumping," Alex whispered. "People told me I should have come when I was called in August because all the judges are on vacation then."

"Cornelia Winslow!" the clerk called.

"Here!" Libby said, raising her hand.

Alex's head swung around. "Oh, no! I can't lose you now!"

She burst out laughing. She waited and, sure enough, about fifteen names later, the clerk called, "Alexander McCalley!"

They gathered up their belongings, went together to the waiting room across the hall, and sat down. "So far so good," Alex said.

Their panel ended up being a massive group of sixty, which, someone whispered, meant it had to be a murder case. It took a big panel to find a jury both sides could agree on. The group was led up the EMERGENCY ONLY staircase to the sixteenth floor and then forced to wait in the drab hallway for an hour. Libby and Alex chatted for a while—he was not married; he was from upstate New York; he restored brownstones for a living; he was thirty-six—and then he went down the hall to make a call at the pay phone. Libby pulled out a book to read and a young guy in a pinstripe suit sidled near her, smiling, pushing his glasses higher on his nose, and said, "Annoying, isn't it? How they hurry us up only to make us wait?"

Libby glanced up and smiled.

"Remember me?" he said. "The one you rescued from the jury room door yesterday?"

Libby hesitated and then decided to tell the truth. "No, I'm sorry, I don't." He looked so disappointed she said, "Well, maybe I do. Refresh my memory."

As he talked, Libby looked him over—an immaculate Wall Streeter, it seemed. Blue pinstripe suit, quiet red-and-blue tie, black tasseled loafers. "Oh," she said, looking at his shoes again, "did you have on black tie Oxfords yesterday?"

"Uh, yeah."

"I remember now," Libby said. "I just didn't see you—I saw your shoes."

He looked a little confused at this response, but smiled slightly and moved away.

Shortly after Alex returned, the guard announced that they could enter the courtroom. Libby assumed this was a higher court, since it was very large and had windows. Although it was rather chilly outside, the windows were open and a fan was going. The sixty of them piled into the gallery with all their belongings. The judge was a very attractive black woman, in her fifties or so, with a commanding presence. The prosecutor was a white man, his assistant a white woman, the three defense attorneys were white, and surprise, surprise, the defendant was white. And young. In his forties, Libby thought. And rather good-looking.

"Oh, my God, Alex," Libby suddenly gasped, "isn't that 'the poor little rich boy'?"

Libby was not alone in thinking she recognized the defendant; everyone in the gallery was whispering now, too. It had been a famous case at the time, maybe two years or so before.

"Yep," Alex confirmed, "that's him."

That is *he*, Libby instinctively corrected in her head.

Alex gave a low whistle. "This is going to be some trial." He looked at her. "And we stand a very good chance of being chosen for the jury."

"We do?"

"He's entitled to a jury of his peers," Alex reminded her. He nodded to the people around them in the gallery. "Look at what they have to choose from."

Libby looked around. There were an awful lot of older people, and there was a tremendous spectrum of ethnicity.

But her, a juror on a murder case? No, they'd never pick her. She read the newspapers every day and lawyers thought she couldn't tell the difference between fantasy and reality.

Judge Williams made some introductory remarks about the trial and then introduced the people who would be involved:

The defendant was James Bennett Layton, Jr., who stood up and turned toward the gallery. He looked to be in his early forties, and had blond hair, blue eyes, a few early creases in his forehead and around his eyes.

Mr. Layton's lead defense lawyer was then introduced, Arnold N. Geiggen. He stood and turned to the crowd. He was pushing sixty and was very short, which surprised Libby because when she had seen him on TV (he was a star defense lawyer in these parts), he looked a lot taller. He had two assisting attorneys, George Kennett and Carole Feiner.

The assistant district attorney prosecuting the case for the People of New York was Kevin MacDonald, who also stood and turned to the crowd. He was about six foot two and, like the defendant, fairly young, around forty, and pretty good-looking, with strawberry-blond hair and blue eyes. (Smart, Libby thought, to make sure the prosecutor was young and good-looking, too. Both the defendant and the prosecutor reminded her vaguely of Dan Quayle.)

And, finally, the assistant counsel for the prosecutor was introduced, Kathryn Schnagel. She was everything the others were not—tiny, skinny, and rather homely, with an enormous nose, small squinty eyes behind horn-rimmed glasses, and mousy brown hair. She turned around and looked carefully at the crowd, as if to dare criticism.

The judge asked if anyone knew any of these people. Immediately a hand shot up. "I do, Your Honor," said an older woman.

"And you are?" the judge inquired.

"Evelyn Riley."

The judge looked over the top of her reading glasses. "And whom do you know?"

"The prosecutor, Your Honor, Mr. MacDonald. I used to baby-sit for him when he was a child."

Everyone burst out laughing and the prosecutor whipped around, squinting at the woman. And then he gave a slight smile, which quickly vanished. (This was a murder trial, after all.) "Yes, Your Honor," he said gruffly. "Mrs. Riley knows me."

A ripple of laughter through the courtroom.

Mrs. Riley was excused from the case.

The judge proceeded to explain that the charge against James Bennett Layton, Jr., was murder in the second degree for willfully causing the death of Sarah Elizabeth Cook, also known as Sissy Cook, on February 10, 1994.

Judge Williams asked for all those jurors who had a problem serving on a case that might last three weeks to raise their hands. Almost two-thirds of the group did. The judge then told those people to move over to the other side of the courtroom so their cards could be pulled from the pool. After fifteen minutes or so, this was accomplished, but instead of questioning those jurors about what their excuses were and then dismissing them, which was customary, the judge announced that they would select the first panel of jurors.

There were loud groans from the segregated group. This judge was going to make them sit there until *she* was ready to talk to them, which clearly was not going to be for a while.

Libby smiled to herself. She kind of liked how this judge was handling herself.

The first panel of jurors was called and Cornelia Winslow was #11.

The judge asked some preliminary questions to get things moving. What did each juror do for a living? In what part of the city did each juror live? Where was each juror born? How many jurors were married? How many years of schooling did each juror have?

The defense attorney then introduced himself to them as Arnold Geiggen. He walked and talked as if he had won the case already and merely needed the jurors to wrap things up. It took him about an hour to reach Libby. He smiled at her and she reflexively smiled back. "Ms. Winslow, isn't it?"

"Yes."

"You write novels for a living."

"Yes."

"And do you write about murder in your novels?"

"No," Libby said.

"Do you write about crime at all?"

"If I do, it's about white-collar crime."

His eyebrows went up. "Are these romance novels?"

"No. Although they do have a romantic story line in them—usually. Well, I guess they all do."

"And have you ever heard anything about this case?"

"Yes, sir, quite a bit—in the newspapers, on TV, the radio, when it happened."

"And do you have any reason to think you cannot listen to the evidence given in this courtroom and make a fair decision about my client's innocence or guilt?"

"I don't think so," Libby said honestly. "But it's difficult to know. There were a lot of conflicting reports at the time."

"Yes, indeed," the attorney agreed. "But is there some reason why you feel you could not be a fair juror? That you feel biased or convinced one way or the other about the facts of this case?"

"I don't know enough about the case to have any opinion about it one way or the other," Libby said, raising her hands in a gesture of helplessness.

Geiggen smiled. "And would you take the word of a police officer over another person?"

"I might," Libby admitted. "Depends on the situation."

"Well, when would you?"

"I would take the word of a police officer over another person in a time of emergency, for example. An accident, let's say; I would listen to a policeman or woman over just about anybody."

"And what about in a court of law?"

"I don't think so," she said, "but then, I can't be sure. It would depend on the evidence, I guess."

He went on in that vein for another five minutes, after which he merely nodded, looked her straight in the eye, smiled, and said, "Very good, thank you.

Much to Libby's chagrin, when the prosecutor questioned her, the story came out again about how her ex had stolen one of her cats. This courtroom found it even funnier than the last one.

"He stole your—*cat?*" MacDonald said.

"He knew it would upset me more than anything," she answered. "He could have stolen the other one, but Sneakers is a lot lighter."

More laughter.

The prosecutor tried to restore sobriety, but even he had to keep going to sate his curiosity. "But you called the police."

"Yes."

"And they got your cat back."

"Yes, they did."

More laughter.

"So would you call the police again, Miss Winslow, if a crime occurred?"

"Oh, yes," she said quickly, "I believe in reporting crimes, regardless."

"Regardless?"

"Regardless of what they are."

"Why is that?"

"So we at least get an idea of what's really going on in the city. In terms of crime."

He nodded. "Miss Winslow, do you know any lawyers?"

"Yes. My father's one."

"Is he a criminal lawyer?"

"No, he has a general practice, wills and estates and contracts and things."

"And where does he practice?"

"In a town called Greatfield, Ohio. It's about sixty miles from Columbus."

"And that's where you're from?"

"Yes."

"How long have you lived in New York?"

"It's coming up on six years now."

"And you've always been a writer?"

"No, I was a teacher for four years. In Cleveland."

"What grade?"

"Tenth."

"And what did you teach?"

"English."

"Did you like teaching?"

"It was very frustrating because of where I was teaching."

"Why was that?"

"It was an inner-city school and the kids just did not want to be there—and neither did most of the faculty, I'm afraid."

"But you didn't grow up in the city," the prosecutor continued.

"No. Greatfield is—oh, gosh, I think the population is maybe around nine thousand? Ten thousand? It's primarily a farming community."

"Was there much crime there?"

She had to laugh. "No, not unless you could count drinking beer out near the town airstrip."

The prosecutor nodded, pacing. Suddenly he stopped and turned to her, looking directly into her eyes. "Do you believe in sending people to prison?"

"If they've committed certain crimes, yes."

"How bad does the crime have to be before you send them to prison, in your opinion?"

"Mr. MacDonald," the judge said, "I don't think it's necessary to ask Miss Winslow to define the finer points of law."

"I'm sorry, Your Honor," he said to the judge. "Let me rephrase that." He whirled around. "Miss Winslow, would you have a problem finding someone guilty of murder in the second degree if you knew that without a doubt such a verdict would send that person to prison for as long as twenty-five years?"

"I have absolutely no problem with that," Libby said firmly.

Evidently the prosecutor liked how she said that; he thanked her and moved on. Evidently the defense attorney suddenly had his doubts, for his head had jerked up at the tone of her voice as she answered. Libby met Geiggen's eyes without flinching. She would be fair, she thought. She really would be. She'd try to be, anyway. Geiggen looked back down at his pad and made a note.

Three jurors were selected to serve out of that first panel of twelve. The first was a woman named Adelaide, a kind of fruit-loopy lady who had feathers in her hair. The second was a black guy in a sharp suit who looked as though he was planning to murder them all, he was so angry about being chosen. He had, when interviewed, said he might be biased in his verdict just to get the case over early. And so he was chosen! And the third was Cornelia Winslow.

The three were asked to stand and be officially sworn in. Everyone was then excused for lunch—that is, everyone except all the people who said they could not serve on this jury. They had to stay and wait in line to talk to the judge, who was, clearly, bent on punishing them.

"And Ms.—" The judge looked at her notes. "Ms. Freid, Mr. Millerton, and Ms. Winslow."

The jurors looked at her.

"Since we will not finish jury selection today, you are excused for the rest of the day. You are not to discuss this case with anyone or amongst yourselves. Please return to this courtroom at nine-thirty tomorrow morning. Thank you."

A guard came over to hand a yellow slip to each, which, he explained, would allow them to skip the line for the metal detectors in the morning.

STATE OF NEW YORK
UNIFIED COURT SYSTEM
JUROR'S PASS

JUROR'S NAME: Cornelia Winslow [*was filled in by hand*]
FACILITY: 100 Centre Street
COURT: Supreme   PART: 62
EXPIRES: Nov. 10, 1995
ISSUED BY: Carla J. Williams   DATE: 11-8-95

On the back of the pass was a number to call if something absolutely catastrophic happened to them. (Read, get here on time no matter what, or else.)

Alex was waiting for her outside the courtroom. "Well, you did it," he said. "Congratulations."

"I don't believe it," she murmured, shaking her head. It was just beginning to dawn on her. She was going to be a juror on a murder trial. A *murder* trial.

"The prosecutor loved that bit about having no problem sending someone to prison," Alex told her.

Libby could only nod, feeling a little bewildered. And a little scared, too. A *murder* trial?

By the time Libby called her parents that night, it had sunk in. "Guess what? I'm a juror on a murder trial!"

"You say that as though it's good news," her mother sighed. "Tom! You better pick up. Your daughter's on a murder trial."

"A murder trial!" her father said, picking up the extension.

"On the jury, Dad," Libby laughed.

"I know on the jury," he said, "but I'll be damned if I can figure how the prosecution ever let you on."

"Why?" Libby asked.

"Well, honey, it's just that writers and females are notorious for sympathizing with the enemy, so to speak."

"Writers and *females?*" Libby screeched, bursting into laughter.

"Are you still coming home for Thanksgiving?" her mother asked.

Libby simmered down. "As far as I know."

"Did you want to be on this jury?" her father asked.

"Well, sort of," Libby said. "I thought it would be a good thing to participate in the system for once."

"And Hal is definitely not coming?" her mother asked.

Libby paused. "No, Mother. I told you, we split up months ago."

"Oh, that's too bad. You shouldn't be alone at your age." In a minute, Libby knew, her mother would get to the part about the dangers of living alone, that she could become one of those awful people who smacked their lips when they ate.

"Don't worry, Lib," her father said, "your mother never liked Hal, anyway. She was scared your children were going to be dim-witted." He laughed.

"I never said dim-witted," Mrs. Winslow protested, "I said they would be odd, growing up with a father like that."

"Mother!"

"Well, he *was* odd, Libby."

"He was not *odd*, Mother."

"He lived like a vampire, let's start with that!" her mother argued. "I never saw the man in daylight hours once. And he wouldn't eat bread and he hated ice cream. And remember, Tom, the time we got up at Libby's and he was drinking? At six in the morning!"

"He had just come home from the studio!" Libby cried. But it was in vain. Once her mother got on a roll, there was no stopping her. She was not, evidently, the least bit impressed by her daughter serving as a juror on a murder trial.

4

ON THURSDAY morning Libby felt like part of the aristocracy because she had her magic yellow juror's pass now, enabling her to bypass the line for the metal detectors. Many, many pairs of envious eyes followed her as she sailed through security, flashing her pass. The pass did nothing, however, for the crowds in the elevators or how many stops they made on the way up to 16, the top floor.

She was excited this morning. Regardless of what anyone else felt about it, she felt honored to be on a jury.

Alex McCalley spotted her as she approached the courtroom and came bounding over to her. "Guess who's Juror Number Five!"

"Hey, that's great," Libby said.

He smiled. "I think so. Anyway, they picked two other jurors, so it's six down, six to go. And then the alternates."

As Libby and Alex and the throng of prospective jurors waited outside the courtroom in the hall, nine-thirty came and went. Every few minutes after that an armed guard would come out of the double doors and bark at everyone to stand to one side of the corridor. Then, as the guard continued down the hall, two more officers would appear, leading a male prisoner, clad in prison grays and handcuffs and leg irons, down the hall between them.

"Sentencing day," someone said.

At ten-fifteen, another large group of jurors from the central jury room were brought up to join them, extending the crowd another fifty feet or so down the hall.

"What's taking so long?" someone sighed at ten-twenty.

"Oh, no, they'll never choose me," a woman said, voice reverberating down the hall with classic lockjaw inflection. "I know exactly what to say to get off."

Libby glanced over. The woman was around sixty, about five foot eight, and had pure white hair, still cut as though she were in boarding school. She was wearing a black cashmere sweater, one long strand of pearls, pearl earrings, a red Scotch plaid skirt with pleats on one side, and classic black pumps. Libby tended to agree with the woman; people like her usually had a talent for getting their way.

They weren't brought into the courtroom until ten-thirty. As Libby and the other jurors took their designated seats in the jury box, the judge apologized for the delay, but explained that sometimes they had double duty in the courts and this morning something urgent had come up.

Adelaide, Juror #1, had earrings in the shape of black high-top sneakers dangling from her ears; Juror #2, the black accountant, practically scowled at Libby when she said good morning; #4 was a big red-faced guy in his forties who, Libby could swear, smelled vaguely of stale liquor; #5 was Alex; and #6 was a very pale white man, balding, about fifty years old, with rather thick glasses.

Another jury panel was selected to sit in seats 7 through 12. No one from that panel was chosen, eliciting groans from the courtroom gallery. Out of the next panel, they selected #7, a young white guy with slicked-back hair who barely looked old enough to drive, much less serve on a jury. Another panel was drawn, and from this one a juror was selected and sworn in as #8, a big German lady who, in another life, Libby was sure, must have been a Viking queen (complete with blond braids and antlered helmet).

Finally, at one-fifteen, they were dismissed for a forty-five-minute lunch.

"Shall we get something to eat?" Alex asked her.

"Sure."

And so they went a couple blocks away to a little coffee shop Alex knew and had a quick tuna sandwich and soup. "I like women with an appetite," he told her, watching her eat.

"Well then, you're going to like me a lot," she told him.

"I already do," he assured her.

Libby only laughed, flattered.

When they returned, they were promptly led back into the courtroom and another panel was called. Time started to drag unmercifully now, as the same questions from the morning were asked over and over. The lawyers selected one juror from this group, #9, a young white woman Libby thought she might like. Her name was Melissa and she was in advertising. Novelistically speaking, she was what Libby would have described as a modern-day business heroine, with glossy black hair, large green eyes, a nice figure, and a very sleek suit and heels.

They struggled on, everyone but the lawyers and the defendant fighting yawns. (Libby accidentally made eye contact with the defendant once, and tried to keep her face impassive. He, on the other hand, looked directly at her, as though he would beg for her help if he could.) She wondered what it had been like for him after all this time. To be in jail.

The lawyers started arguing at the bench about something, and several times a guard had to go over to the gallery and tell the prospective jurors to be quiet.

Now it was four-fifteen. Libby dropped her face in her hands and rubbed her eyes, sure there couldn't be any makeup left on them by now.

Finally the group at the bench dispersed and the court officer announced that all three jurors on the last panel were excused. Everyone in the gallery groaned. No one chosen from this panel, either. It was four-twenty and Libby thought they might be dismissed for the day, but the judge was determined to move this case along and another panel of three was selected. One potential juror was rather interesting. She had been robbed at a car rental agency where the robbers had locked her in a utility closet with four strangers. When Geiggen asked her if she thought she could be a fair juror, the lady said yes, of course she could be, the only problem was that in this case the defendant looked far too much like the robber who had locked her in the closet to find him anything but guilty.

There was laughter mixed with groans. This lady wasn't getting picked, that was for sure.

Nor would the young woman with the bangle pierced through her eyebrow; or the piano turner, who, whenever he was asked a question by Geiggen, looked at him in blank astonishment and said something like "Snoo?"

At five-fifteen, they were finally dismissed for the day.

"Miss Winslow, how are you?" the doorman said as Libby swung in under the awning of her building.

"It's good to be home," Libby told him. In the lobby she saw Al, one of the security men, standing next to the concierge's desk.

He waved. "Hey, how are you?" Like the other security guys, he was a former NYPD detective, now retired. Libby was soaked with perspiration from her subway ride and knew she looked dreadful, but it didn't matter since Al, as good-looking as he was, was happily married and the father of small children—which was why he retired from the force, he told her once, because he had wanted to live to see them grow up.

"Oh, Al, you'll never believe," she said. "I'm a juror on a murder trial."

"Let me save you some time, then," Al said. "He's guilty."

"Al!"

"I'm telling ya, Libby, if the case has gotten this far, he's guilty."

"How do you know it's a he?"

"It's always a he in this town. Is he black?"

"No, as a matter of fact, he's white—white as driven snow."

"White?" Al said, frowning, blinking, thinking. "I must know the case, then. Did he murder someone black or white?"

Libby cringed. "We don't know if he murdered anyone yet, that's why there's a trial! Oh, come on, Al, don't do this to me."

Al looked at her. "Seriously, Lib, do you *know* what it takes to go to trial for murder in this town? You practically have to have the judge present for the murder."

"I'm not supposed to talk to anyone about it."

"Okay, okay," Al said. He scratched his head. "I just don't know how the hell a prosecutor would let you get on a jury. A *writer*?"

"That's what my dad said."

Suddenly his eyes grew large. He snapped his fingers and pointed at her. "You're not sitting on the Layton trial, are you?" From her expression he knew he was right. He slapped the concierge desk. "Oh, man! Are you ever in for it."

"Al, I'm serious," she said sharply. "I'm not supposed to read the papers, I'm not supposed to watch or listen to the news—and I'm absolutely positive I'm not supposed to be listening to an ex-cop talk about it!"

He smiled. "Look, I won't say anything." He touched her on the arm. "It just could be a long case, that's all. You do exactly what you're told to do. I'm sure you'll be a great juror." And then he cracked up, saying to the concierge, "How the hell did they let a *novelist* get through?"

"And they asked me if I held anything against policemen," Libby muttered, making a mental note to cancel her newspaper delivery for the next couple of weeks.

"You're not off jury duty *yet?*" Jerry whined as William got off the elevator at Connors, Morganstern. Jerry, standing with some others, was leaving for the day. The married ones would be going off to homes in the suburbs; the single ones, like Jerry, would be going off to the gym to play squash or lift weights.

"Not yet," William said.

"William's on goddamn jury duty, can you believe it?" Jerry said to the others. "I guess some people must make enough money they don't have to worry about making money for the firm anymore."

"Oh, who knows, Jerry?" William said, turning around. "Odds are you'll be praying for a fair and impartial jury yourself someday soon."

Laughter and guffaws.

"Can you believe that guy?" he heard Jerry say. "What an asshole."

There were several messages on Libby's answering machine. The first was from her literary agent. "Oh, darn, I'm sorry to have missed you, Lib."

Oh, yeah, sure, she thought. He knew she was on jury duty and he had known she wouldn't be there. So, clearly, the news was not good. If it was good, he would have caught her before she left this morning, or waited to call tonight.

"I don't know what to tell you about a new contract," he said, "which is to say I don't know what to tell you about money. I think we have to sit tight for a while until we find out how *Smiles Meeting* did."

Jerk. He couldn't even get the title of her novel right. That's it. She was going to fire him. She pushed the Skip button.

"Rosa? Alo, Rosa?" the next message said. She hit Skip. The third message was a dial tone. The fourth was Hal. "Libby, I really think we need to talk. So we don't have to be afraid of running into each other."

Who was afraid of running into him? There's no way she was interested in anything he did, or any of the people he hung out with.

No, thank you. Three years had been quite enough.

The last message was from Kitty Darnell, wanting to confirm their meeting for tonight. Tutoring was the last thing Libby felt like doing tonight, but Kitty was so close to getting her GED—high-school equivalency diploma—she had to call her back and say sure. If Kitty could work, raise a child, and go to school, Libby could survive one day of jury duty, for heaven's sake. At any rate, it was their last session for the semester.

"You're late," Bonnie warned Melissa. "First you let them pick you for a murder trial, and now you're going to piss off the only clients who'll accommodate your new schedule as a good citizen."

"I know I know I know!" Melissa cried, frantically trying to key in the last of the revised copy into her computer. "Just let me finish this!"

"They're at the restaurant," Bonnie warned.

Melissa didn't answer. She just kept typing. Writing like this—with no time to think—often brought out her best. She finished her thought and logged off the computer, scooped her mail folder into her leather briefcase, and took the big black portfolio from Bonnie.

"They're at the China Grill," Bonnie said. "Car twenty-three is waiting downstairs."

"Thanks," Melissa said, walking out.

"So you won't be here tomorrow morning?"

"Not if we're out late," Melissa said.

"But you'll come in after you're dismissed for the day?" Bonnie said.
"Yes."

"But it will be Friday and no one will be around," Bonnie sighed, clearly not pleased with whatever additional work this might mean for her.

"If it's so important," Melissa said, walking backward down the hall toward the elevator, "people can call me over the weekend. Thanks a million for staying so late, Bonnie."

"You're welcome. Hey, I better warn you—the old guy, Sal, wanted to know if you were married."

"What did you tell him?"

"That if you were, your husband must have divorced you by now because you hadn't been home in months."

With the trading desk weirdly quiet, William pushed his chair back to stretch. And then yawn. And then to take off his glasses to rub his eyes. He looked at his watch. Eight twenty-seven P.M.

Two hours more and Betsy should be asleep. He could sleep in the den again then and say he hadn't wanted to disturb her.

"Hello?" Kitty said over the top of her book.

"I'm sorry," Libby said, covering a yawn. "It's being in court all day."

They were sitting at the worktable in Libby's study, going over Kitty's algebra assignment. Kitty's son, Malcolm, was watching a *Sesame Street* video in the living room and playing with the blocks Libby kept for the children of her friends.

Kitty cleaned for several people in the building, and after a chance conversation with Libby in the laundry room several months ago, she had taken Libby up on her offer to review her lessons with her whenever she felt the material was getting past her. "Why would I offer if I didn't love teaching?" Libby had asked her. And now Kitty was just a few weeks from the test for her GED. Next would be taking SATs, and then college courses.

"Girl, you been talkin' to that mother of yours again?" Kitty asked.

Libby was a bit startled. "Last night."

"And now you're de-*pressed*. How many times do I have to tell you, just because she gave birth to you—"

Libby held up her hand to silence Kitty. "I know."

"But you're a writer! You publish books! She should respect you!"

Libby smiled and shook her head. "It's not my mother, Kitty—at this point, it's me. She'll never change. I can, though. I don't have to let her get to me."

"Listen to me, she'll poison your life if you do. And if I ever knew any woman who deserved a life of *love*, girl, it's you!"

Melissa nearly fell on her head trying to get out of the cab with the unwieldy portfolio containing the storyboards, but pulled herself together and walked into the China Grill looking, she hoped, confident and at ease. The clients on their cat food account had been more than understanding. Melissa was serving on jury duty, so could we meet for dinner, and then maybe go on to the theater? And let the agency put them up for the night at the Plaza? Wonderful, the clients had said. And so Melissa and Roger—the account executive—were serving as hosts tonight for the Cat People, as they called them, who were in from New Jersey. Melissa would pitch the campaign as they wined and dined them, then they would whisk them off to the theater, and afterward, drop them off at the Plaza with the boards, where Roger would return in the morning to discuss them.

Roger saw her and stood up, waving, as though lost at sea. The clients simply stared at her. Three men, one woman. As she approached, the men stood up. They remained standing until the maître d' took the portfolio from her and she could sit down.

"Very attractive," said the short man with the purple nose, who Melissa knew had to be Sal Borno, the founder of the company. If Melissa's research was right, he used to be in hot dogs and had switched to pet food after new federal guidelines were issued about what could and could not be used to make hot dogs.

"Mr. Borno," Melissa said, holding out her hand, "how wonderful to meet you."

"Call me Sal," he said, covering her hand with his own.

Roger introduced her around the table: Ted Smith, the president, a nice-looking youngish guy; Ron Romero, marketing director, about fifty; and Christine Harrington, a looker around forty, the media director.

Melissa quickly slid into her Mademoiselle Charming routine, telling funny stories, complimenting everyone at the table (she had done her homework on each), and reintroducing the major concept of their campaign. Old Sal was delighted (and half in the bag) by the end of dinner; Ted Smith was easy to handle since he would go along with anything Sal liked; and Ron Romero and Melissa were on the same wavelength. Christine Harrington was the only one Melissa had her doubts about; she had remained aloof and noncommittal, though vaguely amused.

They went off in a waiting limousine to the theater, very appropriately to *Cats*, through which Sal managed to sleep soundly.

William unlocked the front door and let himself in. It was quiet. She was asleep. Thank God.

He went into the den and undressed as quietly as he could, then pulled out the sofa bed. He grabbed a pillow and blanket from the closet and threw himself down.

And fell asleep.

After Sal had his nap at *Cats*, Melissa and Roger tried to drop the Cat People off at the Plaza, but Sal, suddenly revived and bright eyed, insisted they come to the Oak Room for a nightcap. Melissa knew better than to refuse. Until the media contracts were signed and the billing approved . . .

And so they sat there, Sal getting smashed all over again; Roger, Ted, and Ron getting into a discussion about football and sports bookies; thus leaving Melissa, sipping mineral water, listening to Christine Harrington go on and on about the future of interactive TV. She got so technical, Melissa finally had to laugh and say, "How on earth do you know so much about this?"

Ron leaned toward them. "Didn't tell her about the degrees, did you?"

"Ron, come on," Christine said, looking annoyed.

"MIT," he said to Melissa.

Melissa looked at her. "Really?"

Christine Harrington looked like what Melissa had come to expect most successful "media" women to look like: She had blond hair, wore good clothes and jewelry, was thin and attractive and stylish—and very pretty in a stressed-out way. Media women did not, however, as a rule receive degrees from the Massachusetts Institute of Technology.

"Please, let's just let it lie," Christine said, finishing her glass of white wine.

"Just wait until you hear the whole story," Ron said.

"Ron, I'm serious," she told him.

He pulled back and, from behind Christine's back, winked at Libby before returning to the guys.

Now, of course, all Melissa could do was wonder what the whole story was. "I have to admit, Christine, you certainly don't talk like any media buyer I ever met before."

Christine looked down at Melissa's glass. "I was wondering . . ." She raised her eyes. "What kind of advertising person you are that you don't drink."

"One that used to get into a lot of trouble," she said honestly, laughing. "Actually, someday, if you really want to hear it, I'll tell you all about it. Otherwise," she added, gently mocking her, "please, let's just let it lie."

Christine laughed.

Her eyes met Melissa's. And held. She was no longer laughing, only smiling.

Melissa didn't know where to look. And so she kept looking into the blue eyes that were looking at her from across the table, knowing that this was a mistake, this was surely trouble.

But she kept looking, anyway.

5

ON FRIDAY morning, promptly at 9:30 A.M., jury selection for *The People of New York v. James Bennett Layton, Jr.* resumed.

The defendant, Libby noticed, seemed vulnerable this morning. She wondered what was going on in his head. At his side, the three defense attorneys looked calm, collected, even relaxed. At the prosecution's table, nearest to the jury, MacDonald was solemn, absently toying with a lead pencil, listening and watching the proceedings, lips pursed into a line. His associate was wearing a terribly unflattering green suit today and was up to her nose in file folders.

Three potential jurors were called to fill the empty seats and Geiggen started firing questions. Since there were only three, it didn't take very long, perhaps forty-five minutes. MacDonald barely bothered with two of the jurors, focusing on the one extremely good-looking young Hispanic guy, around thirty, who said he worked as a limousine driver. His focus was on whether or not Mr. Doñez thought murder was justified, and Mr. Doñez got into a bit of a scuffle with him over whether killing someone in, say, self-defense was murder at all.

"Are you saying, Mr. Doñez, that murder in some cases is justified?"

"What I'm saying is," the young man said, "if someone tried to kill me, and I defended myself, and that guy died, I don't think that's murder."

"But if someone hired someone to murder someone else—"

"There's no excuse for that!" he cried.

The prosecutor looked at the Jurors #1 through 8, as if to make sure they heard this point and knew it was worth remembering.

"Thank you, Mr. Doñez," MacDonald said. "No further questions."

Dayton Doñez was chosen as Juror #10. Libby had already nick-named him Romeo. He was awfully good-looking.

Two more potential jurors were called, and neither was chosen. Two more were called up, but neither of them was chosen, either. (One didn't speak English very well, and the other, every time she was asked a question, had demanded of the judge, "Do I have to answer that? I want to know my rights!")

It was now twelve-thirty, but instead of breaking for lunch, the judge pushed on for another selection. After the next round, a sweet-looking white woman, in her fifties, named Bridget—married, a nurse—was chosen and sworn in as Juror #11.

"Ladies and gentlemen of the jury," Judge Williams said, "we will now break for lunch. Please do not speak of the case with anyone or dis-cuss it amongst yourselves. Thank you. Please be outside this courtroom promptly at two-thirty."

"Well," Alex said outside the courtroom, "it looks like we're going to be here for a while." He smiled, steering her toward the elevators with one arm, carrying his shearling coat in the other. "I'm not unhappy about it, how about you?"

"What happens to your business, though, Alex?"

"It's *my* business," he explained, leading her onto the next elevator, "so I just continue to pay my salary."

He took her to a restaurant in Little Italy. It wasn't open for lunch, but Alex tapped on the window and a big burly man came to the door to welcome them. He was the owner.

"This man," the owner said to Libby, pointing to Alex, "is the most honest man in New York. Everyone tell me I gotta spend ten thousand dollar onna stupid staircase to make inspection. He come, and a week later, the job done for two thousand and I pass inspection, no problem."

Alex made noises of humility as the owner escorted them to the back dining room, where a very old woman was watching a soap opera on a big TV over the bar.

"Mama! Can you turn it down!"

His mother was either ignoring him or not hearing him.

"Mama!"

Libby touched the owner's arm. "It's all right. Please let your mother watch it as it is. It won't bother us."

They sat down in a booth, set with a traditional red-and-white-checked tablecloth, and shared a large bottle of Pellegrino water. They ate green salads and spaghetti with meat sauce. Alex seemed surprised and pleased when Libby ordered the same thing he did. "You eat red meat."

"Oh, yes," Libby said. "But only maybe once a week now."

"Do you like steak?"

"Is the Pope Catholic?" she asked.

"We'll go out for a steak one night," he promised. He looked around, smiling. "This isn't much of a place to look at, but the food is simple and good."

He was right; the food was good, and with Mama's soap opera raging in the background ("Days of Our Lives"), they talked about the State University of New York at Binghamton, where Alex had gone to school, and Ohio State, where she had gone. Alex's father had died when he was ten (he had fallen off a ladder while painting the house and broken his neck), and he had one younger sister. His mother had remarried and was living in Casanovia, New York, wherever that was.

Back in the courtroom, Libby felt so sleepy from the spaghetti she almost nodded off in the jury box. Now they were calling possible jurors one by one, and it wasn't until the fifth that they chose a Brazilian bombshell named Elena who was a wife, mother, and secretary.

Now, the judge explained, they would be calling four potential jurors up to begin their effort to find four alternate jurors, in case anything happened to any of the main jurors during the course of the trial.

Libby thought Clay, the black accountant next to her, Juror #2, was going to explode with frustration. "I've served a week already," he said under his breath. "A week!"

More prospective jurors were brought up from the central jury room and the officer of the court called four more candidates to sit in the chairs in the second row that trailed all the way over to the window. From the first group they selected an older white woman, a housewife named Basha, as Alternate Juror #1. They proceeded to call three more jurors, the second of whom Libby recognized as the snooty white-haired lady she had heard boast the day before about knowing how to get off.

Today Mrs. Snooty was wearing a simple navy blue dress, and those long pearls again with the matching earrings. She also had an enormous diamond on her left hand, as well as several glittering bands.

"Mrs. Smythe-Daniels," Geiggen began, "you said you live in the East Fifties."

"Sutton Place," she said in a voice that sounded something between Julia Child and the Queen of England.

Geiggen smiled. "Yes. You also said you are retired."

"Yes."

"What kind of work did you do when you were working?"

"I was a volunteer at a variety of institutions—the Metropolitan Museum, Meals on Wheels, Church of the Heavenly Rest. And, of course, I had my two sons to bring up."

"They're grown now?"

"Quite," she said. "One is thirty-eight, and one is thirty-five."

The defense attorney nodded. "And you keep busy now . . . ?"

"Of course I keep busy," she said, insulted.

"I meant, what do you do now to keep busy?"

"I am a member of DAR." She looked at the rest of the jury. "Daughters of the American Revolution," she added, as if they were all clearly heathens of the very worst sort. "I also enjoy listening to Rush Limbaugh on the radio."

"That's it," the black accountant muttered. "She's off."

But, shockingly, after twenty minutes more of questioning by Geiggen and then MacDonald, Mrs. Smythe-Daniels was *not* off the hook, and when the two other jurors were excused and she wasn't, she audibly gasped, slapping her hand over her pearls in disbelief. "You must be joking!"

Libby had to smile.

"No, Mrs. Smythe-Daniels, it is no joke," Judge Williams assured her from the bench. "Please rise so the officer of the court may swear you in."

Two more potential jurors were called. The first was a young woman, who Libby knew within minutes would never get selected (she belonged to the NRA and shot a pistol at a firing range with her boyfriend), but the second, yet another nice-looking, unmarried, white man in his late thirties, a computer programmer named Stephen, seemed like a good bet.

He was, and he was sworn in as Alternate Juror #3.

It was ten minutes past six. The judge was determined to finish jury selection. They only needed one more, and the next prospective juror called was William Seymour Klein. He turned out to be the short Wall Street–looking guy who had tried to talk to Libby in the hall the other day. Geiggen questioned him for about twenty minutes. He had grown up in Skokie, Illinois, went to Cornell, had an MBA in finance from NYU, was some kind of analyst at Connors, Morganstern; no, he didn't watch much TV; yes, he read a lot; his favorite writer was Cormac Mc-Carthy (no, he wasn't a fan of violence, but he was of good stories); no, he had not paid much attention to the press coverage at the time of the murder; yes, he could be a fair and impartial juror.

"Why? Because, as an analyst, I'm trained only to deal with facts."

MacDonald spent only about ten minutes with him, grilling him about his feelings about the police.

William Seymour Klein was selected to serve as Alternate Juror #4.

Jury selection was now complete, Judge Williams announced, and the potential jurors in the gallery were excused. They were to report back to the central jury room on Monday morning. The gallery quickly cleared out, and not without some noise. When the last had departed, it was eerily quiet, and the sixteen jurors in the box exchanged looks with one another as the court officers finalized their jury rosters.

Finally, they were dismissed, too, but were escorted out of the courtroom and down a short hall to what the guard explained would be their home from now on.

The guard took out a bunch of keys and unlocked the door. The jurors filed in, each frowning a little as they inspected their domain. Beige walls. No pictures. There was a metal screen in front of the men's and ladies' rooms. A long table. Sixteen chairs were crammed in, some with arms, some not, some wood, some plastic, all of them depressing. At the end of the room was a window. One part of it was open, the other had an air conditioner jammed into it. Below the window a cast-iron radiator was hissing, and next to it, a bare coatrack jutted out from the wall.

"Good God," Mrs. Smythe-Daniels said.

"No danger of Paige Rense calling on us here," Melissa, the young advertising woman, said, making Libby laugh. Paige Rense was the famous longtime editor of *Architectural Digest*.

They all took seats as the guard introduced himself as Chuck, and proceeded to explain what the procedure would be for them from now on.

They were to report here every day. They were to come to this room whenever there was a recess in court. Unless Judge Williams instructed otherwise, they were free to leave the building for lunch, but otherwise they would spend all their time in this room. There was a pitcher for water on the table, he pointed out, and they were not to ask *him* for water, because he'd only get it from the same place he got water for the judge—from the sink in the bathroom right over there. He then handed a yellow pass to each so they could bypass the metal detectors on Monday.

Looking at her new pass for next week, Libby wondered how anyone in the judicial system could know for sure if any of the jurors were who they said they were. Not once in this entire process had anyone ever asked her for an ID. For all they knew, Cornelia Winslow could have paid someone to show up at jury duty for her. Then she wondered what would happen if someone was found not guilty in a trial, only to find out later that one of the jurors had been an imposter. What happened then?

The guard finished by instructing them to report to this room at nine-thirty sharp Monday morning. Alex and Libby and Melissa-in-Advertising walked out together, chatting, and took the elevator down. They went outside and then Melissa stopped dead in her tracks, taking hold of Libby's arm. "Isn't that the defendant?" she asked.

Libby and Alex followed her eyes.

Sure enough, it was James Bennett Layton, Jr., climbing into the back of a chauffeur-driven car.

"Yeah," Alex confirmed. "With Geiggen, his lawyer."

Melissa looked at Libby. "Sure doesn't look like a prison transport to me."

"Oh, he's out," Alex said.

"He's *out?*" Libby said. "He's on trial for murder and he's not even in jail?"

"He must be out on bond," Melissa said.

"Anyway," Alex said, steering them away, "we're not supposed to talk about it."

"Right, of course, sorry," Libby said. She glanced at Melissa and knew she was thinking the same thing. How guilty could the guy be if he wasn't even in jail?

6

WILLIAM PRAYED everyone would have cleared out for the weekend already. Announcing that he was actually sitting on a jury was not going to go over well, although he was rather curious to see Jerry's reaction to it being the Poor Little Rich Boy trial. More specifically, he was curious about Jerry's reaction to it being a young, wealthy white guy on trial, who was accused of hiring someone to kill a woman just like those Jerry aspired to date.

"Jerry's gone?" William asked a trainee.

"Yeah. He's going to Dick's bachelor party."

"Oh, right," William said. Dick was a bond trader. His party was going to be in Bal Harbour, Florida, this weekend. Years ago William might have widened his eyes and asked, "They're all flying from New York to Florida to have a party?" But not now. He was well acquainted with the excesses on the Street. Thankfully, most people working there did not live like Jerry. Their wealth was discreet, invested in houses and property, in raising families, in creating peaceful retreats that compensated for the harshness and killer pace of the business.

Still, there were quite a few Jerrys, the ultimate consumers of anything and everything. They were wine connoisseurs by twenty-five; they did not ski, they helicopter-skied; they had gone around the world at least once (in ten days or less); they bought in East Hampton; had played at least ten of the top twenty-five golf courses; owned one practical car (with four-wheel drive) and one fun car like a BMW convertible; and always had some beautiful body to sleep with.

The strangest thing was, soul-sick Jerry and others like him seemed a lot happier than William. It was almost as if at birth their capacity for individual thought and emotion had been shut down and replaced by a complete reorientation to embody a collective perception of what was desirable and what was not. Along those lines, living was easy. All one had to do was make the money and spend it fashionably and lavishly to feel good and to be admired—which was to say, make mere mortals sick with envy.

But if there was one thing that got to William about Jerry and his kind, it was their complete inability to understand what an act of charity was. Oh, sure, Jerry wrote big checks to good causes—but only under one of two conditions: that it was tied to a black-tie dinner where all the partners would see the table Jerry had bought tickets for, or that his name would be printed on a program where lots and lots of important people would see it.

As William's mother would say, that wasn't charity, that was public relations at best and social climbing at worst. His mother was one of those women who had slaved for years as a volunteer on Hadassah projects, who had pounded it into William's head since he was knee-high that one always shared one's good fortune with others who were in need—and certainly didn't go around advertising it. On her first trip to New York to see her son as "the Big Shot," she had enjoyed the black-tie dinner for the benefit of a city charity, but later, over brandy, after his father had gone to bed, she gently reminded her son, "Charity is an act of the heart, Willie, and is freely given. And while the dinner tonight was lovely, I hope you are giving to causes that won't ever help your career."

He heard her. And he did give. Heck, he made a damn fortune, and although he would never turn his back on declaring a contribution as a tax deduction, he generally did request anonymity for the thousands of dollars of donations he made. (Last year, it had been a little over forty thousand dollars, about eight percent of his income.)

Wall Street was treating him incredibly well financially, but William longed for the banking days of his paternal grandfather. In his day, William Seymour Klein, Sr.'s, being a banker meant being able to finance the building of dams, TV stations, hospitals, bridges—anything and everything that could and would be of use to the public in some way. That's what Grandpa Will had done, and it was at his knee that William had learned what goodness could come from viewing money as a tool, as opposed to a collectible to take out of circulation. Before Grandpa had died, though, the crazy eighties' Shortcut-to-Riches schemes so sickened him that he declared the world was going to hell in a handbasket and he'd rather be dead than see it.

And then he died. A day or two after the Keating S&L scandal broke, as a matter of fact.

Sigh.

Even just four days away from his usual nonstop workaholic pattern was giving William time to think about things for the first time in months. And yet thinking, he knew, did nothing but stir up nameless longings and faint aches of loss for something William knew not even what. It was not enough to want Betsy out of the apartment once and for all. It was not enough to simply dream of building something someday, like his grandfather had done. And it was not enough to have these thoughts temporarily, only to shut his mind down later when it became too painful, the repetitive cycle kicking in, working, working, working, hoping that someone or something might someday drop down out of the sky and bring new meaning to his life.

"He's guilty," the night handyman told Libby as she entered her building.

"Oh, no," Libby groaned, "not you, too."

"Oh, yes," José confirmed, grinning, looking up from the paperwork he was doing at the edge of the concierge desk. Libby liked him. (He had once saved Sneakers, who had fallen behind the refrigerator and gotten stuck.)

Libby looked to Larry, the concierge, who held his hands up. "Don't blame me, I haven't said a word!"

"Read my lips," José said, pointing to his mouth. "Gillll-teeee."

The phone in her office rang. Melissa looked at her watch. Who would be calling at nine o'clock on a Friday night? She picked it up. "Hello?"

"How did I know you'd be there?" a woman's voice said.

Melissa didn't have a clue as to who it was.

"This is Christine calling, the cat lady," she said with a laugh.

Melissa hesitated. "The—?"

"The cat lady of the Cat People," Christine said. "We know what you people call us there. Sal loves it because it implies there is no greater authority on cats."

"So how did you like the boards?" Melissa asked, grabbing a pen to take notes.

"They're good," she said brightly. "Although frankly I think we were all much too hung over today to come to a decision." Pause. "I don't usually drink that much, although I can't vouch for Sal. But then, it's his company—was, at any rate. But it's his subsidiary to run."

"Someone owns you guys? I didn't realize."

"Harding-Buckner Mills. It won't matter to you, though, Melissa, don't worry, the Cat People will still pay all the bills for your campaign."

Melissa laughed politely.

"Anyway," Christine said, "I wanted to tell you what a big hit you were with everyone. Even if the campaign needs revising, we all agree we want to work with you."

"Are you saying the campaign needs revising?" Melissa asked.

"A few things, I think, here and there. It's a matter of semantics, mostly, but we won't have formal feedback for you until next week—at least, until the boys are sober again."

Melissa laughed politely again.

"Melissa." Her voice had softened considerably.

"Yes?"

"You're really terrific—you know that, don't you?"

"Thank you."

"I mean it. As a person, you're super. I like you a lot."

"Thank you," she said again.

"So I'll call you next week—just as soon as I have something for you."

"Okay." Then Melissa snapped out of it. "Oh! Since the trial's started, it's best you try me here after six-thirty. But you can always leave me voice mail. I call in. Or you can talk to Bonnie."

"Great. Listen, have a great weekend. And get some rest, Melissa, you work too hard. You need to have fun once in a while, too, remember."

Melissa smiled. "Will do." She hung up and looked at the phone for a minute. Then she shook her head and turned back to her computer.

Marty really was a sweetie, but Libby wondered if he would ever really understand that she was not interested in him romantically. When he had asked her to attend a dinner party with him, she said no, she didn't think it was a good idea, but then he almost pleaded with her, saying it was a publishing dinner and he really needed a date like her in order to go and feel comfortable. It was his new boss who had invited him. This Libby could identify with.

When he showed up at a quarter to eight with flowers, she groaned inwardly, wondering if she was going to have to explain her feelings—or lack of them—yet again. Marty had been a sales executive at Haverhill and, after a painful divorce, moved to another firm and started calling Libby. At first, it was simply as a friend, to have a cup of coffee, that sort of thing, but one time Marty arrived half-lit and weepy for their friendly chat and she had a hell of a time making him go home, telling him no, she wasn't going to make him a man again.

Other than the flowers, though, Marty didn't seem to be romantically inclined, either. First of all, he refused a drink before they went (good sign), wanting to be at his best for the dinner. It was in a gorgeous East Side apartment near the United Nations, with windows overlooking the East River. It was all publishing people and the hosts were very nice to Libby, and soon she was genuinely enjoying herself.

Later, enjoying a cognac after dinner, looking out at the river, Libby thought this apartment had to be the most romantic place she had ever been. And then she wondered if she was going to spend the rest of her life visiting romantic places with men she felt not the least bit romantic about.

And she wondered, not for the first time, if something was wrong with her.

When Marty took her home, she let him see her to her apartment door. She tried something a friend had suggested. When that awkward moment came as to whether or not she would let him kiss her, she smiled and said, "Marty, give me a hug. It was a wonderful evening."

It worked. He hugged her and she hugged him back and sent him on his way, not unhappy.

Mission accomplished. Thank God. And tomorrow she could sleep in.

William did not get home until ten. Betsy was waiting for him in the living room, fighting mad.

"You can't just end this, William," she announced.

"I didn't just end it, I tried to talk to you about it months ago, and when you continued to refuse to talk about it, I told you I would help you find a place of your own."

"You're being stupid and ridiculous as usual," she told him.

He walked past her into the bedroom. While he was getting undressed in front of his closet, she burst in, crying, "You never do anything, William! You're such a letdown, such a never-will-be! You can't even handle a relationship! You're thirty-three years old, for God's sake. What are you, gay?"

He wished he were. It certainly would make this a lot easier.

He glanced back at her over his shoulder. "The issue, Betsy, is that I cannot and will not go on living like this."

"Take this jury thing!" Betsy nearly shrieked, ignoring what he had said. "None of our friends do all these strange things! And you do them all the time. A lot of our friends wonder how I put up with you."

"Look, I'll sleep in the den awhile longer," he told her. "And I'm more than willing to have this be friendly while you're still here—"

"Still *here!*" she screamed. "I *live* here! This is my home!"

"But you've got to look for a place to live," he continued. "I'm more than willing to pay for a broker's fee and the deposit on a place, and a mover. So plan on leaving on the first."

"The first?" she said, dumbfounded. "You mean three weeks from now?"

"A broker will find you a great place, no problem." He glanced at her again while hanging up his suit pants. "I'll also pay your credit card bills one last time."

She went into the bathroom and he went out to the kitchen to call for Chinese food. He had to eat. He had to try to function. He couldn't give in now. While he was on the phone, Betsy came in, gently took the phone from him, and hung it up. "I have dinner for you," she said quietly. "I fixed that garlic chicken you love."

He felt bad. He turned around. "Betsy, please understand, I want to be friends. I care about you—I really care about you—but neither one of us was ever really in love."

She said nothing, but rested the side of her face on his shoulder. He wrapped his arms around her and just held her, standing there. "I just loved being with you, that's all," she murmured. "I don't want this to be angry, either." Her hand was now on his crotch.

They just stood there, not saying anything, Betsy stroking him through his khakis. He was starting to get hard. He couldn't help it. They hadn't had sex in weeks. Betsy might have a lot of problems, but being sexually attractive was not one of them.

When she led him into the bedroom, every alarm bell in his head was ringing, but the ache in his loins was worse. She pushed him down on the bed and crawled on top of him, undressing him, taking special care with his underpants. She threw her robe off, revealing that she was naked underneath, then crouched over him to brush her ample breasts back and forth over his body.

He was as hard as a rock.

He turned her over and climbed between her legs, angling himself into position. He closed his eyes and sank himself into her, making her call his name. He lowered his head and started pumping away, but when he opened his eyes it was to see Elizabeth Winslow staring at him from the back of that book.

"What's wrong?" Betsy asked him.

"Nothing," he said, closing his eyes, trying to continue.

But it wasn't working. He was losing it. Fast.

"I'm sorry," he finally said, rolling off of her. "I'm sorry, Betsy, I just can't do it."

She lay there, blinking, looking at him.

"I'm sorry," he said again, and he got up and went into the bathroom.

"You goddamn son of a bitch, I hate you!" Betsy suddenly screamed, and she threw his ten-year anniversary gift from Connors, Morganstern, a Steuben-glass bull. It smashed into the door and thudded down onto the carpet.

Unbroken.

7

MONDAY MORNING the children were absolutely determined to KO Mom's trip to New York because it meant the arrival of the dreaded Mrs. Montell. "I do all my homework," Peter complained, "and she *still* won't let me watch TV."

"Then I take my hat off to her," Jill said, finishing their lunches and closing up their lunch boxes.

"She cooks liver, Mommy," Katie said.

"Liver's good for you," said Rusty, Jill's husband, all dressed and ready to go.

"She's here! She's here!" Peter warned.

As a last-ditch effort, the little monsters locked themselves in their bathroom.

"We're going to kill ourselves," Peter promised through the door.

"Good," Rusty told his son, "then we don't have to pay a baby-sitter. Jill, while the kids are killing themselves, I'm going out to the garage and starting the car."

"Oh, Petey, for heaven's sake," Jill said, smiling nervously at Mrs. Montell, who was standing there, watching, with a severely disapproving expression on her face. There were two ways for Jill to play this: scream at them, which would work, she knew, but would also lower her parenting skills even more in the eyes of Mrs. Montell, who never raised her voice; or two, graciously coo at the door like this and get nowhere.

"We're going to hang," Katie said, "like that boy did."

"What boy?" Jill asked, frowning. "What are you talking about, Katie?"

Mrs. Montell had disappeared down the hall toward the kitchen.

"The boy who hanged himself," Peter explained, giggling.

God only knew what this was all about! Ever since that Jack moved in up the street, a charismatically evil twelve-year-old, Jill's children were learning all kinds of amazing new things.

"Excuse me, Mrs. Tompkins," Mrs. Montell said, pushing her to the side and inserting the triangle end of the bottle opener into the lock and turning it. Voilà, the door was open.

The children screamed and scrambled into the bathtub.

"Out!" Mrs. Montell commanded.

After a moment of silence, the two young hooligans came out, heads down.

"Hurry up, now, you'll be late for school," Mrs. Montell said matter-of-factly, walking back to the kitchen.

"Come on, you guys," Jill pleaded to the children in a whisper, "be nice. I don't want to go into New York either but—"

"But why her?" Peter cried.

"Because she's the only one I can trust." Jill bent over to kiss Peter on the forehead and then Katie. "Because, my rotten little darlings, I'm very upset about Aunt Sissy and I want to make absolutely sure my babies are safe and sound while I'm in the city."

"Babies," Peter spat, walking down the hall. But Jill knew she had gotten through to him; there'd be no more trouble from him. No other kid at school had a beautiful aunt who had been murdered.

"Everything okay?" Rusty asked her in the car.

"Everything's fine," she said, trying to pull herself together. There was only so much she could share with Rusty about this trial business. While he wanted to support her, he was also worried what impact the trial would have on her emotionally. Sissy's murder had been a shock she had not yet recovered from, and the idea of resurrecting all the painful details again, day after day in court, made Rusty nervous.

"Corporate attorneys don't deal well with murder," Jill remembered a family friend saying after Sissy had been killed. "That's why Rusty's a corporate attorney. You can't expect too much of him, Jill."

They were late getting to the station. They parked down in the big pay lot and then raced up the slope and up the stairs to the platform to jump on the seven thirty-two, which had just pulled in.

High heels were not made for this track event and Jill longed for her sneakers.

"Quick," Rusty said, "grab a seat before the next station." All hopes of sitting with her husband on the way in were dashed. Worse yet, she had to sit in a middle seat, making the men on either side of her sigh as they swung their newspapers a little farther to the sides to let her get in and sit down.

The train reached Grand Central on time, and Rusty took her by the arm through the mob at the track, across the middle of Grand Central and then—fighting the tides of people that were coming up—down the stairs into the Lexington IRT subway station. He pushed a token in her hand, led her through the turnstile, and then, still fighting the crowds, steered her down to the platform of the 4 and 5, showing her how to wait to the side as the passengers flowed out of the car, and then how to push her way into the lurching express that stopped first at Fourteenth Street and then, hallelujah, City Hall/Brooklyn Bridge. Rusty pulled her off the train just in time (she was waiting for an older man to get off first and the doors nearly closed her in). He walked her through the station to the exit that came up in the middle of Centre Street, escorted her to 100 Centre Street, flashed the special pass sent to them from the District Attorney's office, took the elevator up with her to the sixteenth floor, pushed her through the crowds there, and delivered her to the outer doors of the courtroom, where Jill heard him tell the guard she was the victim's sister, Mrs. Jill Cook Tompkins. The guard promised Rusty that he'd watch out for her.

"Okay, honey," Rusty said, handing her a bag of tokens and a map, "call me if you need me." And he was gone.

"Mrs. Tompkins," the guard said, "please follow me. I'll take you to Ms. Schnagel of the DA's office."

Cornelia Elizabeth Winslow, Juror #3 on the trial of *The People of New York* v. *James Bennett Layton, Jr.*, flashed her pass at the guard and sailed through security. In her hand she carried a cup of coffee; in her bag she carried no work, only five back issues of *The New Yorker*.

This morning she headed for the south bank of elevators, hoping all the jurors would follow the signs and be on the north one. No such luck. It was just as crowded. As they groaned upward from floor to floor, a man suddenly demanded, "Fucking son of a bitch, how long do we have to put up with this!"

A woman sighed and said, "You can say that again," and everyone laughed.

Everyone but Libby and a courthouse guard got off on 15. He smiled at Libby. "On a case?"

Libby smiled back. "Yes."

"Which court?"

"Part sixty-two? Judge Williams?"

"Oh," the guard said as the elevator reached 16, sounding serious. "Well, just remember, don't stop to talk to anyone, go straight to the jury room."

Vaguely puzzled, Libby said thank you, got off the elevator, and turned the corner down the hall. She nearly fainted when she saw the mob scene waiting at the other end. Another jury selection? No, no—it had to be something else because suddenly a lot of these people were staring at her as she approached.

"She's a juror, I bet!" a guy cried, making a beeline for her, others following behind.

Libby didn't know who or what all these people were, but she knew enough not to say anything except "Excuse me" and push her way through the crowd to the hall leading to the jury room. She turned the doorknob and hurried in, a little taken aback by the silence inside. Heads rose to look at her. She could have mistaken it for a Bible study class if she hadn't known better. "My God," she couldn't help but exclaim, "what is going on outside?"

"The celebrity murder trial of the month evidently," said Melissa, the pretty woman in advertising.

"Oh, no," Libby said.

"Oh, yes," Alex said, motioning for her to sit next to him. "We've hit the big time. All those guys out there are press—trying to get into *our* trial."

"Oh, no," Libby said again, putting her bag down on the table and going over to the rack in the corner to hang up her coat. The Wall Street guy, who was all smiles, nodded to her. He was sitting in the corner by the window, reading, naturally, *The Wall Street Journal*. "William," he said.

"What?" she said, sitting down next to Alex.

"My name's William."

"And I'm Libby." She smiled.

"What's all that about?" Alex asked Libby in a whisper. "What did he say?"

"FYI," Melissa said, leaning over the table in Libby's direction, "from now on, the only newspapers we can read are the ones they provide us with."

"I figured as much," Libby said, starting to feel the excitement in the air.

"It's a carnival," huffed the lady who had tried to get off jury duty, Mrs. Smythe-Daniels, who was sitting down at the other end of the table. "In which they expect us to participate. Ridiculous!" She was wearing her long string of pearls again, and the matching earrings.

The door crashed open and the Brazilian bombshell burst in, Juror #12, with the red-faced drinker #4 behind her. "Ay! What ees thees out there?" she exclaimed, and everybody started talking at once.

Chuck the guard came in shortly after that and they all froze, silence falling over the room, the jurors all looking vaguely guilty, as if they had been caught at something. "Okay, ladies and gentlemen," he announced authoritatively, producing a clipboard, "I'm taking attendance. Juror Number One, Adelaide Freid."

"Here!" said the lady who wore feathers last week, raising her hand and standing up. She was tall and slim, with short dark hair, in her mid-forties, Libby would guess. She was wearing a purple wool bag-dress today, with pink warm-up leggings and—Libby stretched under to the table to see—red high-top sneakers.

"As Juror Number One," the guard told her, "you are Madame Foreman of the jury. You will be responsible for all communication with the court on behalf of your fellow jurors."

Libby exchanged looks with Alex and choked back a laugh.

"Okay, Juror Two, Clay Millerton?"

"Here." It was the hostile black accountant, isolated in a corner with coffee and some sort of work sheets balanced on the top of his briefcase. He was thin and his head was kind of oddly shaped, and his perpetual frown did not help his appearance—but his suit and tie were impeccable. His dark skin was velvety and beautiful.

"Juror Three, Cornelia Winslow."

"Here," Libby said. "But could you call me Libby?"

He smiled. "I'll try, but the court will always know you as Cornelia."

"Juror Four, Robert Shannon."

"Here." It was the drinker, looking as though he were on vacation to-day, in blue jeans and an argyle vest. "Call me Bob."

"Juror Five, Alexander McCalley."

"Here!" Alex said, raising his hand.

"Juror Six, Rupert Slotnik."

"Here." He had to be the palest human being Libby had ever seen, and she wondered if he had a skin condition that didn't allow him to be in the sun.

"Juror Seven," the guard read, "Ronald Levinson."

"Here," said the young turk, whose new hairdo—slicked straight back—didn't add any new sense of maturation to him.

"Juror Eight, Debrilla Riff—riff—"

"*Rrrifff*-ten-stalll," the heavy, white Viking lady said in a heavy German accent.

"Okay," the guard said, "Debrilla Rifstenstahl is here. Juror Nine, Melissa Grant."

"Here," Melissa-in-Advertising said. Today she was wearing a brown Donna Karan suit, and Libby couldn't help but wonder if she had bought it wholesale. She looked pretty young to be able to afford those kind of clothes.

"Juror Ten, Dayton Doñez," the guard read.

"Here!" said Dayton, the young Romeo in his thirties. He was truly beautiful, in the sense that only gorgeous Latin men who knew how to dress could be.

"Juror Eleven, Bridget Bell."

The sweet-looking housewife timidly raised her hand. "Here."

"Juror Twelve, Elena Sartoza."

"I am here!" said the Latin bombshell.

"Alternate Juror One, Basha Mendyzak."

Silence.

"Basha Mendyzak?" the guard asked, looking around the room.

"Which one was she?" Alex asked Libby.

"I'm not sure."

"She was a retired teacher, I think," Melissa-in-Advertising said. "She was chosen the day I was. She had ten grandchildren or something?"

"Kind of heavy?" Alex asked.

"A little."

"Basha Mendyzak is not here yet," the guard said, marking this down with his pencil. "Okay, Alternate Juror Two, Eleanor Smythe-Daniels."

Mrs. Smythe-Daniels sniffed and touched at her pearls. "Here under protest."

People laughed, which seemed to confuse Mrs. Smythe-Daniels for a moment. And then she smiled slightly, too.

"Alternate Juror Three, Stephen Cadalonee."

"Cada*lone*," the nice-looking computer programmer said. Libby hoped to ask him sometime about various computer systems. It was time for her to upgrade the system she had. That is, if she ever earned any money again.

"Alternate Juror Four, William Seymour Klein."

"Here!" Wall Street William said, raising his hand. He was wearing a gray pinstriped suit today, and a gray-and-blue tie. Oh, right, Libby remembered, he was the guy with the black tie Oxfords.

"Okay, so we're just waiting for Basha Mendyzak," the guard said, turning and walking out.

A half hour passed and any good will on the part of the jurors went out the window, so to speak, where Dayton Doñez, alias Romeo, was hanging outside to smoke a cigarette.

"Where the hell is she?" Bob the drinker asked.

"If we can get here on time, she can get here," said Elena the bombshell with a toss of her head.

"You were late," Ronald with the slicked-back hair pointed out.

"How would anyone know with that clock?" Alex asked. All heads turned to look up at it. The hands were frozen at ten-forty.

Everyone was sinking into a lousy mood, each, Libby speculated, thinking about his or her own effort to get here on time—and for what? To wait around in this depressing place. Chuck the guard came back in. "Basha Mendyzak is at the dentist's," he announced. "It was an emergency."

"Yeah," Alex said, "and the dog ate my homework."

Everyone laughed.

"No, seriously," Chuck said, "it sounds pretty good—a broken crown. That can really hurt."

"So what are we expected to do?" Mrs. Smythe-Daniels demanded to know.

"Wait," Chuck said cheerfully. "You can go down to the cafeteria and get some coffee or something, but tell me if you go. I need to know where you are if the judge calls us into court."

After he left, the group talked a bit, complaining. Wall Street William disappeared to use the phone; Melissa-in-Advertising asked if anyone wanted coffee and took a few orders; Slicked-Back Ronald announced he wanted everyone to call him Ronnie (and Libby wondered if he ever forgot and ran his hand through his slicked-back hair and, if so, what did he wipe his hand off on afterward?); Dayton the Romeo finished his cigarette and started to close the window, but everyone protested because it was too stuffy, leave it open.

"It's so strange," Libby said to no one in particular, "but *I* feel incarcerated."

"That's because you are," Clay, the black accountant, said, speaking for the first time.

"I need water," Adelaide announced, Madame Foreman, standing to reach for a plastic cup and the bronze-colored water pitcher in the middle of the table. "It is very important to maintain proper hydration in an institutional building."

"No amount of water can protect you from the asbestos in this one," Alex observed.

All eyes turned to him. "Just kidding," he told them. Adding, under his breath to Libby, "But there's no way I'd work in this building every day."

"And what is it that you do, Madame Foreman," Mrs. Smythe-Daniels inquired of Adelaide, "that you are so concerned with proper hydration? Are you in . . . irrigation, perhaps?"

"I teach dance," Adelaide said, sitting back down with her water. "Modern, interpretive, and a little jazz."

"Oh, I see," Mrs. Smythe-Daniels said. "An *artist.*"

Adelaide looked around the table. "She sounds exactly like my ex-husband." People laughed. Adelaide turned back to Mrs. Smythe-Daniels. "My ex had trouble expressing his emotions, too."

Mrs. Smythe-Daniels's eyes grew quite large. "Indeed," she said, clearing her throat and abruptly opening an issue of *Town and Country* to read.

"You suppose she's really at the dentist?" Slicked-Back Ronnie asked Debrilla the Viking lady, who thus far had said almost nothing.

"Vhy vould she lie?"

"To get out of this," Ronnie said. "This trial could go on forever."

"Oh, dear, I hope not," Bridget, the nice-looking housewife, said.

"Maybe she's getteeng her hair done for the reporters," Elena the bombshell suggested, looking in a hand-held mirror at her own.

"They're not allowed to take pictures of us," Alex said.

"That's good," Libby said, although thinking what a great publicity angle for her dying novel it could be. AUTHOR BOOK TOUR DETOURED TO MURDER TRIAL, she imagined. There she would be, smiling and waving a copy of *When Smiles Meet* from the jury box.

Melissa-in-Advertising came in and handed out coffees and teas. To Bob the drinker she handed the requested can of Coca-Cola. "No Basha yet, huh?"

"No."

A minute later, Wall Street William came back in. "No Basha?"

"No Basha," Libby told him. He took off his jacket, hung it on the back of his chair, and sat down. He was pretty short by Libby's standards, but he had a nice chest and shoulders. He also wore very expensive, well-fitting white shirts.

"Basha is a Russian name, I tink," Debrilla the Viking lady said. "Mendyzak, Polish."

"She ees your friend?" Elena asked.

Debrilla frowned. "Vhat?"

"You said that like she ees a friend of yours or something," Elena said, gesturing and making her charm bracelet jingle.

"Surely I will go mad," Mrs. Smythe-Daniels said suddenly.

"This is kind of like sitting in the waiting room of a Berlitz school, isn't it?" Melissa-in-Advertising asked Libby.

Chuck the guard poked his head in. "Is she here?"

"NOOOO!" they all yelled.

The door closed again.

"How long do we have to wait for what's-her-name?" Slicked-Back Ronnie said.

"Who?" Stephen the computer man said, waking up.

"Basha," Wall Street William said.

"Basha Mendyzak," Debrilla the Viking lady repeated.

"What ees thees magazine?" Elena asked Mrs. Smythe-Daniels, peering over her shoulder. "May I look at eet when you're done?"

"I *will* go mad," Mrs. Smythe-Daniels said positively.

"This jury is awfully young, don't you think?" Melissa said to Libby and Alex.

"Basha's the oldest, I think," Libby said.

"Older than—?" Dayton the Romeo asked, nodding toward Mrs. Smythe-Daniels.

Mrs. Smythe-Daniels leaned forward to look down the table at him. "Are you addressing me, young man?"

"No," Dayton said cheerfully. "Ma'am," he added.

They waited and waited. At eleven forty-five, Chuck finally came in to take them into court. Outside, the hallway had been roped off, so that the crowd of people had to wait about sixty feet down the hall. The courtroom, however, was packed. As the double doors were opened by guards, Libby was a bit overwhelmed by all the people. She looked back at Alex, who winked.

The jurors self-consciously filed through the courtroom. At the jury box, it became a major traffic mess, since Adelaide, who was supposed to be the first juror to go in, was the last to come into the courtroom and Clay, the hostile accountant, was bound and determined to wait until she got there before the rest of the first row went in, thus blocking the second row of jurors from getting into their row. After a bit of a scuffle and reshuffle and an indignant "Good God!" from Mrs. Smythe-Daniels, the dance macabre ended and the jurors got into their correct rows in the correct order at last.

Judge Williams, looking tired, scanned her eyes over them and then looked down at her notes.

"The jury is now present," an officer of the court announced for the benefit of the court stenographer, a woman who started "typing" on a strange little machine with a large band of paper on it. While her fingers flew over the keys, her body gently bobbed up and down over the machine, as if she were playing the piano.

"Ladies and gentlemen of the jury," Judge Williams said in a loud, clear voice, "it seems that one of the jurors has sustained a dental emergency. She tried her best to get here, but, as you have so patiently experienced for yourself, she has been unable to. Therefore we have no choice but to adjourn and reconvene tomorrow morning promptly at nine-thirty. I apologize for the inconvenience and thank you for your patience. I wish to remind the jurors that you are not to discuss this case with anyone or amongst yourselves, refrain from watching or listening to the news, and confine your newspaper and newsmagazine reading to those periodicals provided to you by the court each morning. Thank you."

The guard gave them a signal and the jurors stood up and filed out in much better order than they had come in.

Once in the jury room, several jurors exploded while collecting their stuff. What a waste of time. What the hell was this? A whole day lost for someone's stupid tooth. Why couldn't they use one of the alternates? Who had to pay for this fiasco? Them, the taxpayers, that's who!

"Can you believe this?" Wall Street William said to Libby, holding the jury room door open for her as she was leaving.

"It's really a waste, isn't it?" Libby agreed. "But I guess that's what we have to do if we're going to have a fair trial." She looked at him. "I have to admit, I'm pretty impressed by how they run things by the book."

"When everything else seems to be going to hell in the world," he finished for her. "I am, too."

Six guards were in the hallway to keep the crowds away from the departing jurors.

"Libby!" came a shout. It was Alex, who was waiting ahead for her at the elevator. "Come on, I'll walk you to the subway."

This prompted a kind of unspoken face-off with Wall Street William.

William retreated, saying, "I forgot something in the jury room. I'll see you guys tomorrow."

Libby felt a twinge. "William—"

He turned.

She smiled. "I'll see you tomorrow."

In the elevator, Alex said, "Guys like that bug me."

"Guys like who?" Libby said.

"You know, that William." Alex looked around the elevator to see who was on it. Whatever it was he had been about to say, he decided not to. "Are you into rich guys?" he asked her instead.

People looked at Libby, waiting to hear her answer.

She only smiled. "I'm quite capable of supporting myself, thank you."

Alex smiled. He lowered his mouth to just beside her ear and whispered, so that she could feel the warmth of his breath. "Good. Because I've got a car, a half-interest in a brownstone, a cabin upstate, and some money in the bank, but I can't compete with that kind of guy. And I don't know of any honest way I could."

"I like you just the way you are," Libby told him, thinking, You know, he's exactly what Mother would choose for you.

"I've got a motorcycle, too," he said. Their faces were maybe four inches apart now.

"It's too cold to ride now," Libby said, meeting his eyes.

"How could it ever be cold with you around?" he murmured.

She knew she was supposed to feel flattered, but she didn't. And she wasn't sure why. "Oh, it can get pretty cold," she assured him. "Just ask my ex."

"Ah, the ex, the vicious catnapper," Alex whispered, leaning even closer.

II

TRIAL

8

AFTER Libby pushed her way through the crowds to arrive in the jury room on Tuesday morning, November 14, she found that yesterday's missing juror, Alternate #1, Basha Mendyzak, age sixty-something, was stretching her mouth to every degree possible to prove that she had indeed suffered greatly from a particularly murderous back molar. Basha had also evidently reapplied her ruby-red lipstick prior to Libby's arrival, transferred some of it to her fingers, and then, apparently, transferred it to the water-jug handle, because after Libby sat down and poured herself a plastic cup of water, she found the color of Basha's lipstick all over her hands.

Wall Street William smiled at Libby and leaned across the table to offer his handkerchief. "It's okay," Libby said, "I've got some Kleenex."

"Look," Alex said, holding up the Metro section of *The New York Times*, from which some small article had been neatly cut.

"You theenk that is sometheeng," Elena the bombshell said at the end of the table, holding up the New York *Post*, "look at thees!" The whole second and third pages looked like Swiss cheese, to say nothing of the news banner on the front page.

"Charming," Mrs. Smythe-Daniels sniffed, touching at her pearls. She was in a black skirt and white angora sweater today. "Murder, the press."

Libby smiled. She herself was dressed in Armani blue jeans today, a turtleneck, blazer, and clogs. Alex was in a flannel shirt, corduroy pants, and boots. William was in a dark blue suit. Melissa-in-Advertising was wearing a short blue dress that looked fabulous. Adelaide, a.k.a. Madame Foreman, was wearing a yellow leotard, blue-jean skirt, yellow warm-up socks, and shoes that looked dangerously close to Persian slippers. From her ears dangled pink-and-purple peace signs.

Chuck the guard came in to take attendance. It was now ten-fifteen. Juror #4, Bob the drinker, was not here yet.

They waited and waited, and Chuck came in and out about once every five minutes, looking more and more stressed, asking, "Is he here yet?"

"NOOOOOO!" they would all chorus, tired and cranky already.

Madame Foreman then announced, "In the future, I will expect all of you to be here on time. Is that understood?"

There was a bit of stunned silence created by this sudden assertion of power, to which Clay the hostile accountant slowly raised his head to respond. "Is that supposed to scare me?"

"No!" Elena barked, moving closer to her new friend in power, Adelaide, Madame Foreman. "Eet ees to make you get here on time! Thaz all!"

"I *have* been here on time, goddammit!" Clay exploded. "In fact, I've been the only goddamn person on this jury who's *always* here on time!"

"The case has lasted two days," Slicked-Back Ronnie muttered. "Big fucking deal."

Clay glared at him. "Just make sure you get here on time."

"Yeah, or what?" Slicked-Back Ronnie asked him, giving him the wise-ass look of a fourth grader.

"Come on, you guys," Wall Street William said. "We're all under stress. If we're going to yell at anybody, let's yell at the guard."

Just then Chuck the guard chose to come in again. "Is he here?"

Following instructions, Slicked-Back Ronnie dutifully yelled, "No, he's not here! And you can go tell the judge that she has no right to keep us locked up in here just because of some jackass retard the lawyers picked to sit on the jury!"

Chuck smiled, amused. "I'll be happy to deliver your message to Judge Williams, Mr. Levinson."

Slicked-Back Ronnie deflated instantly. "We just don't know why we have to sit here doing nothing," he mumbled, looking down at the table.

"Look," Chuck said, "the guy's gotta get here sooner or—"

Just then, out from behind the guard, Bob appeared, red-faced, puffing, huffing out an apology but no explanation. Libby caught a powerful whiff of Listerine as he hurried to the only seat open, away from the table against the wall.

"Not to be rude or anything, Bob," Alex said after Chuck left, "but if you're late like this again, I'm going to toss you out the window and be done with it so we can use one of the alternates."

Bob looked vaguely stricken by this and looked around the room. Everyone avoided his eyes, hoping the message got through.

There wasn't an available seat left in the courtroom. And it was warm. After the jury filed into the jury box—with mercifully more organization today than they had yesterday—Judge Williams called Bob up to the bench to speak to him and Chuck the guard opened the window by the jury. Once Bob was reseated in the box, the judge announced that if any juror was chronically late, he or she could and would be fined.

The trial finally began. Charges against the defendant, James Bennett Layton, Jr., were read: violation of New York Penal Code 125.25, murder in the second degree, for willfully causing the death of Sarah Elizabeth Cook on February 10, 1994.

Murder.

Libby remembered again why they were here, serving on a jury.

She looked at the defendant. He was sitting there calmly. If he had any expression, it was one of faint bewilderment, as if he couldn't imagine what he was doing there.

Nineteen months ago the woman had been murdered. Nineteen months ago Libby had been thirty-two and was planning to get married; now she was thirty-four, her book was returning from bookstores in droves, and she was a single woman with cats.

This is a murder trial! she reprimanded herself. Pay attention!

MacDonald, the prosecutor, rose from his table to address the jury. He was so slow, methodical, and deliberate in his delivery that Libby couldn't help but wish for the state's sake that he had taken a couple of acting lessons. Despite the dramatic contents of his opening statement, his monotone was dreadful.

The defendant, MacDonald explained, James Bennett Layton, Jr., by sixteen known as Benny to his fast-track friends—"Benny as in Benzedrine—"

"Objection!" Geiggen screamed, on his feet in a second.

"Sustained," Judge Williams said. She looked at the prosecutor and raised one weary eyebrow. "You know better, Mr. MacDonald."

"I'm sorry, Your Honor."

"The jury will disregard that remark and it will be stricken from the record," Judge Williams announced.

The stenographer nodded. She stopped her machine, searched through her tape, and then struck something out with a pen.

MacDonald continued. James Bennett Layton, Jr., the jury would learn, was from an extremely well-to-do family on Long Island. He went to the best schools, and his parents gave him everything a son could wish for: a boat, a car, sporting equipment, unlimited lessons at whatever interested him. The defendant married young, had three children, and lived in the house his father bought for him near the family mansion in Locust Valley. Mr. Layton senior also employed his son in the family business in New York City, where, it was explained, the defendant might stay as many as four nights a week in one of his parents' corporate apartments on Park Avenue.

The defendant, the jury would learn, used drugs from the time he was an adolescent, and by the time of his arrest, had spent, borrowed, and stolen hundreds of thousands of dollars from his family. The defendant also indulged in endless extramarital affairs. There was one woman, however, who refused to be involved with him, the victim, Sarah Elizabeth Cook, better known as Sissy Cook.

The prosecution, MacDonald said, would prove that the defendant had one date with Sissy Cook, who was a professional model, and that after that one date, Sissy Cook would have nothing to do with him. But the defendant persisted. He called Sissy Cook, sent flowers and gifts—all of which the victim returned—and began following her. He hired a private investigator to watch her movements. And then, one fatal night at the nightclub Belle's, on Wednesday, February 9, 1994, the defendant attempted to talk to and touch the victim in an inappropriate manner and the victim lost her temper and said some insulting things to the defendant.

The defendant, the prosecution would prove, stormed out of the club and drove his car to Jersey City, where he picked up a hired killer. At 2 A.M., Sissy Cook left the club with her roommate. As they came out, the defendant drove up in his car and a man jumped out of the passenger side, asked the defendant which woman did he want, aimed a nine-millimeter gun at Sissy, and shot her three times in the chest and then once in the face. He then jumped back in the car and the defendant drove off.

The prosecutor paused.

The shooter had not been caught, he explained. But the man who had hired him to murder Sissy Cook was. And that man was the defendant, James Bennett Layton, Jr. They had eyewitnesses, they had proof; the People would prove their case beyond a reasonable doubt.

After a stunned silence lasting several moments, it was the defense attorney's turn. Arnold Geiggen stood up and slowly walked over to the jury box, paused, and then looked Libby directly in the eye. "I hope the prosecutor has enjoyed his time in fantasyland, because it's going to cost the state big time when we win this case."

"Objection, Your Honor!" MacDonald yelled. "Defense is in fantasyland!"

"Sustained. Mr. Geiggen, please confine your remarks to the facts of the case as you know them. Mr. MacDonald, you will watch your remarks, too, please."

"Yes, Your Honor," both lawyers mumbled.

Geiggen then started in on his version of the case. The story he had to tell was very different indeed. It was true Jim Layton had gone out with the victim, he acknowledged. It was true that she said a lot of unkind and untrue things at the club, which everyone heard. It was true that Mr. Layton left the bar that night very angry, choosing to leave rather than continue participating in the spectacle. It was *not* true, however, that he drove away that night, because Mr. Layton's car had in fact been stolen while he was in the club! Mr. Layton had then called the police to report the theft and then taken a cab to his parents' apartment.

The next thing Jim Layton knew, Geiggen explained, he was being arrested for hiring some kind of hit man. The state had not caught the murderer, who, incidentally, witnesses say was black. The state, Geiggen said, was under incredible pressure to arrest somebody, and so chose to create a case using a carefully orchestrated arrangement of circumstantial evidence against Jim Layton. And now, he said, walking back and forth in front of the jury box, the state was under more pressure than ever to convict Mr. Layton, not only because they had not found the murderer, but because Jim Layton was white—

"Objection!" MacDonald thundered, jumping to his feet. "The People request a sidebar."

"Counsel will approach the bench," Judge Williams said.

They did, the lawyers and assistants glaring at one another while they waited for the stenographer to unattach her machine from the stand and lug it up to the bench to record the confidential remarks. A few minutes went by as Judge Williams tried to help the stenographer find a resting place for her machine on the bench so she could operate it there.

MacDonald whispered furiously to the judge; Geiggen rose on his tip-toes to whisper something; all the assistant attorneys craned their necks to hear. This went on and on; the jurors started yawning for lack of air. Finally a loud hiss from Judge Williams sent all the attorneys back to their tables and she announced they would break for lunch.

She reminded the jurors that they were not to visit the scene of the crime unless taken there as a part of the trial. A general buzz broke out in the gallery at that. "Jurors will refrain from discussing this case with anyone or amongst yourselves. I also remind you not to read, listen, or watch any form of communication or press concerning this trial. Court will resume at two o'clock."

Libby had expected Alex to ask her to have lunch with him, so of course he didn't. She ended up going out by herself to get some soup and fruit to bring back to the jury room. Melissa-in-Advertising was there, work-ing furiously away on a laptop in the corner; Stephen the computer man was reading *The Alienist*; Basha was doing some needlepoint; and Day-ton was smoking a cigarette out the window, listening to music on his Walkman. Libby sat down and started flipping the pages of the censored newspapers.

At a little before two, the other jurors came streaming in: Debrilla the Viking lady (who had been shopping at Century 21); poor pale-faced Rupert; Adelaide and Elena, who showed earrings they had bought off the street; Mrs. Smythe-Daniels, who had taken advantage of her loca-tion to argue a ticket in traffic court down the road (to no avail); Slicked-Back Ronnie, who had been shopping at Tower Records; Clay the hostile black accountant; Bob the drinker, who seemed in better shape now; Alex, and then, a moment later, a puffing William, who had dashed all the way down to his office. Last but not least, sweet-looking Bridget appeared.

At two o'clock they were taken back into the courtroom, where the judge announced that the prosecution would now call its first witness.

"Excuse me, Your Honor," Geiggen said, jumping up.

"Yes, Mr. Geiggen?"

"I didn't finish my opening statement."

She looked at him a moment. Then she looked down at her notes and nodded. "Mr. Geiggen will resume his opening statement."

All Geiggen did, however, was walk over to the jury box to say that his client was innocent and that if there was the slightest doubt in the prosecution's case against him, then the jury was duty-bound to find him innocent. Because this was America, blah, blah, blah. And then he thanked them and sat down.

The first witness for the prosecution, Jill Cook Tompkins, was called to the stand. A guard disappeared out the back door of the courtroom and they all waited a few moments before the door opened again and a woman—in her late thirties, Libby guessed—entered. She was well dressed, a little heavy but very pretty all the same. Her hair was brown, shoulder-length, streaked; it was an expensive cut. She didn't look like a New Yorker, though. Libby didn't know what she looked like except that she didn't belong in a courtroom like this.

The woman walked up to the front, stumbled a little getting into the witness box, and raised her right hand to be sworn in. On her left hand, Libby could see, was a large diamond ring and a wedding band. After she was sworn in, they told her she could sit down, which she did, and the judge instructed her to state her name for the record. She cleared her throat and said, "Jill Cook Tompkins. T–o–m–p–k–i–n–s." The guard poured her a glass of water and put it down in front of her, for which she thanked him.

"Good afternoon, Mrs. Tompkins," MacDonald said.

"Good afternoon," she said softly.

"Mrs. Tompkins," Judge Williams said, "I'm sorry, but you'll have to speak up."

She nodded, clearing her throat again, and took a quick sip of water. Libby was nervous for her.

"For the benefit of the jury, Mrs. Tompkins," MacDonald said, "I'd like you to answer a few questions so they could know a little about you."

She nodded.

"How are old are you?"

"Thirty-six."

"And are you married?"

"Yes, for eleven years."

"Do you have any children?"

"Two, a boy, Peter, who's ten, and Katie, who's seven." A quick smile. "She's a girl."

"Yes." MacDonald strolled over to the jury and leaned on the far corner of their box, out of their line of sight, forcing them to focus on the witness. "And do you have a job?"

"Uh, well, I'm a full-time mother and homemaker, but I do volunteer work as well. Two days a week."

"Did you attend college?"

"Yes, I graduated from Mount Holyoke."

"Very good, Mrs. Tompkins. And now I would like you to tell the jury what your connection is with this case."

She turned to look at the jury, eyes landing on Libby. "The victim— Sissy—she was my baby sister."

MacDonald let that sink in before proceeding. "You say 'baby sister.' Why is that?"

"Because she was—well, kind of an afterthought for my parents. She was seven years younger than me." She smiled slightly. "And everyone used to call her Baby when she was little. Except for me—I called her Sissy, and that name stuck." Her eyes squinted suddenly, as if she had felt a sudden pain. "My father still calls her Baby, though. I mean, refers to her, since she's . . ." She didn't bother finishing and reached for her water.

"Could you tell us a little about your sister? What she was like?"

She swallowed and put the cup down. "To be honest," she said, looking back at the jury, "Sissy was pretty spoiled when she was little. She was absolutely beautiful from the time she was born, and when she smiled or laughed, she could get away with murder." Her expression froze and the color drained from her face. She leaned forward, holding her face in her hand. "I'm sorry," she said.

She was crying.

In a moment she had pulled herself together, wiping her eyes with a handkerchief and accepting a refill of water from a court officer.

"Can you continue?"

"Oh, yes," she said, sighing. "I'm so keyed up and nervous. It's been such a long time since Sissy was murdered."

"Objection, Your Honor," Geiggen said softly, standing up. "I respectfully request the witness be instructed to confine her answers to the questions asked."

"Sustained." Judge Williams looked down at the witness. "Mrs.

Tompkins, please try and answer only the questions Mr. MacDonald asks you."

"Yes, Your Honor."

They went on, and the witness described how mischievous and full of life Sissy had been, and how wherever she went people fell in love with her. She explained that while Sissy was extremely bright—with an IQ scored at 126—she had little use for school. She was an avid reader, however, loved art and music and dance, and was a great sports enthusiast. She skied, played tennis, and, when she lived on the West Coast, had taken up surfing and kiting.

"What's that?" MacDonald asked.

"Kiting? I don't know what the real name for it is. It's when you go up on the top of a mountain and then run off it and sail around hanging from a big kite."

There was a chuckle in the courtroom.

"Hang gliding?"

"Yes," she said, smiling. "That's it."

And then they went into the negative things, presumably to get anything less than pleasant about the victim out in the open before the defense asked her about it.

"Your sister was once arrested in California, is that correct?" MacDonald asked.

"Yes," Jill said seriously, nodding, "when she was twenty years old. For driving under the influence of drugs."

"What was the penalty?"

"She lost her license for a few years—but the good part was, she didn't hurt anyone and she went into the Betty Ford Center, where she was treated for an addiction to pills and cocaine."

"Was Sissy ever in trouble for drugs again?"

"No, sir, never after that. Drugs scared her. She used to say she didn't even know she was addicted until she got to the police station after she was arrested—because she went into withdrawal there and nearly died."

"Did she serve a sentence?"

"No, I think the modeling agency she worked for at that time got her off somehow."

"Did you know she was arrested at the time?"

"Not until she went into the Betty Ford Center. Then she called me. She wanted me to bring our parents out for a counseling session."

"And did you go?"

"Oh, yes," she said, nodding. "It was very important to her—and important to us as a family. I remember it all very well, because my son was just a few months old—and he came, too."

"So your sister never had problems with drugs again."

"That's right."

"Did she have friends who used drugs?"

"Not friends, no. She used to say how much it bothered her, all the drugs that people used in her industry. But she had a rule about that kind of thing, that if anyone was using, they were out of her personal life. She wouldn't, for example, even let pot—marijuana—into her apartment."

"So it's highly unlikely your sister would have dated someone who did drugs."

"I'd say it was next to impossible."

They moved on to her sister's career, which had been very successful—when she felt like working.

"Sissy would work all-out for about eight months, and then she would take four months for herself and travel." Sissy had been twenty-six when she was murdered. Almost twenty-seven. No, she had never been married, but Sissy always said she would get married to have children and that wouldn't happen until she had retired from modeling.

"Did your sister have any plans for employment if and when she retired from modeling?"

"Oh, yes, she had a lot of plans," her sister said. "As I said, she wanted to have a family, but she also wanted to start a special kind of modeling school."

"How would that school be special?"

"She said that pretty girls had to learn about certain things long before adolescence."

"Such as?"

"Weight management—with the emphasis on the dangers of anorexia and bulimia, and of drugs. She was already doing some counseling through the agency she worked for, because she'd see these kids and could see the trouble they were either already in or headed for."

The testimony lasted through the afternoon to almost five o'clock, when MacDonald ended his examination by asking about the defendant.

"Had your sister ever mentioned the defendant to you?"

"Oh, yes, she did. She told me he was bugging her—following her around, sending her stuff, accosting her in the street—but that it wasn't just the usual weirdo stalking her—because she got a lot of those, because of her looks, you know. Anyway, she said—"

"Now, when was this, Mrs. Tompkins?"

"Well, it was several times over that last fall she was alive. November and December for sure."

"And what did she say to you?"

"Which time?"

"Well, let's begin with the last time."

"The last time was the last time I talked to Sissy—" Her voice broke. She sipped water and continued. "She said that he—the defendant— was a real pain because he was from this really rich and powerful family and that he kept running around telling people stuff that wasn't true, and because of the family he came from, they believed him."

"Did she say what he told people that wasn't true?"

"Objection, Your Honor, this is hearsay."

"Your Honor, I'm simply asking the witness what her sister told her."

"Overruled. Mrs. Tompkins, you may answer the question."

"I'm sorry, what was the question?"

"Did Sissy tell you what it was the defendant was telling other people that was not true?"

"Well, for starters, he told her boss that she was his girlfriend."

"Anything else?"

"He also told her boss that she was upset with him because he had made her have an abortion. And that she was back on drugs."

"Objection, Your Honor, this is hearsay!"

"I'll redirect, Your Honor," MacDonald volunteered. "Mrs. Tompkins, could you tell the jury what objections your sister had to the defendant?"

"Objections? Sure. He used drugs; he was married; he was a liar and a cheat, if not crazy; he was obsessed with her and stalked her and hired a private investigator to follow her around when he couldn't."

"And what was your sister's basic feeling about the defendant?"

"If Sissy had been capable of hating anyone, she hated him." She paused and swallowed. "But more than anything, she was afraid of him."

MacDonald let this hang in the air. And then, finally, he said, "Thank you, Mrs. Tompkins, I have no further questions."

Court was dismissed for the day.

All was silent in the jury room. Libby got her coat and bag and walked out with Alex, but they didn't speak. Libby didn't think any one of them would be speaking a whole lot tonight with anyone.

A person had been murdered, and now they had an idea of what she had been like. Real.

9

T HE SILENCE of the previous day carried over to Wednesday morning. Libby was the second to last to arrive in the jury room, at nine fifty-eight, and as she sat down people murmured some discouraged-sounding hellos. Alex held up the *Daily News*; the entire headline and cover copy had been cut out, leaving only a frame with the logo, a sports score, the weather box, and a plug for a celebrity interview.

"Does anyone feel as awful as I do?" she asked.

"Worse," Melissa answered from across the table.

"Ess verrry de-presseeng," Elena agreed. "Thees whole theeng."

"Ve are not to discuss the case!" Debrilla said.

"Oh, pooh!" Mrs. Smythe-Daniels said, giving her pearls a jerk.

With a sigh, Bob the drinker slumped down on the table to bury his face in his arms, while Clay the accountant, sitting next to him, made a face and waved to clear the air around him.

"Jurors, all present?" Chuck the guard asked, poking his head in.

"Yes—er, no," Adelaide said. Even she seemed down today, and was wearing a remarkably conservative black flannel skirt and sweater. She was also wearing the red high-top sneakers again and red-and-white-striped leggings, but still, the point was clear, the outfit was worn out of respect for the deceased.

"Okay, let's just run through the roll," Chuck said, looking at his clipboard. "Adelaide Freid."

"Here!"

"Clay Millerton."

"Yes."

"Cornelia Winslow."

"Here."

"Robert Shannon."

A mumble came from inside his arms somewhere.

"He's here," Adelaide said, pointing at him.

"Alexander McCalley."

"Here."

"Rupert Slotnik— Oh, he's out," Chuck muttered, crossing something out on his clipboard.

"What do you mean he's out?" Clay the accountant demanded.

Chuck hesitated. Finally, "It's not for me to say."

"Why not?" Elena asked.

"He probably killed himself to get out of this," Clay muttered.

Libby caught Chuck's startled look at Clay. "Oh, my God," she said, "he didn't, did he?"

"Forget it, just forget it," Chuck said. "Don't worry about it."

The jurors looked at one another, spooked.

"Okay . . . Ronald Levinson," Chuck resumed.

"Present."

Chuck the guard looked at Libby. "Look, he didn't kill himself, okay?"

"Somebody do it for him?" Alex asked.

Chuck ignored him. "Debrilla Riff—Rifften—"

"RRRiffftenstall," she rolled off her tongue.

"Here," Chuck said. "Uh, Melissa Grant?"

"Here."

"Dayton Doñez."

"Here."

"Bridget Bell."

"Here."

"Elena Sartoza."

"Good morning, I'm here!"

"Okay, the alternates. Basha Mendyzak."

"Here."

Chuck looked up. "How's the tooth?"

"Better, thank you."

"Thank God," the guard sighed. "Eleanor Smythe-Daniels."

"Yes."

"Stephen Cadalone."

"Here."

"And William Klein."

"Here."

"Okay, jurors, let me just go tell the judge you're here." The door closed.

Silence. And then Libby blurted out, "You don't suppose he died, do you?"

"Who?" Alex asked. "Oh, Rupert? He certainly didn't look very healthy."

"They're not going to show us pictures of the body, are they?" Sweet Bridget fretted.

"Of Rrrrupert?" Debrilla asked.

"The veecteem, seely!" Elena said.

"They might," Melissa said.

"Do we have to look?" Bridget asked squeamishly.

"But they might not show us," William said. "It depends if they were ruled admissible or not, and you can bet the defense has tried to keep them out."

"Ve are not to discuss the case!" Debrilla reminded him.

"Ya-voll, Herr Commandant," Alex said under his breath.

"Okay, jurors," Chuck said, opening the door. "Let's go."

It was strange going into the courtroom. On one hand, Libby felt dreadfully self-conscious, fully aware of the eyes that were trying to absorb every nuance of her and the rest of the jurors. On the other, there was definitely a surge of power in the courtroom as they came in, and Libby, feeling that power, felt compelled as a juror to mask her face of any telltale emotion.

Mrs. Tompkins, sister of the victim, was still sitting in the witness box.

"All jurors are present and accounted for," a court officer announced.

"Very good," Judge Williams said. "And may I commend the jurors for being here on time this morning. It is as it should be." A pause while she scanned her notes. "All right. This morning we have one juror who has been excused from the trial for medical reasons, Juror Number Six, Rupert Slotkin. And so the first alternate juror, Basha Mendyzak, will now be Juror Six. Mrs. Mendyzak? Would you please move down into seat number six."

Basha moved down into the last seat of the first row.

"All right," Judge Williams said, "we may now continue. I must remind the witness, Mrs. Tompkins, that you are still under oath from yesterday."

The witness nodded.

"Mr. Geiggen? The defense may begin their cross-examination."

"Thank you, Your Honor," Geiggen said, rising and walking behind the prosecution's table to stand by the jury. "Good morning, Mrs. Tompkins."

"Good morning," she said politely.

"The examination by Mr. MacDonald yesterday was quite thorough and I hope not to keep you long. There are one or two points, however, I wanted to ask you about." He walked back to the defense table to look at his notes. Libby could see the witness bracing herself. Geiggen walked back to the jury box. "Mrs. Tompkins, you said your sister had many friends."

"Yes."

"And she had lived in New York for how long?"

"Five years."

"How many friends do you think she had, approximately?"

"I'm sorry, I don't understand."

"Just an estimate—how many friends do you think your sister had in New York?"

"Do you mean good friends or acquaintances?"

"Well, let's start with good friends, people she might call and chat with, or have a cup of coffee with, or might see a movie with."

"Oh, I'd say twenty-five or so."

"And how many acquaintances do you suppose she had?"

"Oh, heavens," the witness said, rolling her eyes, "I have no idea. In my sister's profession, she met literally hundreds of people."

Geiggen nodded, turning to look at the jury as he asked the next question. "And so it's safe to say that your sister had met at least three hundred people since she moved to New York?"

The witness thought a moment. "Well . . . at least that."

"Very good," Geiggen said, turning around. He walked closer to the witness box. "Your sister was an extremely beautiful young woman, is that correct?"

"Yes."

"I mean, she was beautiful in a way that the whole world seems to agree on, not just beautiful to those who loved her?"

"That's correct."

"Mrs. Tompkins, in your testimony yesterday," he said, walking quickly over to the defense table and picking up his notes, "you mentioned that your sister often had problems with—and I think these were the words you used—'the usual weirdo stalking her.' Did you say that?"

"Yes."

"And then you explained, quote—because she got a lot of those, because of her looks, you know—end quote. Did you say that?"

"Yes."

"And this was true? That because of your sister's great beauty, it was not unusual for her to have some weirdo stalking her?"

"*Stalking* may be too strong a word. Following her, certainly, sending her stuff, that kind of thing. Unwanted advances and, well, weirdos."

"How many times would you say your sister was the subject of unwanted advances?"

"I have no idea."

"Well, would you say it was more than five times?"

"Oh, yes."

"More than ten?"

"Yes."

"Close to fifty times?"

"More, I would think," she said, sipping her water.

"And why is that?"

She looked at him. "Did you ever see a picture of her?"

He nodded. "Yes, Mrs. Tompkins, I have. And may I say she was one of the most beautiful women I have ever seen in my life."

The witness nodded, eyes starting to glisten.

"Thank you, Mrs. Tompkins, that is all," and he started back to the defense table.

Everyone seemed a bit surprised that this would be the extent of the cross-examination, even the judge, who said, "Mr. Geiggen, are you reserving the right to recall this witness?"

"No, Your Honor, I think Mrs. Tompkins has been through enough already."

The whole jury seemed to let out a collective sigh of relief.

"Thank you, Mrs. Tompkins, you may step down," the judge said. "Mr. MacDonald, are you prepared to call your next witness?"

"Yes, Your Honor. The People call Detective Brenda Watts."

A court guard left to get the next witness as Mrs. Tompkins took a seat in the back row of the courtroom, holding her forehead in her hand for a moment. Then she lowered her hand and looked straight ahead.

The guard came back in and went up to the judge. The judge called the counsel up to the bench. Minutes passed as the stenographer and the legal group gathered to discuss something. When everyone had returned to their places, Judge Williams looked up at the clock and said, "The witness is on her way here, and so, jurors, today you get to have a long lunch. May I remind you that you are not to discuss the case with anyone or amongst yourselves. Court will resume promptly at two o'clock. Thank you."

"Would you like to have lunch?" Wall Street William asked Libby in the jury room.

"I'm sorry," she said, "but I already told Alex—"

"Oh," he said quickly, "sorry."

She smiled. "Don't be sorry. Thank you—for asking."

Alex came over to hand Libby her coat. "Ready?"

"Yes," she said. And then, "But Alex, can William come along?"

It was evidently the wrong thing to say. Alex looked absolutely disgusted with her. But then he shrugged and looked around. "Melissa? Would you like to join us for lunch, too?"

Poor Bob the drinker was standing right there, all by himself, listening to this. If they had any decency, Libby knew, they would ask him to come along, too. Welcome to junior high school. "Bob? Would you like to come to lunch?"

Alex laughed and turned to address the whole room. "A group of us are going over to Amsterdam's for lunch. If any of you would like to come with us, please do."

William, Melissa, Bob the drinker, and Slicked-Back Ronnie accepted, the others declined, and Mrs. Smythe-Daniels looked at them as though they had all lost their minds.

Amsterdam's was a pleasant restaurant, and happily they had no trouble getting a table for six. Libby and Alex somehow ended up at opposite ends of the table, as hosts, and William and Melissa quickly moved in to either side of Libby, leaving poor Alex with Slicked-Back Ronnie and Bob the drinker, who had, somehow, a beer in front of him already.

While they were looking over the menu, Libby looked at William. "I want to ask you a personal question."

"Sure." He was smiling.

"Why are you called William?" When he flinched slightly, she quickly added, "I mean, instead of—well, Will? You look like a Will."

"I'm actually—if you can believe it—William Seymour Klein *the third*," he explained. "My grandfather *was* Will—that's what people called him. And so my father was Willie for a long time, but when he got older, he wanted people to call him Bill. And so by the time I came along—"

"It was going to be Willie, Billy, or William," Melissa said.

"Exactly! And so my mom went for the more important-sounding version."

Libby was laughing.

"My grandfather was a great guy," he continued. "He was from Germany—a stereotype, I guess, since he was a banker. But the great kind, you know? He came to Chicago with his wife and kids and he built bridges and highways and buildings and even whole cities—or at least that's the way he told it. His favorite story was how he financed running electricity into South Chicago." He shook his head. "But the best part of Grandpa Will was how so very proud he was of being an American." He looked at Libby. "Of what America was, you know? Represented?" She nodded and he turned to Melissa. "He would say that you never really knew what freedom was until it was taken away from you. But in his case, he got it back."

Libby was amazed by the transformation in William as he told this story. His blue eyes were shining bright, his cheeks were flushed, his whole being seem to swell with pride, and best of all, his was a smile full of genuine love and affection.

"He passed away?" she asked him.

"In 'eighty-nine." He folded the menu and put it down on the table. "Sometimes I think the savings and loan crisis killed him. He absolutely could not believe what had happened. It worried him that people wouldn't notice that most of the crooked S and L bankers were not Jewish." He looked at Libby again. "He was worried about anti-Semitism—like in the Germany he knew." He shook it off then. "Sorry."

"No," both Libby and Melissa protested.

"It's so nice to meet someone who values his family," Melissa said. "Or who has someone in the family worth mourning the loss of, I guess. I don't know, it seems like nobody listens or remembers what their grandparents had to say."

"I was lucky," Libby said. "I had a grandmother who was just absolutely wonderful."

"You're from Ohio, right?" Will said.

"Yes."

"And you?" he said to Melissa.

"Los Angeles."

"Really?" Libby said. "Aren't any of us from New York?"

The waitress came to take their order. Salads for the three of them.

"So what are you guys talking about?" Alex said from his end of the table.

Poor Alex. Libby felt bad. Bob now had two beer bottles in front of him and Slicked-Back Ronnie was talking a mile a minute to Alex, who was clearly not listening, but looking miserably across at her, as if to say "How could you leave me down here?"

"Not much!" she answered cheerfully. She turned to William. "Listen, back to your name."

He looked at her.

"I think that now that your grandfather is no longer with us, that you should—and I think he would be pleased beyond belief if you did this— have at least some of your friends call you Will from now on. Because you look like a Will. I mean, now that I know you, I don't think you're a William at all. In fact," she confessed, "I think between the pinstriped suit and the William, I wasn't sure I'd like you at all."

He looked at Melissa. "Well, you see it was like this, kids, back in 'ninety-five, when I was on jury duty, even though I was almost thirty-four years old, I decided over lunch one day that a strange woman I met was right and I should—"

"I beg your pardon!" Libby laughed. "Strange woman?"

"A strange famous woman novelist I met," he continued, "was right, that I should change my name to Will. And so I did."

"Libby's right," Melissa said. "Will *will* sell better. I should know."

"Hey, I'm not disagreeing," William said. "I used to say to my mother that the only people called William were kings and butlers, neither of which I aspired to be—" He broke off because Bob, sitting on the other side of him, had suddenly dived under the table. William lifted the tablecloth to look. "Are you all right?" Bob murmured something and William let the tablecloth fall back down. "He says to pretend he's not there and not to look," he reported.

"Oh, no," Melissa said, "this isn't going to be like President Bush in Japan, is it?"

"What's he doing?" Libby asked William.

Now Alex was looking under the table. "Just crouching down there," he said, dropping the tablecloth, "with his finger over his mouth, shushing me."

"I think he's hiding," William said, eyeing a man who was being seated in the corner. He went back down under the table and said something. Bob said something back. William looked over at the corner and then said something under the table again. Slowly Bob came back up into his seat, and when William said "Go!" he got up and raced out of the restaurant.

"Owed him money, huh?" Alex said.

"I don't know, but I do know we've got an extra steak sandwich coming now," William observed.

"To say nothing of the tab for two beers," Alex muttered.

"I'll cover it," William offered.

"I didn't say that so you'd pay for it," Alex said, sounding annoyed.

Lunch was served and was cheerful and pleasant until Melissa and William started telling Libby how wonderful it must be to be a writer. Libby didn't feel up to explaining how her career was going to hell and so she merely smiled and murmured, yes, she had been very fortunate. After they finished eating, William excused himself, saying he needed to call his office.

Alex quickly moved down the table to slide into his seat. "Ah, the better half of the table—smart, beautiful women."

They talked about Melissa's job for a while, her having moved from Los Angeles to San Francisco and then to Chicago before landing in New York. She was very nice, Libby thought, but there was something about Melissa that seemed—well, guarded. She talked easily enough about her work, but thus far had made absolutely no reference to her personal life. Funny.

Libby noticed it because it was her nature to draw people out to talk about themselves, their lives, their experiences. It was a most valuable asset for a novelist, one that fed her an ongoing stream of new information and ideas. So when someone like Melissa could gracefully rebuff Libby's probes, it had to be from years of practice.

"Here he comes," Alex said, eyeing William as he came up the stairs and approached the table. "Took your seat, I figured you wouldn't mind."

"No, it's okay," William said, moving to sit in Alex's. He stopped then and came back to get his glass of mineral water.

"Did you call your girlfriend?" Alex asked him.

"What?"

"You have a girlfriend, don't you?" Alex asked him.

William hesitated, looking confused.

"You live with someone, don't you, William?" Alex continued.

"Uh, yeah," William said, moving to take Alex's old seat.

"I knew it," Alex said under his breath. He looked at Libby. "I bet he didn't tell you that part."

10

THEY walked back to the courthouse from Amsterdam's, the cool air feeling great. They flashed their passes at the door and took the elevator up. When they arrived at 16, Chuck the guard was waiting for them at the elevator bank. "Go directly to the jury room," he said forcefully. "Do not speak to anyone, is that clear?"

"But we have two minutes," Alex protested, looking at his watch.

"Just go!" the guard said.

Puzzled, the group made its way down the hall toward the jury room, Alex and Melissa leading the way. "It's not the way it sounded," William murmured to Libby on the way.

She looked at him. "What?"

"It's not the way it seems. I—we're—in the process of breaking up," William said.

"Oh, that," Libby said, pretending she didn't know what he was referring to. But she did. And it annoyed her how annoyed she felt with Wall Street William.

When they went in the jury room, Elena explained why the guard was upset. "Deeckson—"

"*Dayton,*" Debrilla the Viking lady corrected.

"Somebody offered heem ten thousand dollars to tell what was goeeng on een here during the trial!"

"Oh, my God," Libby said.

"And now he ees een with the judge," Elena finished.

Clay the hostile accountant made a sound of disgust. "Ten, they offered him ten. If it was one of you," he said, nodding his head in the direction of those who had just come in together—Libby, Alex, Melissa, William, and Slicked-Back Ronnie—"it would have been twenty-five at least."

"Vhy?" Debrilla asked him.

" 'Cause they're white," Clay said. "So the press'll think they cost more."

"Oh, I don't think that is true," Sweet Bridget said.

"Wait a second, wait a second!" Libby said. "Let me get this straight. Who is 'they'? A reporter?"

"I theenk so," Elena said.

The door opened and Basha and Stephen the computer man came in, asking what was going on, why was the guard so upset. Everyone began talking at once, during which time, Mrs. Smythe-Daniels came in to join the fray. About five minutes later, the door opened again and it was the guard with Dayton.

"Okay, okay, settle down," Chuck said as Dayton took a seat by the window. "The judge has the press in the courtroom now and she's telling them if any one of them is caught trying to talk to a juror, she will charge them with contempt of court, throw them in jail, and ban the press from the courtroom entirely."

Everybody started talking at once again.

"Yeah," Chuck confirmed, "some slimeball caught Mr. Doñez outside at lunchtime and offered to buy his story. To his credit, he came straight back and reported it immediately."

"Good for you, Dayton!" Libby said. Several others echoed her.

"The judge is going to talk to you about it when you go back into court," Chuck continued, "but she asked me to tell you this: If anyone approaches you on any aspect of this case in any way, you are to come to me or any officer of the court and report it. Otherwise, it could mean a mistrial."

They were all silent a moment. It had not occurred to any of them that anyone might want to pay them money for serving on this jury. Ten thousand dollars, regardless of Clay scoffing at the amount, was a lot of money. A windfall.

"From now on," Chuck said, "you will be entering and exiting the building by another entrance. And, I repeat, if anyone, *anyone*, approaches you to discuss the case, you are to report it immediately."

In five minutes, they were led back into the courtroom, where Judge Williams looked very angry indeed and launched into a tirade about the press. She ended with, "Ladies and gentlemen of the jury, if anyone, I repeat, *anyone*, other than an officer of this court or myself approaches you about any aspect of this case, you are to report it immediately, and the violator will be prosecuted to the extent of the law. Have I made myself clear?"

Heads bobbed up and down. Even Mrs. Smythe-Daniels looked submissive.

"Very well," Judge Williams said, "the prosecutor may proceed and call his next witness."

The prosecution then called Detective Brenda Watts.

People cleared their throats and shifted position, settling down as Detective Watts made her way through the courtroom to the stand. She looked a little like Sharon Gless from "Cagney and Lacey," though not so attractive. She was sworn in and then questioned about her credentials. She was from Manhattan Homicide. At the time of the shooting, nineteen months before, she had been a police officer for six years. She had been a detective now for a year and a half.

When MacDonald got to the night of the shooting, the jury became interested in what she had to say: the call at 2:04 A.M. to the precinct that there had been a shooting; the officer and her partner's arrival on the scene at 2:12 A.M.; the victim declared dead at 2:26 A.M. by EMS workers; the preservation of the crime scene, the interviews of the witnesses.

Outside the courthouse, a construction crew started jackhammering and the judge ordered that the windows be closed, which was unfortunate since within minutes everyone in the jury box was yawning for air.

MacDonald then started introducing photographs of the sidewalk where the shooting had occurred. After the initial shock of seeing blood all over the ground in the first photograph (which they were not shown, but saw in passing as MacDonald flashed it at the witness), there was nothing terribly interesting about the rest. They went through six photographs in near identical procedure, and when MacDonald whipped out yet another picture of the crime scene, only shot from a different angle, Libby started to yawn. At this rate, they'd be here until Easter.

Libby's legs were aching from the awful seat. Although it swiveled, it was too high off the ground to be comfortable—and she was five foot seven! Who was it made for? She heard the jurors in the row behind her squirming in their seats, too.

"Your Honor, the state wishes to introduce this photograph into evidence as People's Seven," MacDonald said.

"Please let defense counsel examine the photograph," the judge said.

As he had done six times before, the court officer took the photograph over to the defense table. Geiggen looked at the front, and the back, shrugged, and handed it back. "Defense has no objection."

The guard wrote something on the back of the picture. "Photograph has been entered into evidence as People's Seven," he said. He handed it back to MacDonald, who handed it back to the detective in the witness box.

Libby heard Slicked-Back Ronnie let out a big yawn in the back row.

"This photograph," MacDonald continued, "People's Seven—what is it of?"

"It's of the sidewalk where the victim was murdered," the detective replied.

"Objection!" Geiggen screamed, leaping to his feet. "And requests that counsel may approach the bench."

Judge Williams glared at him. "What *for?*"

"A sidebar, Your Honor, to discuss a point of law the jury should not hear."

She looked as though she might throw the gavel at him. She sighed and then said, "We will take a short recess. The jury will return to the jury room, and may I remind you that you are not to talk to anyone about this case or amongst yourselves. Thank you."

The jurors were beside themselves in the jury room. "Does anybody know what is going on?" Alex wanted to know.

Dayton was sniffing the air. "Something smells good."

"It's a steak sandwich," William said. "I put it on the radiator to keep it warm. You interested?"

"Yeah, man, I'm starved," Dayton said, reaching for the bag. "I never got lunch. Turned down ten thousand bucks and the court can't even give me a sandwich. What do I owe you?" he asked, almost into the sandwich already.

"Nothing," William said.

"Pass him some napkins," Libby said, handing them to Alex.

Bob, whose steak sandwich it was supposed to have been in the first place, suddenly announced, "I think the cop's lying."

"*What?*" Melissa cried. "How can you think that? We haven't even *heard* anything yet!"

"Those pictures," Bob insisted, "there's something funny about them."

"Well, I *know* there's something funny about someone in this room," Alex muttered, provoking some laughter.

"I can't make heads or tails out of those pictures," William said. "They all look like the same bloodstained cement." He glanced at Dayton and grimaced. "Sorry."

Dayton, his mouth full with the sandwich he was clearly enjoying, waved it off, William was not to worry.

"Vee have been instructed *not* to discuss the case!" Debrilla the Viking lady said.

"You needn't shout, my dear," Mrs. Smythe-Daniels said quietly. "But she's quite right, we shouldn't be discussing the case."

As if on cue, Chuck the guard came back in. "We're going back in."

Dayton choked down a little more of the sandwich, wiped his mouth with a napkin, and followed everyone to the courtroom. "Thanks, man," he said to William out in the hall. "I was about to faint."

Once they were settled in the jury box, MacDonald resumed his questioning of the policewoman. As far as Libby could tell, the only difference now, after the sidebar held at the bench, was that when MacDonald repeated the question he had asked before, "And this photograph—People's Seven—what is it of?" the detective said, "It's the sidewalk where the victim was shot" instead of "It's the sidewalk where the victim was murdered."

"And the sidewalk is . . . ?" MacDonald said.

"In front of Belle's, the nightclub where she was shot."

"And the nightclub was located where?"

"At Sixty-four West Fourteenth Street, Manhattan—between Fifth and Sixth Avenues."

"I meant, Detective Watts, where was this part of the sidewalk in relation to the nightclub?"

"It is—it was to the right," she said. "Or west of the front door. Or the left, if you were coming out of the nightclub's front door. The right front door."

Libby was going to scream. She couldn't follow this!

"Detective Watts," MacDonald said, dragging over a huge poster board that had been leaning against the prosecution's table, "if I showed you a ground plan of the Fourteenth Street block west of Fifth Avenue—"

"Objection, Your Honor!" Geiggen called, jumping to his feet. "No such ground plan has been entered into evidence!"

Judge Williams sighed, looking as deadly bored and tired as the jury was. "Yes, Mr. Geiggen." Wearily she looked over to MacDonald. "The prosecution will please offer the ground plan into evidence."

"Your Honor, the People wish to introduce this ground plan into evidence as People's Eight—no, Seven—as number Nine, Your Honor."

"People's Eight, you were right the first time," the judge said. "Will the officer of the court please give the ground plan to defense counsel for examination."

"Yes, Your Honor." The officer quickly took the big floor plan from MacDonald and brought it over to the defense table, where all four (the defendant included) looked it over.

Geiggen finally looked up to nod at the guard. "Defense has no objections to the ground plan being entered into evidence."

Libby covered her mouth and yawned again.

The court officer dropped his pen on the floor. He picked it up and marked something on the corner of the ground plan. "Ground plan has been entered into evidence, Your Honor, as People's Seven."

"Eight!" Elena and Ronnie supplied simultaneously from the jury box.

There was a ripple of laughter through the courtroom, and the judge stared at the jury box until the court stenographer strained forward and said, "Excuse me? People's what?"

"PEOPLE'S EIGHT!" the guard shouted across the room.

"Thank you," the stenographer said, resuming her rhythmic motion over her machine.

The court officer then brought the unwieldy diagram back over to the prosecutor. MacDonald took it in his hands and squinted, as if checking to make sure the defense team hadn't done anything to it while he wasn't looking.

Now there was the sound of a candy paper being unraveled in the second row of the jury box. The judge glared at the jury box again and the sound stopped. She then turned back to the prosecutor. "You may continue with your examination, Mr. MacDonald."

"Detective Watts," MacDonald said, "looking at this ground plan—Your Honor? May I put People's Eight on the easel so everyone can see it?"

"Yes," she said.

"Objection, Your Honor!" Geiggen cried, standing up. "Are we going to have to sit here until Christmas waiting for the assistant DA to prepare his case?"

"Overruled," the judge said quietly. "Mr. Geiggen's comment will be stricken from the record and disregarded by the jury." She looked at the defense attorney. "Mr. Geiggen, you will cease to make comments like that in my courtroom. Have I made myself clear?"

"Yes, Your Honor. I apologize, Your Honor."

The direct examination staggered on, the members of the jury sinking lower and lower in their chairs, seeking oxygen.

An hour later all that had been accomplished was the entrance of photos 1 to 15 and the ground plan as evidence, and also some documents concerning fingerprints, which Libby was sure no one understood the point of since she certainly didn't.

The jury was almost swooning by now. The judge, looking rather faint herself, finally interrupted MacDonald to suggest breaking for the day.

"Your Honor?" MacDonald said. "May I respectfully submit that I only have a few more questions for this witness and would like to ask them before we stop?"

Judge Williams's eyes narrowed slightly and then she nodded. "You may finish your direct examination."

"Detective Watts," the prosecutor said, drawing himself up to his tallest, "could you please tell the jury what information the female eyewitness on the scene gave you?"

"Yes. She gave me a description of the man she had seen driving the shooter to and from the scene of the shooting."

"And where was this witness standing at the time of the shooting?"

"Next to the victim, Sissy Cook."

The jury was awake now. Everybody was.

"And can you repeat the description she gave you at the scene?"

"Your Honor?" the detective asked. "May I refer to my notebook?"

"Yes, you may."

The officer flipped through her notebook. "Suspect was a white male, about thirty-eight years old, light brown hair, clean shaven, and was driving a gray or silver two-door Jaguar with a black convertible top, New York license plate with the first three letters three-el-eight."

"And was the witness given a photo ID of the suspect?"

"Yes. We conducted a photo lineup with the witness later the same morning." A description of a photo ID ensued: how five photos of men who looked like the defendant were put in with one of the defendant. MacDonald entered into evidence a yellow card that had six pictures on it and then gave it to the detective, who then explained that the marks on the back indicated the result of the photo ID.

"And who did the eyewitness select as the man she saw driving the shooter to and from the scene of the crime?"

Reading off the back, the detective said, "Number four."

"Detective Watts," MacDonald said, "could you please tell the jury whose picture was number four in the lineup?"

She pointed. "The defendant's, James Bennett Layton, Jr."

The prosecutor paused for a long moment and then murmured, "No further questions, Your Honor."

The jurors piled out of the courtroom, nearly trampling one another to get some air.

"One witness!" Clay the accountant cried in the jury room, kicking a chair in frustration. "Two hours and forty-five minutes—and for what purpose?"

"To set up the crime scene," Stephen the computer man explained.

"Shhh!" Debrilla said. "Vee cannot talk about the case."

"Deed you see the getup on that cop?" Elena asked Adelaide. "Wasn't eet unboleevable?"

"Now, now," Mrs. Smythe-Daniels said, gathering up her belongings, "one needn't criticize our only line of defense against the criminal element."

"Yo, but Ellie," Dayton the Romeo said to Mrs. Smythe-Daniels, "what the hell was she talkin' about, anyway, with all that fingerprint stuff? I didn't know what the heck she talkin' about."

"Ellie?" Mrs. Smythe-Daniels said in wonderment. "*Ellie?*"

Libby and Melissa looked at each other and burst out laughing.

Chuck came in to explain to them again that from now on they were to come and go through the entrance on the south side of the building.

Another pass was handed out, this one blue. He reminded them once more that if anyone tried to talk to them about the case, they were to report it immediately.

Alex came over to Libby, slipping on his coat. "I'll walk you to the subway."

"Great."

After saying good night to the others, Libby and Alex strolled out onto Centre Street. It was cold; the sun had gone down long ago.

"I have to apologize," Alex finally said.

"Good heavens, what for?"

"Oh, that stupid thing I pulled at lunch with William."

Libby smiled. "How did you know he lived with someone?"

"I didn't," Alex said, "not for sure. But I know his type." He looked at her. "Look, it was stupid. But—" He stopped walking to turn to her. "Truth is, Libby, I was a little pissed off you asked him to come along. I know it's childish, but that's how I felt—and I apologize for acting that way. It won't happen again."

Libby felt her face growing warm. Alex's interest in her was becoming difficult to ignore. Under normal circumstances she'd probably be interested in him, too, but they had to serve on this jury together. And for some reason, she didn't know why exactly, he made her feel uneasy. Maybe he was just too good-looking.

Or maybe she was just too jaded.

II

———

He's guilty," the doorman whispered to Libby as she walked past him.

"I don't want to hear it!" she snapped. "Mack, I'm serious. I don't mean to yell, it's just that it's getting pretty stressful."

"Yeah, sure, sorry," Mack said, slinking outside, his feelings hurt.

Libby sighed and turned around and went back out after him. At this rate she'd be fighting with all the building employees—and it was a big building. "Mack," she said, touching the sleeve of his uniform. "Please, don't take it wrong. I'm just burnt out."

He looked at her out of the corner of his eye. "Yeah, okay," he said. And then he winked. All was forgiven.

"Hi, Libby," said Nick Albanese, Libby's favorite night security person, standing in the lobby by the concierge desk. Like Al, he, too, was a former NYPD detective. She had nicknamed him Nick Danger the day she met him. He had that kind of smile.

"Listen, Nick Danger, I'm warning you," she said, "I don't want any grief."

"About what?" he said, baffled, holding his hands out. And then he got it. "Oh. I know what you're talking about. Al told me."

"I've got a package for you, Miss Winslow," the concierge said. "Hang on." He disappeared into the back room.

"He told me he gave you a hard time," Nick said.

"Normally I wouldn't care, but this—" She shook her head. "It's too depressing as it is."

"Yeah."

She looked at him. "So you're not going to say anything?"

"You mean, tell you that he's guilty?"

"Nick!"

"All right, all right," he said, holding his arms up to fend her off. "I swear I won't say anything."

"Here we go, Ms. Winslow," the concierge said. "Sign here."

Her package was from Random House. A friend had sent her a book. That was nice. On the other hand, in her mailbox was nothing but bills and a flyer about a new dentist in the neighborhood, which only reminded her about the unpaid bill sitting upstairs for the one she had. She took the elevator up to her floor, let herself into the apartment (from which Sneakers promptly escaped, so she had to go down the hall to get him), and listened to the messages on her answering machine. "Call me call me call me!" her publicist, Barbie, sang. And then later, "Call met at this number!" and then yet another message from Barbie, "Call me at home as soon as you get in!"

It must be good news, Libby thought. And that would be welcome. Feeling a little surge of hope, she called Barbie's home number.

"Libby!" Barbie cried. "I've been waiting for you! Guess what? Guess who's going to be on 'Oprah' after all?"

"Me?" she said.

"Yes! Your airplane ticket will be at the American counter at La Guardia tomorrow morning."

In one split second Libby's whole world had brightened; in the next she was seized by a sickly dread. "Tomorrow?"

"They had a cancellation and you're going to fill in and tape the show. Isn't this fantastic? We've been on the phone all day to the reps to roll out the books—"

"Wait a minute, Barbie—"

"They think _When Smiles Meet_ could hit the best-seller list after this!"

"Barbie! Barbie, wait!" Libby nearly shouted. "I can't go tomorrow. I'm on a murder trial. We have to call and explain. I could do it Saturday, though."

Dead silence.

"Libby," the publicist said quietly, "you cannot be serious."

Libby felt her throat tighten horribly. "But what can I do?"

"You can fucking go, that's what you can do!" Barbie told her.

"But I'm on the Poor Little Rich Boy trial."

"You're filling in—get it, Libby? If you don't come tomorrow, they don't want you at all."

"Barbie—"

"Just call in sick tomorrow."

No. She could not do it. Not even for this. There was no way she could not show up for court, not after that awful day when Basha had to go to the dentist.

But what about your life? Fifteen dollars a day serving on a jury isn't going to cut it.

Maybe she _could_ call in and say she was sick. . . . Maybe they'd put one of the alternates on the jury. Maybe—

"Libby? Are you there?"

Libby took a breath. "I'm sorry, but I can't go," she managed to get out.

"Oh, holy shit, you've got to be kidding!" Barbie cried. "You're going to fucking tell me that you can't go out and do 'Oprah'? Jesus Christ, Libby, you call in sick, you do whatever you have to do, but you have to get out there! We've fucking pulled every string in the book to get you on! You've _got_ to be there tomorrow!"

"No, I'm sorry," Libby said quietly, "but I can't. It's just not possible."

"Unbelievable!" Barbie yelled before hanging up on her.

Libby slowly hung up the phone, walked into the bedroom, fell facedown on her bed, and sobbed with frustration. Missy and Sneakers curled up next to her, purring supportively.

"What is happening to my life?" she asked, clenching her fist.

"Mom!" Peter cried, bolting from the kitchen table to hug his mother.

Jill laughed, staggering back, receiving Peter with one hand and closing the door to the garage with the other. "What's this sudden display of affection?"

Peter looked up at her. "She's making us eat liver," he whispered.

"Good evening, Mrs. Tompkins," Mrs. Montell said, continuing to eat.

"Hi, Mom," Katie said weakly. She looked as though she had been crying. A large piece of liver was on her plate, congealing.

"Peter," Mrs. Montell said sharply, "your dinner is getting cold."

"Yes, Pete, finish your dinner, darling," Jill said. "Let me go upstairs and wash up and then I'll be down."

"Mom," he whined.

"Go," she told him.

Obediently, he trudged back to the table.

"Mr. Tompkins called to say he would be late," Mrs. Montell called after Jill.

"Yes, I know, I talked to him while I was in the city."

"But he called again," Mrs. Montell said. "He won't be home until near midnight."

Darn. Well, it probably couldn't be helped.

"I saw that, young man!" Mrs. Montell said.

"But Duncan loves liver," Jill heard Peter say quietly.

Duncan was their Labrador retriever.

William spotted them at the table in the back of 15 Irving Place. Betsy and her brother, Jeffy, and his wife, Martha, waved at him. He couldn't believe Betsy had talked him into this. "Please, it's Jeffy's birthday," she had said. "Just let us take them out to dinner this one night. I'll tell them later we're splitting up, but not tonight. He's going through a hard time as it is."

And so William was here to take Jeffy out to dinner, although how a thirty-one-year-old could still be called Jeffy was beyond him. "I'm sorry I'm so late," he said when he reached the table.

"I've explained," Betsy said quickly, which meant *Don't say anything because what I've told them is not what you would tell them.*

Jeffy worked for Betsy's uncle at some kind of beer-importing firm and, as far as William could tell, did little but sample the goods. He had gained at least twenty-five pounds since he started working there. His wife, Martha, whom he married five years ago, had delivered two children already, but to William's eye looked anorexic now, she was so thin.

Twice already William had helped to bail Jeffy out with credit card messes that to him seemed incredible, particularly since the couple and their children were living rent-free in a house Betsy's parents had bought for them as an investment. How could people live so casually? he wondered. Just go ahead and have children without regard as to who would support them?

"Wow, William," Jeffy said under his breath after taking a huge gulp of red wine, "this is some trial you're on. You're not going to convict him, are you? I mean, it's pretty clear he's being framed—even so, she sounded like a bitch the world's better off without."

William looked at him.

"They've got to get a white guy for something, that's what they're thinking. After the Menendez brothers and O.J., they went after this Layton guy like vultures." He took another gulp and swallowed, wincing as though the action pained him. "It's getting so bad in this city, I practically had to break Martha's arm to come in tonight. She's terrified of ending up like the Central Park jogger." He threw down the rest of his wine and attacked the bread. "Some black guy shoots some bitch and a white guy's arrested for it and put on trial," he garbled through the bread. "If that doesn't sum up what a mess the world is today, I don't know what does."

"I'm not allowed to discuss the trial," William said. He turned to Martha. "How are the kids?" he asked. "Did you bring any pictures?"

"Mom?" It was Peter, in his pajamas. Jill was in hers, too, lounging in bed, watching television. She was supposed to be doing some cleaning, but she was too wiped out after court today.

She flicked off the TV with the remote control. "What is it, honey? You should be in bed."

Peter came over and climbed onto the bed next to her. She put an arm around him and he curled up, resting the side of his face on the covers over her thigh as she stroked his hair. "Mom," he said in a whisper, "did you see the man who killed Aunt Sissy?"

Jill felt her throat constrict slightly. "Yes, honey, I did."

Perhaps the strangest aspect of the trial was that Jill had never really been close to her sister, certainly not close the way she knew Peter thought she had been, which was the way Peter was close to Katie. Quite frankly, she and Sissy couldn't have been more different. While Jill had largely done everything she had been told to do from Day One—get good grades, be popular, win student elections, be a cheerleader, attend Mount Holyoke, get a job, marry, have children—Sissy had gone straight from expulsion from Emma Willard in her senior year to modeling in New York and "dating" a married man some twenty years her senior, which led to her move to Los Angeles, her arrest at age twenty, and then her stay at the Betty Ford Center.

Still, Jill had never once envisioned Sissy being murdered on the streets of New York before reaching the age of twenty-seven. If for no other reason than Sissy had always been so very lucky.

Well, as lucky as a beautiful woman could be who knew how to manipulate people with it. And Sissy had.

"Will they put him in the electric chair?" Peter asked.

"He will go to prison for a very long time, darling, so he can't hurt anyone else." Jill paused. "That's why I'm going to court. To make sure the authorities get all the information they need to convict him."

Peter thought about this for a moment. "Did they bring him into court in handcuffs?"

Jill hesitated again. There was no way she was going to tell her son that the man who was responsible for the murder of his aunt had been walking around on bail for almost two years.

"No one comes into the courtroom in handcuffs," she finally said.

He thought about this for a moment, too. And then, "Mom, *why* did he kill Aunt Sissy? The kids at school keep asking me."

Why did he kill her. Well, she could tell Peter the truth and explain that Layton hadn't actually murdered Sissy with his own hands, but had driven off to some drug-infested neighborhood instead to hire some drug thug who would shoot Sissy down in cold blood for him. And that Jim Layton had been so helpful to this nameless assassin as to drive him to the scene, point out her sister, and help him get away.

Sissy. Oh, God, poor Sissy.

Jill remembered when she was eight and her mother caught her carting a screaming one-year-old Sissy down the driveway in her red Radio Flyer wagon. "Jill! Where are you going with your baby sister?"

"Nowhere," Jill had answered.

"I saw you going somewhere—now answer me."

Lewisboro Library

Date charged: 5/18/2013,10:27
Title: Jury duty : a novel
Item ID: 31032150375877
Date due: 6/8/2013,23:59

To renew, please call
(914) 763-3857

Jill could remember mashing the red rubber toe of her Keds sneaker into the driveway as Sissy continued to howl. "Dr. Field's," she admitted. He was a doctor down the street.

"Dr. Field's!" her mother exclaimed, stooping to pick up Sissy in her arms. "There, there, sweetness. Jill, why?"

"Because she's broken, Mom, or something. She never stops crying! Something's the matter with her."

Little Sissy. So blond. So blue-eyed. Her mother's little angel. The apple of her father's eye. They had spoiled her rotten, of course. All of them. It was no wonder Sissy had had so much trouble getting her act together. For the longest time she simply didn't have to. And then when her family wouldn't spoil her anymore, she had gone elsewhere to find people who would.

And there had been many. The world was like that when it came to an amazingly beautiful young woman who knew how to oh-so-subtly seduce. Who, it had never seemed to matter, so long as Sissy got what she wanted.

And then she had finally sorted everything out. And then . . .

"Mom, Mom," Peter whimpered, "please don't cry." He was sitting up now, looking at her, lower lip trembling.

Her office phone rang at nine-thirty and Melissa stared at it a moment before picking up. "Hello?"

"Ms. Grant? Lobby security. There's a Miss Christine down here who would like to talk to you."

There was the sound of the phone being handed over. "Melissa?"

"Christine? What on earth are you doing here?"

"Oh, I had to have dinner with a CBS rep," she said. "I figured you might be up there and I wanted to offer you a nightcap."

"I haven't even had dinner," Melissa said.

"Then I'll buy you dinner and a nightcap," Christine said. "We can go to Zazu's across the street."

It was clear to Melissa that Christine Harrington had already enjoyed a bit of wine tonight, but she was perfectly lucid and funny while discussing the cat food campaign with her—which they did while Christine sipped a glass of white wine and Melissa ate some soup, salad, and warm bread, too tired to wonder at Christine being here at this hour of the night.

She was in her early forties, Melissa decided. Even in this flattering light Melissa could see the years on her face. Actually, the lines rather suited her, gave her a sense of mature beauty, of power. Anyone could be attractive in this day and age, but few women could look as though power truly suited them. Christine was one of those.

But MIT scientist turned New Jersey cat food marketing executive? Well, they all had their pasts, didn't they? Certainly Melissa had hers.

"Jeffy looks so fat," Betsy said, having already shed her coat and shoes and throwing herself down on the sofa. "I wonder what the hell she's feeding him."

"Something she's obviously not eating herself," William said. "She looks skeletal."

"Do you suppose she went to the ladies' room after dinner to throw up?"

"Do you want a nightcap?" he asked, moving toward the kitchen.

"No thanks." After a moment: "Jeffy's unhappy, I know he is. Look at all the weight he's gaining. I bet she's not having sex with him anymore. I bet she has some kind of problem with it."

"She's probably just tired," William said. "A three-year-old and a one-year-old would make anyone feel sexless."

"No," Betsy said, "I think it's something worse. Some sort of neurotic tendency. She's always struck me as a traumatized child."

He came out of the kitchen with a small snifter of brandy. She looked up at him and smiled. "Thank you for coming tonight."

"It's all right," he murmured, standing there, smelling the brandy and then tasting it.

"Are you going to your parents' for Thanksgiving?"

"Yeah," he said. "I got a flight today."

"Must have cost you a fortune," she said. She patted the sofa next to her. "Sit a minute."

He hesitated.

"I won't do anything," she said. "William, look, I'm already looking for a place. After Mom and Dad come next week, I'm out of here, all right? I just think it's important we stay friends."

After she finished dinner, Melissa walked Christine to the parking garage, but finally had to speak up. "Look, Christine," she began, "no offense, but I can't let you drive back to New Jersey this late. Not after all the wine. I mean, I can, but I'm afraid I won't."

Christine's eyes blazed a moment—and Melissa thought maybe she had gone too far—but then Christine smiled slightly. "What are you suggesting that I do?"

There was something in the way she said this that made Melissa blush, but fortunately they were outside under the streetlights where things like that did not matter. There was something going on with this woman that was getting hard to ignore. Even if she wanted to. "I'm going to call for a car—to drive you home."

"Okay," she said. "But only on one condition."

"What's that?"

"You drive my car out tomorrow night to our offices, and we go over the storyboards there. Okay? Then I'll send you back in a car."

"Well, I have the trial—"

"Take my car tonight," Christine said, "and park near the courthouse. When you get on your way, give us a call—there's a phone in the car."

They went on to the garage, where Melissa called for a car, on the agency account, to drive Christine home to Montclair, and Christine paid the attendant to bring her car down for Melissa to drive. When it arrived, Melissa murmured, "Oh, wow, I'm going to have to park this in a precinct to hold on to it." It was a brand-new navy blue Lexus.

"You can drive, right?" Christine asked her, laughing.

"Oh, I can drive, all right—I'm from California, remember," Melissa said, walking over and surveying the car admiringly. "It's fighting off the carjackers I'm worried about."

A black Lincoln Town Car pulled up outside the garage. "There's your car," Melissa said, walking Christine over and opening the door for her.

Christine smiled at her. And then touched the side of Melissa's face for a moment. "You're very sweet," she said. "And thoughtful." And then she got into the car.

Melissa waved good-bye, took a deep breath, and then turned around to face the Lexus.

"I'll take it if you don't want it," the garage attendant offered.

She smiled and walked over to tip him.

Sometime during the drive downtown, Melissa finally started to think straight. Christine Harrington was making subtle overtures to her that she could—and *should*—pretend she didn't understand. But she did understand them—she had since the night they talked in the Oak Room bar—and not only did she have an ironclad rule about getting involved with a client, but felt nothing but panic at the prospect of dealing with her attraction to *any* woman, even if it was such an extraordinary one like Christine Harrington.

"Women," as Melissa thought of it, was something she had only "done" on her most drunken nights in the last year of her drinking. That's how hard she had always resisted her feelings in that direction. Given the life-style Melissa had always envisioned for herself—one of the mainstream—to cross sexual lines seemed at best unproductive and at worst an invitation to be forcibly dragged out of the mainstream and shoved into a psychological ghetto.

Who, in their right mind, would volunteer to be a minority?

She sighed, stopping at a red light, gripping and regripping the leather-covered steering wheel.

She had dealt with none of this in sobriety. Her method of coping was to have dated a guy for a while to reconfirm what she already suspected, and then to simply shut down sexually until the day she was ready to deal with it. As they said in AA, some issues you simply had to put on a shelf until you were sober long enough to deal with them (without freaking out and running back to the bottle). When Melissa was ready, they had told her, she would be able to take any issue down from the shelf, examine it carefully, and then figure out where it fitted in with her new life, or if it fitted in at all, and how then to proceed.

And now one of the most attractive women Melissa had ever met in her life was making overtures to her.

Hell, she hadn't taken this off the shelf—the damn thing was leaping down into her lap!

Jill heard the taxi in the driveway, motor idling, the thunk of the door closing, and the sound of the car backing out over the gravel. Moments later there was the sound of a key in the front door. A minute later, Rusty was coming upstairs, coming in through the door, pulling at his tie. "You shouldn't have waited up," he said wearily, coming around the bed and throwing his briefcase into the chair in the process.

"I couldn't sleep," she said, lying. She had fallen dead asleep after putting Peter back to bed. Then she had set her alarm to appear to be waiting for him at midnight.

He was a very good-looking man, her husband. Six foot two, reddish brown hair, blue eyes, a warm and friendly smile. He had played football in high school. Not in college, but that didn't matter. He still looked the part.

Rusty gave her a kiss. He smelled of stale alcohol. "Tell me about court while I get undressed."

And so she did, as he undressed—tossing his shirt and underwear into the hamper—went to the bathroom, washed his hands and face, brushed his teeth, and came back out in cotton pajama bottoms.

"So my part is done," Jill said.

He made a sighing sound as he crawled into bed. Once settled, lying on his side, he said, "Thank God, Jill."

"But I'm still going to go," she told him. "MacDonald wants me to sit in the courtroom every day so the jury remembers my testimony."

"I think that's a lousy idea."

"Honey, if it'll get him convicted . . ."

He reached for her hand and held it, closing his eyes to sleep. "I just don't want you hurt anymore," he whispered.

He shouldn't let her do this, he thought. But oh, it felt so good.

His belt was undone, pants unzipped, his shorts pulled apart, and Betsy was going down on him. And he just sat there, arm still across the back of the sofa, hand still holding the snifter, letting her do it, up and down, up and down, slow and then fast, trying everything to make him hard.

And now she was succeeding.

Her mouth was warm and wet, her tongue swirled around him, and he wondered idly where she had learned this since she had never done this to him before. The thought made him falter a second, but her hand tightened on him, slick with saliva, and her mouth plunged deeper and he knew if this kept up, he would come soon.

He balanced the snifter on the couch back and then gently brought Betsy's face up to his. Everything was wet. He pushed her back on the couch and felt under her skirt. She had on self-holding stockings and could just slip off her panties and push up her skirt.

She was very wet and very hot. And it was a good fit, sliding into her, perhaps the best, he thought, starting to grind into her, the best since the very first night they had done it, way back before he realized he was being taken hostage.

12

SHE LOOKED down at the street from the living-room couch. What was it, four in the morning? Five? Yes, five. It had to be five because the man was down in the street unhitching his coffee wagon from behind his battered station wagon. He always started work on the sidewalk at five. And what day was it? Thursday.

Libby pulled her robe closer around her and curled up against the couch. She had awakened in a sweat, panicked about something, something she couldn't remember for a minute or two. And then she remembered it. That everyone at Haverhill Publishing would be furious with her for not flying out to Chicago today to tape "The Oprah Winfrey Show." That her career was in a downward spiral. That *When Smiles Meet* would be considered an even bigger disaster than before.

Down below, a city bus was pulling over on the far side of the street. The driver shut off the lights, got out, and crossed the street, hailing the coffee man.

Libby loved the peace of New York at this hour.

Sneakers leapt up onto the back of the couch, did a short catwalk, and then dove into her lap to burrow a bed in the folds of her robe. A few minutes later Missy came sauntering in, pretending to be disinterested, but soon ended up sleeping on the couch next to Libby, resting the side of her face in the arch of Libby's foot.

She felt scared. Money did that to people when it was running out.

The driver jogged back across the street to his bus with a paper bag in his hands. A few moments later, the bus roared to life, the lights came blazing on, and with a final wave to the coffee man, he drove the big city bus down the street.

Libby envied the driver's sense of purpose, his unerring instinct about what to do next.

When Libby was waved through the special southern entrance to the courthouse at nine forty-five, she heard the unmistakable address of Mrs. Smythe-Daniels calling behind her. "William! Good morning."

"Good morning, Mrs. Smythe-Daniels," she heard William say.

Libby turned around. "Oh, look," Mrs. Smythe-Daniels said, "it's Cornelia. Good morning."

"Good morning."

Mrs. Smythe-Daniels looked at William and then back to Libby. "If I didn't know better, I'd have to say the two of you were out together last night. For two young people, you both look simply awful."

"Thank you," Libby said with a weak smile. "It's nice to know you think I can still get a date when I look this bad."

Mrs. Smythe-Daniels threw her head back and laughed a high, whinnying laugh, then headed off in the direction of the courthouse cafeteria.

"Thank you," William said to Libby.

"For what?"

Oh, boy, he did look awful. Behind his glasses his eyes were swollen, the bags underneath blue-gray. "It's nice to know you would ever consider me as a date."

She laughed a little. "Yes, well, life is short, William."

"Yeah, I know."

His tone was so discouraged she had to stop walking. "Are you all right?"

"Oh, hell, I don't know!" he said, digging his hands into the pockets of his overcoat. He looked at her. "I'm supposed to be breaking up with my girlfriend, and then last night— I— Oh, hell, I don't know!"

Libby looked at her watch. "Come on, we should get upstairs," she said, leading him to the elevator. "Look," she said a moment later, under her breath so only he could hear, "if it's any consolation, I was fool enough to give in and do exactly the same thing the night before I was leaving my ex."

William looked at her, startled.

She met his eyes and smiled. "If you're the one who's leaving, then they're the one who's going to do their damnedest to want to do it just one more time. So don't feel bad—we all go through it. It's the last trap to get through. Somehow it seems too mean to reject them to the last— reject them on every count."

He was so surprised, he couldn't respond.

"Anyway," she said, pushing the elevator button, "if you think you've got problems, I was asked to be on 'Oprah' today to save my career and I had to turn it down."

"Well, at least you didn't sleep with her last night so you wouldn't reject her completely!" he joked and they both burst out laughing. "Seriously, though, are you in a jam? Can I help?"

"No," Libby said, shaking her head. "It's just a case of an almost-miracle. You know, the kind that sends you soaring with hope only to dash you down harder and lower than before."

"I'm really sorry," he said.

They got on the elevator. She glanced over at him. "Was it very bad this morning? For you, I mean?"

"This morning? Forget this morning," he said. "It was last night. It was interpreted as recommitment." He sighed and shook his head. "I'm not very proud of myself this morning."

"I know the feeling," she told him. After a moment, she added, "But what are you supposed to do? If it isn't working, it isn't working. I mean, I stayed far too long with my ex—basically because I had already invested so much time and energy I didn't want to have to start over."

"She was going to stay just for a week," he said, "and then she never left."

"Oh, one of those," Libby said.

"No," he said quickly, "don't think badly of her. I mean, what kind of jerk would let it go on like this for fourteen months?"

"Fourteen months," Libby murmured. "It could be worse. That's not very long. She'll be okay."

Most everyone on the elevator was listening to them by now, but since William didn't seem to care, Libby decided why should she.

"Well, I do have one suggestion," she said under her breath.

His eyebrows went up.

"Write it off as William's last mistake. And from here on in, have people you like call you Will. Like your grandfather. That way you'll be able to tell the bad guys from the good guys, and if they try to move into your apartment, you tell them no, sorry."

He smiled. "What are you going to call me?"

"What do you want me to call you?"

"Will," somebody in the back of the elevator urged.

When attendance was taken in the jury room, three jurors were missing: Alex, who arrived shortly thereafter; Romeo Dayton, the limo driver, who arrived after that and promptly climbed up on the windowsill to have a cigarette with his coffee, and Bob the drinker, for whom they were waiting now.

"Do you suppose this is what President Nixon's newspapers looked like toward the end?" Stephen the computer man said, holding up the *Daily News*. The newspapers were really bad this morning. The *News* had very little of its first three pages left. He looked down the table. "What's the *Post* look like?"

Basha held it up. People laughed. It looked as though a kindergarten class had attacked it with scissors.

"Did anyone check the obituaries for Rupert Slotnik?" Melissa asked.

"He's not in it," Libby reported. "So at least we know he didn't die."

"He had a stroke," Adelaide said. "But he's okay. I found out from the guard."

"That's too bad." Pause. "But if he had died," Sweet Bridget asked, "would they have put that in the obituary? That he had been serving on this jury?"

A few laughed.

"God, a stroke," Libby murmured.

"Where the devil is that man Bob?" Mrs. Smythe-Daniels demanded to know.

"He's going to get fined," young Slicked-Back Ronnie said, sadistically rubbing his hands together. "That'll teach him."

"I do not un-dare-stant vhy everyvune is not here on time!" Debrilla cried.

"Yes!" Adelaide echoed authoritatively. Today Madame Foreman had miniature bowling shoes hanging from her ears.

"I do not un-dare-stant vhy everyvun here has an ax-cent!" Ronnie cried.

Some people snickered, but Elena was not amused. "I am just as good a ceeteezen as you, Mr. Hotshot Executeeve Trainee. Probably bet–*tor*."

He looked hurt. "I wasn't implying you weren't. It's just there are all these accents. The, uh—German lady—"

"Debrilla," Melissa supplied, glancing up from her laptop computer.

"And you," Ronnie said, nodding to Elena, "and then, you know, the lady down the table who was at the dentist. Isn't she Russian or something?"

"*Russian?*" Basha said in a clipped, accentless voice. She hadn't spoken much since the first day and so this had the desired effect. "I beg your pardon."

"Because I was born een Brazeel?" Elena said. "Thees makes me not as good? They called me to jury duty, deedn't they?"

"They called you for jury duty," Alex said, "because you registered to vote."

"That's how they got us?" Melissa asked. "You mean if I hadn't re-registered when I moved to New York, I wouldn't be here?"

"I knew it was a mistake to register," Dayton said from outside the window.

"Oh, come on, Dayton," Libby said. "It is never a mistake to register to vote. The only mistake is *not* to vote."

"Here, here," Mrs. Smythe-Daniels said. "Although I dare say there are a lot of people I wish who wouldn't."

"The mistake we made after registering," Alex continued, "was to send in the jury card."

"What jury card?" Melissa said.

"After you registered in New York, didn't you get something in the mail that confirmed your address?" Alex said. "And said that if you destroyed it, or didn't send it in, that it would be under penalty of law?"

"If I had thrown that away, I never would have been called?" Melissa said.

"I should hope you would have been called to a jail cell," Mrs. Smythe-Daniels said indignantly.

"So when do we get paid?" Dayton said, coming back in through the window.

"A couple of months after the trial," Stephen the computer man said. "Fifteen a day plus two-fifty for transportation."

"One would think there are better uses for our tax money," Mrs. Smythe-Daniels said.

"Speak for yourself, Ellie," Dayton said. "I'll take what I can get."

Mrs. Smythe-Daniels looked at Dayton, amused, as if he might be her pet or something. "Eleanor," she said. "You may call me Eleanor, young man, but this Ellie business simply has to stop."

Dayton smiled his best Romeo smile. "But you're too young to be called Eleanor—hell, Ellie, people'll think you're Mrs. Roosevelt out of the grave."

"That's the idea, I think," Melissa said quietly, in such a way that Mrs. Smythe-Daniels didn't hear it.

Libby's end of the table laughed. She hazarded a look at Mrs. Smythe-Daniels, who was, much to her surprise, beaming at Dayton. Good Lord, she was playing the coquette!

Bob the drinker came bursting in. He looked absolutely awful. Drawn, pale, red eyes, near to collapsing.

"You were supposed to be here at ten o'clock sharp, bub!" Elena exploded, elbowing Adelaide.

"Yes!" Adelaide cried, little bowling shoes swinging.

"I'm sorry, I couldn't help it," Bob said, reaching shakily for a chair.

He did look awful and Libby wondered if he didn't have the flu or something.

"Okay, everyone, into court," Chuck the guard announced.

The courtroom was packed to the rafters again; the defendant looked meek today. The judge looked positively furious.

By now they knew the order in which they had to file into the jury box, and after Alex pushed Adelaide to the front, they did this with almost military precision.

"The jury is present, Your Honor," the officer said.

"Yes, indeed," she said, glaring down at Bob the drinker in seat #4. Then she moved things along, announcing that it was time for the cross-examination of the prosecution's witness, the Cagney police lady from the day before. The detective, who had been sitting in the box when they came in, was reminded that she was still under oath. Geiggen got up and walked over to the jury box, smiled at the jurors, and then turned to smile at the detective. "Good morning."

"Good morning." There was a microphone in the witness box today and the detective's words boomed across the courtroom.

"We have a microphone today, Detective Watts," Judge Williams said. "So you won't have to speak up as loudly as yesterday."

Next to Libby, Bob's head started curling down toward his lap. A nudge from the other side made her turn to look at Clay the hostile accountant. She followed his eyes down to his hand, which was offering an open pack of Life Savers. He nodded toward Bob. Libby took them and nudged Bob.

"How long have you been on the police force, Officer Watts?" Geiggen asked.

"It's Detective Watts," she replied. "Seven years."

Bob had taken one red-eyed look at the Life Savers and shaken his head, and now clutched his stomach and dropped his head all the way down into his lap. Even the witness turned to look at him, which made Geiggen turn around to look, too. "Your Honor," he said, "I believe a member of the jury is ill."

Judge Williams tried to see over the edge of the jury box. "Mr. Shannon, are you all right?"

Bob only shook his head, clutching himself.

"I think he's in pain, Your Honor," Libby said.

Judge Williams sighed, but said gently, "We will take a short recess. The jury is reminded not to discuss this case with anyone or amongst yourselves. The guard will please assist Mr. Shannon."

As the rest of the jurors filed into the jury room, Bob the drinker was taken down the hall somewhere. They had been in the jury room for maybe ten minutes when Melissa came in. "I have the distinct feeling Bob won't be coming back. He's pretty sick. My guess is pancreatitus or a bleeding ulcer."

Sure enough, after forty-five minutes had passed, they were called back into the courtroom, where the judge announced that Juror #4, Robert Shannon, would be unable to serve as a juror for health reasons and that Alternate Juror #2, Eleanor Smythe-Daniels, was now officially Juror #4. "I suppose they think this some kind of honor," Mrs. Smythe-Daniels muttered, moving down into the seat next to Libby.

Suddenly Libby felt her spirits lift. Thank God she hadn't called in sick today. Thank God she had played it fair and square. Maybe her career was going through a rough patch, but she would never have to deal with the guilt from knowing the kind of havoc her absence would have caused had she called in sick and flown out to Chicago to tape "Oprah."

The cross-examination of Detective Watts resumed. Geiggen seemed to be asking the same questions that MacDonald had covered the day before, putting the jury to sleep, but then suddenly he came out with "Detective, isn't it true when the same eyewitness went to an actual police lineup, that instead of picking the defendant, she picked a police officer?"

"OBJECTION!" MacDonald thundered. "Defense is saying this to confuse the jury. No such evidence is in the trial, Your Honor!"

"Sustained," Judge Williams said. "Mr. Geiggen . . ."

"Yes, Your Honor?"

She sighed heavily, gave him a look of disgust, and said simply, "Behave."

Laughter rippled through the courtroom.

"Yes, Your Honor," Geiggen said, turning to make a face of mock-terror to the jury. Then he turned around and resumed his questions.

"Detective Watts, you very thoroughly described for us yesterday how the police conducted the investigation of the shooting of Sissy Cook. But despite the department's best efforts, the police did not—and have not—caught the person who actually shot her. Is that correct?"

"Yes," Detective Watts said, eyes beaming hate.

"So for all intents and purposes, you have no murder suspect."

"Objection, Your Honor!" MacDonald said. "Defense knows his client is on trial for murder in the second degree. It has not yet been established who the murderer is, or whether in fact it could be his own client—"

"OBJECTION!" screamed Geiggen. "Prosecution is inflaming the jury with prejudicial information!"

"What prejudicial information?" MacDonald yelled. "It's no secret your client's on trial for murder!"

Judge Williams was banging her gavel. When there was dead silence, she said, "Counsel will approach the bench." While they argued in whispers up there, Clay offered Libby a Life Saver, which she gratefully took. Her stomach was killing her after all this screaming and unpleasantness.

After an angry two minutes at the bench, the judge dismissed the jury for lunch and told them to come back at two. As for counsel, they were to meet in her chambers immediately.

Jill had to get some air. Court this morning was nothing but frustration. Maybe Rusty was right, maybe she should just go home. But MacDonald said her presence was important. What had he said? "You're the only person who can sit in for your sister in the courtroom. The jurors will look at you and see her, and that is very, very important."

She pushed her way through the crowds in the lobby to exit the front of the courthouse. Vans with microwave antennas were parked along the street. "That's the one!" she heard someone yell. "She's the sister!" and Jill started to panic as a sea of reporters, photographers, and camera people came running toward her.

"Is it Cook? Miss Cook?" a reporter said.

"Her name's Tompkins," someone else said.

The swarm was around her, the lights of the TV cameras making her squint. Jill recognized a reporter she had watched for years on CBS and the reporter seemed to know it, for she quickly asked, "Mrs. Tompkins, do you have confidence in the prosecution's case against James Bennett Layton?" and then shoved the mike in her face.

"I'm sorry, but I can't discuss the case," Jill said, trying to move, but she was hemmed in from all sides.

"Will anyone else from your family be testifying?" someone from Fox News asked.

"I'm sorry," Jill said, shaking her head, "all I can tell you is that I'm here because my sister was murdered."

"Do you know about your sister's past love affairs?" someone yelled.

"Her what?" Jill couldn't help but make a face of disgust. "How dare you!"

"Does that mean yes?" one reporter in the back asked.

"Why aren't your parents here, Mrs. Tompkins?"

"If they were physically able to be, they would be."

"Can you tell us what your sister was really like, Mrs. Tompkins?"

"Are you staying in the city, Mrs. Tompkins?"

"What hotel is she in?" one reporter asked another.

Jill's head began to swim as her body went numb and the lights started to close in on her. Suddenly there was a hand on her arm and a voice barking, "Mrs. Tompkins will not be answering any questions whatsoever until the trial is over."

"You're Schnagel from prosecution," someone said.

"Let Mrs. Tompkins through!" Kathryn bellowed.

For someone so tiny, Jill thought, she packed a lot of punch. She supposed she had to. "Back off, I say!" Kathryn yelled. "Here, Jill, in here," and Jill was pulled back into the courthouse and up some stairs. "I told Kevin we needed to make arrangements for you. Goddamn it, those people are animals."

The reporters were stopped by the guards at the foot of the stairs and Kathryn steered Jill into a room where there were six uniformed city cops sitting around watching TV. In the next room was a variety of desks and chairs, where various people were being questioned. Some people had handcuffs on. Jill knew what this was. This was the central booking office for criminal cases. She had been called here the night Sissy was killed. The police had brought James Bennett Layton here to book him and for the officers to be interviewed by the DA's office to determine what the charges were.

"I'm so sorry, Jill," Kathryn said. "I promise, I'll make sure you're protected from now on."

At one time Jill hadn't liked Kathryn very much. She had lacked warmth and seemed bossy and bitchy at best. But Jill did now. Because someone finally had seen that she needed protection. Support.

After all, she was just a mom. Murder was not something she did.

The sun had warmed the day to a surprising degree, and so Libby and Alex ordered sandwiches at a deli and went outside to eat on a bench in a small park behind the courthouse. Libby was feeling a bit uncomfortable because Alex seemed so determined to find out about her past romantic life, why she had never married.

Watching some courthouse workers playing basketball on the court, Libby ate her sandwich slowly and explained to Alex that she just hadn't met the right person yet. Otherwise, as far as she knew, she was perfectly normal.

Alex burst out laughing, spraying crumbs of kaiser roll and nearly choking. Libby looked at him. "Normal is being a novelist?" Alex whooped. "Libby, wake up—nobody lives the way you do."

Huh. She supposed he was right. "Well, what about you? You're thirty-six and you've never been married. A lot of people would say that isn't normal, Alex."

"It is if you haven't met the woman you'd like to be the mother of your children. That's why I want to get married—to have a family." He paused and Libby looked up from her sandwich, meeting his eyes. They were blue and intense. His expression was sincere. "I don't want a normal woman for a wife. I want someone extraordinary. I want my kids to have the best." He smiled. "Someone like you, maybe."

Libby lowered her eyes and took another bite of her sandwich— turkey, lettuce, tomato on whole wheat—and thought about this. Maybe she was normal after all, because, she thought, most normal women would agree that what Alex had just said was a very effective line. Very effective. But still, there was something off about him. Something that just didn't sit right.

One Police Plaza was not far from the courthouse. It took a little doing, but Melissa found what she was looking for. She took a seat in the back and opened the yogurt she had bought on the way and started to eat it. She should be working, but she knew she needed to be here, too.

The meeting had already started, and a woman was swearing her boss was going to drive her back to drink. Melissa smiled. The first six months, *everything* had been going to drive her back to drink, too. Now, two and half years later, things had settled down to a dull roar.

A young man was now sharing about how upsetting it was to see all the drug dealers hanging around City Hall at lunchtime, but how it was now none of his business since he was no longer a client.

"My name's Chuck and I'm an alcoholic," a man on the other side of the room said. "And I just had to hear myself say it. Today, where I work, I came full-face with the disease. I had to walk this guy out of where I work, knowing full well the guy's a drunk, and knowing there's nothing wrong with him that a drink wouldn't fix—and that in all probability this guy wants to drink a whole lot more than do what he's supposed to be there doing, and so he's decided to use his hangover as the early stages of some terrible disease for which he can be excused so he can go home and drink."

People burst out laughing. Melissa was sitting up, craning her neck, trying to see.

"So I take this guy out and call for an ambulance—which is procedure—but all the while I'm just dyin' to blow the whistle. 'Hey! This guy's fakin' it! You guys are too easy to fool!" But it's none of my business, I think to myself—if he wants to screw the system, fine, let him, I've got enough problems keeping myself in line. But, man, the point is, you can't con a con—and I sure as hell felt like bustin' this guy's ass 'cause I can't con anybody anymore—so I guess maybe I'm kinda jealous."

More laughter.

Melissa got a glimpse of him—and pulled back.

It was their guard. From the jury room. Chuck. The one who had taken Bob out this morning.

Will felt his heart speed up as his eyes roamed the paperback fiction stacks at Barnes & Noble. He slowed at the W's, saw Wouk, backed up and—there she was.

Elizabeth Winslow.

He picked up the book and looked at the back. "Funny, warm, delicious," a quote said, "just the story to warm even the most cynical heart." The blurb read:

Can a very successful woman find true love in this day and age? Amanda Sinclair, the smart and beautiful heroine of this novel, has come to be-

lieve not. But Amanda soon finds that she doesn't know everything . . .
particularly when it comes to love.

Will smiled. And then went up to the front of the store to find her
new book.

13

A FTER TELLING Libby she was the kind of woman he would want to
be the mother of his children, Alex went dashing off to buy some
athletic socks on Canal Street, leaving Libby to stroll back to court
alone. She was feeling better now. Alex was not the most intellectual
man she had ever met, but it was nice to feel not only desirable, but worthy of motherhood.

When she reached the sixteenth floor and was making her way toward the jury room, someone called, "Libby!"

She whirled around. Down the hall was William—Will?—waving a
shopping bag at her.

"Look what I've got!" He hurried over and opened the bag. Libby's
heart skipped when she saw her first novels—in paperback—and *When
Smiles Meet* in hardcover. She would never get over the thrill of having
been published, existing in print. But then Will said, "I wanted to do my
part to compensate for 'Oprah,' " and then she felt that sinking sensation again in her stomach.

"Oh, that," she said, feeling foolish for feeling so instantly crushed
again.

He looked pained. "I'm sorry, Libby, I shouldn't have—"

"Oh, William, I'm fine, I'm just being silly."

He touched her arm. "Will. And you're not being silly. I could tell at
lunch at Amsterdam's you're worried about your career."

Whatever he was saying didn't quite register, because she suddenly
had a thought. "If you were me," she said, walking past him down the
hall toward the pay phone, forcing him to follow or be abandoned,
"would you call 'The Oprah Winfrey Show' and tell them why you
couldn't come today? Or would you trust the publicist who hung up on
you?"

"I'd call," he said. He looked at his watch. "I'd call right now, in fact, before court resumes."

She had already whipped a pen and pad out of her bag and was picking up the phone. "Chicago area code."

"Three-one-two," he readily supplied.

She punched in the number of her telephone credit card from memory. "Yes," Libby was saying into the phone, "for Chicago. The number for Harpo Productions?" A minute later she was smiling at Will, holding for one of the producers of "The Oprah Winfrey Show." "Do you really want me to call you Will?"

The trial resumed at two o'clock, and with the exception of some feedback problems from the new microphone (rendering the jury almost on the floor, at one point, clutching their ears), the last leg of the cross-examination of Detective Watts went smoothly. Geiggen was brief and courteous and the jury absorbed the following information:

Yes, there had been an eyewitness to the shooting in front of the nightclub. She had been standing right next to the victim when it happened. Yes, she had successfully ID'd the defendant as the getaway driver in a photo lineup hours later, but yes, Detective Watts had to admit it, there had been some problem with a police lineup identification at the precinct the next day, but—as Judge Williams explained at that point—that lineup was not part of the evidence of this trial. The photo ID was, however.

Oh course, all Libby could wonder about was whether or not it was true what Geiggen had said before, that the witness had picked a cop out of the actual lineup, even though they had been instructed to forget it.

She was in much better humor now. As she had suspected, the producers of "Oprah" hadn't gotten an accurate account about why she couldn't be there today. ("Gosh, maybe you'll come after the Poor Little Rich Boy trial is over!" the producer had said. "Sure!" Libby responded. "You know, as an insider on the jury, what happened in the jury room," the producer added. "Oh," Libby said, losing her smile. But at least they had the real story now, that she was a good citizen doing her duty, not a prima donna author who couldn't be bothered.)

Finally, Detective Watts was excused and the prosecution called its next witness. Libby hoped that *some* witness would provide a little narrative to this story soon, because it was very hard to get an overview of what had happened the night of the shooting.

Beside her, Mrs. Smythe-Daniels took the moment to shift her lady-like self, and Libby sat up a little straighter.

When the next witness was brought into the courtroom, murmurs broke out. Marybeth Shaeffer was a tall, slim, and absolutely gorgeous brunette, and Libby wondered if she hadn't seen her somewhere before. After she was sworn in, it was revealed that yes, indeed, Marybeth Shaeffer was a professional model. She had also been the best friend and roommate of the victim, Sissy Cook, and had been with her at the time of the shooting.

As MacDonald led her through the examination, they learned that Marybeth was from a small town in Nebraska. She had attended the University of Texas for two years, but then moved to New York City when offered a modeling job. No, she had never been arrested. No, she had never witnessed a violent crime before.

She and the deceased had met at their modeling agency. She was a lot younger than Sissy, only twenty-one at the time they met, but they hit it off and so when Sissy asked her if she would like to share her spacious two-bedroom apartment on the East Side, Marybeth gratefully accepted. What was Sissy like? Warm and funny and caring. Couldn't cook worth beans, but then they were never encouraged to eat much anyway (laughter). She was smart and hard-working and full of fun. She was also generous. Sissy's parents lived in Florida and the Christmas before she had died, she had taken Marybeth with her to stay at their house. It had been wonderful. They had gone to church on Christmas Eve and then had turkey and presents and everything. She had been invited that next Christmas, too, but then Sissy had been murdered.

"Miss Shaeffer," Mr. MacDonald said, "could you please tell the jury what happened on the night of February ninth of 1994."

"Well . . ." she began.

"Could the witness please speak up?" Geiggen asked from the defense table.

MacDonald looked pissed, but Marybeth Shaeffer leaned toward the microphone and began her story. She and Sissy had gone out with the executives of a clothing firm they were modeling ads for. They had eaten supper and then gone to Belle's, the nightclub, indulged in a glass of wine and were dancing, having a nice time, when suddenly, around midnight, the defendant showed up.

"And what did he do?" MacDonald asked.

"Both Sissy and I were on the dance floor, and so I saw what happened." She paused, eyes starting to tear slightly. "The defendant came out on the floor and tried to cut in on the man who was dancing with Sissy."

"And what did Miss Cook do?"

"She told him to get lost."

"And why did she say that?"

"Well, she hated him."

"Objection, Your Honor!" Geiggen cried, jumping to his feet. "It's pure speculation on the witness's part."

"No it's not," Marybeth shot back. "I lived with her!" There was some laughter, quickly stifled by the judge.

"Overruled, prosecution may continue."

"What had Miss Cook told you about her feelings in regard to the defendant, Miss Shaeffer?"

She rolled her eyes. "What didn't she tell me? She hated him. She told me she went out with him once and that he was very abusive and—well, that he was, you know, all talk and no show."

"What do you mean by all talk and no show?"

"She said he was impotent."

Geiggen stood up. "Objection, Your Honor, that's pure hearsay."

"No eet's not," came from the back row of the jury box. Elena. The judge glared in her direction and then returned her attention to the lawyers.

The defendant looked utterly impassive.

"Your Honor," MacDonald said, "this line of questioning is directly linked to the motive for the shooting, and since the victim obviously cannot speak for herself, we must rely on what she confided to her best friend at the time."

"Objection, Your Honor," Geiggen said. "How are we to know who the victim's best friend was?"

"Counsel will approach the bench," the judge ordered, and after a brief shouting match (in whispers), the stenographer lugged her machine back into place and the trial resumed.

"Miss Shaeffer, could you share with us the reasons the victim gave for disliking the defendant?"

"She said she saw him that one time and afterwards found out he was married, which he hadn't told her, and he had kids, which he hadn't told her, and he was a drug addict, which he hadn't told her, and maybe even dealt drugs—"

"Objection, Your Honor! Hearsay again!"

"Sustained."

"What else did Sissy Cook tell you about the defendant?" MacDonald persevered.

"That he had started harassing her."

"Harassing her how?"

"Oh, calling, sending flowers, waiting for her at the agency, following her at night sometimes, that kind of thing."

"Was Miss Cook scared of him?"

"Not in the beginning," the witness said. "She said he was such a loser that he couldn't even stalk her right."

The defendant's face remained expressionless.

"I told her to be careful," Marybeth continued. "And then later, she said I was right, she should have worried, because he was getting worse."

"Was she scared of the defendant then?"

"Yes. Very."

The examination went on, and Marybeth described how the defendant wouldn't leave Sissy alone on the dance floor, how he grabbed her arm, how the man Sissy was dancing with said, "Hey, wait a minute," and how the defendant shoved him and jerked Sissy by the arm, and how the music stopped and everyone heard Sissy yell, "Let go of me, you drug-dealing, impotent son of a bitch!" And then how the executives the models had been with grabbed the defendant and were joined by a club bouncer to escort him to the front door.

"Did the defendant say anything as he was taken out?" MacDonald asked.

"Yes. He said, 'You'll get yours, you slut.' "

MacDonald waited as Marybeth took a sip of water.

"And what time did you leave the club, Miss Shaeffer?"

"At two A.M. Sissy and I stayed on to talk to the owner of the club for a minute, inside, while the men went outside to find a cab."

"What happened next?"

"We went outside." Her voice broke at this. She took another sip of water.

"Are you able to continue?"

She nodded.

"What happened then?"

"We went outside and saw the men in the street, trying to find a cab, and we walked toward the curb." She swallowed and frowned, squinting as if seeing the scene in front of her. "And then we heard this squeal of tires—you know, like in the movies—and we turned to look. And then Sissy grabbed my arm and said, 'Oh, no, it's Jim Layton. That's his car.' "

"Could you see the car?"

"Yes, because it was bearing right down on us. It was a Jaguar, gray, with a black convertible roof."

"And what happened then?"

"I pulled Sissy back from the curb—"

"And where were the other people?"

"The men had scattered because of the car tearing down the street. I think one of the bouncers from the club was behind us, by the door."

"Continue."

"I pulled Sissy back as the car came down toward us. And then the car stopped and a man got out—a black man, who had trouble getting out, I remembered, because he was very tall and big and the car was very low to the ground."

"Continue."

"So he got out and then bent down to look in the car, and the driver was saying something, pointing at Sissy. And the black man looked at us and said, "The one in the red?"

"He was referring to what, Miss Shaeffer?"

"Objection, Your Honor," Geiggen said. "How could the witness know what the man was thinking?"

"Sustained," Judge Williams said without looking up from her notes.

"Let me rephrase that, Miss Shaeffer," MacDonald said. "What red— Strike that. Was anyone wearing red outside the club?"

"Sissy was," she answered. "She was wearing a bright red trench coat. Really bright. It looked great on her."

"Was anyone else wearing red?"

"No, sir."

"And what happened then, after the man asked the driver of the car, 'The one in the red?' "

"He—the black man—pulled out a gun and the bouncer behind us said something like 'He's got a gun!' and then suddenly he was right there, the shooter, standing in front of us."

"What happened then?"

Her face screwed up in agony. And then, slowly, she opened her eyes. "The shooter shoved me to the side—I was in heels and I fell. And then I heard Sissy scream and I looked up and saw him fire at Sissy."

At this she broke down. When she was ready, they went on.

"How many times did the shooter fire?"

"Four. He went just blam-blam-blam—and then she fell—and then he looked down and shot her again—in the face." She broke down completely this time, sobbing.

The prosecution asked for, and got, a short recess.

It was very quiet in the jury room. The jurors didn't even look at one another, but just sat there. Chuck came in after a while and led them back into court.

"I know this is very difficult, Miss Shaeffer," MacDonald said, "but it's very important that the jury understands what happened."

She nodded miserably.

"Do you remember what happened immediately after the shooting?"

She nodded, taking a breath. Looking down at her lap, she said, "I couldn't see very well, but I could see the shooter get back in the defendant's car—"

"Objection, Your Honor," Geiggen said quietly. "The car in question has not been established as belonging to the defendant."

"Sustained." Judge Williams looked down at the witness. "Miss Shaeffer," she said gently, "please continue, but simply say the car."

Marybeth nodded and looked at MacDonald. "The shooter got in the same car again and it drove off."

"You said you couldn't see very well. Why was that?"

Her head bent again and she said something.

"I'm sorry, Miss Shaeffer," Judge Williams said, "but please try and speak into the microphone. I know it's very difficult, but it's very important."

She took another breath and leaned forward. Her face was a wreck. "Sissy's blood was all over me— The side of her head—" She broke down again, holding her face in her hands, sobbing.

"Your Honor?" MacDonald said quietly.

She nodded. "We will take another short recess. The jurors are not to discuss this case with anyone or amongst yourselves. Thank you."

In the jury room Dayton went straight to the window to up and light a cigarette; Melissa refilled the water pitcher and nearly all the jurors took a glass when she offered one; Libby went in to the ladies' room to dampen a paper towel and bring it back to the table to hold as a compress to her forehead. "I'm getting a little light-headed," she admitted.

"It's truly awful," Mrs. Smythe-Daniels agreed.

"I know this sounds dumb," Slicked-Back Ronnie said, "but this is the first it's really sunk in that this is about murder. I mean, real murder."

Will was sitting in the corner, silent.

"Can I get you a Coke or something?" Alex whispered to Libby. "You need a little sugar?"

"It can help," Clay added, appearing by her chair, holding out his Life Savers. His voice was surprisingly gentle. "This isn't easy for any of us."

"Thanks," she said, taking a Life Saver and putting it in her mouth.

When they were called back into the courtroom, the witness looked considerably better. That is, the worst of her ruined makeup had been removed and there was a hint of color in her cheeks now.

"Miss Shaeffer," MacDonald said, "before the shooting, did you have any trouble seeing what was happening?"

"Not at all," she said. "The streetlights were very bright."

"And when you saw the Jaguar driving toward you, could you see anything inside of it?"

"Oh, yes," she said quickly, nodding, seemingly grateful to talk about anything but the shooting itself. "I could see the driver, and I could see the shooter. I didn't recognize the shooter, though. He was a stranger to me."

"But did you recognize the driver of the car?"

"Oh, yes."

"And is that person in the courtroom now?"

"Oh, yes," she repeated. She pointed. "It was the defendant, Jim Layton."

"Thank you, Miss Shaeffer, that will be all," MacDonald said.

Judge Williams stopped the proceedings for the day, advising that court would resume at ten o'clock the following morning.

14

Libby came home utterly wiped out. She scarcely spoke to the gang in the lobby and they knew from her expression that it was not a night to joke with her.

Upstairs in her apartment she mechanically opened her mail and then, giving in, picked up each cat briefly to pet them and then fed them both. She brought her bills into the living room and sorted through them. Since she felt so awful anyway, she thought she might as well deal with these.

A bill from her dentist for redoing two fillings with gold ($1,200); a health insurance bill for the next quarter, January through March ($712.58); her car insurance for the quarter ($650); and on January 15 her estimated tax payment of $3,500 would be due. In her savings account she had two months' rent and about $300 to eat with. Forget Con Edison, New York Telephone, and her charge cards.

No, jury duty at fifteen dollars a day was not going to cover it. And no one was beating down her door with a new contract.

It was time to call Uncle Greg, her mother's brother. Uncle Greg was some sort of investment adviser in Chicago. She had never known him terribly well, but at her mother's urging, she'd had him invest part of her IRA, and her savings over and above the prudent reserve she always kept. She figured the savings had to be around twelve thousand dollars at this point.

Uncle Greg was glad to hear from her. Yes, he had heard she was on the jury of a murder trial. But then he was less glad to hear that she would be needing to use some of her savings soon.

"I told you, Lib," Uncle Greg said, "that this was not money you could get back the next day. It's tied up in investments."

"Well, I guess why I'm calling is to say that it's time to sell the investments because I'm going to start needing the money in about six weeks."

A sigh. "How much of it?"

"All of it, I'm afraid." Pause. "Uncle Greg, believe me, I had no idea my rainy day was going to come so soon."

"But don't you have a new contract?"

"Well, that's just it, it's going to be a while. Or that's what they tell me. Anyway, I'm not going to touch my retirement stuff or anything."

"You sure as heck better not!" Uncle Greg said.

He was deeply annoyed with her, she could tell. But then again, Uncle Greg had always seemed annoyed with her. She was too loud and unpredictable for his temperament, her mother said, but that didn't mean he didn't love Libby. (Sure. Like sister like brother.) "Listen, Lib, we may have to take a big loss if you sell now—the securities market hasn't been what it has been."

"I don't expect a great profit or anything."

"Well, you're not getting any."

"But on that thing you sent me last year it said my ten thousand was worth about twelve."

"And is worth only about seven thousand if we sell now," he said.

"Seven!"

"It's very complicated, Libby, it's in a derivative investment, and you have to wait it out."

"The point is, I can't wait on it. This isn't my IRA—you were supposed to put it into something liquid."

"You wanted a high return, Libby, what else can I tell you? If you needed this money to pay your rent, why the hell did you send it out here?"

"Because you told me to!" she said, getting angry, too. She took a breath. "Look, Uncle Greg, I apologize. I just sat in the courtroom all day hearing about a murder and right now I'm all over the place. Why don't you just tell me what it is the money's in, and I'll think it over for a few days."

"You could borrow on it," her uncle said. "And get around five thousand."

Now it was worth five thousand?!?

Libby controlled her temper and merely took down the name of the securities her money was in—or what was left of it was in—and thanked her uncle for his time.

Melissa got lost trying to find the damn cat food offices and didn't arrive there until close to eight. They were in a huge office complex owned by Harding-Buckner Mills off Route 22 in Short Hills. She parked the car and was grilled in the lobby by the security guard.

"Christine Harrington? No way," he said at first. "I'm not bothering her."

"Well, how am I going to see her if you don't call her and tell her I'm here?"

He looked at her a moment, scanned the security cameras, and then looked back at her. He squinted. "She's expecting you?"

"Yes. My name's Melissa Grant. Just as I wrote it there in the registry."

He debated, inflating his cheeks while he thought. "Okay," he said finally. He picked up a phone, punched in a number, and waited. His back went ramrod straight. "Yes, Mrs. Harrington, I have a Melissa Grant from S. Wiley—" He smiled nervously. "Yes? Yes, all right, I'll send her up." He hung up. "Sorry for the third degree, but she's got top security clearance."

"How come?"

He ignored Melissa's question and pointed. "Take the very last elevator to the top floor. I'll turn it on for you."

"I don't see any other way," Will said, continuing to pack his suitcase. "You need time to find a place, I understand that. I just don't want any more misunderstandings."

"My parents are coming next week for Thanksgiving, William!" Betsy yelled, furious. And well she should be, he thought. He had let her seduce him last night and tonight he arrived home announcing that he was moving into a hotel until she left. "What am I supposed to tell them?"

"The truth," he said, going to his dresser and taking out a pile of pressed and folded dress shirts.

"I can't tell them the truth," she said wildly, "they think we're getting married next summer!"

At this, Will had to turn around. He sighed, dropped the shirts on the bed, and walked over to her. "Betsy," he said, holding her by the shoulders, "you have to tell them. You'll need their support in this. You know they'll understand when you say that I wasn't the right person for you."

"But you are!"

"You know that's not true," he said, dropping his hands and returning to the suitcase. "Listen, just tell your parents I wanted to raise our kids Jewish—they'll be dancing in the streets."

"But I'm supposed to have them here all by myself?"

"Then cancel—let them use the tickets for something else."

He sensed her approach before she actually hit him. "I hate you! I hate you!" she seethed, pounding his back with her fists.

"Hi," a voice said from the end of the darkened hallway.

"Hi," Melissa said, startled. She had stepped off the elevator into what looked like someone's living room; attached to it was this long, dark hallway, lit only by emergency exit lighting. "Not to be rude, Christine, but where the heck are we?"

Christine laughed, a gentle, confident laugh, and came down the hall to greet her. "We're in one of the executive suites. Follow me. I have things set up in the conference room. Sorry about the lights, but we're pretty strict about conserving energy. No reason to light up the whole place just for us."

"Is Sal and everyone here?" Melissa said.

"Not tonight. We really don't need them," Christine said, opening a door that flooded light into the hall.

Inside the conference room a TV and VCR were set up. The agency storyboards were lined up against the far wall. On the table was a legal pad of handwritten notes.

"Okay, let's start with the first TV commercial," Christine began.

Melissa took off her coat and sat down to work.

"Jill?"

"Yes, hon?" she said, finishing the last of the pots. She placed it in the rack by the sink and dried her hands on the dish towel. "The kids okay?"

"Oh, yeah," Rusty said. "They finally settled down—I think they'll sleep now."

Jill sighed and leaned back against the kitchen counter, brushing a strand of hair off her face with the back of her hand. "I'm sorry, Russ, I know this is messing up their schedules. They're all out of whack."

"It's you I'm worried about," her husband said, going over to the refrigerator and opening the door. "You want a beer?"

"White wine."

"Okay."

"Let me just run upstairs and kiss the kids good night."

"Meet you in the den," he said.

Rusty was right, the kids were pretty well settled down. Katie was already asleep, clutching her little Bambi (whose head badly needed reinforcing before it came off altogether), and so Jill merely kissed her good night before moving on to Peter's room. He was still awake, but barely, curled up on his side in his Yankee pajamas. "Going to have sweet

dreams, darling?" she asked him, sitting on the edge of the bed. He nodded, eyes closing. "Did you say your prayers?"

"With Daddy."

"That's good, sweetheart, sleep tight." She kissed him on the temple.

"Daddy said to pray the trial would be over soon."

"Yes, darling."

"I told him I hated Mrs. Montell." At this confession his eyes flared
open a moment in defiance and then closed again.

Jill smiled. "Well, I guess tomorrow we'll have to say a prayer for Mrs.
Montell then, too."

"That's what Daddy said." And he was asleep.

Rusty was in his easy chair in the den, beer at his side, feet up on the
ottoman. He held out his arms to her and she instinctively climbed into
his lap. "I have to go on a diet," she said apologetically.

"You don't have to do anything," Rusty said, rubbing her back and
handing her a glass of wine from the side table.

She took a sip and then kissed him. "It was horrible today."

"I figured."

Jill took another sip of wine. "I wish we could stop right here. The jury
would hang him."

"And they will, honey. These things just take time."

She sighed. "Yes." She looked at him. "Do you suppose when it's all
over we could go away?"

"Sure." He smiled. "With or without the kids?"

"Oh, maybe half and half. Florida," she said, taking another sip of
wine. "We can go with the kids to Disney World, and then drop them
off with Mom and Dad—then we can sneak off for a few days."

"Mmm," he said, kissing her neck. "Let's go now."

She smiled, put her wineglass down, took his face in his hands, and
kissed him full on the mouth. "Darling," she murmured, hoping the
buzz of the wine would temporarily give her energy she knew she did not
have on her own, "let's go upstairs and make love." It was so odd, how
she had these sudden sexual urges these days. Grief, she supposed. It
had been like this after Sissy's funeral.

"Darling, come," she whispered, standing up and pulling on his hand.

Their lovemaking was intense. Whether it was the wine or the grief,
Jill didn't care, but her body felt wired and she urged Rusty on, the two
of them climbing, and she climaxed in a way she hadn't in over a year.

"Jill, darling," Rusty panted in her ear afterward. "That was so good, darling. You feel so close, so good. So soft. Mine."

"I love you," she murmured, holding him in place on top of her.

"I love you," he said, resting his face in the side of her neck.

Christine had some very good suggestions for revisions in the cat food campaign, and once Melissa got over the initial annoyance she always felt when a client wanted to make changes, she realized Christine knew her audience better than the agency did. They worked until almost ten-thirty, at which time Christine called for a car to drive Melissa to Manhattan. "My turn to send you off," she said, helping to gather the boards for Melissa to take back.

Christine disappeared briefly and came back with her coat and a briefcase. They went down in the elevator together, talking business details, and signed out with the guard.

"Oh, before I forget," Melissa said at the front door. She took Christine's car keys out of her coat pocket and handed them to her.

"I really appreciate this, Melissa. Thank you. Oh, there's your car."

"Our car for you last night wasn't nearly so glamorous," Melissa protested, seeing the full-size limousine that was waiting.

"You might have saved my life last night," Christine said, walking her over.

"No," Melissa said, embarrassed. She felt Christine's hand on her arm. Melissa looked at her. She looked very pretty in the light of the parking lot. Younger. Happier. Something.

Melissa's mouth was going dry. She had not made this up. The attraction was mutual and in spades.

Electric was more like it.

"I wanted you to know, Melissa," Christine said quietly, "that from now on, all decisions regarding the campaign will come through Sal."

Melissa swallowed. "I don't understand."

Christine smiled. "I had hoped you would. Sooner rather than later."

She was gazing into Melissa's eyes the same way she had that first night in the Oak Room bar. Melissa wondered what the hell to do now. Christine was evidently happy to go on standing there, the two of them staring at each other under the parking lot lights, waiting until she said something.

"I—I do," Melissa managed to say. "But—" She sighed, shrugging, indicating the helplessness she felt.

After a moment, Christine murmured, "Go home," and stepped forward to kiss her gently on the cheek. "I'll call you." Then she opened the car door for her.

Melissa climbed in, pulling the portfolio case in behind her. Once she was settled in the backseat, she looked up. And tried to smile. "It's so complicated for me, Christine."

"Life's complicated," Christine told her. She winked. "I'm older, I know."

Once the door was safely closed, Melissa watched Christine walk toward the Lexus. She pushed the button to make the window slide down. "Christine."

She turned around.

"The guard told me you had top security clearance around here. Why is that?"

Christine smiled, walked back a couple of steps, but didn't answer.

"Let me put it this way," Melissa said. "Why do I get the distinct feeling that you might *own* the cat food company?"

Christina laughed. And then she shook her head. "No, Melissa, I don't own the cat food company. I'm part owner of the *company* that owns the cat food company." And then she waved, laughing, walking to her car, calling good night over her shoulder.

15

THE TEMPERATURE had taken a plunge the night before and so everyone on Friday morning, November 17, was wearing coats and hats and gloves. Despite it being freezing outside, the jury room was stifling. The ancient radiator was blasting away and Chuck confirmed that there was no way to turn it off. He showed the jurors how they would have to open the window and turn on the air conditioner if they wanted to stay alive.

Everyone this morning, Libby noticed, looked nearly as dreadful as she did. Whether it was from the graphic testimony from the day before or the fact that everyone's radiators had been turned on full-blast last night, she didn't know, but they all had swollen eyes.

She herself had had a very uneasy night, dreaming that she had to testify about the murder, and she kept trying to explain that she hadn't seen it, but everyone kept telling her that she couldn't lie, she had to tell them what happened because she was the only one who knew.

Will gave her a tired little wave during roll call, which she returned. Melissa seemed a million miles away. Only Alex seemed to have any life in him this morning, but he, too, was subdued, sipping his coffee and reading the sports pages of the *Times*.

They were taken into court at ten on the dot. The witness from the day before was still on the stand, Marybeth Shaeffer, and she was reminded that she was still under oath. Defense counsel Geiggen then began his cross-examination. He was surprisingly gentle, asking questions that seemed rather innocuous, but as lunchtime approached Libby realized that he had quietly established that Marybeth Shaeffer had sought psychological help for a number of problems in the past—anorexia, bulimia, cocaine, one suicide attempt—and was wholly dependent on contact lenses that could and sometimes did severely irritate her eyes late at night. And, on that note, the jury was dismissed for lunch.

"Gee whiz," Libby sighed outside the courtroom to Alex.

"And people wonder why no one wants to testify," Clay grumbled.

Libby turned around. This was a first. Clay was talking. Meeting her eyes, Clay apparently remembered that he was supposed to be the hostile black accountant, because he then pushed ahead of her into the jury room without further comment.

"You come to court to tell what you saw at the scene of a crime," Alex said as they entered the jury room, "and the next minute they're advertising your personal problems."

"Vill they put it in the papers, you think?" Debrilla the Viking lady asked.

"Of course," Alex said in disgust. "They put all horrible things in the paper."

"I know we cannot talk about the trial," Elena began.

"So don't!" Stephen the computer guy snapped. Everyone turned to look at him. Everybody seemed to be changing personalities today. Clay was nice, Steve was snapping at everyone, Alex was saying things like "They put all horrible things in the paper," and Debrilla wanted to talk about the trial.

"Let me tell you what I theenk," Elena said, hand on her hip. "I theenk that Go-gen guy ees a fuckeeng asshole."

"Geiggen," Eleanor Smythe-Daniels said, suppressing a smile as she slipped on her mink coat.

Madame Foreman, struggling with her coat, rose to the occasion. "We can't talk about the trial," she reminded them. Today she had little purple hair clips all over her head in the shape of lightning strikes.

Libby and Alex took the elevator down together. They didn't have much time for lunch, Alex pointed out, looking at his watch. "And I have to go to the bank and do some stuff."

"Go on, then," she said. "I'm just going to get something around the corner."

"Well, okay," he said reluctantly. "But only on one condition."

"What's that?"

"You'll have a drink with me tonight after court."

She hesitated. "I can only do a short one, okay?"

After he ran off, Libby wandered outside, debating what to do. It was freezing. Get some lunch and bring it back, she thought. But the idea of voluntarily returning to sit in that jury room was not very appealing.

"Have any ideas for lunch?" a voice asked from behind her.

She turned around. It was Melissa. "Absolutely none," she answered, "but you're welcome to join me and freeze to death while trying to decide."

They set off together, Libby glad for the company.

Few of the eateries around the courthouse encouraged sitting down, and so they ended up at some sort of noodle shop off Canal Street where they could at least get a table. Libby took Melissa's suggestion and ordered a huge bowl of vegetable and noodle soup. It was actually very good, and hot and nourishing. Bypassing good manners, Libby thought it was time to penetrate the protective sphere around Melissa.

"Don't you find it odd that so many of us on the jury are unmarried?" Libby asked her.

Melissa barely glanced up from her bowl. "No."

That certainly flummoxed Libby for a moment. "Well, of course you're younger."

Melissa laughed, looking up at her. "And you're very old?"

"Well—how old are you?"

"Twenty-nine."

Libby made a face. "That's younger. When you're thirty-four, twenty-nine's a lifetime ago."

"I've read one of your books, you know," Melissa told her. "I liked it very much. The one about Amanda? It was great."

"Thank you."

"I guess her preoccupation with being single applies to you, too," Melissa added.

Libby jerked her head up. "Excuse me?"

"Amanda was always wondering about people who weren't married. And now here you are, too."

Oh, brother, this was not the way this conversation was supposed to go. She was supposed to be finding out about Melissa, not getting outsmarted and cornered about her own neurosis bequeathed to her by her mother.

Libby took a big gulp of water and put the glass down with a thump. "I was with a guy for three years and I was going to marry him. The only problem was, he was playing around and, looking back, I'm not sure I liked him all that much to begin with."

Melissa winced. "Ouch. I'm sorry."

"Oh, don't be. The first year maybe, you could feel sorry for me. The next two years, well, I did that tour of duty by myself."

"You'll get married, Libby," Melissa said casually, "but it will only be to someone who's absolutely right for you."

"How do you know?"

Melissa smiled. "Ten years of psychotherapy. You begin to be able to tell the difference between women who are looking to be taken care of and women who are genuinely seeking a partner."

"Alex said I would make a great mother," she blurted out, laughing then to cover up. Why had that popped out? To show Melissa that Alex thought she was attractive, so she wouldn't think she was in need of ten years of psychotherapy? (Although she had undergone three years of it, while teaching back in Cleveland. One of the great things about teaching was the benefits package, which was the least every Board of Ed could do since the profession was sure to drive a person crazy.)

Melissa patted her mouth with her napkin and picked up the check. "I'm not sure Alex would be a whole lot more reliable than your ex." She looked at Libby. "I'm sorry, it's none of my business."

"No, that's okay. I know what you mean. There's something a little off about him, isn't there?" Melissa nodded. "And what about you?" Libby continued. Was it her imagination or was Melissa blushing slightly? "You know, are you living with a guy who's cheating on you or anything?"

Melissa smiled and shook her head. "No. That's far too advanced for me. At least right now."

"Why?"

"You are very nosy, Libby, you know that."

"Yes," she admitted.

Melissa sighed, sitting back in her chair. "Okay. Truth is, the last couple of years, I've been trying to get my life back together. I had a very bad drinking problem. Since I was a teenager."

"Did you go to a rehab?"

Melissa nodded.

"And you don't. . . ?"

"No, nothing. No alcohol or drugs."

Libby beamed. "That's wonderful! You must feel like you're starting your whole life over. And you're young enough to do it."

Melissa made a face and stood up. This was not a topic she was evidently comfortable with.

As they were walking back to the courthouse, Melissa said, "I didn't mean to be short with you back there. It's just that I'm in the middle of something that's got my head going a hundred miles an hour."

Libby's ears pricked up. "I knew there was a man in this somewhere!"

Melissa laughed, shaking her head. "Well, sort of." After a few steps, she said, "There's someone I've met through work. A client."

"You like him?"

"Yes. At least, I think I do. It's complicated."

Libby smiled to herself. That meant yes. Big-time. "So what's the problem? Is he married?"

Melissa stared at her for a moment. "No. At least, I don't think so. God, I never even thought of that."

"Then that's the first thing you have to find out," Libby instructed.

"It's just that . . ." Melissa was clearly wrestling with something. "I'm not absolutely sure if I'm imagining the signals I'm getting."

"You're not imagining them," Libby assured her, "not if you're already battling ethics."

"And he's older," Melissa added.

"Old enough to be your father?"

"No!" Melissa laughed. "He's like forty."

"Well, if you don't want him, I'll take him!" Libby laughed. "But look, seriously, the first thing we've got to do is find out if he's married."

Melissa looked at her as though she wanted to say something more.

"What is it, Melissa? Is there something else?"

She smiled and shrugged. "It's nothing," she said, and left it at that.

Of course, Libby could only wonder then what else there was for Melissa to worry about. Well, if this case dragged on as long as it looked like it might, she'd probably find out.

Back in the jury room, they found Dayton explaining to Clay, Adelaide, Elena, and Ronnie how the crack dealers operated outside in the square in front of the courthouse.

"Right in front of the courthouse?" Ronnie was saying in disbelief.

"Only in front of family court," Dayton explained, "because family court's where all the customers are."

"Dear God!" Elena cried. "Those poor cheeldren!"

Will arrived with a brown paper bag. He gave Libby a questioning look, and she smiled, patting the seat next to her, normally Alex's. He sat down and unwrapped a sandwich.

"And how are you doing?" she asked quietly. He shrugged. Whatever he said would be heard by the others, Libby realized, and so she thought to talk in vague generalities to find out what was going on with his girl-friend. "Did you figure out that problem? With your apartment?"

"Yeah, I'm staying somewhere else for a while. Until after Thanksgiving."

"You'll feel better very soon."

He looked at her. He must have had a sleepless night. "After yesterday's testimony, though, I must admit, at one point last night I thought, Does it really matter? Maybe I should just be grateful with the way things are."

"With being unhappy?"

He gave an ironic smile. "I guess you're right."

"Will, I'm no expert, but I do know it's easier to stay miserable and not have to change anything. What's hardest is what you're doing—starting over again."

"And I don't want to be miserable anymore." He looked at her. "I really don't. It's a habit I get into at work as it is." He looked across the table at Melissa. "How are you on relationships, Melissa?"

"Been buying drugs at family court, have you?" Melissa asked him. "What does anyone in advertising know about relationships?"

They all laughed.

"I'm going to tell her not to wear that fur coat anymore," Adelaide suddenly vowed. All heads turned. "It's very cruel what they do to minks."

"And it's not cruel to murder a person?" Clay muttered.

As the gang continued to discuss minks and murder, Libby took a piece of paper out of her bag. "Will? May I ask you a financial question?"

His eyes lit up. Clearly this was an area he did not feel unsure about.

Libby explained to him about the money she had placed in the hands of a nameless investment adviser, about how she would be needing the money soon, but how the adviser said that if she sold now, her twelve thousand dollars was only worth about seven, or that if she borrowed on it, it was only worth around five. "He says it's in this," and she handed the paper to him.

"Oh," he said without barely looking at it before handing it back. "Well, one thing, Libby, I'd fire the adviser immediately. He's an idiot for putting any of your money in that." And then he explained that this type of financial instrument would fluctuate wildly, hardly a good idea for someone who's rainy day money might be needed on short notice. "And you've seen the statements on this all along?"

She shook her head no. "As matter of fact, on this money I'm not sure I've ever seen more than one."

"What?"

"Well, on my IRA stuff I have, but not this. I mean, he was just sort of taking care of this with some of my parents' money."

Will looked deadly serious as he said, "Libby, something's not right here. If I were you, I would gather together every statement you do have from this guy and show them to me."

"Would you mind?"

"Not at all. But Libby, I've got to tell you, this makes me awfully nervous for your parents, too, if this same guy is handling their money. Who is he?"

"My mother's brother."

"Oh, no," Will said.

"Oh, yes," Libby confirmed.

When the trial resumed at two, Geiggen took his time rummaging through papers on his table to find one in particular. He slowly read it, glancing up at the witness once, and then walked back toward the jury box with a sense of seriousness. "Miss Shaeffer," he began, "in your pretrial testimony, you said that Miss Cook had said something that made you turn and look at the oncoming car."

She thought for a moment. "Yes."

"In the transcript it says you said, 'Sissy kind of gasped and said, "Oh, shit, it's Jim Layton, that's his car," and I turned and saw the gray Jaguar coming toward us.' " He lowered the papers. "Is that an accurate statement?"

She nodded. "Yes."

"And in this trial, you said basically the same thing, but that the victim saw the car and said, 'Oh, no, it's Jim Layton. That's his car.' "

"Yes," she said.

"One question," he said with a wave of his hand, as if it were a mere trifle. "Who told you to clean up Miss Cook's language for the trial?"

"Objection, Your Honor!" MacDonald roared. "Defense is making accusations, not cross-examining!"

"Defense is trying to get to the truth, Your Honor, and it's right here on the court record, the first time around, under sworn testimony, that Miss Shaeffer quoted Miss Cook as saying, 'Oh, *shit*—' "

"That's enough, Mr. Geiggen," the judge said. "Counsel will approach the bench."

As the lawyers battled it out at the bench, and the stenographer valiantly tried to get everything on the record, Clay leaned close. "Feeling better today?"

Libby nodded, murmuring, "Yes, thanks."

She scanned the faces in the gallery. It was an intimidating lot. Who was press and who were interested parties was impossible to tell. The most impressive person, though, was the victim's sister. Jill Tompkins sat rigidly straight through everything, every minute, every hour, eyes never wavering from the proceedings in front of her.

Libby wondered what the defendant felt when he saw her sitting there.

"All right," Judge Williams said as the crowd of lawyers at the bench cleared away. "That last objection was overruled, and Mr. Geiggen will continue with his cross-examination."

"I repeat, Miss Shaeffer," Geiggen said gently, "who instructed you to clean up the language of Miss Cook for this trial?"

"No one," she said angrily. "When I was asked if that's exactly what she—"

"Excuse me, Miss Shaeffer, when *who* asked you?"

"After the hearing, Mr. MacDonald asked me if I was absolutely sure those were the words Sissy used. I told him I thought so, but I wasn't absolutely positive."

"Then why did you swear those were her words in the preliminary hearing?"

"Because that's just what popped in my head!"

"So," Geiggen said, taking his time, walking over in front of the jury, "if that sentence hadn't popped into your head, you would have just remembered Miss Cook saying, 'Oh, no, it's Jim Layton. That's his car.' "

"Yes!" she said, glaring at him now.

"Fine," Geiggen said. He walked back to the defense table to look at a piece of paper and then came strolling back to the witness. "So, Miss Shaeffer, the one thing we do know for absolutely sure is that Miss Cook saw the car and told you it was Jim Layton driving."

"Yes," she said.

"And until Miss Cook told you it was Mr. Layton driving, you didn't know who was driving."

She hesitated. "I recognized his car. He had parked outside our apartment enough times to spy on her."

"But did you recognize it was his car before or after Miss Cook told you it was Jim Layton driving it?"

She hesitated. Finally she said, "After, I think. Because right after we heard the squeal of the tires, she saw it was him—he—him."

"And your sworn testimony is that it was Mr. Layton you saw behind the wheel of the car."

"Yes," she declared.

"And if in later testimony you hear, Miss Shaeffer, that given the lighting conditions, the angle of the approaching car, and the resulting shadows, that it would have been impossible for you to have seen who was in the driver's seat—"

"Objection, Your Honor!" MacDonald cried, standing up. "No such testimony has yet been given."

"Sustained," said Judge Williams. "Mr. Geiggen, you will please confine your examination to the evidence as it pertains to this witness."

"Yes, Your Honor," he said obediently. He took a walk back to the defense table again and then came over to stand in front of the jury. "Miss Shaeffer, you previously testified that you and Miss Cook had first gone to dinner with agency clients."

"Yes."

"And did you have anything to drink at dinner?"

She paused. "We had some wine."

"So you had drunk more that night than just the one glass of wine you said you had at the dance club."

"Well, it was just wine. I mean, maybe a glass at dinner and then, two hours later, a glass at the club."

"But still, Miss Shaeffer, there was alcohol in your system, wasn't there?"

"Objection, Your Honor! Defense is lecturing the witness."

"Overruled."

Marybeth looked up at the judge. "Am I supposed to answer?"

"Yes," the judge said. "You are to answer if the defense attorney is correct, that you had some alcohol in your system."

"Yes."

"Didn't you previously testify, Miss Shaeffer," Geiggen resumed, "that less than a year before that, you had been treated in a drug rehabilitation program?"

"For cocaine, yes."

"But isn't it true that in such a program alcohol is considered a drug, too?"

"Objection, Your Honor! The witness is not on trial here."

"Your Honor, I think the mental and emotional state of the witness at the time of the shooting is crucial," Geiggen said. "Defense believes it crucial to know if Miss Shaeffer was suffering at the hands of her addictive personality."

"Your HONOR!" MacDonald yelled. "OBJECTION! Defense is saying whatever he wants for the benefit of the jury!"

"Counsel will approach the bench." After several minutes of arguing, the lawyers cleared the bench. "The objection is sustained," the judge announced.

"All right, then," Geiggen said, his voice taking on a decided edge now. "Miss Shaeffer, let me sum up. You went out with the victim, Miss Cook, with some agency clients. You were wearing your contact lenses, which sometimes irritate your eyes when you get tired. You went to dinner, where you drank some wine. Then you went to a dance club, where you had another glass of wine. Then, when you left the nightclub at two o'clock in the morning, you heard the squeal of tires, turned to look, and Miss Cook gasped and said, 'Oh, no, it's Jim Layton. That's his car.'"

"Yes!" she nearly cried.

"Very good," he said, softening. He walked over to the jury box to glance down at his legal pad, left on the shelf there. He bit his lip for a moment and then looked up at the witness. "Miss Shaeffer, at the time of the shooting, you had been Miss Cook's roommate for how long?"

"About eight months."

"It was a two-bedroom apartment?"

"Yes."

"And you basically came and went as you pleased?"

"Yes."

"But on the night of the shooting you two had gone out together."

"Yes."

"Did you do that often?"

"With business clients, yes."

"I see," he said, glancing down at his notes. He looked up. "Tell me, while you were living with Miss Cook, did she date anyone?"

"Occasionally."

"Did she have a steady boyfriend?"

Marybeth shrugged. "I don't know. I suppose she had seen a couple of men more than two or three times, but I wouldn't call that steady. You know, being serious or anything."

"Could you tell the jury some of the names of the people she went out with?"

She shrugged. "I don't know their last names. I met them in passing."

"So, for example, you met . . ."

"There was Jonathan, a photographer she had met through work."

"And was she serious about this Jonathan?"

"Not very. He was just a friend. They went out dancing occasionally."

"Did any of the men stay overnight at the apartment?"

"Objection, Your Honor!" MacDonald said. "The defendant is on trial, not the victim."

"Your Honor, it is crucial we establish if there could have been other people in the victim's life who wished to see her dead."

"Nobody who came to our apartment!" Marybeth snapped.

The judge sighed, clearly on the fence. "Overruled, but defense will be careful to confine his questioning to evidence that pertains to this trial."

"Miss Shaeffer, I repeat the question, while you were living with the defendant, did any men stay overnight at the apartment?"

She thought for a full minute. "To my recollection," she said, "there was no man who stayed all night in our apartment."

There was a slight buzz in the courtroom and the judge ordered silence.

"Then we are to believe," Geiggen said, "that while the victim readily admitted to having met the defendant at a luncheon once and had gone to an apartment alone with him that same night to get sexually involved, that never once did any man stay overnight in your apartment?"

"That's correct," the witness said defiantly.

"All right, then, Miss Shaeffer, let's return to the men who did visit the apartment—but who did not stay the night."

The witness nodded. "I told you about Jonathan. And there was Paul, an old friend of hers."

"Paul—?"

"I don't know his last name."

"Did you know what this Paul did?"

"I think he was in sporting goods. I think she met him through work—way back, when she first started."

"And was Paul a suitor?"

"No."

"Miss Shaeffer, was there any man in the apartment while you lived there who was a suitor?"

"I'm sorry, I don't understand."

"Was there any man who came to the apartment to see Miss Cook who was something more than a friend—who was a boyfriend, a lover, or who wanted to *be* her boyfriend or lover? And I have to remind you, you are under oath."

"Objection, Your Honor!" MacDonald said, but he didn't give a reason.

Judge Williams was thinking. After several moments, she said, "Overruled."

"Thank you, Your Honor," Geiggen said. "I repeat, Miss Shaeffer, was there a man who came to the apartment to see Miss Cook as a lover?"

She sighed, thinking. "I wouldn't call him a lover."

"Did this man come over to the apartment?"

"Yes."

"And did he go into Miss Cook's bedroom with her?"

She hesitated. "Yes."

Geiggen let this sink in with the jury and then asked, "Was it your impression that Miss Cook engaged in sexual activity with this man?"

"Objection, Your Honor!" MacDonald yelled. "This line of questioning has nothing to do with the murder!"

"How will we know, Your Honor, until we get to the truth?"

The judge took a deep breath. "Counsel will approach the bench."

A particularly vicious argument seemed to be taking place, and members of the jury exchanged looks with one another. Then Geiggen seemed to be arguing with his own assistants. Finally the lawyers broke it up.

"In regard to that last objection," Judge Williams said, "it is sustained."

Geiggen took a moment to collect his thoughts. Then he looked at the witness. "Did this man—who you saw go into Miss Cook's bedroom with her—come to the apartment more than once?"

"Yes. Twice."

"And then he stopped coming?"

"Yes."

"Do you know why?"

"No."

"Do you remember when this was?"

"It was in the middle January—of 1994."

"Three weeks before the murder?"

"About that, yes."

Geiggen took a few steps over to look at the jury as he asked the next question. "Miss Shaeffer, do you remember the name of this man?"

"Objection, Your Honor!" MacDonald thundered.

"Your Honor," Geiggen said, whirling around, "I am merely trying to establish for the jury that there was yet another man in Miss Cook's life who may have had some romantic grievance with her."

"Your Honor, the defense is deliberately trying to lead the jury into what he knows is a false direction!"

"Your Honor," Geiggen pleaded, holding out his arms, "how can the jury come to an informed decision if they don't know of the incidents that led up to the murder of Sissy Cook?"

"He's doing it again, Your Honor!" MacDonald shouted, and Libby wondered *what* was Geiggen doing again? And *what* the hell was going on!

After a long pause, Judge Williams said, "Objection overruled, but Mr. Geiggen, you are not to lead the witness, do you understand?"

"Yes, Your Honor, thank you, Your Honor," he said. He walked over in front of the witness and said, "Miss Shaeffer, do you remember the name of the man who visited Sissy Cook in her bedroom—"

"Objection, Your Honor!" MacDonald was one step away from a fit.

"Overruled," Judge Williams said. She looked down at the witness. "You may answer the question."

Marybeth Shaeffer looked at Geiggen. "She only introduced him by his first name."

"Do you remember what that name was?"

"Yes," she said. "His name was Rusty."

16

S HE WAS trembling so violently, the guard had to put his arm around her waist while he wrestled with the keys to unlock the door. He got it open and helped her inside. There was a lounge in the corner and he helped her over to it. She immediately threw herself down, near fainting, and the guard deftly swept her legs up on it. "I'll get you some water."

Jill closed her eyes, panting for breath.

The guard helped her sit up to sip some water, lowered her back down, and placed a wet paper towel on her forehead. "Please don't move, Mrs. Tompkins. Please, just rest here." He left the room.

Immediately Jill curled up on her side, holding herself, and let out an agonized cry. It hurt so much she could not even cry. She still couldn't breathe; she could hear herself panting, like Duncan, their dog.

There was a quiet knock, the jangle of keys, and then someone came in. Jill didn't say anything, but simply lay there, on her side, face against the wall, eyes screwed shut. "I have some brandy, Mrs. Tompkins," Kathryn, the assistant prosecutor, said. "I think you should have some of it."

"I don't know what to do," Jill heard herself whimper, crouching tighter, holding herself.

"But you will," Kathryn said. "Give yourself time to get over the shock."

Jill felt her hand on her shoulder. The grip was firm but gentle, and she was glad for it.

"Please, take a sip of this."

Jill turned over and let Kathryn hold a paper cup to her mouth. She took a sip and the liquor burned down her throat. In a moment she didn't feel faint anymore, only numb. She took another sip. More burning. She raised a hand to her forehead. The compress was gone. Kathryn was pressing Kleenex into her hand. Jill looked up at her helplessly.

"The most important thing to remember," Kathryn said, "is that Geiggen knew exactly what he was doing in there."

"Then it's true," Jill croaked. She didn't even recognize her voice. She didn't even recognize her life. Suddenly she had no husband, no family, nothing. Everything had been taken from her.

"I don't know," Kathryn said forcefully, rising to her feet. "It could be that your husband simply visited. As Marybeth said, how would she know?"

"Oh, she'd know," Jill said, pressing the tissues into her face. Suddenly she clenched her teeth. "Goddamn you, Sissy," she hissed. "Goddamn you—" and her voice broke and she slammed her hand on the lounge.

Kathryn let her rant and sob for a while. And then she tried again. "Mrs. Tompkins, I'm not trying to minimize your pain in any way, but I want you to be aware that Geiggen is banking on you reacting this way. And if it works—what he's done—then he knows you won't come back to court anymore. Which is exactly what he wants. He's trying to drive you out of that courtroom. So the jury won't see you anymore."

Jill looked up. "How could she have done it? Our mother was dying. That's where I was—in Florida, sitting in a hospital, while Sissy and Rusty—" The tears came forth violently and she doubled over.

After a minute, Kathryn said, "You don't have to worry about your husband being subpoenaed."

Jill's head jerked up at that. "What do you mean?"

"Being subpoenaed to testify in court."

"You mean, in front of the press?"

Kathryn nodded. "You don't have to worry about that—it won't happen."

"How can you be sure?"

"We settled all that in the preliminary hearing."

Jill stared at her. "You mean—you *knew?*"

After a moment, Kathryn nodded. "And we established that your husband could shed absolutely no light on anything having to do with this case."

"How?" Her voice was cold now. Sharp and cold, the way it had been after Jill once overheard a neighbor make a snide comment about her son. "How did you know?" she demanded. When there was no answer, Jill took the cup of brandy from her, swallowed what was left in it, and sat up. "You *talked* to Rusty about it, didn't you?"

Kathryn nodded.

"Well, then you better go talk to Rusty again," she told Kathryn. "And when you do, tell him he needs to find a place to live." And then she burst into tears again.

"It was the sister who ran out," Mrs. Smythe-Daniels said, slipping her fur coat on. "She looked positively dreadful."

"Wouldn't you after listening to how your sister was slain?" Melissa asked.

"No, I quite agree," Mrs. Smythe-Daniels said. "And that defense attorney is positively ghastly." She glanced over at Debrilla, who was putting on her large green cloth coat.

"I agree, it vas awful," Debrilla said, "trooly awful."

"Death is death," Stephen the computer guy sighed, picking up his briefcase, "and it's going to happen to all of us. Maybe Sissy was just luckier to go that way."

"That ees the seekest theeng I have ever heard," Elena told him. "Have a good weekend, effereebody."

"Come on, Ellie, I'll walk you out," Dayton the Romeo said, offering his arm. "Let's give the press something to talk about."

Mrs. Smythe-Daniels threw her head back and laughed her whinny laugh. And accepted Dayton's arm.

After she went out, Adelaide vowed, "I will talk to her about that coat on Monday."

"Ready?" Alex asked Libby.

"In one second," she said. "I'm just writing something out for Basha." It was the name, address, and phone number of a periodontist she had gone to once. Now that Basha's new crown was finished, she was supposed to go to someone for gum treatment and Libby had sworn by the doctor she had gone to.

"I'll be outside," Alex said.

"I'll be there in a minute." Libby handed the paper to Basha, explaining a little more about what the doctor was like.

While Basha was thanking her, Will edged over, waiting in line. "I just wanted to tell you to have a good weekend."

"I'm going to try. Listen, thanks for backing me up on calling 'Oprah' yesterday. I feel a lot better."

"Anytime. But Libby, about your uncle."

She sighed, letting her shoulders sag. "Oh, right, that."

"I think you better talk to your parents this weekend. Tell them you think they should gather together whatever papers they have on the investments your uncle has made for them and have their accountant look at them."

"Now, how am I going to do that without calling Uncle Greg a crook?"

"Come on, you're a novelist—and a very good one—you'll think of a way." His expression grew serious. "But do it, Libby, for their sake. Just to make sure things are on the up-and-up. You said your parents are retired, didn't you?"

She nodded. "I guess you're right."

"And look, I'm staying right now down at the Vista Hotel." He handed her a piece of paper. "Call me if you have any questions, okay? Truly, I'd love to help." He smiled. "In return for having such great books to read at the hotel to take my mind off my problems."

"Thank you," she said softly. It was a very kind thing to offer. To say, too. About her books. And she appreciated it.

"Where would you like to go?" Alex asked her.

"Good heavens, I have no idea, not in this part of town."

"Well, I know a place, over on Franklin. Dionne's."

Given the fact that her head was filled with thoughts about Uncle Greg, her parents, and her career, Libby found it hard to think of something to talk about with Alex. Finally he said something about going fishing over the weekend and she asked several questions to keep him talking. By the time they were served their drinks, Libby knew a lot more about bass and pike and lakes, streams, and rivers in northwest Connecticut and southwestern Massachusetts.

"Tell me about Hal," he said suddenly.

"Oh, brother, what's there to say?" she said, sipping her white wine. "We thought we fell in love, we moved in together, we wanted to break up within a year, but tortured each other for another two." This summary wasn't quite correct, but it would do for the moment.

"What did you like best about him?"

"In the beginning?"

He nodded.

"His sense of calm in a life that had no structure. Being a professional musician is a hard road to take, even after you get pretty successful, which he is. You know, having club dates and then no work—work twenty-three straight days and nights on an album and then nothing. There was no way for him to plan on anything. He had to live day by day professionally, something I very much admired." She gave a bitter laugh. "Of course, I didn't realize that I was mistaking severe narcissistic self-involvement for calm." She met Alex's eyes.

"Why did you stay, Libby?"

She dropped her eyes. "I wanted to settle down."

"I see," Alex said, nodding.

They talked about his business for a while and he promised to take her to one of the houses he was renovating. Soon. After a second drink, he insisted on riding the subway with her uptown. He could catch a crosstown bus; he didn't like the idea of her traveling alone.

"At seven o'clock?" she laughed.

But he did travel with her uptown and at her stop, one arm hanging from the strap, he bent to kiss her lightly on the cheek. "I'll see you Monday."

"Good luck fishing." And the subway doors closed and the train pulled out and Libby, feeling strangely uneasy, climbed the stairs to the street.

What was it Melissa had said? That she had a feeling Alex wouldn't be any more faithful than Hal had been? Was that what bothered her about him?

III

CONFLICTING
EVIDENCE

17

O N MONDAY morning, Libby was walking to the jury room when she was nearly knocked down from behind by the prosecutor MacDonald. "Mrs. Tompkins!" he called, excusing himself to Libby, but pushing her out of the way all the same. The jurors had been instructed time and again not to talk to anyone connected with the case—the lawyers included—but the judge hadn't said anything about watching the prosecutor chase down a star witness who, when he caught up with her, whirled around and glared at him as though she would like to hit him.

"Yes, I'm here," Libby heard her say coldly, "no thanks to you, Mr. MacDonald." And then she pushed past him and went into the courtroom.

MacDonald saw Libby looking at him, and he abruptly turned away. *Now, what was that all about?*

In the jury room, people did not look very happy, either. As Elena said, "How long do we have to do thees? My life is crazee. My keeds theenk I have abandoned them." And Adelaide worried aloud that no one was going to get her dance students to come back to her if she was gone so long they found another teacher.

"Can't you give lessons at night?" Libby asked her.

"Teach after being in here all day?" Adelaide asked. "This place is like a vampire for creativity."

Libby had to admit, she had tried writing this weekend to utterly no avail. All she could think of was court and this case. That and her uncle Greg and the pending demise of her career. Alex, sitting next to her, was not very happy, either; he had caught a cold while fishing and his throat was killing him. Debrilla said her boss was very annoyed that she was still on jury duty, for he had to hire a temporary secretary. Ronnie said no temp could fill in in his capacity as executive trainee. When Stephen came in, he looked absolutely exhausted. Sweet Bridget was fretting over how to get organized for Thanksgiving. Melissa then came in looking—well—not very well rested, and remained quiet, merely sipping coffee and flipping through the Monday editions of the papers, which were less shredded than usual. Basha volunteered that after years of resisting it, over the weekend she had learned to knit because she was determined to accomplish something while sitting on this jury, and no one was going to defrost her freezer for her (?), and she held up four rows of red that she said was going to be a bedspread.

Last to arrive this morning, just under the wire, was the unlikely threesome of Mrs. Smythe-Daniels, Dayton, and Will. "We went to get some great coffee," Dayton announced, promptly going to the window and climbing up on the sill to light up a cigarette.

"A cappuccino for you," Will said, handing Libby a brown paper bag.

"Why, thank you."

"There's one for you, too, Alex," Will added, taking off his coat.

Alex was frowning. He looked at Libby. "What's this?"

"I don't know. But the proper response is thank you, I think."

"Thanks, William," Alex said suspiciously.

Will was in a very good mood this morning. He had enjoyed his first peaceful and productive weekend in months and months. After spending Saturday morning giving Betsy all the furniture she had purchased for his apartment (with his money), all Will had done was work at the office, work out at the gym, and, back at the hotel, relax and read Libby's novels.

The only problem, if it could be said to be a problem, was fellow juror Libby Winslow, and that reading Libby's novels was a lot like spending time with Libby herself, and so, the more he read (like late into last night), the more he felt this funny feeling inside that maybe he was treading into dangerous waters because he thought she was unlike any woman he had ever met.

And it scared him. Particularly when, last night, he had called his parents and mentioned that Libby was on the jury and that he was reading one of her novels, and his mother said she loved Elizabeth Winslow, too.

"Really, you've read one of her books?"

"I've read all three," she said. "Patsy Goldenson loaned me the new one just the other week." She laughed. "They may be a little racy for an old dame like me, but I think she tells a good story."

"She's really nice."

"Well, you can tell that," his mother said.

Will didn't know whether his mother really meant this, or whether she was simply so happy over the news of his breakup with Betsy and the fact that he was coming home for Thanksgiving that she would have been enthusiastic about anything.

"What deed you get, café au lait?" Elena asked Mrs. Smythe-Daniels, peering over the edge of the bag she had put down on the table. Mrs. Smythe-Daniels ignored the comment and sat down, slipping off her fur coat behind her. Adelaide was staring at her from across the table, and after she had looked back at Adelaide three different times, Mrs. Smythe-Daniels finally said, "May I help you with something?"

"Do you know how many animals died to make that coat?" Adelaide asked.

"Good morning, jurors!" Chuck said, swinging in to take attendance. "I trust you all had a good weekend."

There were boos and hisses in response, and even Clay had to laugh, they sounded like such a depressed bunch of hooligans. Chuck took attendance and then, wincing, announced that since the trial was behind schedule, the judge had decided that court would be in session on Friday, the day after Thanksgiving. Immediately the room broke out in an uproar.

"No way!" Dayton yelled.

"I demand to see the judge!" Mrs. Smythe-Daniels said, pounding her fist on the table.

"I'm going to Los Angeles for Thanksgiving," Melissa said. "I can't fly back in time for Friday!"

"I'm going to Illinois!" Will said.

"Ohio," Libby said, raising her hand.

"My nieces are coming from Frankfurt, vat am I to do? Who shall look after them?" Debrilla demanded to know.

"You tell that judge there ees no way we are comeeng hee-er on Frrri-day!"

"Look, I'll tell the judge, but I can't—"

"Just you go tell that judge she don have no jury for Frrriday!" Elena instructed.

Melissa had to wonder whether she even wanted to go home to L.A. for the holiday. On the other hand, spending four days in the office—which she knew she would do if she stayed here—seemed depressing.

She knew who she wanted to see this weekend. And the worst thing was, she had been invited to do something about it. But she had been paralyzed.

"Maybe you'd like to get together over the weekend," Christine had suggested last night. She had reached Melissa at the office (of course) around nine o'clock. "Maybe you could come out or I could come in."

Melissa had said she was sorry, but she was going home to L.A. for the holiday.

When she hung up with Christine, she could have kicked herself. She was dying to see her, to follow up on whatever this was, to do something other, for God's sake, than keeping herself in this emotional deep freeze.

This was no way to live.

But she was scared. Probably, if she admitted it, not much more scared than she would be if she had these feelings for a man. Any violent emotion scared her; it always had, since she was a little girl; before, however, she had been able to drink that fear into submission so she could at least pretend to participate in the world that way. Like a young woman falling in love.

"Ladies and gentlemen of the jury," Judge Williams said, "I understand there is some problem about the Friday court session."

All heads in the jury nodded.

"When we break for lunch, each of you is to submit in writing your reasons for not being able to attend."

"Have you no family, Your Honor?" Mrs. Smythe-Daniels blurted out.

Judge Williams glanced down at her seating chart and then back at the box. "Mrs. Smythe-Daniels, I do indeed have family, but I also have been appointed to uphold the laws of the Constitution of the United States, and it is my obligation to give as speedy a trial as possible, and trust me, there has been nothing speedy about this trial to date. Have I made myself clear?"

Dead silence throughout the courtroom.

"You will submit your grievances in writing," she repeated. "And now, Mr. MacDonald, the people may call their next witness."

Frankly, at this point Libby was rather hoping the judge *would* hold court on Friday so she didn't have to go home. Her mother was very upset with her. Trying to explain to her mother that she didn't think Uncle Greg was a crook, exactly, but perhaps a bit of a gambler with their savings had not gone over very well this weekend. "Mother, all I'm saying is that I think you should check to see what he's invested your money in, that's all."

"He's my brother!" she protested.

"The only reason why I said anything was because I tried to get some of my money back—and if yours is similarly devalued, or even just tied up, I think you should at least know about it."

"Well, that's just fine, Cornelia Elizabeth Winslow!" her mother had said. "Why don't you talk to your uncle about this over the Thanksgiving table and tell the whole family while you're at it!" And then her mother hung up on her!

Her mother did call back a half hour later to apologize, but with the additional comment that ever since Libby had moved to New York she had grown cynical and untrusting, and it was truly a shame, her mother thought, that her daughter had chosen to let herself become such a hard woman. It was no real mystery—was it?—why she couldn't settle down.

"Your Honor," Prosecutor MacDonald said, "the state calls Kareem Johnson."

Kareem, it turned out, was the six-foot-six bouncer at the club who had been standing behind Sissy Cook when she was shot. He was twenty-three. He had grown up in Harlem. No, he had never been arrested for anything. He had worked as a bouncer for four years. He was going to Hunter College part-time, majoring in physical education.

Entered into evidence were photographs of a silver Jaguar with a black convertible top, which, the witness said, he thought was the same one since it had the same first three letters of the license plate he saw the night of the shooting, 3L8. No, he couldn't really see the driver. Yes, he saw the shooter all right, a dark-skinned black man, about six foot two or three, short dreads—

"Could you explain to the jury what dreads are?"

"Dreadlocks. Tightly braided hair. But these were short. Maybe three inches on the side. Up top, I don't know what his hair was like 'cause he had on a Chicago Bulls baseball cap."

The testimony went on and got more and more graphic as Kareem described how he tried to warn Sissy Cook, but she stood there, frozen, until the gunman shot her the first time, and how, after that, she crouched, trying to cover herself, and how he blasted two more times, and how she fell on the ground and the gunman took a step forward, then, pointing straight down into her face, blew it off so there was nothing left.

Libby heard a whimper next to her. To her surprise, it had come from Mrs. Smythe-Daniels, who was now fumbling with the sleeve of her sweater to pull out some tissues tucked there. She pressed them to her eyes.

Libby didn't blame her, this was just god-awful.

Kareem said that after the gunman hopped in the car, he ran after the car to try to get the license number. Then he ran back and grabbed Marybeth Shaeffer, who was paralyzed, lying next to the victim, blood and bits of her friend's flesh splattered all over her. He had pulled Marybeth into the club and tried to wipe the worst of the bloody mess off her with a towel from the bar.

In the gallery, tears started running down Jill Cook Tompkins's face, but she did not do anything about wiping them away. She just sat there, letting the tears stream mascara down her face, dripping off her chin and falling to stain her white blouse. She never took her eyes off the jury.

It had crossed her mind over the years that Rusty might cheat on her on one of his business trips. Certainly it seemed to be a standard in the town they lived in, that just as soon as the man made a certain amount of money, it was then only a matter of time before his wife had to make a decision: Would she be willing to put up with the carousing so long as it wasn't in her face, and, in exchange, continue raising the children, running the household, and, for all intents and purposes, maintain a sense of family despite the faithlessness of her husband?

But dear God, Jill thought, she was still in her thirties. Granted, maybe she had put on some weight, but she was still one of the prettiest women in town.

Sissy. Every time she thought of her, her heart convulsed. She knew she was hating Sissy, hating Sissy so much right now, because she knew if she hated Rusty the way she wanted to, there would be no hope whatsoever of having any family left between them.

She had begun to wonder whether maybe her sister had gotten what she deserved, to be shot down dead on the streets of New York.

Kathryn Schnagel must have called ahead on Friday and warned Rusty of what was coming, because somehow he had beaten her home. The children were with Mrs. Montell somewhere, or so he had said, standing there in the middle of the kitchen, looking hangdogged and stupid and helpless, and all she could think was how stupid he was when it came to sex, how stupid he was to think he would never have to pay for what he had done, that she would never have to pay, that the kids wouldn't have to pay—

"You're just like all those other losers Sissy used," she had said, walking past him into the living room to take off her coat. "At least James Bennett Layton had a drug problem, what the hell was your excuse?" He hadn't answered, so she had gone ahead and hung up her coat in the front hall closet.

It had only been once, he said. The first time he had gone over was just to have a drink. The second time was when it happened, and he realized what he had done and bolted. The third time he had gone there was to sit down and talk to her about it, and to take responsibility for it, and to, as unpleasant as it was, agree to never allow the opportunity to arise again.

Jill had said nothing, but her mind raced with possibilities. She could visualize Rusty with Sissy; she had a good idea what their sexual encounter had been like—spontaneous, hot, illicit, passionate—two tremendously good-looking people giving in to years of attraction.

And that's what made her feel so sick. When it came down to it, her husband was no different than the rest. He was nothing special. He was not the one and only she had thought he was. He was just like any of five hundred thousand men she could have married and had the same family with, or any one of millions who couldn't think beyond their hormonal reaction to the looks of her sister.

She had made him stay at the Howard Johnson's for the weekend, pretending to the kids that he was away on a business trip.

"You've got to give us a chance, Jill," he had said. "I know you need a couple days to think right now, but—"

"But you don't think it will be good for the kids to see us apart," she had finished for him. "Is that what you were going to say? That you think we should stay together and work this out?" When he nodded, she literally sneered at him in disgust and went back to the front hall closet for her coat. "I'm going to go pick up the children. When I come back, I want you out of here."

Geiggen's cross-examination of Kareem Johnson, the bouncer, was brief and to the point. He dragged over the easel holding the prosecution's ground plan of the street outside the club and went over with Kareem where he had been standing at the time of the shooting. Once that was established (again), Geiggen said, "And your testimony is that you could not see who was driving the Jaguar."

"Yes, sir. I couldn't see in through the glare of lights on the wind-shield."

"So it could have been anyone behind the wheel."

The witness shrugged helplessly. "I guess."

"Thank you, Mr. Johnson, that will be all. Your Honor, defense maintains the right to recall this witness."

The judge explained to Mr. Johnson that this meant he was not to be in the courtroom at any time during the rest of the trial, and that he was not to read any papers or watch or listen to any news that had any bearing on this case.

They went straight to the next witness, which surprised Libby since they usually broke for lunch between twelve and twelve-thirty, and it was twelve-twenty already. "The state calls as its next witness George Kelly."

Kelly was a nice-looking executive somewhere in his forties, Irish, with a dark head of black hair, brown eyes, and a glowing, pink complexion. It turned out he was a Southerner, from Atlanta, who was a vice president of the clothing firm Sissy Cook and Marybeth Shaeffer had done magazine ads for. Yes, he was married, had children. He was also one of the men who had taken the models out for dinner and dancing. His version of events on the night of the shooting was very similar to Marybeth Shaeffer's and Kareem the bouncer's, only at the time of the shooting he had been down the block. The Jaguar had, in fact, almost hit him because he had been in the street trying to find a cab. But no, he did not see the license plate, and no, he did not see the driver.

"Let's return to the nightclub," MacDonald said. "You were dancing with Miss Cook when the defendant appeared?"

"Yes."

"And what did he do when he came up to you?"

"He shoved me from behind and grabbed Sissy."

"What happened then?"

"Sissy pulled away from him and screamed at him to leave her alone."

"What exactly did she say?"

"As I recollect, it was something like 'Leave me alone, you drug-dealing son of a bitch.' "

"And how did the defendant respond?"

"He said she was going to get it."

"Mr. Kelly, can you describe for the jury what the defendant looked like that night? There in the club?"

"He was a mess. He was in some nice clothes—gray flannels, I think, a blue blazer, Oxford shirt—but there was something all over the blazer." He illustrated with his hands. "Like something spilled, or—" He hesitated.

"Or what?"

"Well, I thought maybe he might have thrown up on himself earlier. It looked like that. I was surprised they had let him in the club. Because he looked so crazy. His eyes were all glassy and bloodshot."

"Did Miss Cook say anything to you after he was shown out of the club?"

"Yes. She told me who he was—you know, a Layton—which explained why they let him in, I guess. And she told me he had been stalking her, and it was a real problem because he was a drug addict and was strung out and crazy half the time."

Libby looked at the defendant, who sat there calmly, watching, betraying no emotion. He did look like Dan Quayle, she decided.

"I asked her if she had called the police, and she looked at me like I was crazy."

"Why was that?"

"She said his father *was* the police, or might as well have been for all his pull in the city."

"Thank you, Mr. Kelly, that will be all."

The jury was dismissed for lunch.

"One thing," Alex said to Libby as they walked across the street to the deli, "and I promise I won't say anything more about the trial this morning." He casually put his arm around her, resting his hand on her shoulder. Since it was cold and they were both wearing heavy coats and gloves, it didn't really count, Libby didn't think. Or maybe it did. At the next corner, she gently slid out from under his arm.

"What's the one thing?"

"If Kareem's twenty-three and has been a bouncer for four years, that means he was an illegal minor in the club for two of those years."

"Never thought of that."

"I don't know if the prosecution's done the best job, you know?" Alex said. "And of course the defense isn't going to say anything about Kareem's credentials since he swears it was impossible to see who was driving the Jaguar."

Libby sighed. "It does seem like Geiggen's a lot smarter and a lot more comfortable in court than MacDonald."

"And I wish that woman at the prosecution's table didn't always look as though she's watching MacDonald learn how to drive," Alex said. "Something's up in this case, something weird."

"I know what you mean," Libby said.

18

IF THE morning court session had been tough, the afternoon was a killer. First Geiggen cross-examined George Kelly (the dancing executive, as Libby thought of him), which ended up in a screaming match as Geiggen tried to steer the witness into admitting that he had been seeking to seduce the victim that night.

"Objection, Your Honor!" MacDonald yelled. "The witness is not on trial here!"

"The witness is in a unique position to shed light on the personality of the victim and the variety of men she used and discarded," Geiggen argued.

"OBJECTION! Now the defense is saying whatever he wants to the jury, Your Honor!"

"I must say, Mr. Geiggen," Judge Williams said with a sigh, "one could think you were deliberately trying to incite a mistrial."

A mistrial? Libby thought. And go through all of this again?

"Never, Your Honor," Geiggen said.

"Yes, well, we'll see, won't we?" Judge Williams said. "At any rate, the objection is sustained and you will confine your questions to this witness as it pertains to this trial."

"Yes, Your Honor," and then Geiggen of course promptly asked, "Did you ever sleep with the victim, Mr. Kelly?" and the judge blew up, calling a recess and summoning Mr. Geiggen to her chambers.

"Would you like some water, Ellie?" Dayton asked Mrs. Smythe-Daniels.

"No, thank you," she said quietly.

People exchanged looks. All the life seemed to have drained out of Mrs. Smythe-Daniels and the jurors weren't used to it. Even Adelaide didn't say anything as Mrs. Smythe-Daniels shivered—although it was anything but cool in the jury room—and pulled her mink up around her shoulders.

On her way out of the ladies' room, Libby stopped at that end of the table and gently placed her hand on Mrs. Smythe-Daniels's shoulder. "Can I get you anything?"

Mrs. Smythe-Daniels looked up to smile gratefully. Then she reached up to pat Libby's hand. "Thank you, dear, but no."

Stephen the computer guy went out to use the phone. The rest of them just sat there, waiting.

When they were finally called back into court, Geiggen finished up his cross-examination peacefully, established nothing new, and Mac-Donald called the other executive who had been there the night of the shooting, Robert Girstein. He had less to say than George Kelly about what happened that night, but basically confirmed everything the other witnesses had said.

When Geiggen got up to cross-examine him, he asked, "Mr. Girstein, how would you describe the victim, Sissy Cook?"

"She was very nice and very beautiful."

"Had you known her long?"

"No, just since she did the shoot for the campaign."

"Did you know anything about her before you met her?"

"Only that she was a great model and had the look we wanted."

"You didn't have any friends who knew Miss Cook?"

"Well, yes, I did. One friend of mine had met her before."

"Had he met her through work?"

"I believe so, yes."

"And had this friend of yours gone out with Miss Cook?"

"Objection, Your Honor," MacDonald said. "This line of questioning has nothing to do with the shooting."

"Your Honor," Geiggen said, "it does have to do with the shooting because I am establishing just how many men could have been responsible for it."

Judge Williams looked like she just might climb down and biff Geiggen. "Counsel will approach the bench."

As they did so, a rash of clicking noises broke out in the jury box. It was the sound of Life Savers against teeth. They had all picked up Clay's habit now, stocking up each morning on different flavors. The sugar helped to keep them awake for short periods of time.

The cross-examination dragged on, Geiggen eventually scoring points by having the witness say that almost every man who came near Sissy Cook would start to fall for her, she was that attractive and smart. And no, it would not surprise the witness if she had many unwanted suitors.

The next witness called was an EMS worker, Jocko Ramirez, who was asked to detail the sequence of events after the ambulance arrived, what they found, and what they did. It was, from beginning to end, horrible to listen to, about the blood, the position of the victim, the condition of her head, face, neck, chest, and hands, and how, after ascertaining she was dead, switching their attention to Marybeth Shaeffer, who at first they thought had been shot because she was covered with so much human carnage.

Mrs. Smythe-Daniels didn't lose it this time, but someone in the second row started to. Libby heard someone sniffing and turned to see that it was Elena. Then Libby looked out in the gallery and saw that Mrs. Tompkins, the sister, was sitting there, tears streaming again, too. She wasn't the only one; other women in the gallery had also begun to cry.

But Libby only felt sick.

The cross-examination went quickly and the judge mercifully called it a day. She also announced that she had reconsidered her position and court would not be in session on Friday, and therefore the jury was free to travel where they wished for the four-day weekend. However, she reminded them, they were not to discuss this case with anyone or amongst themselves, and they were not to expose themselves to any reports of this trial in any of the media.

Despite the promise of the holiday, depression had almost physically disabled the jury. They had been sitting in the box only five full days, but the trial stretched out before them, guaranteeing only further boredom, horror, and disgust. The holiday, too, only served to remind them that they had to come back, and that the trial would go on.

And on, as long as it took.

"I cannot hack eet," Elena was telling Mrs. Smythe-Daniels as they got their coats and belongings from the jury room. "Eet is so awful, the waste, the violence."

"I could not agree more, my dear," Mrs. Smythe-Daniels said softly.

Alex walked Libby to the subway. "Maybe we could have a drink before you leave for the holiday."

"I'm sorry, Alex, I'm just not up to anything tonight."

"No, neither am I. I have go uptown and reenforce an archway anyway. I meant maybe tomorrow."

"Let's see how we feel," she said, feeling a complete lack of enthusiasm.

"Buck up," he told her, "you've got your whole life to live." And then he gave her a big hug, lifting her up off the ground.

And Will, standing behind them, saw it.

"Mrs. Tompkins?" Kathryn Schnagel called as Jill was getting into the car that would drive her home to Connecticut.

Wearily she turned around and waited, watching the young lawyer hobble over in her too-high heels under the streetlight. Once Kathryn reached Jill, though, she just stood there, not saying anything.

"You're going to catch pneumonia," Jill told her.

Kathryn seemed to be struggling with a decision. Finally she met Jill's eyes. "I did something highly unethical."

"Not with my husband, I hope," Jill said in a bitter little joke.

"After your sister's murder, part of the evidence logged was a letter to her from your husband. That's how the police knew to interrogate him." She thrust an envelope at Jill. "When we were through with the letter, it should have been returned to your husband, but I was afraid he might destroy it."

Jill didn't understand what she was trying to say.

"I figured he would destroy it because he wouldn't want to run the risk of you finding out what had happened." Then she seemed to be on surer ground, some of the tension leaving her face. "But in case you did find out—if it came out in the trial, which it has—I deliberately held on to the letter. Because I knew if you did find out, and if I were you, I would want to be able to read the letter he wrote to your sister."

Jill took the letter and studied the young lawyer's face. "You could be in a lot of trouble for this."

She nodded. "Yes. But it would be worth it, I think. If it helps you." And then she turned around and went back into the courthouse.

"Christine?" Melissa said, gripping the phone in her office.

"Well, hello, what a nice surprise," she said. "How was court today?"

"Rough, actually. And upsetting. Very upsetting."

"I'm sorry to hear that."

"I can't believe you're still in the office," Melissa said. It was seven-thirty. The deal she had made with herself was to call Christine's office number and if she wasn't there, then that was that. But if she was . . .

"It's a busy time for us. We've got a lot going on in the spring—you know, with the mating season and everything."

This was not really a joke, Melissa knew. Christine did the media buying for all the Harding-Buckner Mills companies, whose business it was to feed not only cats, dogs, horses, cattle, birds, and zoo animals, but people, too, through their general foods group. It was the only way she felt comfortable being involved with the companies, she had explained to Melissa, in the one area she knew something about—media. Her brother and sister, on the other hand, were the hard-core business fanatics, and had been running things ever since their father had died.

"Uh, the reason I called," Melissa began.

"Yes?"

"Would you—rather, could you—if I don't go to California this weekend after all, would you still like to get together?"

"Oh, Melissa, I wish I had known," Christine said. "As you know, I asked you—"

"I know, I'm sorry, I just—"

"Just what?" she asked softly.

Melissa sighed. "I just don't know what I'm doing, Christine."

There was a long pause on the other end. "I don't want you to do anything you don't want to do, Melissa. It's essential you know that. And that getting to know each other better has nothing to do with anything else." Now she sighed. "The only trouble is, I've got plans for this week-end now, and I'm not sure I can get out of them. But let me work on it, okay?"

"Okay."

Another pause. "Melissa—are you all right?"

Melissa regripped the phone. "Christine, may I ask you something?"

"Sure."

"You're not married, are you?"

"Ah. Well, yes. Actually, I'm still in the process of getting divorced."

"Oh."

"Look, Melissa, it's complicated, and I want to explain the whole thing to you. Just let me try and clear one night this weekend. And then we can sit down and really talk, okay?"

When Melissa got off the phone, she felt the strange sensation of having separated from her body. Her body, however, dutifully picked up the storyboards and walked them down to Roger's office. "The revisions look great. Someone should go out and get the final okay from the Cat People tomorrow."

"Great," he said. "Do you know what director we want to use?"

Melissa sat down and discussed production plans with Roger, all the while her heart continuing to pound.

Will wasn't sure when he had ever felt this depressed. Seeing Alex Mc-Calley casually take Libby Winslow into his arms and hug her was like having the wind knocked out of him. He saw it and tried not to see it, and he had veered pathetically across Centre Street through the traffic, just wanting to get away. The only thing worse would have been for Alex to see that he had seen.

McCalley hated him, that he had known since Day One of jury duty. Will assumed it was his clothes, something Alex considered a contest: the big, good-looking, athletic man who chose to make his living restor-ing old houses, and the smaller, average-looking four-eyes who made plenty on Wall Street. They didn't call men like Alex McCalley blue-collar anymore; his sister had tried to explain it to him once, something about the influx of talented women into the executive workforce send-ing what would otherwise have been young white-collar executives back into upper branches of blue-collar industry.

Whatever, Alex hated him and Alex had fallen for Libby and obviously the feeling was mutual. And why not? Libby made good money and wasn't seeking anyone else's; Libby was great-looking and of course would be attracted by Alex's classic good looks (besides, she was from the countryside of Ohio, where, Will bet, all men looked like Alex Mc-Calley); and Alex was single and Libby was single, while he, Will, was merely an intruder, some nerd from Wall Street who had shown up for jury duty while in the process of throwing his old girlfriend out on the street.

Well, that wasn't exactly true, either, but at this point, did it matter?

Because he had lost out. And he hadn't even gotten a chance to try.

And worse yet, no matter how crazy it seemed even to himself, Will was pretty sure he was starting to fall in love with Libby Winslow. Or maybe with the woman who had written her books.

Were they one and the same?

He would never know now, would he.

19

COURT ON Tuesday morning, November 21, was mercifully dull. The owner of the nightclub and a bystander who had driven by at the time of the shooting were both examined by the defense and cross-examined by the prosecution without incident. Lunch was only forty minutes, and in the afternoon two police officers were called to the stand.

The first officer described the call that came into his precinct at 2:15 A.M. from the defendant, James Bennett Layton, Jr., who said his car had been stolen earlier that night at the club.

"This was a good thirteen, fourteen minutes after the time of the shooting, is that correct?" MacDonald said.

"Objection, Your Honor," Geiggen said. "The officer is not here to testify about a shooting in another precinct."

"Sustained."

"No further questions, Your Honor," MacDonald said.

"Officer," Geiggen said, taking his turn, "for the benefit of the jury, could you please tell them what the defendant said to you in his phone call."

"That he had been looking all over the neighborhood around the club for his car," the officer said, "and finally gave up."

"And what did you say?"

"I asked him why he didn't know where he had parked his car."

"And why did you ask this?"

"Because he sounded kind of looped. Drunk, or on drugs or something. I figured he just couldn't remember where he parked it."

"He sounded drunk or on drugs," Geiggen repeated.

"Yes."

"So, to you, Officer, he did not sound like a man who had just carried out a finely timed assassination"

"Objection, Your Honor," MacDonald said, rising. "There's no proof the murder was a finely timed assassination."

"Sustained," Judge Williams said.

Geiggen didn't bat an eye. "Let me put it this way, Officer, did the defendant sound like someone capable of carrying out a series of deftly executed driving machinations, timed to the split second?"

"No," the officer had to say.

"Fine. Thank you. No further questions of this witness, Your Honor."

The next witness called was Detective Joseph Cleary, who had been an arresting officer of the defendant at 4:45 A.M. at 912 Park Avenue. The defendant had been docile, even meek, he said, "as if he had been waiting for us to come get him."

"One more thing, Detective," MacDonald said. "You were apprised that the defendant had called the police to report his car stolen."

"Yes."

"And did you do any follow-up on that information?"

"Yes. We examined the phone records for the Park Avenue apartment to see if a call had been made from there to the precinct as the defendant claimed."

"And what did you find?"

"That no phone calls whatsoever had been made from that apartment until the time of the arrest, at four forty-nine A.M., when the defendant asked to call his lawyer."

On the cross-examination, Geiggen went right back to the issue of the condition of the defendant. What had he been like?

"He was very disoriented, dopey. We had to repeat things like four, five times before he would understand."

"In your expert opinion, Detective, would you say the defendant was under the influence of drugs or alcohol?"

"Objection, Your Honor, the witness is not a doctor or scientist," MacDonald said.

"Your Honor, if a senior member of the New York City Police Department is not an expert in people drinking or on drugs, I don't know who is," Geiggen said.

Laughter in the courtroom.

"Objection sustained," Judge Williams said.

"Detective," Geiggen said, "did the defendant seem to you to be capable of carrying out a number of expert driving maneuvers that night?"

"I don't know," the detective said.

"Do you not know, or do you not want to say?"

"Objection, Your Honor, defense is badgering the witness."

"Sustained. Mr. Geiggen . . ."

"No further questions, Your Honor," he said, walking back to the defense table.

"Does the prosecution wish to redirect?" the judge asked.

"Yes, Your Honor." MacDonald stood up. "Detective Cleary, you testified that after you arrested the defendant, he telephoned his lawyer."

"Yes."

"And he called from the apartment?"

"Yes."

"Did he look up the lawyer's number before he called?"

The detective thought a moment. "No. He just picked up the phone and dialed."

"So although the defendant appeared to be dazed and confused, under the influence of drugs or alcohol, when it came to calling his lawyer, he simply snapped up the phone and punched in the numbers without a second thought."

"Yes," the detective said.

"No further questions, Your Honor," MacDonald said.

"A glass of Chardonnay," Libby told the waitress, "but also the largest glass of water you can find, please."

"Make mine a Dewar's and water," Alex said, "and please find the other largest glass of water you can find."

"Oh, boy," Libby sighed, rubbing her face, "I am wiped out. This trial is just the most depressing and debilitating thing I've ever sat through."

"That building is not a well building, as we say in the trade," Alex said. "There's no air, for starters."

"There's no happy ending anywhere," Libby said as if she had not heard him. "No matter what happens, a twenty-six-year-old woman is dead and her family has to live with it. No matter what happens, Mrs. Layton and the Layton kids have to live with the fact that their husband and father is a louse and a cheat and a druggie and possibly a murderer."

Alex held a finger to his lips. "No more, Libby. Let it go. You can't let it eat at you."

"I guess you're right. But if I dream about the trial again tonight . . ."

As the drinks were brought to the table, Alex smiled. "Listen, I don't want to talk about court anymore. I want to talk about you."

"Me?"

"Yes," he said, "and how very beautiful you are."

"Hi, Melissa," Bonnie sang as she turned into her office. "You're just in time. Roger's back with the boards from the Cat People and wants to see you."

"Great," Melissa said, taking off her coat and hanging it up.

"You have a hundred million phone messages," Bonnie continued. "Anything interesting?"

"One that's a bit discouraging, if you ask me. I think that Christine Harrington expects you to work over the weekend."

Melissa carefully walked over to her desk and put down her briefcase. "Why, what did she say?"

"She wanted to know your schedule, and then when I said I thought you were going to Los Angeles, she said she thought perhaps you weren't. Anyway, she wants you to call her about this weekend."

He didn't mean to follow them, but they were walking downtown, the same direction as his office, and so Will, in a sort of stupor, followed behind, watching.

Alex McCalley couldn't possibly value Libby the way he would.

But Alex McCalley obviously had her now, just like the Alex McCalleys of the world always did. He was the kind of man women went for. He was the kind of man everything in their culture told women to go for.

He felt awful. He almost wanted to go home to Betsy.

————————

After dinner, when the kids were settled in front of the Disney Channel, Jill sat down at the kitchen table and took the letter out again.

Dear Sissy,

All I can say is how sorry I am. It was my fault. I knew how lonely you were. I knew how lonely I was. So when I came back that next day I knew what it was for.

How can I make you understand how much I value you? That's what's worst about this. Because you're family, because I have always loved and cared for you as the person you are.

When I say family, I mean our family, Jill's and mine. Do you understand the difference? That the way I love Jill and the way I love my kids are different, but that as a family there is a different kind of love, an unconditional love, which I have always felt for you, too.

Jill is to me like a part of me, and to ever do again what we did would be like killing part of myself, and committing suicide for my family—you included.

Do you understand? How I could love you and find you attractive and warm and loving, and know that the only truly loving thing I can do is stop right now? Right where it has started, and say, Sissy, that I love you, I respect you, you are part of my family, but I must be true to my family because they are everything to me?

You told me I was still in love with Jill and always would be—I think that's true. But I'm sure Jill would tell you about her frustrations of being married for so long, of the boredom, the feeling of being taken for granted, the despair that things can never be the way they were in the beginning. I've often wondered if she hasn't erred too somewhere along the line. Certainly enough men in our town would give anything for the chance.

But that is beside the point. The point is, I am so sorry for the way I acted, and I can only hope and pray you'll forgive me and that you will continue to love and respect your sister and your nephew and niece the way they do you. And the way I do. If you feel that you must tell Jill what I did that night, I will understand, but I beg you to say that it was with anyone but you—your roommate or someone. Because it will tear Jill's heart out that you were involved, because, you know, she thinks the world of you. And she should go on thinking the world of you.

Rusty

She didn't know. She just didn't know.

Typical Rusty when emotional, begging for forgiveness, dying to take the blame, instructing Sissy not to tell his wife, but if she did, to nail him to the cross as a martyr to preserve their relationship as sisters.

Oh, Rusty!

If only she couldn't see how it happened. She having been away for almost a month with the kids, and when he came down to Florida it was to find her in such a state she couldn't be touched; his thrill of having a drink with beautiful Sissy and then thinking the next day, what could the harm be in swinging by her apartment again? To cheer himself up? Flirt a little? Feel wanted? And then having a drink or two and bam, Sissy letting loose in a sexually impulsive moment—and then, twenty minutes later, Rusty racked with guilt already, going back to Sissy's the very next day, letter in hand, feeling awful.

The worst part was, Jill could imagine Sissy looking at him as though he were crazy. Because to Sissy, Jill knew, what they had done would have been nothing. Meaningless. Simply an act. A mistake. Something to be forgotten.

She called Howard Johnson's and told her husband to come home.

20

ON WEDNESDAY morning, Libby lugged her suitcase into the jury room, not in the least surprised to find several others already lined up by the coatrack. Given the holiday ahead, everyone was in a much better mood this morning than usual; they were all uncharacteristically chatty. Mrs. Smythe-Daniels was going out to Greenwich to one of her sons' houses for the entire weekend; Elena was having family to her apartment for Thanksgiving dinner; Debrilla's nieces from Frankfurt had arrived last night and they would travel to Philadelphia tomorrow to be with family; Dayton was going to his grandmother's in the Bronx; Basha was going to her daughter's in New Jersey; Sweet Bridget was having Thanksgiving at her apartment and her husband was going up to Boston to pick up her mother and bring her down; Alex was going to Binghamton; Clay and his wife were having Thanksgiving at their home for the first time (instead of her mother's); Slicked-Back Ronnie was going to his parents' on Long Island; and finally, there were the flyers: Libby to Ohio and Will to Chicago.

Only Stephen the computer man did not volunteer what he was doing; instead he stared down at one of the papers, pretending not to listen.

"Stephen," Elena said, peering down the table, "where are you going for Thanksgeeving?"

He looked up. "Uh, maybe to a friend's. I'm not sure."

"You can come to my house," Elena told him. "We are goeeng to have so much food. Turkey and beans and rice and roast beef and all kinds of theengs."

The room went silent, partly out of amazement at Elena's generosity to someone they were pretty sure she had never even spoken to before, and partly out of concern about how scarlet Stephen's face and neck had turned. "Thanks, but no." He smiled. "You're nice to ask."

When people resumed chatting, Libby moved closer to Stephen. "Melissa and I were going to have lunch today. I wish you'd join us." She hesitated. "Really, I wouldn't ask unless I meant it."

He squinted slightly, searching her face. "I—" And then he smiled and shrugged. "Sure, okay. I'll come. Thanks."

Jill checked her watch. Nine fifty-five A.M. The courtroom was full, as usual. As usual, she had entered and taken her seat without looking at anyone. Looking straight ahead at the judge's bench, she had a lot to think about.

Rusty was back in the house, which was, frankly, a relief. He had offered to sleep in the guest room, too, last night, if she felt uncomfortable.

"I just want to get through the holidays," she'd told him with a sigh. "I just want to give the kids the holidays and get through this trial and then we can deal with whatever we have to deal with."

"I was thinking maybe we could go see someone," Rusty had said, sitting on the edge of her side of the bed. This night, wisely, he was wearing all of his pajamas.

Fear ran down her back. "For what?"

"Talking this through."

"Is there something more than what you said in that letter?"

He shook his head. "No."

"So what would we talk about in front of a stranger?"

"Just sort all of this out."

She shook her head. "I can't believe this is you talking, Rusty. I can't believe you'd really go. I mean, I know you're saying this now, tonight, when you're still feeling scared and guilty, but later . . ."

He looked at her with an expression of confusion. "But we have a lot to sort out, Jill. A lot more than just this."

Then she had felt a decided chill. Was he leaving her? Suddenly the tables were turned. She had wanted him out of the house and debated whether or not to take him back, but what if he didn't want to come back? What if he was sick of their life? "What do we have to sort out?"

"Like why you're never very interested in what I do," Rusty said quietly. "Why I bore you so much, Jill. Why everyone else's husband in this town seems worthy of your attention and not me."

Everyone in the courtroom was asked to rise as Judge Williams entered and took her place on the bench. Kathryn Schnagel had told Jill that trials were usually only as good as the rapport was between the judge and jury, and his or her ability to lead them through all the mumbo jumbo and tricks and endless legalese to do their duty: to hear the evidence given in court and discuss the case until they were unanimous in their vote of whether the defendant was not guilty or guilty.

Jill's feeling about the judge was fairly positive. Kathryn said she had a history of being fair, and was a stickler for court etiquette.

Something was up this morning. As soon as court was officially in session, the prosecution stood and made a motion to reevaluate a decision that had previously been made which barred certain evidence from the trial.

Oh, that, Jill thought, feeling a sickening slide of anxiety in her stomach.

Perhaps the most outrageous aspect of this trial was that in the preliminary hearing, over a year ago, Geiggen had objected to certain evidence being included on the grounds that it had been confiscated by the police without a warrant. Technically Geiggen was right—morally, it was an outrage. The issue was a mess, since the police had had a valid warrant for the apartment at 912 Park Avenue where they arrested Layton, but *not* for the apartment next door, also a Layton corporate apartment, where key evidence tying the defendant to the murder had been found.

There was also a problem with evidence found in the Jaguar, since there was some physical evidence—fingerprints on the steering wheel—indicating that it could have been stolen as the defendant claimed.

Geiggen had consulted just about every major defense lawyer in the country when drafting his argument (some three hundred and ten pages), and in the end the court had ruled that the evidence from the second apartment and everything but the fingerprints on the wheel of the car was inadmissible, which meant that although the police and everyone else knew there was physical evidence that directly linked Layton with the shooting, the jury would never hear about it.

The prosecution's motion to bring some of that evidence into the trial did not get very far. Judge Williams had little choice but to reconfirm the earlier ruling, since nothing in the prosecution's argument had changed substantially.

Jill recrossed her legs and checked the pocket of her blazer for tissues. There could be a lot of tears today, and the jury didn't need to know that hers were ones of frustration.

"The prosecution calls Carl Wilgins," MacDonald announced at 10:40 A.M., after the jury had finally been brought in. Judging from the expressions of people in the courtroom when they were brought in, Libby knew something pretty heavy must have been discussed. Everyone looked keyed up, angry, uncomfortable, unhappy. The sister, Jill Cook Tompkins, was dabbing at her eyes with a handkerchief. Libby scanned the rest of the gallery, wondering, yet again, if the defendant's wife was there. For the life of her she couldn't figure out who she might be.

Carl Wilgins turned out to be a bartender at something called the Sportsman's Bar, where, evidently, the defendant was somewhat of a regular.

"Mr. Wilgins, could you please tell the jury if you ever heard the defendant speak of Sissy Cook."

"Oh, yeah, all the time. He used to bring in magazines and stuff and show me pictures of her."

"And what would he tell you?"

"Oh, lots of stuff. That she was his girlfriend. And then private stuff."

"Could you clarify that, please?"

"Well," the bartender began, evidently embarrassed by the request, "like what she was like in bed."

"Was he graphic in his descriptions?"

"Very," the bartender admitted.

"What else would the defendant talk about?"

"Sometimes he'd talk about a mole she had, or something. You know, something in a private place."

MacDonald turned to look at the jury, as if to say, *Get this—not only did this scum have her killed, he was a sicko cad.*

And yet the defendant seemed unfazed by all this, sitting there, looking on, calm, at peace.

But the victim's sister, Libby saw, was crying in the gallery, clearly angry as hell.

"What was Mr. Layton's mood like when he talked about these things?"

"He was like a young kid. You know, like a horny little—" He looked up in horror at the judge. "I'm sorry, Your Honor."

"You may continue, Mr. Wilgins."

"Um," he said, returning his attention to MacDonald, "I thought he was a pretty sick camper. He wasn't all there. I thought he did drugs—he was just kinda twisted, you know."

MacDonald looked over his shoulder at the defense table as if expecting an objection, but Geiggen hadn't moved; he only sat there, watching and listening carefully.

"No further questions, Your Honor," MacDonald said.

Geiggen did not waste much time. "Mr. Wilgins, in your experience as a bartender, did you think it was possible that Mr. Layton was an alcoholic?"

He thought about this for a minute. "Not really. Um, he would just have a few beers. But he was on something, all right. I mean, he was not in his right mind usually."

"Do you think it's possible Mr. Layton had a drug problem?"

"Oh, yeah, heavy duty. All the signs were there."

Geiggen went on to accentuate the bartender's theory, that Layton was a drug addict, a rich one, half in the bag and half out of his mind, spending lots and lots of money to make people—like the bartender—put up with him.

The next witness called by the prosecution caused quite a buzz. It was Helena Danchione, the woman who had discovered Sissy Cook and signed her with the Danchione agency. She was an older woman, somewhere around seventy, dressed all in black, complete with a black hat. All Libby could think of was when Joan Collins made her debut on "Dynasty" years ago as Alexis to testify against Blake. Helena Danchione had that same kind of sweep and manner.

MacDonald spent quite some time leading Helena through all the reasons why Sissy Cook was so wonderful: After dealing with her drug problem and anorexia, she had been an enormous help with the younger models, identifying who had problems and convincing them to seek help; as a professional she could not be beat—she was extremely hard-working, responsible, reliable, and beautiful. No, she didn't do much TV work; it was a credit to Sissy that she knew her photogenic talent was best suited for stills. No, she was no actress. Sissy had been refreshingly real, open, warm, and full of fun.

How much money had she made in the year before she died? Through the agency, almost seven hundred thousand dollars. Helena knew she sent money to her parents in Florida; she knew she gave heavily to charity—in 1994, Helena knew Sissy had given twenty thousand dollars to an anorexia clinic, ten thousand to an AIDS hospice, ten thousand to Sloan-Kettering for breast cancer research, and had bought a twenty-five-thousand-dollar table at a fund-raiser for a psychiatric center for abused children.

On this note, the judge called for a recess and dismissed the jury for lunch.

"We're having another group lunch," Libby said to Will in the jury room. "Melissa and I were having lunch, and now Stephen's coming and Alex is, too, so why don't you join us?"

Because it will be torture to watch you with Alex, Will thought. "Are you sure Stephen won't mind? I'm not sure why, but he never seemed very keen on me or Alex."

"Oh, he's fine—he said fine. Come on," she urged, "come with us."

After the jury left the courtroom and Judge Williams adjourned the trial for lunch, Jill continued to sit in her seat, letting the crowds pile out before her. When she was finally ready, she stood up and turned, and saw Rusty standing in the back, leaning against the wall, waiting for her.

She went up to him. "What are you doing here?"

"I thought about it," he said, "and I decided I should try and get here when I can. Until it's over." He took her hand.

Her mouth parted in surprise. And then she felt tears come up so suddenly that they spilled down her face before she could catch them. "Jill, honey, don't," Rusty murmured, putting his arm around her. He led her to one of the benches and they sat down while she pulled herself together.

"Can I help with anything?" a court officer asked them.

"Honey?"

"No, no thanks," she said, wiping her eyes.

"Think you could eat something?" Rusty asked her. "Maybe soup and a sandwich?"

"Could we go out? Somewhere I won't be stared at?"

"Sure, honey, we'll find somewhere."

"I need some air, anyway," she said, standing up. "This building is so stuffy. We go this way," she said, pointing down the hall. "Let's take the far elevator, it's usually people from other trials."

They got down to the lobby and Jill led him through the maze of people to the side entrance. As they approached the door, Jill suddenly stiffened. Geiggen and one of the other defense lawyers were standing there.

"What is it?" Rusty asked, trying to follow her eyes. Then she felt him stiffen. "Well, well, the sleazebag himself. I have a thing or two to say to him." Before she could stop him, Rusty had left her side.

Jill couldn't hear what Rusty said to him, but she did see Geiggen raise his hands in front of him, talking a mile a minute, and then he looked past Rusty's shoulder at her as she approached. Geiggen actually smiled. "There she is. How bad could it be?" he said to Rusty. "You know, in my experience, many times it's better if everything comes out in the open." He looked at Jill. "Doesn't he understand it's not what I did that matters, it's what *he* did?"

Rusty slugged him, sending the lawyer crashing back against the wall. Court officers came running and Rusty did not resist as they grabbed to restrain him.

Blood was spewing out of Geiggen's nose and onto his chest. He took out a handkerchief and held it against his nose as an officer assisted him. "Yes, I'm pressing charges!" he barked. "Arrest this stupid ape."

"You'll do no such thing," a sharp voice said. It was tiny Kathryn, madder than hell. "If anything, you'll arrest the counselor for inciting a riot."

"Oh, Christ, Schnagel," Geiggen sputtered.

"The DA's office accepts responsibility for these witnesses—"

"He's not a witness!" Geiggen yelled.

"You'll have to talk to MacDonald," Kathryn told the officer, grabbing Rusty's and Jill's arms firmly. "They're in his custody." She pulled the Tompkinses out the door and pushed them toward Jill's car and driver. "Take them home to Connecticut," she instructed the driver. "Stop on the way and get them something to eat, but don't let them come back here." To Jill, as she pushed her into the car, she said, *"Don't* let him hit anybody else—have a good holiday—come back on Monday," and then she closed the door on the couple and waved them off, laughing for the first time Jill had ever seen.

Over lunch Libby told Will about how much she was dreading seeing her uncle Greg over the holiday. Will insisted that she should tell her mother that he, Will, was now her investment adviser and that Libby should blame all her inquiries on him. So caught up in this idea, he gave her his business card at Connors Morganstern and wrote his parents' number in Chicago on the back. At the slightest hint of trouble, Will said, she should call him. And for heaven's sake, play dumb. If her uncle went ballistic, she should just say, "Look, will you just talk to my adviser on the phone right now and answer his questions? Then it will be all cleared up." And if he wouldn't, at least Libby's mother would see this.

While they were talking, Will had missed what was being said on the other side of the table, but when he and Libby were finished, the table suddenly got very quiet. And then Stephen excused himself to go to the men's room.

"He was telling us about his friend who's in the final stages of dying. Of AIDS," Melissa told them.

"I think it's his lover," Alex added.

"Oh, no," Will murmured. Maybe this explained Stephen's aloofness toward him and Alex, being how neither Wall Street nor blue-collar culture was known for being terrifically open to gays.

"It's the end, he thinks?" Libby asked.

Melissa and Alex nodded.

"Makes you stop and think, doesn't it?" Will said.

"About what we have now, the time left to us, certainly," Melissa said.

Will saw Alex reach over to squeeze Libby's arm. And not let go of it.

On the way back to the courthouse, Stephen stopped in a gift shop to find something funny for his friend in the hospital. Melissa and Will walked on together, Libby and Alex behind them.

"I was just thinking what Stephen's holiday is going to be like," Melissa said.

"I know," Will sighed.

After a few paces, "Do you ever feel useless? Self-involved?"

"On Wall Street? Every day."

"I'm serious."

"So am I. So I write a lot of checks. Donations."

"That's it, isn't it?" Melissa muttered.

"What?"

"Our occupations. There's no time to spend anywhere but in them."

Will laughed. "Hey, listen, ask your mom, that's the way it's been for men always—the women did the social work."

"So you do know what I mean," she said.

"Oh, yeah. I think that's why people have kids—so they don't feel so selfish. They live like we do but say they work so hard for their sake."

Melissa gave a smile.

"When I go home," Will continued, "my mom will make me and my father and whoever else is around go to a homeless shelter on the South Side to serve Thanksgiving dinner."

"Really?"

"Oh, yeah. She's one of those—very community-oriented. She's great."

"My mother will have Thanksgiving catered by Valducci's," Melissa said. "She hates to cook and so do her friends, but it's the maid's day off. Not that I know why she bothers, they're all anorexic, anyway."

"Really? She's like a Hollywood wife?"

"Not quite so bad, but bad enough." She smiled. "But thanks, Will, you've given me an idea about how to spend the holiday."

"So you're calling me Will, too?" he said.

"Absolutely. It suits you." She turned around. "Libby? I need to talk to you for a minute."

Alex reluctantly left Libby's side and walked ahead of the women with Will.

"Remember the client I told you about?"

"Of course I do!" Libby said, eyes bright. "What's going on?"

"Well, I'm not going to Los Angeles this weekend. I'm having dinner with—him—on Saturday night."

Libby's eyes widened. "That's great."

"Great?" Melissa said. "I am completely freaked out."

"Why? Oh, no, he's not married, is he?"

"No. Well, yes. He says he's in the middle of a divorce."

"Okay, Melissa, listen to me—you've got to check that one out carefully. The world's full of men who are supposedly getting divorced."

"He's not like that, I don't think."

"Yes, well, you just make sure the story checks out. *Before* you do anything. Hear me?"

Melissa laughed. "I've got my very own personal romance adviser."

"What better choice," Libby laughed, slinging her arm through Melissa's, "than she who knows how the plot should go?"

"Yeah, well," Melissa sighed, "at some point I'm going to have to talk to you about the casting of the characters."

Before Libby could ask her what that meant, Alex turned around. "Are you two finished gabbing yet?"

21

I S IT my imagination, or has defense counsel been run over by a bus?" Clay whispered to Libby that afternoon in the jury box.

Libby's eyes widened. Clay wasn't kidding. Geiggen had some sort of splint on his nose, held in place by a big X of adhesive tape. He also seemed to be wearing one of the court officers' shirts and someone else's brown jacket, which certainly did not go with his blue pants. But no one was going to explain anything to them about why the natty defense lawyer was dressed à la Salvation Army, and court resumed with Mac-Donald's direct examination of Helene Danchione.

He asked her if Sissy Cook had ever mentioned the defendant.

"Yes, many times."

"In what context?"

"In the context that the man was a kook, a pervert, and a nuisance."

"Could you please explain to the jury what you mean, Ms. Danchione."

She looked at the jury. "He followed her for weeks. And it got so bad,

I had to hire extra security—at the office, and on Sissy's shoots. You see, the problem was Layton's father was a big shot and it was next to impossible for Sissy to do anything about him without getting further harassed in other ways."

"Harassed how?"

"Well, by certain members of the police department—"

"Objection, Your Honor," Geiggen said. "The witness is speculating. It has been proven before that there is no evidence in this regard."

"Sustained. Mr. MacDonald?"

"Yes, Your Honor. Ms. Danchione, could you explain to the jury what relationship the victim had with the defendant, as you understood it?"

"From Sissy?"

"Yes."

"Well, Sissy was the first to admit that when she first met the defendant, she went back to his apartment—on Park Avenue. And there she said she had a dreadful experience with him, and after that didn't want anything to do with him."

"Did she say what that experience had been?"

"Yes. That she and the defendant had started to get sexually involved, and that when it came time to go to bed, she asked him to wear a condom. He wouldn't. And so she told him, if he wouldn't wear a condom, the whole thing was off, she was leaving. And then he began to yell and shout at her, and started breaking things—and it scared her."

"What did she say happened then?"

"He threw her down on the ground and pulled his pants down."

"For what purpose?"

"She thought he was going to try and rape her, but . . ." The witness shrugged.

"But what?"

She looked at the jury and shrugged again. "He had no erection, none, and so she knew he *couldn't* do that."

"What did she say happened then?"

"Sissy said he went into the dining room and started cutting lines of cocaine on the table in there. So she left."

"Did he pursue her?"

"No. She said he let her go. He was busy snorting lines."

Libby could feel herself starting to whither inside. While some people, like Stephen's lover, were fighting for their lives in a hospital bed, other people were playing Russian roulette with sex and drugs because they had nothing better to do. It was sick. The whole thing. The defendant, the whole stinking trial.

MacDonald was finished with the direct and Geiggen slowly got to his feet and limped over to the jury box. "I hope the jurors will excuse my appearance."

"Mr. Geiggen," Judge Williams said sharply, "you have already been instructed on this subject."

With his back to the judge, Geiggen rolled his eyes. "Yes, Your Honor, sorry, Your Honor," he parroted. Then he turned around and, leaning on the jury box as if he was in pain, started in on Helena Danchione.

"You said that Sissy Cook freely admitted that she went to the defendant's apartment to have sex."

"Well, I don't think she knew she was going to have sex when she went there."

"But you don't really know what Miss Cook thought, do you? You don't know if she went back to the defendant's apartment to have sex, or maybe she even went back to do drugs?"

"She wouldn't have gone to do drugs," Helena said forcefully. "Sissy was very anti-drugs."

"So she would not have gone to the defendant's apartment late at night to do drugs?"

"No."

"But it is possible she went to have sex with the defendant, a man she had met only hours before at a charity luncheon."

"I don't know if—"

"Yes or no, Ms. Danchione, is it possible that Sissy Cook went to the defendant's apartment with him the night she met him with the intent of having sex?"

She hesitated. "Yes."

"And did you consider yourself a good friend of Sissy Cook's?"

"Yes. Extremely so."

"So if anyone would know if Sissy Cook was capable of acting out impulsively in a sexual manner, it would be you."

"One of the people, yes."

"So let me ask you, in all your years of friendship with Miss Cook, did she ever tell you anything that would lead you to believe that she could be sexually impulsive?"

"Yes."

"Objection, Your Honor. Defense is prosecuting the victim—"

"Defense is trying to establish the personality of the victim, Your Honor," Geiggen said quickly, "so that the jury may understand the motive or motives of whoever may have wished to see Sissy Cook dead."

The lawyers were called up for a sidebar. Life Savers were quickly consumed in the jury box. They argued up there for perhaps five minutes, and then Geiggen limped over to take his place by the jury box again.

"Ms. Danchione," Geiggen said gently, "could you tell the jury if Ms. Cook had any other admirers besides the defendant?"

"Oh, yes. She was a very beautiful person, inside and out."

"How many admirers would you say she had—in the time you knew her?"

"At least a hundred. She didn't go out with these men," she added to the jury, "but these were men who tried to get her to go out with them."

"And so there were, in fact, many men whom Sissy Cook had rejected as potential lovers? Is that not correct?"

"Yes. That's correct."

"And weren't there, in fact, many *women* Sissy Cook had rejected as potential lovers?"

She hesitated and then said, "Yes, some. A few."

"No further questions, Your Honor," Geiggen said.

"The state wishes to redirect, Your Honor," MacDonald said quickly, jumping up.

"You may proceed, Mr. MacDonald."

MacDonald stood at his table. "Ms. Danchione, to your knowledge, did Sissy Cook ever have any kind of sexual relationship with a woman?"

"No, never."

"And to your knowledge, had any rejected lover of Miss Cook's ever stalked her?"

"Besides Jim Layton?" the witness asked.

"Yes."

"Not that I know of."

"Thank you, that will be all."

Geiggen staggered to his feet. "Defense wishes to re–cross-examine the witness, Your Honor."

"Proceed, Mr. Geiggen."

Slowly and painfully, Geiggen limped back over to stand in front of the jury box. "Ms. Danchione, you said that no rejected lover of Miss Cook's—besides the defendant—had ever stalked her."

"Yes."

"Let me ask you, then, had any men *ever* stalked Miss Cook?"

"You mean, men she didn't know?"

"I mean any man that was anything but a rejected lover," Geiggen said. "It could have been a complete stranger."

"Well, yes," she admitted.

"And had Miss Cook *ever* been stalked by a woman?"

"Uh, yes."

"How many people, would you say, Ms. Danchione, had in some way stalked Miss Cook in the years that she worked for you?"

"When you say 'stalked' . . . ?"

"You mentioned having to hire extra security. What I'm asking you is, Ms. Danchione, how many people would you estimate tried to make advances toward Sissy Cook in a way or manner that bothered her?"

"You mean if they had to be taken away, or something? From the agency? Or if we had to give their letters to the police?"

"Yes."

"But not just autograph seekers."

"I think you know what I mean, Ms. Danchione, people who fancied themselves attached to Miss Cook in some way, or who desperately wished to know her, or be connected with her in a way that made Miss Cook uncomfortable."

"Yes, I think I understand what you mean now. People whose mental condition or intent would alarm us in some way."

"Exactly," Geiggen said. "Now, how many of those people have there been, would you say, in the years you knew Sissy Cook?"

"Oh," the witness said, looking to the ceiling, thinking. "I'd say maybe twenty."

"Twenty people in all that time?"

"No, about twenty a year," she said.

"You would estimate that about twenty people a year would approach Miss Cook in some way that you or she found alarming?"

"Yes. It's a problem with all the successful models."

"And you knew Miss Cook for—how long?"

"We worked together for eight years."

"And so that means, to your recollection, Ms. Danchione, about one hundred sixty people made unwanted advances of some kind toward Miss Cook in the time you knew her—and that these unwanted advances caused some kind of alarm."

"Yes."

"Thank you. No further questions of this witness, Your Honor."

Judge Williams then moved to end the session, but not before lecturing the jury about what she expected of them over the holiday. "If the football game is on, fine, go ahead and watch, but no newscasts of any kind, no tabloid shows, no newsmagazines, and above all, you are not to read any newspapers until you return to court on Monday. You are not to discuss this case with *anyone*. If you are driving in a car and someone turns on the radio, you are to either have them turn it off or you are to get out of the car."

She cleared her voice. "Now, for those of you who will be flying. There is the matter of news videos, which some of the airlines show."

"Either turn it off or get out of the plane," Clay murmured to Libby.

"Excuse me? Is there a question?" the judge asked.

Silence.

"When you board the plane, you must talk to the flight attendants and explain the situation, that you are serving as a juror on a murder trial . . ."

It went on and on. And then, finally, they were released for the four-day holiday. One would have thought they had graduated from high school, they were so happy.

Will made Libby promise she would call him in Chicago if he could help with the Uncle Greg fiasco, and then Alex quite deliberately made a show of taking her suitcase and escorting her out of the jury room.

Outside, Alex hailed her a cab. He held the door for her and leaned inside to hand her the suitcase. Before she could do anything to prevent it, he took the opportunity to kiss her briefly on the mouth. "Have a wonderful trip."

As the cab drove off, Libby could see Will standing on the sidewalk. And he looked dreadfully upset.

After talking with Will at lunch today, Melissa knew exactly how she wanted to spend Thanksgiving. As soon as she reached her apartment on Tenth Street, she flipped open the phone book, got the number, and then called the Alcoholics Anonymous Intergroup office to ask if there was a Manhattan meeting they knew of that might appreciate some food tomorrow.

"You mean, like, Thanksgiving food?" the person manning the phones said. "Not just junk food in a bag?"

"Yes. I was thinking I could cook a turkey—and stuffing, turnips, green beans, potatoes, gravy—"

The guy let out a low whistle. "Wow, the works—somebody's gonna luck out. Let me check, hang on." A new voice came on the phone, this time a woman's. "This is wonderful! Now let me ask you, do you live uptown or downtown?"

"Down," she said. "The Village."

"I have just the meeting for you. At three o'clock tomorrow, would that be okay?"

"Sure."

"There'll probably be between eight and twelve people. But I don't know that you'll want to go there alone," she added. This meeting, she warned Melissa, was pretty low-bottom and always had one or two wet-brain alcoholics who had been asked to leave other meetings because of their disorderly conduct. But if Melissa wanted to bring some Thanksgiving food to some people who would really appreciate it, this was certainly the place.

But who would go with her? Melissa wondered. She had no friends in AA, really. She had no real friends in New York outside of work, for that matter, which only underlined the uneasiness she'd been feeling ever since going on jury duty. It was, for the first time in years, giving her time to think.

"I'm new in town," she said slowly into the phone, and then thought, Come on, Melissa, at least tell the truth in AA. "Well, actually, I'm not new in town, I just haven't connected here in New York AA and don't really have anyone I could ask to come with me."

"Then we'll send someone over to go to the meeting with you," the woman said without missing a beat, and she took Melissa's address, promising that someone from Intergroup would be there before two-thirty. They would also alert the meeting's present chairman that food was coming—that is, if he had a number where he could be reached, which the chairman of this meeting usually didn't. "Oh, by the way," she added, "it would probably be a good thing if you brought everything they'd need to serve the food with—and to eat it on. You know, paper plates, plastic forks, the works. If you can afford it, it would be great."

Melissa had a ball at the grocery store. Spending money this way felt wonderful.

She used two big shopping carts. She got the biggest turkey they had left—twenty-six pounds—and the makings for stuffing. She got cran-

berry sauce, rolls, butter, milk, cream, herbs, spices, paper plates, napkins, plastic forks and knives and spoons. She got a big clean-up sponge,
paper towels, aluminum foil, plastic wrap, and a big paper tablecloth.
She got a pumpkin pie, two apple pies, and some mild cheddar cheese.
She decimated the vegetable bins. The total was not two hundred dollars, but a little over three (largely because of all the Rubbermaid containers she bought to transport the food). She paid for it all and
arranged for it to be delivered in cardboard boxes that she could use the
next day.

At home she put on a Bonnie Raitt CD and, singing along, started
getting out pots and pans and mixing bowls. She had never really used
this kitchen before. At one time, Melissa had been a really good cook—
not a gourmet or anything special like that, but just essentially good on
all the traditional meals she and her brother would otherwise never have
been able to eat at home, since for years their mother had employed a
maid to prepare the family dinner before leaving every day, and while
the meals had always been healthy, they had also always been *de la Mex-
icana,* i.e., pot roast with red-hot chili peppers, or spaghetti and
chimichanga.

Tonight Melissa wanted to start on a good old-fashioned Thanksgiving dinner. She would set her alarm and get up early to start the turkey;
the vegetables she could make tonight. With the Rubbermaid containers, she could zap each entree good and hot in the microwave before
leaving tomorrow, so it would still be at least room temperature when
served. The groceries arrived from the store, and by eight o'clock the
apartment was full of good smells. The Bonnie Raitt CD had given way
to a Judy Collins, and it was Barbra Streisand who was singing when
Melissa started cleaning up.

For the first time in a very long time, Melissa felt as if she had a life.

22

L IBBY STRETCHED, luxuriating in the softness that only a grandmother's sixty-year-old linen sheets could offer. She was home, in
Greatfield, in her very own bed. It was early, maybe seven or seven-
thirty; she could tell by the light coming in through the windows. For
years she had told time by it.

She smelled coffee from downstairs. The Victorian heating vents between the floors of the house had always left little to the imagination as to what was being prepared in the kitchen. There was no noise yet, though. Her parents were early risers and very quiet, as a rule, until they had read the papers and done the crossword puzzles. In earlier decades, Libby's father would have been making the rounds on this floor by now, pulling Ted and Jimbo and Libby out of bed, as Mrs. Winslow would start breakfast and Louisie Trutmueller, the lady who had helped her mother for as long as Libby could remember, would bring up freshly laundered clothes for the children.

People in town said Diana Winslow maintained airs. And she did. Granted, her grandparents had owned half the county, and her parents had managed to hang on to the farm and the house in town through the Depression, but after Diana Garran married Tom Winslow, they only had the house in town, and yet Diana still acted like she owned the *whole* county, always dressing her children and sending them off to school like they were the President's children or something. But Mrs. Winslow felt her position strongly in the community; social mores had slid drastically in Greatfield since she was a girl. Someone had to set standards and maintain a sense of propriety, and so she had always undertaken the task herself.

Her mother was definitely a character, Libby had to admit. Although she would hardly devote a book to her.

"I hope you're happy," her mother had said to Libby last night when she arrived. Her father had still been outside, putting the car away in the garage out back. "Your uncle Greg isn't coming after all, and I know it's because of this unpleasantness over your money. You can be absolutely dreadful when you want to be, Cornelia, do you know that?"

Trying not to continue to be so dreadful, Libby suppressed the urge to laugh and said, "Listen, Mother, if I were you, I would check to see if there shouldn't be some unpleasantness between you and Uncle Greg over *your* money."

"Don't you dare mention this to your father," her mother warned her as they heard the back door open.

So that was going to be the deal. Libby was not to mention any of this to her father because, in her mother's view, the money in question was from her family, anyway, from the sale of the farm, and so it was not necessarily her husband's business, even if it was the bulk of their retirement money. In return for Libby keeping quiet about it, over the holiday

Libby's mother would only scowl at her like Black Death when no one else was looking, pretending that this behavior was something unusual.

Her mother was very loyal to her baby brother. As Libby's father would say, someone had to be.

"'Morning, my Corny Girl," Mr. Winslow said from the doorway of her bedroom. Only her father could call her that and get away with it. It was a kind of double entendre, living in the Corn Belt as they did.

Libby smiled and turned over on her side, snuggling under the covers. "Hi, Dad."

"Thirty-four going on four years old," he said, coming over to sit on the bed. "It's good to have you home."

"It's nice to be here. I love Grandma's sheets. They're so soft."

"I know. We have to be careful, though, they rip so easily now. You can't thrash around like you did when you were little." He patted her shoulder. "I censored the paper for you."

"Thanks."

"It's a nasty business, that trial you're on."

"There are some nice people on the jury, though. It's not as bad as it could be."

"Corny," her father began. "What's going on between you and Mother?"

"You'll have to ask her, Dad. I'm not allowed to tell."

He frowned and stroked his chin. His was a close shave. He still used an old-fashioned barber's blade, one he sharpened a little every morning on a strap. "Well, let's see, if you're not allowed to tell me . . ." He looked at her. "You're not dating an Arab terrorist or anything, are you? Your mother seems very upset about Arab terrorists this month."

She smiled. "No."

"Then it must be about your uncle Greg."

Libby kept her mouth shut.

"And if it's about your uncle Greg," her father said with a sigh, "then it must be about money. Did he lose yours? The money you gave him?"

"No."

"Good."

"Not all of it," she added.

"Oh, no," her father groaned. "That dope. If he wasn't as pathetic as he is, your mother would never be so attached to him. How much did he lose?"

And so Libby told her father the whole thing, about her book, about

Oprah, about the trial, about money, calling Uncle Greg, what Will told her about the investments Uncle Greg had made, and how he had made Libby promise she'd talk to her parents about the money they had with him.

"Pity your friend Will can't talk to your mother," he sighed. "You know how she is." Which was to say that on the subjects of money, politics, and religion, Libby's mother would never listen to another woman, least of all Libby.

"Well, maybe she could," Libby said, sitting up. "He gave me his number in Chicago. He even volunteered to have everything blamed on him."

Her father's eyebrows rose. He was not so much a lawyer as the local problem-solver these days, and this kind of thing was right up his alley. "Now, that may be an offer worth considering. And he's in Chicago, you say?"

That horrible sickly dread she had lived with for a week was not there. That was the first thing Jill was conscious of when she awakened. The second was that she had genuinely slept. Husband beside her.

Things were going to feel strange for a long time. Things certainly would never be the same.

She was glad he had decked Geiggen, though. (And smiled at the memory.)

And, too, that part in his letter to Sissy, about how he wondered if Jill hadn't had an affair during their marriage, was surprisingly a big help to her. Because that meant Rusty had never viewed her as passive. He saw her as desirable, and was evidently acutely aware of how other men in this town looked at her and how she looked at them in return.

Still, there was no excuse.

Or was there?

Rusty kept talking about how she never seemed very interested in him. She really had not known what he was talking about until he asked her in the car yesterday on the way home from New York to explain what it was he did for a living. Well, he was a lawyer, she began. Corporate work. Having to do with patents and things.

"That's it?" he said.

"Well, what else is there?" And as soon as she said that, she felt awful, because she realized he was right. She really didn't know what he was doing these days.

Inwardly she cringed. He supported their family on his salary alone and she was not even sure anymore exactly what it was that he did.

Yes, well, maybe he was right. Maybe there were things for them as a couple to work on in therapy. And for her to work on by herself.

But right now, she thought, stretching a little and rolling over, on this Thanksgiving morning, she was only experiencing a kind of heartfelt gratitude, and a tide of relief that her husband was in the bed next to her, asleep, and that their children were safely with them in the house, and, above all, that they were still a family.

Given that, Jill felt certain she could deal with almost anything.

"William," Mrs. Klein whispered into his bedroom, "there's a woman on the phone for you and it's not Betsy."

Will rolled over. "Yikes! It's not her mother, is it?"

"It's that writer. Elizabeth Winslow."

He sat bolt upright, covers flying. "What?"

"That's what she said."

Will was halfway down the hall already.

"What's going on?" Mr. Klein called upstairs to his wife.

"That writer woman from jury duty's calling William," his mother whispered over the banister. "Isn't that funny? From jury duty!"

"Anyone but that Betsy," Mr. Klein declared.

In his parents' room, Will had scooped up the phone. "Hello?"

"Happy Thanksgiving," Libby said. "I hope I didn't wake you up. We tend to rise pretty early here in Greatfield."

"No, we're all up here, too," Will assured her while rubbing the sleep out of his eyes.

Jill was tending to the turkey when Peter came bursting in through the door. They had sent the kids outside to have a little morning touch football scrimmage with the neighborhood kids. (Even young Katie had a role as cheerleader, although Peter always complained that his sister had no loyalty whatsoever, she cheered for everyone.) Normally on Thanksgiving they would be expecting friends and relatives, but this holiday, given the trial, everything was different. Even Rusty's relatives were staying away, they who normally would weather anything if it meant free food and good liquor.

"Mom, Mom!" Peter cried. "Roger says Dad's in the paper because he punched some lawyer at Aunt Sissy's trial!"

"Yes, that's right," Jill said matter-of-factly, basting the turkey in the lower oven. "Yesterday. That's why we came home early." She shoved the turkey back in.

"But Mom!"

"Yes, sweetie?"

"Dad hit somebody! It's in the paper!" Peter sputtered. "You always say we're not supposed to hit anyone!"

"Rusty?" she called, straightening up and closing the oven door. "Are you listening to this?"

"Yeah," came from the living room.

"Well, don't you think maybe you better go out and face the neighbors?"

Pause. "I guess."

Jill looked at Peter. "Your father will explain it all to you and your friends." She lowered her voice. "But I'll tell you a secret."

Wide-eyed. "What?"

"I'm not angry with your father, because sometimes, Peter, you just have to fight to protect your family. I know you don't understand it now, but someday you will. Your father has his way of fighting, and I have mine—and both of us are trying to protect what is ours."

The arrival of Libby's brothers, Ted (Edward) and Jimbo (James), and their families gave Libby and her father a suitable screen for organizing Operation Get Uncle Greg. Greg had evidently told Mrs. Winslow that he couldn't come to his sister's as planned because he simply *had* to be in his office tomorrow in Chicago. And so, while Uncle Greg was hiding out in his house in Winnetka on Thanksgiving, he was an unsuspecting sitting duck, never suspecting that his brother-in-law and niece might sic some Wall Street financial expert on him, one who happened to be in Chicago as well.

At eleven-thirty all the Winslows started bundling up. It was time for the annual football game between Greatfield High School and rival Douglaston Township. Even Libby's mother would go for the first quarter, in order to make an appearance. (After all, her father had been a star player for Greatfield in the 1920s, her husband in the 1940s, and her sons in the 1970s.)

Libby was always recognized by townspeople; she had been the high-school homecoming queen of her class, though most of the people who ran up to her now were people she hadn't known very well back then, but who did read her books now. Her mother thought the whole thing was declassé, fussing over Cornelia, for heaven's sake, only because she wrote racy books.

For the life of her, Libby could never figure out what it was that her mother held against her, and why, no matter what Libby did or said in this life, to her mother it was not worth remembering. Teddy, the eldest, had always noticed it, and in recent years told Libby he thought it was simply jealousy over attention from their father. Jimbo disagreed; he swore it was because their mother thought Libby was eerily like her own mother, who, the family knew, she had bitterly disapproved of, too, although no one knew why that was, either.

Had it not been for the proximity of Grandma Garran while she was growing up, Libby knew she would have turned out hopelessly screwed up. Grandma had made her relationship with her mother—or the lack of it—seem very run-of-the-mill, a situation that was nothing to worry about, for if Libby felt that her mother greatly disliked her, Grandma constantly said Libby was the daughter *she* had always desperately wished she had borne, instead of *that* which she had.

"Oh, Grandma, that's mean," Libby would say.

"It's not mean, child, it's the truth. Your mother spent most of her childhood scolding *me*—like the way she does you. Better you understand it now, Libby, your mama surely does love you, but she doesn't like women. Never did, never will. Where she got it from, heaven only knows. Maybe from your great-uncle Floyd, who ran away to Persia."

Greatfield lost, 36 to 0, so it was not such a great game, although Libby had a ball looking at the parade floats with her nieces and nephews. By two-twenty the Winslows had all trooped back to the house and were settled in the living room to watch a proper football game on TV. In the Winslow house there was no den per se, just this enormous living room where they had all assembled for years. To the right of the front door was a small parlor, complete with a tiny gas fireplace, reserved for company. To Libby's knowledge, no one save hysterical clients of her father's ever sat in there.

The telephone rang. "Lib, it's for you!" Jimbo called from the kitchen, adding in a whisper, "It's a booooyyyyyy."

"Oooooooo," Libby's little nieces and nephews said.

"And it sounds like long dissssstannnnnncccce."

"*Ooooooo,*" the whole family said.

"Hello?" she said, acutely aware of her mother's eye on her. She and Louisie Trutmueller were putting the final touches on the Thanksgiving feast. Her mother sensed that something was up; her mother always knew when something was up, and Libby knew this needed to be handled carefully.

"Libby? Hi, it's Will," he said over the phone. Then he chuckled. "Remember me? I'm calling out of the blue, right? This is totally unexpected."

"Yes, right, how are you?"

"Listen, I talked to your uncle, and did just as your father suggested. I told him I was your investment adviser and that your dad had mentioned that he was going to be in the office on Friday, and so, since I was in Chicago and his office was in Chicago, I thought I'd swing by tomorrow."

"And?"

"He freaked. And said forget it, he had very important meetings all day. I asked him about Saturday and he said he was going away to Canada."

"What?"

"I almost asked him, 'With or without the Winslows' money?' " he laughed. And then, recovering, "Oh, Libby, I'm sorry. He's your uncle, I shouldn't say something like that."

"No, it's all right. I agree." Her mother was really giving her the eye now.

"Well," Will said, "I'm afraid this doesn't bode very well. On the bright side, though, your dad told me he knows where all the correspondence with your uncle is. All we have to do is figure out how to get it from your mother without her killing you."

"Yes, I think that's right," she said brightly.

"So I think— Wait a sec." He covered the phone and then came back on. "Libby? My mother would like to talk to you for a minute—about your books. She's a fan."

Before Libby could say anything, Mrs. Klein was on the phone. "Elizabeth?"

"Hi." Libby wondered if any other human being had as many people calling them as many names as she did. Cornelia, Corny, Libby, Elizabeth.

"This is Sally Klein. I just wanted to tell you how impressed I was that William was on the jury with you. He was reading one of your books and I said, 'Why, I've read all her books!' My friend recommended one to me and I've been a great fan ever since."

Libby was smiling. "Well, thank you, Mrs. Klein, that's very nice of you. Will mentioned to me you had read a book of mine."

"*All* of them," she corrected. "And he was also telling me that you're going over a bit of a rough road right now, and I just wanted to tell you not to give up five minutes before the miracle. You're a very talented young lady, and from what my son tells me, a pretty wonderful person, too."

Libby glanced at her mother, wondering why or how she was hearing all this from a fellow juror's mother in Chicago while her own mother was looking daggers at her.

"Libby?" Will said, coming back on.

"Hi."

"Sorry about that, but—"

"Sorry? Are you kidding? It's a gift."

Her mother was now openly staring at her. "Who is that?" she mouthed.

"So, listen, Libby, I was thinking," Will continued, "what do you say to my stopping in on my way back to New York to talk to your mother? Your dad thought that sounded like a great idea and said he'd spring for the ticket changes."

"He did?"

"He said I can fly into Columbus and maybe you could pick me up."

"I—" The thought of Will from jury duty coming to Greatfield, Ohio, to talk to her mother about Uncle Greg's financial shenanigans was too strange for words. In response to her mother's now-frantic curiosity, Libby covered the phone and asked, "Mom, can a friend of mine stay over for a night on his way back to New York?"

"What friend?"

"My friend Will. He's on the jury with me."

"I heard you say Mrs. Klein. Is he Jewish?"

Libby held her temper in check. "Yes."

Mrs. Winslow looked at Louisie and widened her eyes, as if to say the world was surely beyond her, but what could she do? Then she looked back at her daughter. "If you would like him to come, yes, of course he can stay. He can sleep in your grandmother's room." Grandma's room was the only other bedroom in the house besides the master that had its own bathroom. To her mother's way of thinking, this was the basis of all propriety, to keep strange men in bathrooms by themselves, out of sight, out of sound.

"Sure, Will," Libby said into the phone, "my mother says you're more than welcome. You can stay in my grandma's old room, which has its own bath."

"And do I get a tour of Greatfield?"

"If you blink, you might pass it, but sure. When do you want to come?"

"Why not tomorrow?"

When Will hung up the phone, he felt his mother's presence behind him. He turned around.

"You're very sweet on this girl, aren't you?"

"She's thirty-four, Mom, she's hardly a girl."

She nodded, acquiescing on the point. "She's not married."

"No. She lived with some guy for a long time but left him."

"She lives by herself?"

"Yes."

His mother was nodding. "Okay, dear, I'll be sorry to see you go already, but I understand."

Pause. "Do you, Mom?"

There was a twinkle in her eye. "Oh yes, Will, I do."

He stared at her. "You just called me Will."

She smiled. "That's what she called you. Will, she said. So I assume that's what she calls you."

"We had lunch one day and I told her about Grandfather and she said to me later, Why not be called Will now? She said she thought Grandpa Will would like it."

His mother walked over and took his face in both her hands, kissed him tenderly on the cheek and looked into his eyes. "She's a very perceptive young woman."

"Another guy on the jury likes her," he blurted out.

"But another guy's not going to go visit her tomorrow," she said, smiling.

———————

"Oh, gosh, let me help you!" an old geezer cried, throwing his cigarette butt into the street and limping over to the cab. "Kip, come help." A much younger man, in jeans and a battered leather jacket and work boots, more slowly threw his cigarette down and walked over.

"Oh, great, thanks," Melissa said, getting out of the cab. George, the shy young giant of about six foot four who Intergroup had sent over, climbed out of the front seat of the cab. Melissa slid over a big box on the backseat and, with both arms, hefted it to the geezer and the younger guy he called Kip.

The geezer peered inside and smiled, showing several missing teeth on one side. "A whole turkey?"

"Twenty-six pounds," she said proudly. "Somebody named Rocket here?" she asked, reaching into the cab again for another box. This was full of large Rubbermaid containers.

"Yeah, he's inside."

"I'm supposed to bring this stuff to him."

"Kipper, you heard the lady. Bring this turkey inside to Rocket. What's this?" He was referring to the second box, now lodged in his arms. Like a lot of people in AA, he looked kind of thin and frail, but was tough as nails and handled the box easily.

"Sweet potatoes, turnips, sausages, string beans with onions."

"Ah, glory, you be sent from heaven, girlie."

"No, just Intergroup," she laughed. "George, if you could reach in and get the box of drinks."

He did, stretching effortlessly to pick up the box of fruit juices and soda. Melissa took the shopping bags that were full of bread and butter and paper plates, napkins, plastic forks, spoons, knives, and a carving knife. Also included was aluminum foil and paper bags for leftover whatevers.

"Intergroup sent you here? Pretty rough meeting for a girl," the geezer said.

"I called them last night, because I felt like cooking and—"

"They said, 'Do we have a group for you, girlie!' " the geezer said. "A bunch of ol' Bowery boys who think a Thanksgiving spread's a Snickers bar and a pint of Thunderbird! Ha-ha-ha!"

Indeed, they were not in the classiest part of Manhattan. They were a half block off the Bowery, standing outside a church that looked to be abandoned. The stairs leading down to the basement, however, where hundreds of cigarette butts lay, told a different story.

"What's your name, by the way?" the geezer asked her, leading her sideways down the stairs, to accommodate his stiff leg.

"Melissa. And this is George."

"Smoker, here. Not 'cause I smoke, heh-heh. Nickname from the Army. Don't ask, girlie, you don't want to know."

It was pretty dark and pretty grungy down there. Thankfully she had thought to bring some sponges to wipe down the battered table in the back, which had a few open bags of cookies and potato chips on it. There were perhaps seven people sitting in folding chairs, one of whom had turned his chair around to face the wall and, wearing a blanket over his head, was telling some sort of exciting story to the wall.

Wet-brain, the term they used for an alcoholic whose mind was hopelessly damaged from years of drinking.

The chairman of the group, a scruffy-looking fellow named Rocket, came over, eyes nearly popping out of his head at what Melissa and George had brought. The meeting was very small, maybe ten people, tops, he said. Great, Melissa thought, everyone would get leftovers to take with them. They agreed they would set up the food and containers in the back, have the qualification, and then break to eat. The qualification meant a member sharing his or her past and present experiences as it related to their alcoholism and recovery in AA.

"Um, if you need help setting up," Kip mumbled to Melissa, "I could help. Most of these guys shake too much."

"I know the feeling," she said, smiling. And it was true.

This meeting was certainly a far cry from the AA meetings Melissa usually went to. There were a couple of meetings in Manhattan that Melissa knew of where those attending probably represented twenty percent of the city tax money collected from individuals, they had done so well. Some had made the money before sobriety, an awful lot had done astonishingly well afterward. And then, of course, there were those who had simply inherited their money or married it and then had stopped squandering it all since they had come in.

But most meetings were a good mix: a third who were settled into longtime sobriety, people whose lives had become worth envying in a variety of ways; a third who were still in the early years of their sobriety, bitching and screaming and wondering when life was going to be worth living (i.e., would they always be owing money, would they always be scared of parties, would they ever have sex again?); and the final third, the most important of any meeting, the new people, still startled to find that what these AA people had said was true, they didn't have to drink anymore, people whose faces were showing the first bloom of better health since childhood.

Rocket, the chairman of the meeting, came over, looking a bit shy. "Melissa? We were wondering if you would qualify for us. Everybody here's told their story so many times we can tell 'em in our sleep."

"Yeah!" George said, speaking for the first time. "Great idea. We'll set everything up while you qualify."

A few more people straggled in and took a seat. Melissa, sitting in front of the room, nervously smiled, wondering if she had anything to say that would mean anything to these people. Her old sponsor used to say that to tell one's story, all one had to do was disengage the brain and engage the heart. That way it was very difficult to retell all the lies most alcoholics had been telling all their life.

Melissa smiled. For God's sake, if she couldn't tell the truth in an AA meeting on the Bowery, where on earth else could she?

"Mommy! Daddy!" they heard Katie cried. "There's a strange man outside talking to Petey!"

They didn't even pause, but dropped the dishes in the sink and made for the front door. Rusty was out first, bounding across the lawn; there was a man talking to Peter, and there was a woman next to him holding a video camera, filming it. Duncan was there, too, at Peter's side, tail wagging.

"Stay in the house, Katie," Jill instructed. Katie did as she was told, shutting the front door. When Jill glanced back, she could see her tiny face peering out the window.

"Ah, and here are your parents!" the reporter said brightly, and the camera swung in Rusty's direction.

"Dad, this is the guy from the news."

"Turn the camera off," Rusty said.

"And this is Jill Cook Tompkins, the victim's sister," the reporter said, prompting the camera to swing in her direction.

"You heard my husband," Jill said.

"Go in the house, Pete," Rusty said.

"But Dad—"

"Go," Jill told him.

The camera was still running.

"See that line?" Rusty said, pointing to the edge of the front lawn.

"You cross that, and you're in jail. Got it? My family has suffered enough, and every news guy in America understands that but you. Come on, Jill," and he took her by the arm and pulled her back to the house. "Duncan, come!"

The dog knew he meant business and came bounding after them.

"I think you better talk to me!" the reporter called. "If I were you, I would go inside and talk about it, *Rusty*. About you and your sister-in-law and why you slugged Geiggen yesterday. I'm sure you'll agree it would be better to give us an interview than to leave us to our own devices."

Rusty's hand tightened on Jill's arm.

"Your kids have to go to school, you know, and you know how cruel kids can be."

They got into the laundry room and Rusty slammed the top of the washer with his hand. Petey and Katie came running from the kitchen.

"Petey, take Katie down into the playroom, please. Now. We'll be there in a moment. Daddy and I need to talk."

Reluctantly the children went. Jill closed the door to the kitchen behind them and sighed, turning back to her husband. "Now what?"

Rusty had his back to her; she waited for him to say something. And then she saw his back start to quake. And then he dropped his face in his hands and stifled a sob.

She waited.

"Oh, God, Jill, I'm so sorry." And then he really did sob, sort of hiccuping and sobbing, and she went over to put her arm around him.

"We'll get through this, Rusty."

"I'm so sorry, Jill!" He sounded as though his heart was breaking and she imagined that maybe it was. What their children thought of him meant more to Rusty than anything. Anything. And the thought of his son being tormented by other kids at school, telling him his father had—

Still holding her husband, Jill looked over his shoulder out the window.

They were still out there. Waiting.

She imagined they would be there a long, long time.

23

I 'M GOING out there to talk to him," Jill announced on Friday morning, putting her coat on as she came through the kitchen.

Rusty didn't argue. They had been up most of the night, trying to figure out what to do about the reporter parked outside their house, and Jill had insisted she deal with it. And now Rusty was sitting at the kitchen table, watching the kids finish eating the waffles he had made them, looking pale and tired and miserable.

"Why is he out there again, Mom?" Petey asked. "I already told him yesterday what Aunt Sissy was like."

"Your father will explain, while I go out and talk to him."

Rusty was looking at her.

"About the media making money off other people's misfortunes," Jill cued him.

"Oh," Rusty said, and some color came back into his face.

Jill felt very self-conscious walking across the lawn toward them. That damn woman had the video camera on again.

"Good morning, Mrs. Tompkins," the reporter said.

"Good morning." She stopped in front of him and tried to ignore the whirring of the camera. "We're still not sure what it is that you want."

"I want an exclusive interview with you and your family. About your sister's murder, about your reaction to the trial—"

"But I can't talk about the trial while it's going on. The prosecutor explicitly told me not to. You must understand that—that something I do with the press might endanger the progress of the trial in some way."

If the reporter had seemed a little unprepared for her arrival, he was clearly thrown by her sudden frankness. She was not angry this morning, she wasn't scared, she wasn't anything except maybe a little bored by the whole thing because she knew she couldn't tell him much. That's what Jill wanted him to think. That there was no way she would give the man responsible for her sister's death a chance to get a mistrial.

"But you'll talk to me," he said.

"Well, sure," she said. "And I'm talking to you now. Yesterday I'm afraid my husband and I were furious that you went behind our backs to talk to our children. That's not fair game—not in our book. Take us on, sure, but you go near our children and we tend to go berserk."

"Val, turn off the camera a minute." The camera operator complied. The reporter cocked his head to the side. "So it's true, about your husband and sister."

"What's true?" she asked.

"That he—they—well, you know, had an affair."

She forced herself to laugh. "Oh, that's it, is it? Who was it, Geiggen who talked to you? Rusty said last night Geiggen was probably behind this. So I get it now. Because Rusty humiliated him in public, Geiggen's decided to make up stories and sic the press on us." She shook her head. "I expected more of him. He's supposed to be smart. Not pathetic. And certainly not antagonizing to the press. Or does he have an old grudge against you, too? To set you up like this? You'll notice that no one else is here. There's a reason why—there's no story."

"He offered me some pretty convincing evidence," the reporter said.

"Evidence of what?" Jill said, letting crankiness show. "Of my husband having dinner at my sister's while I was away? If that's all it takes, then I guess Geiggen will be sending you back here because I've had an affair with Rusty's brother."

The reporter narrowed his eyes. "Yeah, but what else could you say? Under the circumstances, all you can do is deny it."

"Oh, forget it," Jill said, waving him away. "I give up, you're hopeless. Val, turn the camera back on. Do whatever story you want, but remember that there are laws about making up accusations about people, and my husband's an attorney, so be forewarned that your bosses are sure to hear from us." She turned on her heel and started back to the house.

"Wait, Mrs. Tompkins!" The reporter had hit the property line and was balancing, trying not to trespass, but trying to get her back all the same. "Wait, I'm sorry! Maybe we can still work something out."

She whirled around. "Get a life, will you? What do I want with you when I've got 'Sixty Minutes' and 'Primetime' calling? Run that on your newscast tonight—give free advertising for 'Sixty Minutes' and 'Primetime'!" She went into the house.

"What was that?" Rusty was just inside the laundry-room door, panicking. " 'Sixty Minutes' and 'Primetime'? Jesus!"

"Where are the kids?" Jill whispered.

"In the playroom—"

"Honey, don't worry," Jill said then, not being able to restrain a laugh. This whole situation was getting so ridiculous. They were just a family in Fairfield County with a son and a daughter and a dog, and now her husband was terrified that Ed Bradley and Diane Sawyer were outside. "I only asked him that if those shows were calling, why would I want to talk to him?"

"I don't know, Jill, I don't know," he said nervously.

"I do," she said, taking his hand and pulling him into the kitchen. "I told him that Geiggen's making up stories to torture you since you humiliated him in public. I said there was no evidence of anything except that you had dinner at my sister's while I was away, and so if that's evidence, then Geiggen would be telling him next I'm having an affair with your brother. Sit down, Rusty, we're both going to eat. We'll feel better." She plugged in the old waffle iron, took the bowl of batter out of the refrigerator, and began stirring it with a fork.

"What did he say?" A little shaky, Rusty pulled out a chair and sat down at the table.

"Nothing much, until I made him understand that I know everything there is to know about my sister and my husband and that I am not worried in the least about anything. *Anything.*" She threw a little tap water on the grill to test it.

"But—"

"But what?" She turned around. And then, suddenly, all she could think was enough was enough, she would not let them win, and she rushed to his side, falling down on her knees and taking hold of his arm. "Rusty, get this straight. I meant it. I know everything there is to know. And from now on, that one small paragraph of our lives is to be utterly forgotten. So you went to Sissy's—and so *what?*"

His eyes were searching hers.

"From now on, we have nothing to hide. Got it? They can say what they will, but I love you, Rusty, and I trust you—completely. And should anything ever reach the children, then you know what to say. Sure, you went to Sissy's. No big deal. Your mom will tell you."

"Oh, Jill," he murmured, taking her hands into his and looking down at them. He bent to kiss them once.

"The operative words right now, Rusty, are that I love you—and trust you. I *have* to. It's the only way it can work." She kissed his hand. "Clean slate, both of us."

He reached to hug her, stifling a sob. "You'll never regret it, Jill, never."

Well, they would only find out by going on with their lives, wouldn't they?

"Oh, no!" Petey cried a minute later, walking in. "Smoochie stuff in the kitchen!"

He had it wrong, though. It wasn't smoochie stuff, it was forgiveness stuff. She simply had to forget this, put it behind them, and trust that it was indeed true, that to err was human, to forgive divine.

The strange thing was how utterly normal it felt to pick Will up at the airport. He was like an old long-lost friend, made in another time, in another world, and now he was one of the very few in Libby's life who had ever been to her hometown.

As they drove toward Greatfield and the city gave way to suburbs, and the suburbs to towns, and then, finally, the towns to trees and hills and fields, Will got more and more excited. "It's so beautiful!" he kept saying.

And this was in late fall, when there was nothing to look at.

Clearly, Libby thought, this guy's been in New York too long.

Over Greatfield itself he went crazy. "It's like something out of *To Kill a Mockingbird!*" he said, looking, looking, everywhere, looking.

It was a nice town, picturesque to be sure, with its Victorian houses along Main Street and two-story buildings in town. The town hall was small but had columns. The post office had a granite eagle on top.

One thing that was fairly well hidden was the Wal-Mart, housed in what had been the old high-school gymnasium, a massive brick structure built in 1938 to show off a state champion high-school basketball team. The advent of the store, Libby explained, had put almost all the other retailers out of business, but the people had come to worship it. The merchandise was inexpensive and of good quality. They had gotten into Greatfield pretty easily, by guaranteeing to employ the people they were putting out of business and give them health insurance and other benefits.

It was a dying town, Libby explained to Will, driving around, waving often (her parents' car was well known). She pointed out how many of the houses and buildings were a bit dog-eared, how some were whitewashed, not out of old-fashioned habits but out of pride and a lack of enough money for paint. She explained how ninety-five percent of the town's children left at eighteen and never returned, and how the Elks and Rotary and 4-H Club scholarships had only succeeded in accelerating the attrition, so much so that only the Rotary Club had enough members left to meet.

"But why?" Will said in awe. "Why would someone not want to live here?"

"Will, there's nothing here. No jobs. The farms have all been bought up by grain cartels. We've got one bar, two restaurants, a bowling alley, and a roller rink eighteen miles down the road. And the Wal-Mart."

"Yes, but this is the computer age," Will pointed out. "Anyone with their own business could live here. With a fax and a computer, you'd be all set up. And I'd imagine it would be easy to set up warehouses and things—and you've got a workforce. Like a fulfillment house. Let's say a warehouse for one of the book clubs, the place where they store and then fulfill and ship orders. You can't tell me that wouldn't work out here."

"We're just too far out, Will."

"I saw train tracks."

"For grain shipping."

"Well, there you are!" he said, excited. "And financial people, stock-brokers and things—you can do that from anywhere now."

"Well, you can go find them, Will, and I'm sure the town would be very grateful if you brought them back with you. As it is, my father expects the town to last maybe another ten, fifteen years—tops—before the town services are going to have to shut down. The library and the fire department are already staffed by volunteers, and before long they're not even going to be able to afford to keep the lights on in the schools."

"I'm telling you, Libby," Will insisted, shaking his head, "I've seen it happen in Virginia, and there's no reason why it couldn't happen here."

"Well, as I say, you're welcome to try." The part she didn't mention was how she wasn't sure how Greatfield would react to outsiders in general, much less to people from Wall Street. As a matter of fact, her biggest concern at the moment was how her mother was going to react to Will. She had done her best to pave the way for him. She had to make her mother think she sort of liked Will as a potential boyfriend. Otherwise it could be a disaster.

"Oh my God, this isn't your house, is it?" Will gasped.

"Yes. This is it."

"How could you ever leave here?"

"Easily, trust me," Libby said, thinking of her mother.

"But Libby, it's beautiful, and look at all the property you have."

He was right. It was a beautiful house. Victorian with a wraparound front porch, complete with swing. The windows were large and old, the gingerbread in good repair. The house itself was white with green shutters, the same as it was when it was built in 1881. The driveway ran behind to a circle, where the outer-house was, which is where, Libby explained, in the old days, the cook and gardener (married) had lived. Now it was where her father built models—model boats that he sailed, model planes that he flew. The yard was a rolling green, flecked with brown now, and some of her mother's mums planted for the fall were struggling to hold color.

(Libby had been going to tell her mother about what they were using for cold fall foliage in New York gardens these days, flowering Chinese cabbages—green and purple, and green and white—but she decided her mother would look at her as though she were stark raving mad and so she had not mentioned it.)

It took a good deal of money to keep a house like this, money that largely came from her grandparents' estates on both sides. There was no real money to make in Greatfield, not as a lawyer, as her father was, or as anything else really. If they hadn't inherited money, the Winslows would have had to move nearer to one of the cities, where her father might have gotten a job with a firm. But they did inherit some money and so they hadn't and, as a result, a third generation of Winslows had grown up in the house. Well, actually, it had been two generations of Garrans and one generation of Winslow kids, her mother being the heiress.

Sometimes Libby wondered if the whole town of Greatfield wouldn't have just collapsed if her parents hadn't stayed on here all these years, spending money and paying taxes. And sometimes she had to wonder what would happen after her parents were gone. Her brothers had no interest in Greatfield, nor the means to sustain themselves here. Libby was the only one with a profession that enabled her to live virtually anywhere, but the thought of moving back to Greatfield to be the town's eccentric spinster cat lady held little appeal. And with the shape her career was in right now, about all she could afford was maybe to rent the little house behind her parents' house!

Truth was, though, she loved this town and she loved this part of the country. It was a part of her. And it was with no little pride that she always announced to the world, as she toured in places like New York and Chicago and San Francisco and Los Angeles and Houston, that she was born and raised in Greatfield, Ohio, a town no one had ever heard of—until now, when one of its own was in the spotlight.

Her brothers and their families had cleared out of the house first thing this morning, and so Mrs. Winslow had Louisie Trutmueller come in to change beds and dust and run the vacuum before Libby's new boyfriend came, whose last name, she explained to Louisie, for some reason she couldn't remember.

"Will, before we go in," Libby said out in the driveway, "I think I better warn you that my mother can be a little . . . well, naive. Uh, *stupid*, actually, may be a better word."

"You mean anti-Semitic?"

"Anti-anything that is pro me and critical of Uncle Greg. Bear that in mind and you should do fine. As for the other, the worst it will get is that she'll tell you she voted for Barry Goldwater."

He laughed. "Don't worry. I'm perfectly able to handle myself."

And he was. He handled her mother beautifully, seeing her and smiling broadly and extending his hand and shaking hers with both of his. "Oh, Mrs. Winslow, you're as lovely as Libby said you were. And your home—wow."

"Thank you," Mrs. Winslow said.

Still holding her hand, he said, "I don't know if Libby told you, but I was a little nervous about coming."

"Oh, nonsense, Will!" her mother suddenly cried. "Greatfield may be on the quaint side," she continued, "but we are very cosmopolitan at heart."

Libby and her father exchanged smiles and rolled their eyes at that one.

"Mr. Winslow?" Will asked, as if he had never spoken to the man in all his life, instead of having spent Thanksgiving morning planning and plotting with him about how to overthrow his brother-in-law.

"Will, good to meet you," Mr. Winslow said in a hearty voice, shaking hands. He was about six inches taller than Will, and Libby was glad her brothers weren't here, because they were even taller than her father.

"Klein," her mother whispered to Libby in the kitchen while they got some refreshments, "that's not so bad. Good grief, it could have been Goldfish or something."

"Mom," Libby said gently, putting a hand on her mother's shoulder, even though she knew her mother hated to be touched, at least by her, "just be yourself and let Will be himself and everything will be fine."

"I don't know what I would do if your name was Goldfish, Libby. Now, don't look at me like that—it's not my fault the man who foreclosed on all those farms was Jewish."

"Mom!" Libby took a breath, keeping herself in check. "Look, it wouldn't matter what Will's name was. No one would dare look at any friend or relation of yours cross-eyed in this town, you know that."

Being reminded of her lofty social position seemed to reassure her mother, and her face lost some of its anxiety. And Libby did not feel quite so much like punching her out.

"So, you're in finance, I hear," Mr. Winslow said to Will, "on Wall Street."

"My brother's an investment banker," Mrs. Winslow volunteered, bringing in a tray of coffee and muffins. "In Chicago. He was with a large firm and now is out on his own. He's doing very well," she added.

"Oh, that's great," Will said. "That's what I would love to do some-day—to go out on my own." He took the cup of coffee she offered him, along with a napkin. "Thank you, Mrs. Winslow, this looks wonderful."

"What would you do if you could?" Mr. Winslow asked.

"Truthfully?" Will said, in a way that made Libby pay attention. "I'd like to start a bank and do some of the things that my grandfather did. You know, a real community bank. Build things—bridges, companies, individuals with a dream and a good business plan. Nothing fancy, nothing terribly high-risk, just a good old-fashioned independent bank that tries to make a little profit for everybody."

"We don't even have a real bank here in town anymore," Mrs. Winslow said, "not after the farms went under." She blushed. Libby was certain she was thinking of that "Jew" who had foreclosed on them again. "We just have a branch of a big bank in Columbus."

"Well, it's got money, Diana," Mr. Winslow said. "And they send me a lot of business."

"You have a general legal practice?" Will asked.

"Essentially, yes."

"When we were being questioned as potential jurors," Will said, "Libby had to explain to the court that you were not a criminal lawyer."

"Why, you represented that Steve Hicks when he pulled that highway billboard down," Mrs. Winslow pointed out.

"That's not the kind of criminal they meant, I don't think," Mr. Winslow said.

Later on, Libby was sent to the kitchen to start making lunch. This, she was sure, was so her mother could talk behind her back. And, sure enough, while slicing turkey, she overheard her mother say, "Well, as a matter of fact, Libby's got my brother rather annoyed over the whole thing."

She moved closer to the door to hear better.

"Because, you see, Will, Libby doesn't know what she's talking about. Mind you, she's a bright girl, but she knows nothing of finance. As my brother said, if she did, she wouldn't be in such financial straits right now. You do understand that, Will, don't you? That Libby has gotten herself into some kind of hole, that's how this whole thing started. And now she's got my brother terribly upset."

Libby restrained herself from peeking around the corner and throwing a well-aimed knife into the living room.

"Well, Mrs. Winslow, the thing is, maybe I could be of help to you," Will said. "While I'm here maybe I could help you straighten out everything."

"Don't look to me, Diana," Libby heard her father say. "It's your brother and your money."

"Well, that would be just wonderful, Will. If you don't mind. You see, I just can't go on having Libby shooting her mouth off and getting everybody so upset. Maybe you can explain it all to her, so she'll just stop worrying everybody."

In the kitchen, Libby smiled, and moved back to the carcass of the turkey.

24

IT WAS scary how good Will was with her mother. By the time they had gone to bed last night, it had been decided that Will had to stay over Saturday night, too. Mrs. Winslow wouldn't hear of anything else.

By mid-morning on Saturday the two were closeted together behind closed doors in the parlor. Libby was not above trying to listen. There were old-fashioned sliding double doors that led into the parlor, and they didn't fit together exactly right. Will and her mother were murmuring, though, except for occasional bursts of laughter, and Libby could only wonder if it really was her mother in there with him.

"Come on, Corny, walk into town with me," her father suggested after an hour. They got their coats, told Mrs. Winslow and Will they were leaving, and went out the back door. Her father always came in and went out the back door. He said the front door only gave him the feeby-geebies, remembering the times he had been trying to court Libby's mother and how old Garran's thugs had always been spying on them on that porch.

Not that Grandpa Garran had really employed any thugs, though he had possessed several loyal farm workers who would do double duty in town when needed, like keeping an eye on Diana and her beau while she was staying in town only under her mother's supervision. There was a reason Libby's mother was the way she was, Mr. Winslow had always told Libby. The Garrans really had owned a great deal of the county. ("That's why it's called Garran County, Corny!") Old man Garran had tortured Diana when she insisted she was in love with Tom Winslow and not with the wealthy Albert Haskell, while Diana's mother, on the other hand, thought the only hope for Diana as a woman would be to run away with the milkman or something equally extreme.

"Did Grandma Garran not like Mom?" she used to ask her father.

"Grandma Garran thought your mother was a dreadful stick-in-the-mud," he would say. "But then, there were an awful lot of rumors about your grandma Garran in her day."

In other words, Libby was supposed to understand, her mother had been very mixed up as a young girl, and had chosen to take her father's way of doing things over her mother's—a monumental decision since the two parents couldn't have been farther apart—and yet had later defied her father to love Tom Winslow, which had, in turn, soured that familial relationship as well.

They walked along the sidewalk into downtown Greatfield. There was no real traffic on Main Street since the real thoroughfare, Route 62, ran behind the town, mainly because of the fear that the big rigs would shake the foundations of the old community down to the ground. Libby's father said hello to every person they saw, and they stopped to chat with one or two people Libby knew well from her childhood. They went into the little bank branch, where Libby waited while her father went into the manager's office to do some business. When he came out, he took Libby by the arm and walked her across the street to Lily's, the coffee shop, and sat her down in a booth.

"Well, hi, Mr. Winslow," the waitress said.

"Hi, Alice."

"Good Lord, this isn't that daughter of yours, is it? The one you're always talking about? The writer?"

Mr. Winslow grinned. "Alice, this is my daughter, Corny, alias Libby, better known to her reading public as Elizabeth Winslow. Corny Girl, this is Alice Shepherd."

Libby shook her hand. "You have a son who's attending Ohio State, right?"

Alice's mouth dropped. "Now, how do you know about that?"

"Dad writes me about all the news in the town. And that was pretty big news. Everyone's very proud." The other part of the story was that Alice's husband had died in some sort of bar fight in Columbus ten years ago and that her son, Richie, had had a lot of problems. But he had gotten straightened out and was now at Ohio State, majoring in business.

"I read one of your books, you know," Alice said. "*When Smiles Meet.* I really liked it, but I can't ever get your others, they're always out at the library."

Libby thanked her. This was always the most flattering, when a regular person liked her books.

"Corny, here, I want you to take this," her father said when Alice left. He slid an envelope across the table.

She opened it. Inside was a certified check, made out to her, for twelve thousand dollars.

"At some point you just sign over to me whatever securities Greg has you in."

"Dad, no. Come on, I gave him the money. And it was only ten thousand."

"If he had a brain in his head, it would be at least twelve by now."

"But Dad, I gave it to him."

"Your mother bullied you into it and you know it," he said. "And I'd welcome the chance to announce to Greg that your investments with him are now mine, and that he has to answer to me."

Libby had to smile. The image was rather pleasing. "But you shouldn't give me the two thousand extra, Dad."

"And why not? You're still my daughter."

"Yeah, but . . ." How could she say to her father, "You'll have hell to pay with Mom over this"?

"I do have money of my own, Corny," he said seriously. "I know you and your brothers think your mother's family has given us everything—certainly your mother has tried to give you that impression, but it's not true. In fact, while your mother has squandered a lot with that numskull brother of hers, I've been doing rather nicely over the years, thank you." He smiled. "So let me be your father, okay?"

She knew her relief was evident. "This really bails me out, Dad, thank you."

"Your mother has given quite a bit of money to your brothers in recent years, are you aware of that?"

"Well, they have families."

"Corny," he said, "we're leaving you the house. That's the deal I made with your mother."

"Okay, two hot chocolates with whipped cream and candy canes to stir it," Alice announced, plunking them down on the table. She saw the surprise on Libby's face and misinterpreted it. "But your daddy said it was your favorite!"

"It could be a lot worse," Will said as they walked into town that night. Will had performed far above and beyond the call of duty, working with Libby's mother in the morning, both her father and mother in the afternoon, and then with Uncle Greg over the phone for most of the evening before dinner. Now dinner was over and she and Will were walking into town to the movies.

Anything to get out of the house. Anything to get time to think. Libby had heard too much today not to be confused.

"Your uncle's been flipping the money this way and that, churning commissions to the tune of around sixty-two thousand dollars. And he didn't trade in anything worthwhile, either. If he had just let the money sit in a bank at least, it would have made interest. All and all, I'd say your uncle's cost the family about a hundred fifty thousand."

"A hundred fifty thousand!" Libby cried, stopping to look at him. "*What?* The man should be in jail!"

"Please don't tell your mother I told you. She made me promise I wouldn't."

"A hundred and fifty thousand dollars!" Libby cried again. "Good *God!* That sleazy son of a bitch. Do you know how much a hundred and fifty thousand dollars is? Do you *know* what that money could do in a town like this?"

"Yeah, I know," Will sighed. "And I wish I could say I didn't know other people like your uncle in the business. If it's any consolation, I have a very good person in Columbus who your mother has agreed to talk to. I told her I thought for the sake of family peace, that perhaps she should have her own financial adviser. Your uncle is more than willing to turn everything over—he's scared shitless."

"A hundred and fifty thousand dollars!" Libby exclaimed to a tree.

"And then when I told him your father was taking over the investments you had with him, he agreed to send me a full accounting of everything, A to Z, if I could guarantee that that would be the end of it."

Libby turned. "Could my mother go after him?"

"Not really. She signed everything over to him. He had the power to buy and sell as he chose."

"A hundred and fifty thousand dollars." She shook her head. "Will, you're a miracle worker. God only knows what would have happened if you hadn't come."

"I'm just glad to help."

"I owe you—big time."

"You don't owe me anything."

"Well, the least I can do is spare you *Scotty and the Magic Car,* which is about how good the movies get in Greatfield. I think we should go and get drunk at the Cow Palace instead."

"Exactly what I was thinking," he assured her.

Not even in his college days had Will ever been to a place like the Cow Palace. This was one tough old bar with some tough old guys and gals. He and Libby were the youngest ones there by at least ten years, and Libby assured him this was the youngest it ever got anywhere in Greatfield. They sat up at the bar and Libby introduced him to the bartender, whom she still called Mr. Downes because he had been her math teacher in high school. How he had made the transition from Greatfield High to the Cow Palace was not explained.

"Home for the holiday, eh?" Mr. Downes said, wiping the bar down. "Well, what will it be, Libby?"

She looked at Will. "We should get something good."

"Boilermakers?" he suggested.

"I'm not that desperate," she said with a smile. To Mr. Downes: "Do you still make those fruit juice things?"

"Killer Reds? You bet."

Killer Reds turned out to be some concoction of cranberry juice, orange juice, grape juice, vodka, and two kinds of rum. And, indeed, they were killers. After two of them, Will found himself treading the floorboards with Libby, slow-dancing to a sad country tune on the jukebox.

It was wonderful.

It was happening too fast and too out of the blue, but Libby couldn't have cared less. All she knew was that Will was saving her mother from losing any more money, and that her father had come to her rescue with a check for twelve thousand dollars. Certainly she would have to write a letter of thanks to the New York State jury system.

There was so much to think about, here, resting the side of her face on Will's shoulder, barely moving, listening to some poor guy wail about the girl who left him. Although Will would not tell her the amount of her mother's estate that had been with Uncle Greg, he had given her enough information for her to know it had to have been around a half million dollars, far more than she had ever suspected. There was other Garran money, too, she knew, locked up in real estate, in land rentals and trusts around the state, which even Uncle Greg couldn't get his hands on. How he had managed to blow his half of the Garran estate was beyond Libby, but clearly he had if he was shaking down his own sister for what in comparison was minor money in commissions.

And then what her father had said about her mother giving her brothers a lot of money in recent years. Libby wondered how much, and then wondered just how much money did her parents have if they could do all this and still leave their house to Libby as some sort of consolation for what she was missing out on now financially.

Living in New York had taught Libby one thing. WASP families were definitely weird about money, when previously she had thought all families were the same way. If they had money, they didn't show it, and they generally didn't spend it, either—at least not in ways that would raise any eyebrows. If they did, then whatever it was spent on was safely hidden away in some godforsaken place where outsiders couldn't see it.

When Libby stopped to think about it, she wondered why she should be surprised if her parents were very wealthy.

She had always known her mother had money, but it never occurred to her that it might be *real* money, because whatever the amount was, it had never come in her direction except for clothes and schooling. After graduation, she had been on her own, living on her teacher's salary, it never occurring to her to ever ask her parents for anything. Her grandparents' farm had been in trouble and Grandma Garran had been forced to sell; her father's mother had required very expensive care in a nursing home for years and years; it frankly had never occurred to Libby that her family might have emerged from these situations with lots of money still.

She felt Will's arms tighten around her waist. It was nice, comfortable.

And where had her head been that she hadn't wondered about how her brother Ted could afford to buy a five-bedroom house in Shaker Heights when his architectural firm had gone under six years ago and he lost everything? Or how could Jimbo's girls be taking riding lessons and his family taking two exotic vacations a year on his salary as a journalist at a third-string paper? Neither of her sisters-in-law worked outside the home or had any family money. So where had she thought the money was coming from?

Her head was in the clouds as always, her mother would say. Maybe Mom was right. How could she not have noticed the upper-class life her siblings lived on a very noticeable absence of income?

Had her father been trying to tell her something today? Should she be angry? That her mother took delight in spoiling the boys and making Libby find her own way? And that her father couldn't just stand by and watch it anymore?

No, that wasn't it.

Will was so wonderfully warm; he fitted against her so well, in rhythm.

No, what was more likely was that her father saw himself in her, and he wanted to make sure she knew he was perfectly capable of earning money and saving and being there to bail out the family if need be. But that he also loved seeing Libby independent of the quiet power her mother had over the rest of the family. Or the power she thought she had, and the power her father evidently was happy to allow her to think she had—that is, so long as it made her happy.

What a family! And she was supposed to be from the Midwest, land of simple values. But then, if a corporate food cartel was the neighboring farmer, you knew things had changed mightily in recent years, even out here.

"We better go, I think," Will murmured in her ear, coming to a stop. The jukebox was quiet. "We've been gone awhile. I don't want to drop the ball with your mother now."

She agreed, reluctantly, wishing they could just stay here for a year or two more and figure things out. But they put on their coats, said good night to people, and went out into the cold fresh air. They walked home in silence.

When they reached the edge of the Winslow property, Will stopped her. "Would you be angry if I kissed you?"

"No," she said.

He kissed her softly on the mouth. And then kissed her again. And then he cleared his throat and led her to the gate. "This is all so confusing," he murmured.

"No," Libby said, sliding past him through the gate. "It is all so very wonderful."

25

I FIND you rather hard to believe, you know," Christine Harrington said. They were sitting in the balcony tearoom of the Four Seasons Hotel. They had eaten dinner at the Russian Tea Room and were relaxing here now, in the quiet, sipping cappuccinos. It was late. They had been talking for hours.

"You're the one I can't figure out," Melissa said, smiling. "Why you'd be interested in me."

"That's exactly what I mean," Christine said, leaning forward, resting her chin in her hand. "You're young and bright and kind and gentle and beautiful—" She laughed. "And you can't figure out what I would see in you?"

Melissa felt shy again and dropped her eyes to her cup. "I should think you could have pretty much anyone you wanted."

"Oh, Melissa," Christine sighed.

She looked up.

"I understand about your parents, the whole Hollywood upbringing thing," Christine said, "but I still don't quite understand your reluctance to talk about—you know, the years before you stopped drinking."

"Ugh, I knew you were going to say that," Melissa said, bringing her hand to her face. "Look." She dropped her hand, her voice gaining an edge. "It's because even if I make it sound interesting, it wasn't. I know better than anyone else, it was pathetic, disgusting, and repetitive."

"What about your relationships?"

At that, Melissa burst out laughing, looking to the ceiling for help. "Oh, my God," she groaned, bringing her eyes down. "You just don't get it, do you? People don't go into rehabs because the way they're living is pretty, and they have good relationships. They go because *everything* has deteriorated and there's nothing to lose! At least for me that was true."

"Give me an example."

"Okay," Melissa said without emotion. "Let's take tonight. At dinner I would have been charming, but then we'd start drinking and somewhere along the line you would look at me funny and ask me if I was all right."

"Why would I ask that?"

"Because I would all of a sudden be obnoxious and contemptuous and insulting to absolutely anyone who came near me—you, the waiter, the people sitting next to us. Trust me, first you would be shocked, then completely confused about what was going on, then probably terrified that I was schizo or something, and then, finally, in the end, just horribly embarrassed."

"Okay."

"Then, when we'd go outside into the cold air, suddenly I would change back and be warm, and a little shy, and affectionate, and certainly I would make some sort of sexual promises. But first, we'd have to have another drink. So we'd come here—no, I'd want to sit in the bar, where it's darker—and I would have several drinks and you would wonder, Uh-oh, what is going on with this woman? She's turning awful again."

"And would you go to bed with me?"

"Well, yes and no. On one of those infrequent but really bad nights, you wouldn't want me to, because I might have suddenly thrown up all over the place."

Christine grimaced.

"Then someone would have dragged me into the bathroom, where I would then probably proceed to fall on the floor, crawl to the corner, and start wailing for some ex-lover."

"Oh, dear," Christine said gently, a smile hinting.

"On a good night, though, yes, I'd go home with you and I'd tear our clothes off and have sex like a maniac—for only about ten minutes, though. Then I'd start to fade. If you had cocaine, that would be great, because then I would do a couple of lines, finish you off sexually, put my clothes back on, and take a cab over to whatever guy I was supposed to be seeing and crawl into bed with him, so then I could wake up the next morning and pretend I'd never been to bed with a woman."

"I—" Words seemed beyond Christine at the moment.

"We haven't even gotten to the morning yet, when I'd have to try and pull myself together to go to work." Melissa sighed, looking around the lobby of the hotel, thinking how beautiful it was here, quiet, and how wonderful this evening had been. Until now. Until she had to tell her this. "I'll spare you the details about what would go on in the bathroom and cut right to the Valium—"

Christine held up her hand. "Stop. You don't have to tell me anymore, I understand now."

"Do you?" Melissa asked her. "Do you know what it's like for a control freak to be stripped of self-control? What it was like for me to wake up the next morning and find out that I—me, Melissa Grant—had thrown up in public, or passed out dead on the floor, or told some helpless soul they should kill themselves because *they* were pathetic?" She looked off across the lobby. "I don't know which was worse, the physical disgrace or the sexual disgrace. They were the same, you know." She looked at Christine. "It felt exactly the same to me. The horror, then the disgust, then the wanting to die." She shuddered. "So, needless to say, I had to change jobs a lot."

They both laughed at this, the tension broken. Melissa asked the waitress for some ice cream. "Ever since I got sober, I've felt about six years old emotionally. So now when I feel upset, I order whatever a six-year-old would want." She smiled. And then the tears came up from nowhere, and she held her napkin to her face. "Damn it, Christine, I hate this. I feel like such a fool." She sniffed sharply and dropped the napkin. "This is why I hate to talk about it. Because when I hear myself explain what it was like, I know I have no business being here with someone like you. I just—you know—I think, if I just keep my mouth shut, maybe I'll meet someone nice, and then here you are, but I know, deep down, I just don't deserve the chance. Forget the man or woman thing, it's a whole people thing. A decent people thing, and I don't know if I'm trying to scare you away, or if I'm—"

Christine had reached over the table to take her hand. "Darling Melissa," she said slowly, "let me tell you what I see. I see an honest young woman who has made a decision to live, and to be the person she was always meant to be—sincere, kind, smart, talented, beautiful. That's who you are today, Melissa. That's who I see. The past is past. Let's leave it there. All I ask of you now is that you continue with whatever assistance you need to stay away from alcohol, and to stay away from drugs." She paused. "So that you can stay you."

"AA," Melissa said. "I go to AA meetings."

"Good," Christine murmured, hand tightening on Melissa's.

The ice cream arrived. "I brought two spoons," the waitress said.

"Wonderful," Christine said, sitting back in her chair. She picked up a spoon and nodded for Melissa to do the same, which she did.

After eating for a while, Christine put her spoon down in the saucer. "My turn," she announced, patting her mouth with a napkin.

Melissa looked up.

"I, too, have my painful past," she said. "Similar to yours, as a matter of fact, but the other way around. My husband was—is—a terrible alcoholic."

"Really?"

"He was lucky, though, Melissa—unlike you, he had me to clean up his sheets and blankets, and he had me to say that he had the flu, or that he was on very powerful medication whenever he went off at a party and tried to kill someone."

Melissa couldn't help but smile.

"Oh, yes, you're looking at a first-class enabler." And then her expression grew serious. "But I have something far worse to tell you about me."

Melissa waited.

"For years I *welcomed* his alcoholism, because it meant I could discreetly do whatever I wanted." She paused. "You wouldn't be the first woman in my life, Melissa." She swallowed. "Far from it. It's just that now—well, now that I'm getting divorced, the last thing I want are any more sordid little affairs."

Melissa nodded and they were quiet for a while, each thinking.

The waitress brought over the check and Christine took it and scribbled something on it.

"You're a guest in the hotel?" the waitress asked.

"Yes, seven-fourteen," Christine said, signing off on the check.

The waitress glanced down at it. "Thanks very much, ma'am."

Christine grimaced again. "Ma'am," she said to Melissa. "That's got to be the worst—when they all start calling you ma'am." She smiled. "Anyway, we have lots to think about," she said, getting up. She looked over. "Would you like to walk me upstairs?"

Melissa nodded, trying to find her feet. She felt detached from her body again, a sure sign she was terrified. There was something familiar and yet completely alien about this. She was stone-cold sober. This was real. This was happening.

Upstairs on the seventh floor, Christine inserted her key card, the light over the knob turned green, and she opened the door, holding it for Melissa to follow. Once they were both inside, she closed it, put her bag down, took Melissa's bag out of her hand and put that down, and then took Melissa's hands into her own. "I'm not going to suggest you stay. I want you to think about everything we've talked about."

She leaned forward then and kissed her lightly on the mouth—hesitated, and then did it again.

And then she said, while continuing to kiss Melissa—on her cheek—"I want you to know that I'll do my best to take things slowly"—on her temple—"to give you time to get used to things"—on her forehead—"the idea of us seeing each other"—on her temple again—"and seeing how it goes"—and gave her a final kiss on the ear, a gentle, brushing kiss that went straight through Melissa.

Christine then slid her arms all the way around her to hug her, pressing her mouth into Melissa's ear and neck.

She stepped back, taking a breath, holding Melissa by the arms. Her eyes were full of emotion, and Melissa thought she had never seen anyone so beautiful in her life, anyone so vulnerable, so appealing. And so Melissa stepped forward and kissed her back. But Christine suddenly stepped back again, looking worried.

"What's wrong?" Melissa whispered, brushing a strand of hair off Christine's face.

"There's something else you have to know, Melissa," she said. "That I have children."

26

O N SUNDAY morning, there was a knock on the door. "Will?" He
hurried to finish buttoning his shirt and opened the door. Libby
was there. Smiling. "Good morning."

"Good morning," he said.

"Did you sleep well?"

"Very."

"Could I talk to you for a minute?"

"Sure."

She came in and closed the door softly behind her. "I thought I
should say something before I turn you over to your adoring public
downstairs. May I sit?"

He gestured to the bed. She sat on the corner of it while he stood
there awkwardly.

"Last night—this weekend," she began, "has been truly wonderful.
But I wondered if you would understand if I said that so much is going
on—with the trial and everything—that I think we need to wait until
the trial's over before we . . . Well, I don't know. I guess what I mean to
say is, I like you very much, Will. And I'd really like to know you better.
And I kind of get the impression that the feeling might be mutual."

"Oh, yes," he told her, no longer feeling awkward.

Jill came up behind Rusty and kissed the back of his neck. "This was a
wonderful idea."

They were standing at the picture window of their motel room,
watching the kids on the beach. They looked like snowmen, they were so
bundled up. But the wind was fierce and the kids were running around
out there with Duncan, holding their arms out, letting the wind blow
them up the beach.

When the Tompkinses left the house on Friday, they had no idea
where they were going, but within a half hour had agreed to head toward
the water, the ocean, and before long found themselves driving through
a series of ghost towns that were the summer resorts of New Jersey. They
found a motel that was open, right on the beach, and they checked in,
taking two connecting rooms, and paying extra to sneak in Duncan.

Thus far they had seen two movies, gone bowling and roller skating, and now, on this Sunday afternoon after lunch, were relaxing over the papers while the kids were getting blown all over.

"Should we move, do you think?" Rusty said.

Jill froze. Funny, she had been thinking the same thing not so long ago, but now that she had made up her mind to go ahead with her marriage, she felt no need to move.

"Where?"

She felt his shoulders shrug under her hands. "Near the ocean," he said. "Florida. North Carolina. California. Somewhere."

"What about work?"

He shrugged again, but didn't say anything, eyes on the children outside.

Will doubted if he had ever been happier in his life. Nothing could have gone better at the Winslows' over the weekend; no way Libby could be more enticing and lovable than she was.

Mr. Winslow drove them to the airport. Will, he assured him, had done the family a service they could never repay. If there was ever anything, *anything* he or Mrs. Winslow could do for him, he had to swear he would call them first.

Once on the plane, he and Libby smiled a lot, but were a little shy with each other. Real life loomed ahead. Things to deal with. People, places, and things. He called his apartment from the airplane to make sure Betsy had cleared out as promised.

"No answer," he reported to Libby, pressing the phone back into its cradle on the seat in front of them. "At long last, I can go home."

"Where is home, anyway?"

"Just off Gramercy Park. An apartment."

"Do you own it?"

"Yes. Two bedrooms. It's nice. At least, that's one thing Betsy did, make it nice. I never really had time to move in properly. But I gave her most of the furniture."

Libby was looking out the window at the night sky.

"Did I say something?"

"What? Oh, no. I was just thinking about Hal. Living with him. Moving out." She looked back out the window.

Will swallowed. "Do you miss him?"

She turned. "Will you miss Betsy?"

"No."

"I must admit," she sighed, "I miss the convenience of living with someone—more than I should, I suppose. It's not just sharing the bills, it's the habit, the rhythm you set up, not having to think as much about things. You know, socializing, you have the same friends, someone being there when you're traveling—when you live alone, it's all on you. Which is nice, in a lot of ways, but requires a lot more of you in another. And I hate having time to think. About myself, you know? With Hal, months and months could pass without my ever having time to think about how unhappy I was."

"But that's not a good thing!"

"It is if you're trying to finish a book," she said, smiling. "You know, it can be very productive for a novelist to be miserable in a live-in relationship. Then the household's all set up and you can channel all your emotional energy into your work."

"Libby, that's just awful." He was laughing. "What a terrible reason to live with someone. How about being in love?"

"Look who's talking!" she said.

"Look—" He touched her arm. "Libby, all I'm saying is that a person like you shouldn't give up on love. Not you. Of all people, not you."

"Will, be honest, have you ever known passion to last any longer than three months?"

"No, but I'm hopeful that I will—if I fall in love with the right person."

Now Libby was laughing. "Well, I guess we can see why neither one of us is married. I don't think either one of us has had a very promising love life so far, do you?"

"Oh, but I think that might be changing," he told her.

The way he said it made her blush slightly; she only smiled, though, patted his arm, and looked back out the window.

They caught a cab at La Guardia and Will dropped Libby off at her apartment building and continued down to Gramercy Park. He could see that no lights were on in his apartment, which was a relief. He didn't know why, but he had this nagging fear that Betsy might not have given up, that she might still be there tonight, begging him not to break up with her. The cab pulled up and the doorman opened the door, looking at him with blank astonishment. "Mr. Klein."

"Hi, Ralph. How are things? Did you have a good Thanksgiving?"

"You're back," he said.

Will couldn't blame the guy. With all his comings and goings lately, he had to be confused about who was living where and with whom. "She's not up there, is she?"

"No, no, sir—she's not up there now."

Will paid the cabdriver and took the elevator up to his floor. Outside his door, he listened a moment to make sure she wasn't there, and then put the key in the lock.

That is, tried to put the key in the lock.

At first he thought he had the keys mixed up, but then he noticed that near the top of the door there was a whole other new lock in place, not that any of his keys fit the two cylinders below.

What the hell was this?

He dropped his bag and stormed downstairs. "She left this for you," Ralph said meekly, handing him an envelope.

He ripped it open.

Fuck.

She was suing him. And until he dealt with the suit, she was maintaining possession of his apartment.

IV

DUE PROCESS

27

IS THAT our Cornelia?" Mrs. Smythe-Daniels called down the hall of 100 Centre Street on Monday morning. She came sweeping in through the entrance in her mink coat, ignoring the guard who was chasing her. "Oh, my dear, is this *you?*" she said, flinging a hardcover copy of *When Smiles Meet* in Libby's face. "I saw this book on my son's coffee table and I happened to look at it, and I saw the picture and said, 'Why, this is our very own Cornelia! On the jury! That is, unless she has a twin sister,' " and she let out one of her better whinnying laughs. Then she looked at the guard with no small measure of irritation. "What *is* it that you want, young man?"

"Your pass, ma'am."

"Oh, all *right.*"

Everyone passing by in the lobby had stopped to look at them. Mrs. Smythe-Daniels showed the guard her pass, looped her arm through Libby's, and moved them along to the elevators. "My son couldn't get over that I knew you. And so you must be so kind as to autograph this copy for him. You will write something nice, won't you? His name is Malcolm. I'll spell it for you."

By the time they reached the jury room, Basha and Slicked-Back Ronnie were in tow, both of whom seemed as impressed as Mrs. Smythe-Daniels that Libby was really *someone.*

"Libby!" Alex beamed, jumping to his feet and holding a hand out to her.

"That ees not the way he greeted me," Elena remarked to Libby, smirking and elbowing her friend Adelaide in the side.

Alex took Libby's coat from her and hung it up. Libby assumed that the vacant seat next to him was saved for her. It was the last thing she wanted to do, but she sat down.

"So," Alex said eagerly, sitting next to her and resting his arm on the back of her chair, leaning toward her, "how was your holiday?"

"Surprisingly wonderful," she said. "And yours?"

"Oh, it was all right. I actually missed coming here." He lowered his voice. "I missed seeing you."

"Hey, you guys," Ronnie said, "did you know who Cornelia is? Show 'em, Mrs. Smythe-Daniels."

"Well, I suppose if they won't spill anything on it," Mrs. Smythe-Daniels said, slipping off her mink coat. Libby tried not to pay much attention as Mrs. Smythe-Daniels sent her copy of *When Smiles Meet* around the table. Mercifully Melissa came in. Libby jumped up and met her at the coatrack.

"How was Saturday?" Libby asked her.

Melissa made a sound of nervous exhaustion as she hung up her coat.

"That good?"

Melissa turned and nodded, fighting a smile. "Yes. I think so. Oh, heck, I don't know. I mean, I do know." And then her expression turned to a slightly apprehensive one. "Look, Libby, you and I have to talk. There's something I have to explain to you."

"Well, sure," Libby said. "How about lunch?" And then Libby felt her face grow warm. "Actually," she whispered, "there's something I want to tell you about, too—something that happened to me this weekend."

Melissa looked past her. "Hi, Will."

Libby whirled around and smiled—and then frowned. He looked terrible. Absolutely awful.

"Hi," he said quietly.

"Libby," Alex said at the table, "come here, I want to show you something."

"Just a minute," she said. She turned to Will. "What's wrong?"

"I'll tell you later," Will murmured. "Alex is about to slug me."

He was right. When Libby turned around, she could feel the resentment in Alex's eyes. She went over and sat down next to him again, vowing not to tell him about anything. Certainly not that Will had spent the weekend with her in Greatfield, that they had drunk Killer Reds and slow-danced to sad country music, and that her mother had decided to open her entire financial life to him.

"Hi, everybody," Will said to the group as he sat down across the table from Libby. "Did everyone have a good holiday?"

A number of responses came back and discussion began about left-over turkey, not being able to watch the news or read the papers, relatives who tried to talk to them about the trial, etc., etc., etc. "How was Ohio?" Will asked her at one point, showing that he planned to play dumb.

"Wonderful," she said. "And Chicago?"

"Probably the best trip of my life," he said. "The only downer was coming home."

"We can go to BJ's tonight if you want," Alex said to Libby as if Will wasn't there. "Dinner, too, if you want."

"Oh, I can't do dinner, I'm afraid," she said. "I've got to do some work tonight."

"Well, maybe tomorrow," Alex said. "But still, what about a drink?"

Inwardly, Libby groaned. She was going to have to talk to him. Tonight. This had to stop. Alex was not good at taking hints. She glanced over at Will. He had pulled out the *Village Voice* and was skimming the classifieds, and she wondered what on earth he was looking for.

Stephen walked in. He looked awful, too. He mumbled some hellos and then sat down next to Melissa; they started talking in hushed tones.

Alex started cross-examining Libby about what she had done over the weekend, and soon Libby felt annoyed, if not badgered.

Chuck came in to take attendance. "Everybody have a good holiday?"

People mumbled responses, sounding caged and depressed already.

They went through the roster. All were present but Sweet Bridget. When Chuck told them not to worry about her absence, he knew all about it, Ronnie said, "Oh, no, she's not sick or dead, too, is she?"

"Who's dead?" Adelaide, Madame Foreman, asked.

"No, she's fine," Chuck said. "But her husband was in a very bad car accident over the holiday."

"He was going to pick up her mother in Boston," Libby remembered.

"I don't know about that," Chuck said, "but her husband's in pretty bad shape. She's been excused from the trial."

Melissa looked at Stephen. "That means you'll be on the jury, doesn't it?"

"Oh, shit," Stephen said, clamping his hands over his face, "this is all I need. Bill will probably die while we're sequestered."

"Sequestered?" Mrs. Smythe-Daniels said, horrified.

"I thought his name was Rupert," Adelaide said.

"Who?" Elena asked her.

"The guy who died," Adelaide replied.

When they were brought into court, the judge looked none too happy. Once they were settled she announced that Juror #11, Bridget Bell, was being excused from the trial for reasons connected to a family tragedy that had occurred over the weekend, and that alternate juror Stephen Cadalone would now serve as Juror #11. After Stephen moved over a couple of seats in the second row, the trial resumed.

The prosecution called their next witness, Jamal White. The gallery seemed to be interested in this witness. He was a black man wearing colorful robes and a turbanlike hat. He made his way up to the stand, where the guard whispered something to him and he took off the hat. When the Bible was offered to the witness, he shook his head, refusing it. He was sworn in without it.

Jamal, it turned out, was an important member of a Jersey City mosque, who in his spare time worked extensively with youthful offenders, trying to get them on the right path. He himself had been in trouble in Newark when he was younger, but he had been on the right path now for over four years. He had a professional day job as an auto mechanic. MacDonald then began to get serious with his questions.

Yes, Jamal knew of the defendant, he had seen him in his community many times. Yes, some of the boys Jamal worked with knew the defendant rather well.

"Mr. White," MacDonald said, "could you explain to the jury what the defendant's connection to your community was?"

"He bought drugs from the dealers."

"Illegal drugs?"

"Yes, he was a regular with the cocaine dealers."

"Objection, Your Honor," said Geiggen, whose face was healing well from whatever it was that had happened to him the week before. "This is hearsay. Unless, of course, the witness actually sold cocaine to the defendant himself."

"No snide comments are necessary, Mr. Geiggen," Judge Williams said. "But the objection is sustained. Mr. MacDonald, please direct the witness to present only the evidence of what he experienced for himself."

"Yes, Your Honor." Back to the witness. "Could you explain to the jury, Mr. White, why the defendant is so familiar to you."

"A white man in a seventy-thousand-dollar car tends to stand out in our community," Jamal said with a smile.

"Objection, Your Honor. Unless the witness is an auto—" Geiggen smiled. "I'm sorry, Your Honor, I forgot. The witness *is* an expert on cars. Objection withdrawn." And he sat down.

"You were saying, Mr. White," MacDonald repeated, "that a white man in a seventy-thousand-dollar car was very noticeable in your community."

"Yes. And we knew that he was spending large sums of money in the community."

The questioning went on, and Libby started to wonder where this was going. They knew the defendant was a drug addict and had bought drugs all over the place, but what did this have to do with the shooting? Finally it came out.

"When was the last time you saw the defendant in your neighborhood, Mr. White?"

"About one-ten in the morning, Thursday, February tenth, 1994."

"Why do you remember the exact day and time?" MacDonald asked.

"Because the ninth was my birthday and a celebration in my honor was just ending."

"And where did you see the defendant?"

"At the corner of Eighth and Byron Avenue."

"And what was he doing there?"

"He was standing by his car talking to a man."

"Do you know who the man was?"

"I couldn't see."

"And what happened?"

"The defendant saw me and my friends approaching. He got into the Jaguar and so did the other man."

"Did you see anything of the other man?"

"He was dark-skinned and very tall. Six-three, maybe. And I think he was wearing a leather jacket. I couldn't be sure."

"You didn't recognize him?"

"I couldn't see his face."

"What happened then?"

"They drove off."

"And you say this was about one-ten in the morning."

"Yes."

"Mr. White, how long does it take to drive into Manhattan from your neighborhood?"

"At that time of night, twenty-five, thirty minutes."

MacDonald then verified with the witness that he had identified the defendant in a photo lineup. This yellow card, with six photographs on it, was entered into evidence. The witness had also picked the defendant out of a police lineup.

When MacDonald was finished, they went right into the cross-examination. Geiggen got very tough, demanding to know how Jamal couldn't see who the defendant was talking to if he could see well enough to recognize the defendant. Jamal tried to stand firm, but Geiggen forced the issue that had it not been for the presence of the Jaguar, a car he knew well, he might not have recognized who was standing next to it.

"And you freely admit you had seen the defendant many times in your community," Geiggen said.

"Yes."

"Well, if that's true," Geiggen said, turning to the jury and gesturing wildly with his next words, "then of *course* you could pick the defendant's picture out of the lineup. Correct?" He whirled around to look at the witness.

"Why would I pick someone—"

"Yes or no, Mr. White," Geiggen thundered. "Since you had seen the defendant many times before the night in question, you could have picked his picture out—or him out—in any kind of lineup. Is that not true?"

"Yes?" he said, clearly confused now, and looking to the judge.

Geiggen consulted his assistants about something and then went on, hammering the witness about wasn't it true that he had gotten out of prison four years ago because he turned state's evidence against some drug dealers. Jamal said yes, it was. And what about Jamal's relationship with the authorities—was he promised anything in return for his cooperation? How could it be he could safely walk the streets around the drug gangs of Jersey City and not be touched if he was as squeaky clean as he pretended to be?

"Objection, Your Honor!" MacDonald cried on that one.

"I withdraw it," Geiggen said, "and Your Honor, I have no further questions of this witness." The last part he said as if he were spitting snake venom out of his mouth.

They were given a brief recess, which only made Libby feel trapped with Alex in the jury room.

"Don't you feel well, Libby?" he asked her. "What's the matter? Can I get you something? Do you want to talk about it?"

Libby finally got up and went into the ladies' room just to get away him.

Once they were back in court, the next witness called by the prosecution was Police Officer Rod Espada. He was in street clothes (Libby had surmised that police officers weren't allowed to wear uniforms in court), and was a young, pleasant-looking man. He took the stand, was sworn in, and MacDonald started in. Evidently Officer Espada and his partner, both members of the Jersey City Police Department, were on duty in the wee hours of the morning of February 10, 1994, and had been parked in their patrol car near the exit ramp of the Polaski Skyway, on the New Jersey side of the Holland Tunnel. According to Officer Espada, at approximately 12:20 A.M., a silver Jaguar with a black convertible top and a New York license plate starting with 3L8 exited the ramp and turned left at the light, heading east on Smith Boulevard into Jersey City. Why had the officer noticed it? Because the Jaguar had come off the ramp so fast he thought it was going to run the red light at the corner, but the light changed and the car had taken the corner at around forty miles an hour. It was his custom to jot down things like this in his memo book. At that hour of the morning, one never knew if a car like that might not be speeding away from trouble or heading into it.

When it was time for the cross-examination, Geiggen took his time getting to his feet. "Officer, why do you suppose it is that all of the prosecution's witnesses in this case can only ever remember the first three numbers of the license plate of this car?"

"Objection, Your Honor!" MacDonald said.

"Sustained."

Geiggen made a big show of being annoyed with this ruling. Finally, he asked, "Officer Espada, before testifying in court today, did you spend any time with the district attorney to prepare for this case?"

"I came to the prosecutor's office a couple of times."

"And did you testify at the preliminary hearing?"

"Yes."

Geiggen walked around a bit. "Officer, are you married?"

"Yes."

"Do you have any children?"

"Three."

"Objection, Your Honor," MacDonald cried. "Defense is on some kind of irrelevant fishing expedition merely to harass the witness!"

"Your Honor, I am merely trying to provide some background on the witness so that the jury may determine the validity of his testimony."

Slowly, Judge Williams considered this. "Objection overruled."

"Officer, do you and your family live in a house?"

"Yes."

"And do you carry a mortgage on that house?"

"Objection, Your Honor! What can this possibly have to do with whether or not Officer Espada saw the defendant's car on the night of the murder?"

"Objection, Your Honor!" Geiggen yelled. "Prosecution is giving a summation to the jury in the form of an objection!"

They all sat there as the lawyers were called up to the bench for a side-bar.

It was quarter after one. Libby was starving.

The sidebar broke up and Judge Williams said, "The objection has been overruled. The defense may continue his line of questioning."

"Thank you, Your Honor," Geiggen said with a spiteful glare at Mac-Donald. He walked over to the jury box. "Now, Officer, where were we? I believe you said that you and your wife and three children live in a house."

"Yes."

"And now I'm asking, Do you carry a mortgage on your house?"

"Yes," the officer said, "most people do, you know."

"Yes, they do indeed," Geiggen said, smiling at the jury, "myself included." He walked around some more, taking his time. The witness never took his eyes off him.

"All in all, Officer Espada, including travel time, could you tell the jury how many hours this case has taken out of your life?"

"No."

"I see. But perhaps you could explain to the jury that when you traveled from New Jersey to New York City to see the prosecutor, in preparation for a trial, on whose time was that billed?"

"I don't know what you mean."

"Isn't it true, Officer, that you've been well paid for cooperating with the DA's office in connection with this case?"

"Objection, Your Honor!" MacDonald said.

"Overruled. The witness will answer the question."

"No," the officer said.

"Well, then," Geiggen said, "could you explain how you are compensated for your time spent with the DA's office?"

"There's nothing strange about it," the officer began. "When I have to go to court, or I am involved in the preparation for any court proceeding, I am paid overtime—the amount of time over and above my regular work hours and duties."

"And how much is an hour of overtime in your case, Officer?"

"Oh," he said, looking to the ceiling, "I think it's about thirty-four or thirty-five dollars. Thirty-five dollars."

"I see. And so, for example, today, how would your hours of overtime be calculated?"

"It would be calculated from the time I left my house this morning to when I get back."

"Okay, so let us suppose you are released today at three. Then you'll drive back home?"

"Yes."

"How long with that take?"

"Depending on traffic, probably an hour."

"And what time did you leave this morning?"

"Eight o'clock."

"Okay, so let's say you get home at four o'clock today. That would be eight hours of overtime at thirty-five dollars." He scribbled on his pad. "That's two hundred eighty dollars." He looked up. "So, Officer, is it fair to say that you will probably receive an extra two hundred eighty dollars from testifying today?"

"It's not extra," the officer protested, "it's overtime. You know, taxes, pension, everything gets taken out."

"Fine. And now could you please tell the jury, Officer, at what other times you've come into Manhattan recently in connection with this case?"

"I was here all day Wednesday last week, waiting to be called to the stand."

"Did you leave your house at eight o'clock that morning?"

"Yes."

"And when did you get home?"

"With the holiday traffic, not until close to seven-thirty."

"I see. Eleven and a half hours?"

"Yes."

"Okay, so let's see." Geiggen scribbled on his pad.

Espada's face was turning red with rage.

Geiggen looked up. "So last Wednesday, Officer, it is fair to say that you made an extra four hundred two dollars and fifty cents?"

"You're twisting it."

"Just answer the question, please, yes or no. Will you make an extra four hundred two dollars from waiting around last Wednesday?"

"Yes."

Geiggen paused. And then he turned to face the jury. "And so it is also true, Officer, that from just these two days of participation in this trial, you'll be receiving an extra six hundred eighty-two dollars?"

The witness said nothing, fuming.

Geiggen turned around. "Is that a yes?"

"Yes."

"Have you come into Manhattan before in connection with this case?"

"Yes."

"At least two times?"

"Yes."

"More than five times?"

"I don't know," the officer said.

"But we would be able to figure it out from your income tax returns, is that correct, Officer? How many thousands of dollars you've been paid to cooperate with the DA's office in connection with this case?"

"Objection, Your Honor! Defense is way out of line!"

The judge said quietly, "Objection sustained."

"Fine," Geiggen said, looking at the jury and throwing his hands up in frustration. He started back toward the defense table, but then stopped and turned around. "One last question, Officer. You said that you wrote down the first three letters of the license plate in your memo book."

"Yes."

"Is a police officer's memo book considered an official document to be used in evidence?"

"It's used to remind the officer of things that happened."

"To remind the officer so he or she can fill out an official report?"

"Yes."

"*Did* you fill out an official report on the car you say you saw?"

"No. There was no reason to. No crime had been committed—yet."

"So all we have, in terms of evidence, is your testimony and the notation in your memo book that you saw the car—but the memo book, as you have just explained, cannot be considered part of the official evidence."

The police officer looked to the judge for help. None was coming.

Geiggen smiled. "That's all, Officer, thank you."

MacDonald was up like a shot for the redirect. "Officer Espada, did you see a silver Jaguar with a black convertible top and a New York license plate that began with three-el-eight racing into Jersey City at about twenty minutes after twelve on the morning of February tenth, 1994?"

"Yes, I did."

"Thank you, Officer. No further questions, Your Honor."

"I think the cop killed her," Ronnie announced in the jury room.

"Cut it out, Ronnie," Libby said, annoyed.

"Where do you want to eat?" Alex asked her.

"Oh, I'm sorry, Alex, but I already have plans."

"Ready?" Melissa asked, coming over to save the day.

Libby looked at Alex. "We'll have a drink later, okay?"

He nodded, looking upset, but Libby hightailed it out of there.

Outside of the jury room, she looked at Melissa. "I'm not sure what I've gotten myself into."

"He certainly seems proprietary over you these days. I don't know, Libby, if I were you, I'd get rid of him."

"How can I get rid of him when I'm stuck on a jury with him?"

"There are ways," Melissa said seriously. "And I'd do it soon."

"Tonight," she promised. And then she brightened. "But tell me about Saturday!"

As they rode down the elevator and made their way out of the courthouse, Melissa told Libby about the dinner at the Russian Tea Room and drinks at the Four Seasons, about talking for hours and hours, about being able to talk honestly with Chris—Melissa about her troubled past, Chris about his divorce. They even talked about his children.

"Children?" Libby said, going down the courthouse stairs.

"Yes," Melissa said, "two."

"Will he want to have any with you, do you think?" She glanced over at Melissa and stopped. "What? What did I say?"

"Oh, Libby." Melissa cringed. "I've got to talk to you."

"About what?" Libby touched her arm. "What is it?"

Melissa looked around, sighed, and met her eyes. "Libby, Chris is a Christine. She's a . . . she. I was scared to tell you."

"Oh," Libby said. She blinked a couple of times. And then she smiled. "But you're not scared to tell me now."

Melissa looked apprehensive. "Does it bother you?"

"That you felt you couldn't tell me? Yes. But that Christine is a woman who is clearly mad about you? No." She slung her arm through Melissa's and propelled them down the street. "As my friend Kitty says, 'Girl, you gotta understand, *love* is the whole point of the exercise.' "

They laughed and went on to have a quick lunch, during which Melissa told Libby more about Christine, and Libby then shyly confided in Melissa about her having drunk Killer Reds and slow-danced with Will in Greatfield over the weekend.

"With *Will?*" Melissa said wide-eyed. "Will from the *jury?* In *Ohio?*"

After her lunch with Melissa, Libby rendezvoused with Will at one-fifty in the courthouse cafeteria for a quick cup of coffee. There he told about coming home the night before and finding that Betsy had changed the locks on his apartment door while he was away, that he couldn't get in, and that she was threatening to sue him on God only knew what grounds.

"Oh, great," he muttered, looking over Libby's shoulder.

"What?" She turned around to look. "Uh-oh."

Alex was glaring at them from the door. When Libby waved, he gave a kind of sneering smile and walked out.

"I think one of your admirers is upset," Will observed.

Upstairs in the jury room, Libby decided it was best to play the innocent and sit down next to Alex and act as though nothing had happened. Fortunately, in less than a minute they were called back into court.

The afternoon court session was a bit of a letdown. A series of witnesses were called by the prosecution to verify facts. A convicted drug dealer serving time at Rahway State Prison in New Jersey testified for MacDonald that the defendant had been a regular customer of his in 1993 and early 1994. Geiggen didn't try to dispute his testimony, but did point out that where the drug dealer had operated was almost thirty miles from Jersey City. Libby assumed the point of the prosecution was that Layton, through his drug use, was well acquainted with North Jersey drug rings, and would know where to pick up a hit man on short notice; and she assumed the point of the defense was that this witness proved nothing about the defendant's connection with Jersey City, which was thirty miles away.

The next witness was a doctor who verified that at the time of his arrest, Layton had evidence of cocaine, alcohol, and Librium in his bloodstream. Geiggen didn't try to refute this, either.

The last witness called for the day was an old black man, looking very shaky, named Bartley Daily. MacDonald established that Daily had a long alcohol and drug-abuse problem. MacDonald also established that the witness had been homeless for quite some time. After that information was out of the way, his testimony became more interesting.

The witness said he saw the defendant on the night of the murder. The defendant had been coming out of the nightclub, on Fourteenth Street, about midnight or so. The defendant had been ranting and raving when he came out, and had shoved the witness out of his way. Asked if he could make out anything the defendant had said, the witness replied, "He said, 'That bitch will die before morning.' "

MacDonald let these words hang in the air awhile before sitting down. Geiggen then got up and tried, rather effectively, Libby thought, to disqualify the witness by listing his many arrests and hospitalizations and outstanding warrants, and pointing out that the prosecution had provided him with a place to live so he would stay in Manhattan and testify at this trial. When Geiggen was through, however, MacDonald got up again.

"Mr. Daily, could you tell the jury why you remember so distinctly what it was the defendant said when he came out of the nightclub?"

"Sure. When he pushed me, I dropped my bottle o' wine and it broke. And when he said, 'That bitch will die before morning,' I said, 'Man, if you don't get the fuck outta here, *yo'* gonna die right now!' "

There was scattered laughter.

"Thank you. No further questions, Your Honor. This also concludes the prosecution's witnesses."

They were dismissed for the day, advised that the defense would start presenting their case in the morning.

28

LIBBY didn't know what she and Alex talked about on the way over to BJ's, but once they were seated and served their drinks, Alex got right down to it. "What's going on, Libby? Did something happen over the holiday? You seem so different."

She avoided his eyes. "Well, sort of. Yes, I guess."

"As long as it doesn't have anything to do with that little dweeb Klein," he laughed, but he wasn't really laughing, she knew. This laugh sounded like a threat. "Look, Libby, just tell me what's going on." And then before she could say anything he rushed on to say that he had thought she really liked him—as much as he did her. And he had thought, well, and he smiled—a really rather charming smile—that they were attracted to each other. But this morning, suddenly, she seemed cold, distant. What happened?

Libby stammered a bit, trying to explain that while, yes, she had considered herself lucky to have a friend like Alex on the jury—

"*Friend?*" he said, visibly wincing.

She nodded.

He shook his head. "There's got to be somebody else. You must have met somebody."

Cocky, wasn't he?

"Yes," she said. "There is. Someone I saw over the holiday."

"In Ohio?"

She nodded.

"Well, if he's in Ohio, what's that got to do with being here in New York?"

"Well, he's not. In Ohio, I mean. He's here in New York."

"Oh." Alex finished off his scotch and asked the waitress for another. When it came, he took a sip and said, "So did you know this guy before? And then invite him to Ohio? I thought you told me you weren't seeing anybody else."

"Well, I wasn't. We just crossed paths—"

"In Ohio?"

She shrugged. "Yeah."

"Jesus!" he suddenly spat out. "Why can't you just give me a straight answer? Are you in love? Or did you just fuck him?"

She looked at him, stunned. Finally she managed to say, "Neither. But in either case, it's really none of your business, Alex. I'm sorry."

"Jesus," he muttered again, looking around. Then he glared at her, jaw jutting forward. "You really are— I mean, you are the original cock tease, aren't you? You just can't get it together, can you? I mean, what *was* all that bullshit about being in the wrong kind of relationships?"

She had her purse open by now and was pulling a ten out of her wallet, since she didn't have the five she had hoped to find. She put the ten on the table. "All that this is about, Alex, is that I'm sorry if I misled you in any way—and that I hope we remain friends." She stood up. "I'd better go."

"Yeah, you better," he told her. "Before I chuck this drink in your face."

She told herself that, real or imaginary, his feelings were hurt and she shouldn't be angry at his reaction, she should be sympathetic.

Oh, forget it! The guy was a jackass.

At the office there was a message on his voice mail from Betsy's lawyer. Will called him back, but he had left for the day. Mr. Klein could call him during office hours, ten and five, the secretary told him.

"I'm on a murder trial," Will told her. "I can't call during the day."

"Oh, I see, Mr. Klein, and what firm are you with?"

"No, I'm not a lawyer, I'm a juror."

"Oh," she said, as if to say, Right, you're exactly the lowly piece of slime I thought you were.

He tried calling the apartment, but no one answered. This was so stupid. He couldn't get his clothes, he couldn't find Betsy, he couldn't reach her lawyer—

Lawyer. Jeez, he'd better get a lawyer. And then Will began to smile. At long last working with sleazy Jerry might actually pay off. If anyone knew a horrible kick-ass killer lawyer, Jerry would.

The children were already asleep by the time Rusty came in. He looked pretty tired, but smiled as he came in from the garage to the kitchen, where Jill was cutting material for one of Katie's class projects. "Hiya," he said, putting his briefcase down by the oven. He came over to kiss her.

"Hi. You look beat."

"I am." He slipped off his overcoat, threw it over the back of a chair, slipped off his suit jacket, and threw that down, too. "I've got some good news." He loosened his tie, walking over to the refrigerator to get a bottle of beer.

She was watching him, wondering what the good news could be.

He pried off the cap, dropped the bottle opener in the drawer, pushed the drawer shut with his hip, and was about to drink out of the bottle when he caught his wife's eye. He smiled, opened a cupboard, got out a glass, and began pouring the beer into it.

Jill had to smile. It was Rusty's way of trying. To pretend he still cared whether he made a good impression on her.

He took a big swallow, said, Ah, and pulled out the chair next to her to sit down.

"Well?"

"Braxton's going to take over on the Westinghouse case for me."

This meant nothing to her since she still wasn't sure exactly what her husband was working on. Not yet, anyway.

"Which means," he continued, "I've arranged to take a leave from the office until January."

"January!"

"Yeah," he said, smiling, drinking beer. "That way I can go to the trial with you, or I can stay here with the kids. And no matter what, I think I should go see the kids' teachers and stuff—you know, to find out what's going on at school."

Jill was staring at her husband in open awe. Trying to get him to take a week's vacation had always been nearly impossible. Now he was taking a five-week leave to stay at home or go to the trial, and he couldn't look happier. She didn't know what to say, and looked back down at the material in her hand, mechanically continuing with her task.

"We can afford it, it'll be okay," he assured her.

"Oh, that wasn't what I was thinking."

"What were you?"

She sniffed, blinking rapidly, clearing her throat. "I don't know."

He reached over to pull her chin up so he could see her face. "Tell me."

One tear edged out and trickled down her cheek. "I was thinking, He really does love us."

"Oh, God, Jill," he said as if she had hit him. He scooted his chair closer and pulled her into his lap. They held each other, rocking, Katie's material for class getting all scrunched up between them. "You're everything, honey, you're everything to me," he said.

Melissa had been in the office since six, but had accomplished next to nothing. It was starting to get to her, these working hours. Her only colleagues these days were the cleaning people and night security guards. Over four hundred employees at S. Wiley Kearnan, and she hadn't seen more than three of them for weeks.

Her phone wouldn't ring, either. That's what was really bothering her. At this point, she was really just sitting there, looking at it.

But it's your move, Melissa.

She went out to the company kitchenette to get a glass of orange juice. Then she sat down at her desk and made the call. To the home number.

"Hello?"

It was a boy's voice, maybe eight or nine. Oh, God.

"Hi, is your mom there?" she said. "It's Melissa Grant calling."

"Mom!"

"Hello?" Her voice was light and melodic, just as a mother's should be.

Oh, God.

"Christine? It's Melissa."

"Melissa!" she said brightly. "Oh, I'm so glad you called. And I'm so glad you called here."

How could she not respond to how wonderfully happy Christine sounded? "Well, I'm glad, too. And, um, I was wondering if I could invite you to dinner this time."

"When were you thinking?"

"Well, you're the one with, um, considerations at home."

"The kids are going on an overnight to their cousins' house on Saturday," Christine said. "Do you want to come out here?"

"No," Melissa said a little too quickly. "I mean, I could but—"

Christine was laughing. "No, I know exactly what you mean. It's all right, Melissa, I can come into the city." Pause. "Maybe you'll show me your home."

Her home? For God's sake, she rented furniture, what kind of home was that? "Well, I could cook," she heard herself offer.

O N TUESDAY morning, November 28, Libby found herself very reluctant to go to court. Overnight Alex had come to seem like some sort of vague sickness she did not wish to catch. How the situation had evolved over the last three weeks was beyond her.

No wonder they called it a trial.

Alex was in the jury room when she arrived. She said good morning to him and to the others, hung up her coat, and nonchalantly went to the other side of the table to sit next to Melissa. Too late she realized she was now seated directly opposite Alex.

The jurors were quiet this morning. Newspapers were traded silently, coffee cup lids pried off and coffee sipped. Ronnie was eating a cheese Danish in such a way as to make Libby wonder how his mother could have ever let him out of the house.

Would this trial ever end? Would they ever get back to their lives?

Will came in and Libby immediately felt her spirits lift. She smiled and said hello, but then diverted her eyes, horribly aware of Alex glaring at her.

The trial resumed on time with the defense calling their first witness, a detective named José Martinez. Under Geiggen's questioning, the detective explained that since he was on duty at the precinct at the time of Sissy Cook's murder, he had been the original detective in charge of the case.

"Are you saying that Detective Joseph Cleary, who has previously testified in this trial, was *not* the original detective in charge?"

"No. Not until the following day," Martinez said.

Geiggen raised his eyebrows at the jury. "And why was that?"

"I'm not sure," the witness said evasively.

"Well, then, Detective Martinez, perhaps you can simply explain what had happened between the time of the murder and the time Detective Cleary was reassigned to be in charge of the investigation."

"The investigation started."

"Yes, I understand that, Detective. What I want to know is, who told you that Detective Cleary was taking over?"

"The captain. In the early afternoon of the day following the shooting. Actually, it was the day of the shooting—because the shooting happened around two A.M."

"And what reason did the captain give you for pulling you off the case?"

"That Detective Cleary had worked with the assistant DA assigned to this case—Mr. MacDonald—before."

"Detective Martinez, have you ever been the detective in charge of a homicide investigation and then been replaced by another detective, simply because he or she had worked with the assistant DA before?"

"Me? No."

"Thank you, Detective. No further questions of this witness, Your Honor."

"Mr. MacDonald, you may cross-examine the witness."

Kathryn Schnagel, sitting next to MacDonald at the prosecutor's table had slid her pad over in front of him and the assistant DA was looking at it, mouth pressed into a line, shaking his head.

"Mr. MacDonald?" the judge repeated.

He looked up. And hesitated. "No, Your Honor, I have no questions for this witness."

Libby looked at the defendant. He was just sitting there quietly, watching, face placid. Kathryn Schnagel at the prosecution's table, however, was obviously angry with the senior counsel sitting next to her.

Libby glanced out into the gallery. The sister's victim was there, Jill. Today a man was sitting with her. She wondered who he was.

She scoped out the rest of the gallery. Yet again she wondered which one might be the defendant's wife. None of the women quite looked the part.

The next witness called was a Dr. Theodore Kaliptus, a psychiatrist specializing in addictive personalities. He went on and on and on about how the defendant had been suffering all his life from low self-esteem and an addictive personality. At one point, Libby could hear Melissa snicker behind her.

In any event, by the time Dr. Kaliptus was through, the jury was supposed to believe that the defendant, through no real fault of his own save bad genetic material, had been a complete and utter slave to drugs, oftentimes to the point of mental incoherence and physical breakdown. Based upon the medical findings of the drug levels in the defendant's blood at the time of the arrest, and from his subsequent examinations, Dr. Kaliptus said that in his professional opinion, there was absolutely no way the defendant could have planned such an intricate murder, much less been capable of driving *any* car *any*where.

MacDonald's cross-examination lasted until lunchtime, and although he fired questions at the doctor left and right—establishing that he was being paid for his testimony and that he was certainly no stranger to the courts—he did little to counter the doctor's testimony. Essentially it came down to whether or not the doctor could be slanting his expertise for profit, but somehow the point was lost by MacDonald. In fact, by the time MacDonald was through with the witness, Libby found it difficult to imagine the defendant being physically capable of doing much of anything the night of the murder, except leaving the club, losing his car, and taking a cab home.

When they broke for lunch, Libby felt kind of funny. For the first time, she was genuinely starting to have doubts about Layton's guilt. But she shrugged it off, telling herself to keep an open mind.

"Libby?" Alex said softly. "Could I extend a peace offering of lunch?"

She tried to smile. "Of course, but today, I'm afraid, I can't take you up on it." Truth was, hell would have to freeze over before she'd go near him again, but there was no need to be unpleasant.

He looked a little sheepish. "You forgive me? Because I'm really sorry. It was stupid of me to say the things I did. I didn't mean them. I don't know what got into me."

"It's okay, don't worry about it."

"Friends?" He extended his hand. They shook, and then Alex left.

Will came over. "What was all that about?"

"Leave it, Will, everything's fine."

His eyebrows went up. "You wouldn't want to have lunch with me, would you? And read apartment sublet ads? I've got to find a place to live. I can't stay in the Vista Hotel for the rest of my life."

They found a cafeteria-style restaurant, got some food, and huddled together at a small table. It was serious business, Will having to fight for possession of his three-hundred-thousand-dollar apartment, but the two felt warm and happy, and laughed a great deal while discussing it. Lunch was over far too soon.

"The defense calls Alfred Martins," Geiggen announced.

MacDonald and his colleague whispered back and forth and then MacDonald stood up. "Your Honor, the prosecution has no record of this witness."

"Your Honor," Geiggen said, "this witness has only recently surfaced and is instrumental to the defense."

Up to the bench the lawyers went for a sidebar. Libby had begun to worry about the stenographer, who was sagging a little lower with each of these trips with her machine.

When they broke up, Alfred Martins was called as the next witness. He turned out to be a hippie-looking kind of guy, about forty-five, dressed in blue jeans and a striped shirt, and with a ponytail. He took the stand, was sworn in, and then Geiggen started in.

Alfred Martins had been living on and off the streets of New York for the past three years. He had a drug problem. And an alcohol problem. Yes, he had for many years. He had bounced in and out of sobering-up stations, homeless shelters, and the veteran's hospital. Yeah, he had been in the Army. Honorable discharge. Yeah, he was sober now, no drugs or alcohol. It had been about twelve or thirteen days.

"Mr. Martins, could you please tell the jury where you were living in February of 1994?"

He looked at the jury. "I was living in a cardboard box over a heating grate in an alley behind the BurgerKitch on Fourteenth Street. A refrigerator box."

"And can you tell the jury where you were the night of February ninth?"

"I was in the box in the early evening, because it was cold, and I knew I couldn't get any hot food until later, when the restaurants started closing."

"At what time, approximately, did you leave the box?"

"It was maybe a minute before midnight—I know because there's a clock you can see from the grate—it's on the bank across the street—and I always made the rounds for food just before midnight."

"I see. And can you please tell the jury what happened on this night?"

"Sure." He looked at the jury. "I went out on Fourteenth Street and I saw this amazing car. A Jag. I used to have one, a long time ago. Anyway, I stopped and looked at it 'cause it was just the kind of car you have to stop and look at."

"Could you describe it?"

"Yeah. It was gray, a convertible, had a black top. In beautiful shape, too. I was surprised it was parked out on the street like that. And parked crooked, you know? One tire up on the sidewalk. I thought, Oh, man, this guy's had a few."

"And why did you think that?"

"The keys were in it. Just hanging out of the ignition. And the door wasn't locked, neither."

"You tried the door?"

"Sure I did!" He sighed. "But man, I knew if I got caught with a car like that, they'd put me away and throw away the key."

"You were tempted to steal it?"

"I was tempted to drive it away, yeah," the witness said. He looked at the jury. "Who wouldn't?"

"But you didn't."

"No. You know, 'cause I started thinkin'—how weird it was this car was just sittin' there with the keys and everything. So then I thought it might be a setup, you know, that the cops were watching."

"So what did you do?"

"Got the hell out of there."

There was a little laughter in the courtroom.

"And did you see the car again that night?"

"No, sir. It was gone when I came back to my box. About one-thirty."

"And did you see who drove it away?"

"No, sir. But it could have been anybody."

And so on it went, Geiggen continuing to question the witness about his life since the time of the murder and how, barely a week ago, he had heard about an investigator who had been searching for months for anyone who had been in the vicinity of the shooting that night. Yes, the defense was giving him a place to stay. Yes, food to eat. And yes, some pocket money.

MacDonald kept him on the stand all afternoon for the cross-examination, but again, as with Dr. Kaliptus, was having trouble disproving anything he said. At one point, Libby started to get annoyed with MacDonald, because he seemed to be making fun of the man.

"And so we're supposed to believe that you, Mr. Martins, an admitted drug addict, alcoholic, and felon, are here to testify simply because of your burning desire to see justice done?"

"Yeah, so, what if it is?" the witness said. "I got rights."

"Not necessarily, Mr. Martins," MacDonald said. "As a convicted felon you have no right, for example, to serve on a jury because in the eyes of the law you are not *fit* to sit on one."

"Objection, Your Honor!" Geiggen said, sounding shocked. "Prosecution is not only badgering the witness, but sermonizing, and in a most unattractive way. Just because the witness has been less fortunate in life than Mr. MacDonald—"

"That will be enough sermonizing from you, Mr. Geiggen," Judge Williams said, prompting laughter in the court. "Objection sustained. Mr. MacDonald, this is not a hostile witness."

By the end of the day, MacDonald was just about screaming "Liar!" at Alfred Martins. It was not an effective cross-examination, although Libby did get MacDonald's point—that the defense could have dug this guy up from anywhere and paid him to say all this.

Geiggen popped up from his seat to have the last word of the day. "Mr. Martins, did you, or did you not, see a gray Jaguar with a black convertible top parked on Fourteenth Street around midnight on February ninth?"

"Yes, sir, I did."

"And could you repeat to the jury whether or not it was possible for someone other than the owner of the car to have driven it off?"

"Yes, sir. The car was unlocked and the keys were in it."

Kathryn Schnagel had shoved a pad in front of MacDonald again. This time they seemed to agree, for MacDonald nodded and got up to request a chance to redirect his cross-examination.

"Mr. Martins, did the Jaguar you saw have an automatic transmission?"

The witness laughed. "Heck, no. It had a stick."

"A stick shift?"

"Yeah."

"So then it is, in fact, not true that just anyone could have driven the car away. The person would have to have known how to drive a stick shift."

The witness shrugged. "I suppose."

"Do you know how many gears a Jaguar has? You said you had one once."

"Yeah. Five."

"And how many gears does an average stick-shift car have?"

"You mean like a Toyota or something?"

"Yes."

He shrugged. "Four."

"So even a person who has learned to drive the average stick-shift car, Mr. Martins, in all probability has never driven a five-gear car before?"

"I don't know."

"But you do know now, don't you, Mr. Martins, that your previous statement was incorrect? That not just anybody could have driven that Jaguar away? That it had to have been someone who had driven a luxury sports car like that before."

"I don't know," the witness said. "I'm no mechanic."

"Indeed," MacDonald said. "No further questions, Your Honor."

Court was dismissed for the day.

By now, when Libby came home at night, the building staff scarcely dared to say anything but hello. Regardless of what sensational stuff they might be reading and hearing about the trial, they were more intimidated by Libby's expression than curious about her opinion of what was going on.

All except Nick Danger, that was, but even he didn't say anything about the trial. He would only ask, as he did tonight, how Libby was holding up, and how much longer did she think the trial would last, so he could tell people how much longer they needed to be afraid of speaking to her?

She was in good spirits tonight, and sang and hummed around the apartment. She had dealt with Alex. She was very, very fond of Will. She had deposited the check her father had given her and so she could pay her bills.

Will called at about eight o'clock to say that her uncle Greg, as promised, had Fed-Exed complete financial statements regarding the Winslows' money to Will's office, and that Will was now sending them on to her parents.

"I just can't believe how Mom gave you carte blanche on this," she murmured.

"I know it sounds funny, Libby, but I think it has something to do with me being on the jury."

"Yes, well, Alex is on the jury and I wouldn't trust him as far as I could throw him. No, Will, I think the fact that you're an officer of one of the largest investment banking firms in the world might have something to do with it."

Pause. "Everything straightened out with Alex?"

"I hope so. But listen, Will, I don't know why, but he does seem to have it in for you."

"As if I haven't noticed," Will said. "I was thinking of introducing him to Betsy."

They laughed.

"Is there any chance you might want to go to a movie or something with me this weekend?" he asked. "I know what we discussed in Great-field—"

"And you understood what I meant, didn't you?"

"No Killer Reds and slow dancing until the trial's over."

"Well, maybe just the Killer Reds part," she said, feeling a wave of desire wash over her at the memory. She nearly dropped the phone.

Good golly, where had *this* come from?

30

W ISELY or unwisely, she didn't care the next morning, but when Will arrived at the juror room, Libby made it clear he was welcome to the empty chair next to her. Today she was sitting on the same side of the long table that Alex was, and Melissa was placed strategically between them.

The jurors were oddly quiet this morning, as if everyone was scared to say aloud how fast the case suddenly seemed to be progressing. How many more witnesses did the defense need to call, anyway? Particularly after yesterday's effective testimony?

They were brought into court right on time and filed expertly into the jury box. Everybody seemed to know how to do everything in court effortlessly now, whether it was the jury filing into the box or the guard cracking windows for air or the guard adjusting the microphone to avoid feedback.

When court resumed, Geiggen was told he could call his next witness. He stood up and announced, "Your Honor, the defense calls John Russell Tompkins to the stand."

There was an audible gasp from someone in the gallery and Mac-Donald was on his feet in an instant. "Objection, Your Honor. This individual was never subpoenaed to appear as a witness."

"Your Honor, it so happens that Mr. Tompkins is in the courtroom today, and given certain evidence that has come to light, the defense feels it is vital to our case that he testify."

"Your Honor," MacDonald said, "it was determined in the preliminary hearing that there was no cause for this witness to testify."

"Your Honor, the defense can't help it if vital new evidence has come to light since the preliminary hearing."

"Prosecution requests a sidebar, Your Honor."

On this one, the judge sent the jury back to the jury room. They couldn't imagine what the heck was going on. Why would the defense call a spectator to the stand? Tompkins? Was he related to the sister of the dead woman?

"Your books make a lot more sense than this trial does," Basha sighed to Libby in the jury room. In reaction to Libby's quizzical expression, she reached over for her bag and pulled out a hardcover edition of Libby's first novel. "I got it at the library last night. So far I like it. Although I'm not sure I want to read it while you're sitting next to me. What if I don't like the rest of it?"

They weren't allowed back into the court for close to an hour. When they were finally brought back in, it was clear that Geiggen had won the argument and MacDonald was ballistic. Even the judge looked defeated about something. "The defense may call their next witness."

"Your Honor, the defense calls John Russell Tompkins."

There was a deathly silence in the courtroom as the guard went out to get him. John Tompkins came in and Libby recognized him immediately as the man who had been sitting with the victim's sister. Tompkins. Of course, he was her husband. She glanced at the wife. Her face was about as tight as it could get.

They swore the witness in and he spoke in a low, nervous voice. He was a handsome man, with reddish-brown hair and nice blue eyes. Geiggen began in a friendly manner, establishing for the jury just who he was. Married for eleven years to the victim's sister, Jill Cook Tompkins. Father of two children. A patent attorney here in New York City. Yes, of course he had known Sissy Cook.

"Mr. Tompkins, do people call you John, or do you have a nickname?"

He mumbled something.

"I'm sorry, Mr. Tompkins," the judge said, "but you'll have to speak into the microphone."

He nodded, looking sad. "Yes."

"And what is that nickname, Mr. Tompkins?"

"Rusty."

Immediately Libby got it and her blood felt like it was turning to ice.

Rusty. Was this the Rusty who had an affair with the victim? If it was, Libby thought Geiggen should be shot. Jesus God, the wife already had her sister murdered. Now what was he going to do? Publicly humiliate the wife and destroy their family to boot? Or was he going to try and pin the murder on him, à la Perry Mason?

Beside her, Libby could tell Clay had gotten the Rusty connection, too, for his hand had involuntarily clenched and he was leaning slightly toward the witness box.

Geiggen was taking his time, strolling over to the jury box to skim some notes he had left on the shelf there. Rusty Tompkins was starting to sweat, sitting there, waiting. As if he could hear what Libby was thinking—that he looked like a beaten man, guilty as all get out—he suddenly reached for the glass of water, took a sip, and then straightened up, throwing his shoulders back. He looked better, much better, and Libby wondered if the prosecution had coached him during the recess.

"Mr. Tompkins," Geiggen said, "it was previously testified in this courtroom by Sissy Cook's roommate, Marybeth Shaeffer, that the deceased had an affair with a man named Rusty."

"Objection, Your Honor!" MacDonald said. "The witness said no such thing!"

"Your Honor, she testified that somebody named Rusty came over and had sex with Sissy Cook—"

"Objection, objection, OBJECTION, Your Honor!" MacDonald thundered. "There was no such testimony! Defense is making up stories for the jury's benefit!"

Geiggen threw his hands up in exasperation. "Your Honor, how can I ask a question if I can't say what the witness said? I have it right here in my notes that it was Marybeth Shaeffer's impression that they were lovers."

"Mr. Geiggen!" the judge said. "That's enough! The jury is dismissed for a brief recess!" She took a deep breath, let it out, and looked at the jury. "You shall not discuss this case with anyone or amongst yourselves, is that clear?"

Several jurors, Libby included, meekly nodded.

Back in the jury room it was very quiet. At first. And then Libby couldn't help it. "The poor wife, I can't believe she has to sit through this." She caught everyone's expression. "I'm sorry. I shouldn't say anything."

"If we don't get off this fucking case soon, I'm gonna start kickin' down these walls," Clay promised, jumping out of his chair and starting to pace. "We're all getting twisted listening to this crap!"

Attention swung to Dayton, who had pulled the window down and was climbing onto the sill to smoke a cigarette.

They were called back into the courtroom fifteen minutes later. Rusty Tompkins was still on the stand and the judge told Geiggen he could continue.

"Mr. Tompkins," he said, "I will remind you that you are under oath."

Rusty nodded.

"Did you have sexual intercourse with the—"

"Your Honor!" MacDonald yelled. "The People object! The defense is pursuing a line of questioning that has nothing to do with this case! If defense continues like this, we're going to have no recourse but to call for a mistrial!"

"But it does have to do with this case, Your Honor, as I explained before. Defense needs to establish that Sissy Cook had at least one other rejected lover at the time of the slaying."

"Objection, Your Honor!" MacDonald shouted, slamming the table. "Defense is saying whatever he wants! There is no evidence of any of this! I am warning you, Judge, the People will have no choice but to move for a mistrial!"

"Mr. Geiggen," Judge Williams said sharply, "the objection is sustained. You will confine your line of questioning as we previously discussed. The court will tolerate no more shenanigans. Do I make myself clear?"

Geiggen, facing the jury, rolled his eyes. "Yes, Your Honor," he said. Then he turned around to look at Rusty Tompkins. He narrowed his eyes. A full minute went by. "No further questions of this witness, Your Honor," he said, walking back to the defense table and leaving everyone looking a little stunned.

Kathryn Schnagel had shoved her legal pad in front of MacDonald, which he was reading when the judge asked if he wished to cross-examine. "Yes, Your Honor." He took his time getting up, rereading the top sheet of the pad. He took it with him as he walked over to the jury box. He leaned against the shelf there, so that the witness had to face the jury.

"Mr. Tompkins, I want to ask you a difficult question." He cleared his throat, rereading whatever was on the pad, and then looked up. "Did you have an opportunity to pursue a love affair with the victim, Sissy Cook?"

After a moment, the witness nodded. "Yes."

"And could you please tell the jury if you wanted to have that love affair?"

"No, I didn't."

"You're under oath, Mr. Tompkins," MacDonald said.

"Yes, I know," he said solemnly. "And I swear to God, I didn't want to have a love affair with Sissy. I loved—and love—my wife and family too much."

"Did you have any reason to want to harm Sissy Cook?"

"No, none whatsoever. She was a part of our family."

"That's all, Mr. Tompkins, thank you," MacDonald said.

"Do you have any further questions of this witness, Mr. Geiggen?" the judge asked.

"Yes, Your Honor!" he cried, jumping up. But then he stopped, as if finding that his hands were tied. "No, I guess not, Your Honor." He looked at the jury. "You won't allow me to ask what I need to ask to get to the truth."

"Objection, Your Honor!"

"Mr. Geiggen—" the judge said. She sighed. "This witness is dismissed. Mr. Tompkins, thank you. We'll recess for lunch. Court will resume at two-thirty. May I remind the jury that you are not to discuss any facet of this case with anyone or amongst yourselves. Thank you. Mr. Geiggen, I want to see you in my chambers immediately."

"It's over now, it's over, Rusty," Kathryn Schnagel said to Rusty, physically holding on to his arm.

"*Don't* do *anything*, Rusty," MacDonald ordered, moving around to the other side of him. "Jill, talk to him. It's over. It's okay."

"It's not okay," Rusty growled. "You guys fucked up the search warrant, you fucked up the evidence, you swore to me I wouldn't get called and then I am. You son of bitch, MacDonald, it's no wonder Layton's going to walk with you in charge of this case."

"He won't walk," Kathryn Schnagel said.

"Oh, yeah? Everybody knows he is," Rusty said. "Ask my wife. She knows. Look at her. Why the hell do you think she's here every day? This is the only time she'll ever be able to see that goddamn murderer answer to anyone for anything."

"*Shut up*," MacDonald growled, strong-arming Rusty. "Just shut up."

"I feel so sorry for the wife," Libby said to Melissa and Will outside.

"I feel sorry for Stephen," Melissa said. "He's rushing up to St. Vincent's now. He's terrified his lover's going to die while he's here."

"Yeah, poor guy," Will said. "Well, listen, you guys have a nice lunch. I've got to see this lawyer."

"Good luck."

"Yeah, thanks." Will crossed the street to get to the subway entrance.

Libby and Melissa went to a small restaurant they hadn't tried yet. Libby ordered a sandwich and Melissa had soup and a salad.

"Well, come on," Libby finally burst out. "Have you called Christine?"

Melissa nodded.

"Great! When are you going to see her?"

"You're really into this."

"How could I not be? It's so romantic," Libby declared, eyes bright. "Love is love, and I think it's wonderful." She grinned. "It's also kind of fun to see you stuttering and stammering. It's so sweet. You're so damn capable and businesslike otherwise."

Melissa laughed, and told Libby that Christine was coming Saturday for dinner. Their food arrived and they started to eat.

And then Libby froze, sandwich in midair.

"What's the matter?" Melissa asked.

"Hi," Alex said, coming up to their table. "Fancy meeting you here. Mind if I join you?"

"Normally I wouldn't," Melissa said, "but I did have something rather important I wanted to talk to Libby about."

"Oh, you're always talking to Libby about something," he said, pulling up a chair. "Waiter? Could I get a menu, please?" He turned back around, folding his hands on the corner of the table. "So, what were you talking about?"

When court resumed in the afternoon, Geiggen seemed subdued as he called his next witness, a man named Alfonse Catanio. Alfonse was positively enormous. He had to be six-three or -four and at least three hundred pounds. He was a bodyguard by profession and had formerly worked for Baker Street Security. One of their accounts had been the Danchione Agency, where he was often assigned to accompany Sissy Cook on a shoot.

"Was Ms. Cook in need of protection, Mr. Catanio?"

"Yes. Most of the models are. A lot of kooks out there."

He went on to describe several incidents when people had tried to get too near Sissy Cook, and how frightened the model had been.

"And had Miss Cook ever been frightened by anyone she knew?" Geiggen asked.

"Yes, one time I remember." The bodyguard squinted, trying to think back. "There was an ex-boyfriend that was bugging her."

"Did he have a name?"

"Claude something. I don't really know. She only said something about it when some guy was yelling and banging on the door of the studio one day."

"What did she say?"

"That she hoped it wasn't this guy Claude. She was worried he might do something."

"And when was this, Mr. Catanio?"

"January of, uh, 'ninety-four."

"Do you remember if it was early or late January?"

"Late January. I remember because she had had a problem with another guy around New Year's."

"What kind of problem?"

"Same sort of thing. An ex-boyfriend she didn't want to see."

"Was she fearful of this other boyfriend?"

"Well, yeah, because Sissy wasn't very big, you know? She was tall—but very thin and, you know, a girl. A woman."

They went straight into the cross-examination. MacDonald seemed off to Libby, unfocused, aimless in his questions, and by the time he was finished with Catanio, she felt the defense had come off a lot more convincingly. MacDonald had just gone over and over the bodyguard's testimony, to try and trip up the witness, Libby supposed, but he never did, and only succeeded in provoking the judge, at one point, to reprimand him for being so repetitious.

Reasonable doubt.

What was reasonable doubt? she wondered.

31

ON THURSDAY morning, November 30, there were now three jurors reading Libby's books: Basha, Adelaide, and, of all people, Stephen. "Melissa told me I'd like it," he explained, holding up *When Smiles Meet*.

Libby turned to look at her.

"I read it over the weekend, I forgot to tell you. It was great."

"You're not married, are you?" Adelaide asked Libby. "I don't think you could be married and think love can be like this." She held up a paperback of Libby's first novel.

"Like what?" Elena asked her, looking over Adelaide's shoulder as if she might see something dirty right there on the page.

"Being happy and everything," Adelaide said.

Will, sitting next to Libby, laughed out loud.

"And vhat do you tink being in luff is like?" Debrilla asked.

"It's awful," Adelaide said. "Because you're always worried sick he doesn't love you anymore, or he loves you when you can't stand him."

"Or you get mixed up with someone who's not capable of having a relationship," Alex said, leaning forward to look straight down the table at Libby.

"Oooh," Ronnie murmured, "a low blow from the end of the table. Romeo and Juliet are definitely off."

"Cut some slack there, Ronnie," Clay growled.

Libby looked at Clay in grateful surprise.

"It is my opinion," Mrs. Smythe-Daniels said, "that Cornelia knows a great deal about love. And I think her books are simply marvelous." She looked around the table as if to dare a comment to the contrary. Libby smiled in appreciation.

The jury room lapsed into silence after that. Libby scribbled a note to Will.

How are you? [she wrote.]

[He took a pen out of his jacket pocket. The blue pinstripe.]

Okay. Not great, but okay. This lawyer stuff is awful.

Want to have lunch?

Have to go to the hotel for something. Otherwise, I'd love to.

Oh, well.

Come with me. Get a sandwich. There's a bookstore. I forgot some legal papers and I've got to call my lawyer.

Okay. I'll come.

Are you sure?

Sure. We can talk. Tell me what's going on with Betsy.

Ugh.

It'll all work out, Will.

I wonder.

Libby didn't know which she was enjoying more this morning, feeling close to Will or knowing that Alex was watching them. She was beginning to wonder if she wasn't starting to hate Alex. Lunch yesterday had been unbelievable and unbearable. She had thought Melissa was going to dump her salad on his head, he had tried so hard to get Melissa to leave them alone, which, to Melissa's credit, she hadn't.

"Okay, ladies and gentlemen," Chuck announced, opening the door, "I'm here to take you into court."

This morning's defense witness was a good-looking blonde in her forties named Mary Lou Peterson. She caused a bit of a stir in the gallery as she made her way up to the stand. Mary Lou, it turned out, was the defendant's older sister. Once that was established, Libby could see the strong resemblance.

Geiggen went through her background. She had graduated from Smith College. She was married, for fourteen years, had two children, and lived in Locust Valley, Long Island, the same town as her brother and his family. Yes, they were very close. Always had been. Yes, she had always been a confidante of her brother's. Yes, sadly, she had been acutely aware of her brother's problems with drugs. In fact, she had organized two interventions. No, they had not worked. What had worked?

"Why, this whole horrible murder of Sissy," she said, as if the victim had been her best friend.

"Did you know the deceased, Sissy Cook?" Geiggen asked.

"Yes." There was a murmur in the courtroom.

"How?"

"We worked together on a fund-raiser for a center for abused children."

"Did you like her?"

"In the beginning."

"Why just in the beginning?"

"Well, I introduced her to my brother." She made a slight face of disgust. "It never occurred to me she would make a play for him. Certainly not in the condition he was in."

"And what condition was that?"

"He was a drug addict!" She looked at her brother. "Sorry, Jim, but you were, and it wasn't a pretty sight."

The defendant did not make any sign.

"Mrs. Peterson, for the benefit of the jury," Geiggen said, strolling by the jury box, "could you please relate the sequence of events of the relationship between Sissy Cook and your brother?"

"Surely. It was in September, the fourteenth I think. We had a luncheon."

"Excuse me, Mrs. Peterson. Was the defendant at that lunch?"

"Yes, he was. Although Jim was obviously having a lot of problems, I tried to include him in as many normal things as possible. I guess I hoped by spending more time with the family, he would give up the other."

"The other?"

"The drugs. People who did drugs. People who wanted him to do drugs because he had money."

"I see, continue."

"Well, I introduced Jim to Sissy, because, after all, they were going to be sitting next to each other on the podium. They seemed to get on very well during the luncheon, and the next thing I knew, Jim was leaving with her."

"Do you know where they were going?"

"No." She shook her head. "But it worried me. Sissy was supposed to stay and talk to the press. I didn't understand how she could just abandon her responsibilities and slip out with my brother."

"What were you worried about?"

She sighed. "I worried she used cocaine."

"Objection, Your Honor," MacDonald said. "This is not evidence, this is merely speculation on the part of the witness."

"Your Honor," Geiggen said, "what the witness thought at the time is evidence."

"Objection overruled."

"Thank you, Your Honor." Geiggen strolled back to the jury box. "What happened next, Mrs. Peterson?"

"I went home that evening to Locust Valley, where my sister-in-law, Susie, called me. She wanted to know if Jim had come back with me. I said no, he hadn't, but I was sure he would be along soon."

"What then?"

"Then we talked for a while. Susie's been through a lot with Jim—because of the drugs. And the family has tried very hard to help her through it, because we didn't want to see them split up. Jim—when he wasn't high on something—was otherwise devoted to Susie and the kids. And I knew if he lost them, he wouldn't care about his life anymore and would probably do something terrible."

"Like what?"

"Kill himself."

"Did you ever worry he might kill someone else?"

"Only if it was from passing out behind the wheel again."

"You say 'again'?"

She nodded. "God must have been watching over him, because the police would find Jim passed out on the side of the road. Or sometimes he lost his car and would collapse somewhere else."

"Are you saying that your brother was often unable to physically function when on drugs?"

She nodded. "Yes. It was very sad."

"Let me ask you something, Mrs. Peterson, would it seem consistent with your brother's behavior to drive to a nightclub, cause a scene, come out and forget where he parked his car, and take a cab home?"

"He's done it at least ten times that I know of."

"Okay now, continue with your sequence. You said you talked to your sister-in-law the night after the luncheon in September 1993."

"Yes. She called back about midnight, frantic. Jim hadn't shown up yet."

"What happened next?"

"I went over to Susie's house. To calm her down. At least, keep her company. I thought if she knew I was there, she could sleep."

"What happened then?"

"My brother arrived home, in a cab, around two-thirty."

"Did he appear to be under the influence of drugs?"

"Yes."

"What happened then?"

"I tried to talk to him, down in the living room, and he lost his temper." She hesitated, swallowed. "He said it was my fault, I was the one who had fixed him up with Sissy. I asked what he meant. He said I must have known what she was like."

"Did he explain what he meant by that?"

"He said she did drugs, that they went out to a bar, and then they went to my parents' apartment, where she wanted to have sex." She sighed, looking uncomfortable. "He said he didn't sleep with her, but that he had done a lot of cocaine and had a lot to drink."

"And what happened then?"

"Then he went upstairs to bed. And I went home to my house." She picked up the glass in the witness box and took a sip of water.

Geiggen was strolling around, thinking. Finally, "Did you ever hear of Sissy Cook again, Mrs. Peterson?"

She nodded. "Yes, around Christmas. Jim said she had called him to find out if he knew where she could get some good cocaine."

"Why did he tell you this?"

"He was trying to stay off the stuff. And I guess he thought if he told me that someone I had introduced him to was using drugs, I would know how hard he was trying."

"And did you think he was trying?"

"For the holidays, yes. For the sake of the children."

"And did you hear of Sissy Cook's name again?"

"Not until after the shooting."

"When did you see your brother after the shooting?"

"That morning. My husband and I came into New York. Jim was in custody."

"And what did your brother say?"

She took a deep breath. "He kept crying." She took another deep breath, pressed the bridge of her nose for a minute, cleared her throat, and continued. "He said he didn't do it. He said he lost his car or it was stolen, he didn't know, and he had taken a cab to my parents' apartment, and the next thing he knew, the police had come to arrest him."

"Did you believe him?"

With a little cry, Mary Lou brought a tissue to her mouth and said, softly, in a high voice, "Yes. He was so messed up I couldn't see how he could have walked across the street, much less tried to hurt anyone." She started to cry. "He's never hurt anyone or anything in his life, I swear."

Geiggen waited a moment and then said quietly, "Your Honor, I have no further questions of this witness. May I respectfully request that we break for lunch so the witness has time to compose herself before the cross-examination."

"Boy, I tell you, this case is starting to get to me," Libby sighed. "I don't know what to think anymore."

"Welcome to the club." Will looked at his watch. "We do get a two-hour lunch, though. Shall we try and forget it?"

She smiled. They were walking downtown. A few minutes later, the trial seemed a million miles away. Only this seemed real: walking the streets with Will, smiling, talking over the noise. She was amazed how comfortable she felt with him. And happy. She was having fun. Just being with him.

"You know what?" Will began. "I love spending time with you. I mean, everything's terrific—even though everything in my life is a mess."

She laughed, taking his arm as they negotiated the crowds on the sidewalk.

He stopped and looked at her. A few people bumped them, but he didn't care. "It's not just friendship, Libby. What I feel. You know that, don't you?" He looked as though he was afraid she might hit him.

"I know," she assured him.

They walked to the World Trade Center, to the Vista Hotel, in silence, arm in arm.

"The bookstore's on the next level," Will said once they were in the building. "I'll just be a few minutes. I have to find those papers and call this guy."

Libby said she didn't mind coming with him, if he didn't mind her overhearing his phone call. As soon as she said that, she saw a little color gather in his face. She thought, Does he think . . . ?

And, carrying this thought with her into the elevator, Libby felt a definitive rush of desire. She dared not look at him. They went up to his hotel room. It was very small. A single. There was a chair, though, and Libby took it as Will tossed his coat and jacket over the desk and sat down on the bed. "I just have to call this guy," he said, going through a folder of papers.

Then Libby made her fatal mistake. She wondered whether he really needed to hold the folder on his lap or if maybe . . .

He caught her looking at the papers. "Bills of hers I've paid," he explained, reaching for the phone. He dialed, waited, and when he got someone on the line, he started talking, and absently slid the folder onto the bed and hiked one leg up as he bent to take notes.

He was semi-aroused and the sight went straight through her. He finished his conversation and hung up. "What's wrong?" he asked her. And then, as if he sensed what it was, he blushed scarlet and looked back at the folder and then, fatal mistake #2, Libby caught Will looking down at his crotch—an action which had him quickly trying to hide it again with the folder.

Libby couldn't believe this. With all her heart and soul and body she wanted this man, and she wanted him now.

"Will?" she managed to say. She stood up. "Would you hold me?"

He looked as though she had just taken a shot at him, he was so startled. He swallowed. She walked over and he stood up, holding his arms out. He was trembling slightly. She fell into his arms. She slipped off her heels, so she was her true height, pressing the side of her face against his neck. It was an excellent fit.

"Right now," she murmured, "I want you more than I've ever wanted anyone."

He was still trembling. From restraint. He looked at her, holding her. "Are you sure?"

She nodded and kissed him. They had maybe twenty minutes; she knew it, he knew it. If they were really going to do this, it had to happen now. As if reading her thoughts, he was pulling her down onto the bed, kissing her, kissing her neck, undoing her blouse. Her blouse was off and carefully strewn on the end of the bed. There was a small gasp, a groan, as he ran his hands over her bra, undid it, took her into his hands, and then into his mouth. He was kissing her again and it all moved very quickly now. He tie and shirt were off. Her skirt was off. Panty hose were off. He was in an undershirt and boxer shorts, erection pushing out the front. She took off his undershirt; he slipped off her panties; she slipped off his boxer shorts; they were kissing, lying together fully naked. There was a brief exchange:

"I've only been with Betsy. I don't have any condoms or anything."

"I don't have anything, either," she says, wanting him. "I mean, I'm on the Pill, but I don't—you don't have to worry. We can go ahead."

The feel of him entering her took their breath away. The timing was right, the entry was divine, he was not big, but he was wide in a way her body was thrilled with. Most of all, he wanted her, desperately, as much as she wanted him, and she let herself go, not thinking, only wanting to meet his urgency, to let the moorings tear loose, finally, at last, trusting, needing, knowing this was right, that there was something latent between them marked by a desire she had never known.

It was hard and intense and very wet, and after she came—in waves, throbbing around him—he shuddered, crying, "Libby," and then they crashed, holding each other, slick with perspiration and a million other body liquids, faces glued to each other. After a long minute, he raised his head to look at her. "The best," she said, touching his damp hair. She laughed. "Never in my wildest dreams did I ever think I would ever say such a thing, but it's true. I've never been so satisfied in my life." They kissed and kissed, gentle, cuddling, kissing, hugging, until they saw the time and then, frantic, did a hasty washcloth-bath in the bathroom and got dressed, dashing back to the courthouse.

"I'm sorry," Will apologized to Chuck. They were fifteen minutes late. "The subway got stuck. We should never have taken it."

Reentering the jury room was something else, though. All Libby could imagine was that they reeked of sex and hormones. By this time she was filled with desire again, but one look at Alex took care of that. Somehow, she thought, he knew what had happened.

But she didn't care. Looking at Will, she thought, My God, this is it. I've found him. He turned around and smiled. A soft, gentle smile. She felt as though her heart had been infused with all that was love and light in the world.

And maybe it had been.

32

L IBBY tried to pay attention as Judge Williams gave them a short lecture on the importance of the jury being on time. It wouldn't occur to Libby until hours later that the judge had been talking to her and Will.

The afternoon was lost on her. Oh, she heard the cross-examination of the defendant's sister, all right. And much of what transpired registered, but it registered in a digital way, as does a credit card swipe through a self-serve gas pump. Emotionally, perhaps even spiritually, Libby was miles and miles away, lofting in a lovely warm place, full of kind breezes, comfort, and peace, far, far away from this trial.

Jill wondered whether Mary Lou Peterson would go to jail if she was proven to have lied and lied and lied again in her testimony. All she could hope was that MacDonald would do a decent cross. By this time, Jill had a hell of a lot more faith in Kathryn Schnagel than she did in MacDonald. And it hadn't helped to hear Rusty cite chapter and verse all the mistakes MacDonald had made in the trial thus far.

Of course, it was always easy to play Monday-morning quarterback. But Jill's instincts told her that Geiggen was scoring points right and left with the jury; if all he had to do was raise the possibility of reasonable doubt on just *one* point in the prosecution's case, then Layton had a very good chance of getting off.

Jill looked at Juror #3. Cornelia Winslow. Kathryn had shown her a copy of one of her books, written under the name Elizabeth Winslow. Kathryn was reading it; she said any insight into how a juror's mind worked would be invaluable when it came to summations.

Jill wished like hell Kathryn was doing the summation.

"Good afternoon, Mrs. Peterson," MacDonald began, opening his cross-examination of the defendant's sister, trying to be warm—something he would never be in real life, Jill knew.

Mary Lou nodded at him.

"Mrs. Peterson, you testified at length this morning about the sequence of events concerning your brother and the victim, Sissy Cook."

"Yes."

"What I would like to do is retrace the events as you related them, and ask you a few more questions."

She nodded.

He had a legal pad, which he now placed on the shelf by the jury. "You are very open about your brother's past drug addiction. That's good, it helps the jury understand how confusing and complicated this case is."

"Objection, Your Honor," Geiggen said. "Prosecution is supposed to be conducting a cross-examination, not giving a sermon from the mount."

There was some laughter in the courtroom.

"Objection sustained. Mr. MacDonald, please begin your cross-examination. Mr. Geiggen, there is no need for further embellishment from *you.*"

More laughter.

MacDonald went into a careful cross about how the witness had met Sissy, and focused for some time on why Mary Lou had liked her. Sissy had been generous, a hard worker, and was easy to get along with. No, Mary Lou had to admit, she had not noticed any signs that Sissy might use drugs. When MacDonald brought her up to the time of the charity luncheon, where her brother met Sissy, he grew tougher.

"After the time you say your brother left the luncheon with the victim, Sissy Cook, did you ever have another opportunity to speak with her?"

"No."

"And so, everything after that point—including the reason why they left the luncheon together—was told to you by your brother?"

She hesitated. "Yes."

"Did he tell you why they left together that afternoon?"

"No, I don't think so. He only told me about the night. When they went to a bar and then back to one of our parents' corporate apartments."

"I see. So you really have no idea why Sissy Cook left the luncheon an hour early, do you?"

"No. I guess not."

"And you really don't know for sure if her reason for leaving even had anything to do with your brother?"

"I don't understand."

"If, for example, Mrs. Peterson, Sissy Cook left the luncheon an hour early because she didn't feel well, you couldn't deny it, because you don't know why she left."

She shrugged.

"Yes or no?"

"Yes, I guess I couldn't know why she left."

"And you don't know if your brother simply followed her out, as opposed to actually leaving with her?"

"I don't know."

"Very good." He looked at his notes. "Okay, moving on to that evening, in Locust Valley, when your brother failed to return home. You said your sister-in-law, Susie Layton, called to ask if the defendant had returned with you."

"Yes."

"This was about what time?"

"About six."

"Mrs. Peterson, did your brother often fail to show up when he was expected?"

"I don't know if it was often."

"Well, let me ask you, did your brother ever lie to his wife about his whereabouts?"

"Objection, Your Honor," Geiggen complained. "How is the witness to know? She's not the defendant's wife."

"Sustained."

"Okay. Okay," MacDonald said. "Did your sister-in-law ever tell you that your brother had lied to her?"

"About what?"

"About anything, Mrs. Peterson."

"Well, yes."

"Did your brother ever lie to you?"

"Yes. But I've explained—he was very ill."

"While he was ill, Mrs. Peterson, and I remind you, you are under oath, did your brother lie to you more than, say, five times?"

She nodded.

"Yes?"

"Yes."

"More than ten times?"

Hesitation. "Yes."

"What did he lie to you about?"

"His drug use."

"About whether he was using drugs or not?"

"Yes."

"Did he lie about if he possessed drugs?"

"Yes."

"Did he lie about the money he spent on drugs?"

"Yes."

"Did he lie to you about his whereabouts?"

"Yes."

"Did he ever lie about who he was with when he was missing?"

"Yes."

"Okay. Very good." He took his time framing his next question. "Now, about your relationship with your sister-in-law. Did she often call you about your brother?"

"Yes."

"Why?"

"Because they had children, and she was trying to hold together a family and run a household. And so she quite naturally turned to me when things weren't going well."

"I see." Pause. "Did your brother have a job?"

"Yes. He worked for my father's company."

"In what capacity?"

"He was in customer relations."

"Did anyone at your father's company ever call you about your brother?"

"Yes."

"For what reason?"

"You know, the usual things, when someone's sick on drugs."

"Could you tell the jury what the usual things are?"

"Not being able to find him."

"That's all?"

"Yes."

"Mrs. Peterson, did anyone ever call you from your father's company about your brother stealing money from the firm?"

She flushed red and did not answer.

"Is it true that your brother was accused of stealing money from your father's company?"

"Yes."

"More than once?"

"Yes."

"And isn't it true, Mrs. Peterson, that your brother, when caught, lied extensively in an attempt to clear himself?"

Slowly, quietly. "Yes."

"More than once?"

"Yes."

"Okay." He went back to look at his notes, turned a page on the pad and then looked up. "Mrs. Peterson, were you ever called to the Rogers Elementary School because of disciplinary problems with two of your brother's children, Trudy and Michael Layton?"

The witness looked to the judge. "Your Honor," she pleaded, "they're children."

"Answer the question, please, Mrs. Peterson."

Resigned. "Yes."

"Could you please explain to the jury why the school called you and not your sister-in-law, Susie Layton?"

"They couldn't reach Susie."

"Why couldn't they reach her?"

"The phone was out of order."

"And why was the phone out of order, Mrs. Peterson? Do you know?"

"My brother had broken it."

"Broken it? Or ripped it out of the wall and hit his wife with it?"

Geiggen started yelling objections, but MacDonald had scored. The objection was sustained and the judge told the jury to disregard that re-mark, although to Libby, that seemed rather unlikely.

The cross-examination went on all afternoon, Mary Lou Peterson sag-ging lower and lower in the witness chair as MacDonald painted a por-trait of an older sister desperate to bail out her brother's family as he, the brother, systematically stole, lied, and cheated to feed an insatiable desire for drugs. It seemed apparent from the cross-examination that if the murder of Sissy Cook hadn't happened, the defendant and the whole Layton family might well be dead by now, so precipitous was their life as a family.

Wrapping up, MacDonald said, "Mrs. Peterson, you testified this morning that after your brother was arrested for the murder of Sissy Cook, he kept crying and telling you he didn't do it."

"Yes."

"Mrs. Peterson, and I remind you once again that you are under oath, had your brother ever said words to that effect to you before?"

"About what?"

"About anything, Mrs. Peterson. His drug use, his whereabouts, who he had been with—"

"Objection, Your Honor," Geiggen said. "The prosecution is badger-ing the witness."

"Overruled, but prosecution will be more direct in his questions so the witness may answer them."

"Mrs. Peterson, my question is, based on the experiences you had with your brother when he was ill on drugs, did you have any reason to believe he was telling you the truth?"

"I don't know." She was shaking her head.

"Mrs. Peterson, had your brother ever lied to you before?"

"Yes, I told you yes."

"He had lied to you many times about where he had been?"

"Yes."

"He had lied to you many times about who he had been with?"

"Yes."

"He had lied to you many times about what he had been doing?"

"Yes."

"And all knowledge you have of what happened between your brother and Sissy Cook from the time they left that charity luncheon where they first met to the time that Sissy Cook was murdered was told to you by your brother?"

"Yes."

"And your knowledge of what happened came to you only from your brother? No one else told you anything about their relationship?"

"No one else told me anything," she confirmed.

"Thank you, Mrs. Peterson, that will be all."

Geiggen was up in a flash. "Mrs. Peterson, would you say that you know your brother better than anyone else in the world?"

"Yes, I would."

"And do you think he is capable of having someone murdered?"

"*Never.*"

"Thank you, that will be all, Your Honor."

Court was dismissed for the day.

Chuck unlocked the door to the jury room so the jurors could get their things. Libby and Will smiled discreetly at each other, left together, but did not speak until they were downstairs in the lobby. "I don't know what to say," he murmured, allowing her to go out the door first.

Outside, she turned around. "What would you like to say?"

"That I want to be with you tonight more than anything in the world."

"Well . . ." She opened her bag to get out a piece of paper and a pen. She scribbled her address and handed it to him.

"Really?" he said.

"I can't think of anything nicer," she told him.

He grinned. "I've just got to go to the office for a bit and then I'll be up."

"And stay over, won't you?"

He laughed, pleased—thrilled. "What ever happened to judicious discretion and waiting for the trial to be over?"

"We won't talk about the trial."

He walked her down into the subway and to the uptown platform. As the crowds surged onto the train, he kissed her and helped her on. The doors closed, he waved, and the train pulled out.

Someone bumped him from behind. "Out of the way, dweeb," Alex said.

When she reached her apartment, Libby was frantic. What was happening to her? Wasn't this crazy?

No, this was wonderful and she knew it.

"Okay, gang," she told the cats. "Be charming, okay? I like this man. A lot."

Dust. Vacuum. Stack magazines and newspapers. Flowers. Flowers? No time. Shower. The phone rang. "I'm on my way," he said.

"Oh."

"Are you okay?" He sounded worried. "Did you change your mind? If you want to be alone, I'll understand."

"Come," she said. "Please, I'm just scared. And happy."

In less than a half hour, Will was there, handing her a bouquet of flowers, admiring her apartment and making friends with her cats. Libby couldn't believe it, but Missy didn't hide under the bed as she always did, but followed Will around until he sat down on the couch in the living room. She poured him a beer and brought the glass out to him.

"I'm so nervous," she said.

He held up his hand. "Look." There was the slightest tremor.

She handed him the glass; he put it down on a coaster and reached up to pull her down in his lap. She sat there as if she had been doing it for years, and they started to kiss, to whisper, to explore.

Within an hour they were in her bedroom. In another four, Missy and Sneakers slipped in, thinking surely things would have quieted down by now.

33

W HEN Will awakened Friday morning, he couldn't imagine where he was, because his watch alarm had gone off but there was no watch, no nightstand, only a very large tiger cat staring into his face.

Oh, right. He was in heaven. "Hi, Missy Mouse," he said.

He felt a hand slide over his waist and up his chest, coming to rest on his collarbone. He rolled over. "I've got to run to the office before court," he whispered, kissing Libby on the forehead.

She murmured something, eyes still closed. One eye opened. "May I get you some breakfast?"

"It's not breakfast I need," he whispered, sliding on top of her.

Forty minutes later he was showered and on his way. He smiled to himself; long, lazy bouts of lovemaking with Libby were wonderful, but the other was pretty sensational, too.

Libby. He could hardly believe it.

At the office he was happy to find a message on his voice mail from the horrid lawyer Jerry had found him to deal with Betsy's lawyer. His smile was wiped off by the next message, though. It was from Betsy, left at about two in the morning, begging him to meet with her to talk. She said she couldn't stand the way things were, that she *must* talk to him. *Please.* She was staying at the apartment now. She had tried to reach him at the Vista. Where was he? He was to call her, please, and meet with her tonight.

Sighing, he called his apartment. Betsy answered. Before they could get into a row, he said of course he'd meet with her tonight. What about at the apartment, eight o'clock? She agreed, sounding relieved just to hear the sound of his voice.

When he walked into the jury room at ten minutes to ten, Alex glared at him. Fine with him. He chatted with Melissa. And then, at about one minute to ten, Libby came flying in, face flushed. They said good morning. As the morning progressed, Will noticed that the flush in Libby's cheeks did not fade.

Then he realized it was friction burns. From his five o'clock shadow. And he felt happier than he could remember.

When court resumed, Geiggen called the next witness for the defense, Officer Kirk Balis. After he was sworn in, they learned that Balis was with the precinct in which the defendant's car had been found in the early morning of February 10, 1994, down near the end of Morton Street by the Hudson River. It had not been damaged. The keys were in it, still in the ignition.

"And did you dust the steering wheel for fingerprints?" Geiggen asked.

The officer said yes, he had, and then walked the jury through his qualifications and then the fingerprinting process itself. Yes, the witness told Geiggen, there had been another set of fingerprints on the steering wheel of the Jaguar, and the police lab verified they had been left recently. Yes, they had run the fingerprints through the computer, but no, they did not match any fingerprints they had on file.

"And you are absolutely positive that the second set of fingerprints do not belong to the defendant, James Bennett Layton?" Geiggen said.

"Yes."

He turned the witness over to MacDonald for the cross-examination.

MacDonald looked very disturbed and frustrated about something. He asked the officer if the lab could tell whether the second set of fingerprints had been the last set left on the wheel.

"They couldn't tell for sure," the officer said.

"Did they have an educated opinion?" MacDonald asked.

"Objection, Your Honor," Geiggen said, "and I request a sidebar."

The judge agreed and the lawyers went up to the bench for quite some time, arguing about something. Then the judge sent the jury back to the jury room for a short recess.

Libby and Will sat in the corner, chatting quietly, Will filling her in on his talk with Betsy earlier in the morning.

"Be careful with her," Libby warned him.

"I will be," he promised.

Libby didn't say what she was thinking: that the partner leaving always thought he or she was in no danger of getting pulled back into the relationship at a parting-of-the-ways meeting. Didn't he remember the last time he and Betsy "talked"? And how guilty he had felt the next morning?

"I don't want to push," Will said quietly, "but I was hoping we could spend some time together tomorrow. I need to go to the office during the day—"

She was smiling, feeling warm all over, the way she had when she was a child and knew Christmas was coming.

They agreed that he'd call her in the morning, between ten and noon, and they'd figure out what they felt like doing. (As if they didn't know.)

Chuck came in to bring them back to the courtroom. In the hall, Libby felt a presence over her shoulder. It was Alex. "For your sake," he hissed in her ear, "I hope it's for the money, 'cause a puny little squirt like that's gonna be a puny little squirt, if you get my drift."

"To the contrary," Libby said quietly, turning around. "You see, Alex, I already know all there is to know. And I've never been more satisfied." And then she walked into the courtroom, berating herself for saying what she had. It could only cause trouble.

Once the jury was present and accounted for, Judge Williams apologized but said they required more time for the sidebar and so she was going to dismiss them until three o'clock.

By the time she got to the jury room, the thought of a long lunch had Libby half aroused already. As they got their coats, she shyly asked Will if he was going to go to the office.

"I don't know," he said, guiding her by the elbow out of the jury room and into the hall. "If you want to have lunch with me, then we'll have lunch. If you want to come to my office with me, you're welcome to come—"

"And if I suggested," she murmured, "we have room service in your room at the Vista?" She pushed the elevator button and turned around. He was beaming.

"I'd think you were a mind reader," he told her.

Melissa grabbed a subway uptown and then took a cab crosstown to her office. "Hi. I have to leave here at two-thirty," she told a startled Bonnie.

"Fine. You've got ten thousand phone messages," Bonnie said, handing Melissa a sheath of top copies from the phone log, "and you better check your E-mail. There are also messages on privacy voice mail, and . . ."

Melissa looked at her expectantly.

"You can join the department meeting in progress, if you want, in conference room one, so the gang can remember what you look like."

"Just let me hang up my coat," Melissa said, going into her office and hanging it up on the back of the door. She walked over to glance at the mail on her desk, and picked up the phone for her privacy voice mail, those messages only she knew the code to retrieve. One message was from her colleague Roger, wanting to talk to her about a job offer he had. The second was from Christine, just wanting to say hello, and to say how much she was looking forward to Saturday.

Christine. *Come on, Melissa, start breathing.*

She ran down the hall to the department meeting.

"Melissa!" her boss cried as she entered. He turned to the group. "Say hallelujah."

"Hallelujah!" the gang said obediently.

"The trial's not over yet," Melissa said, slipping into a seat, "we just have a recess until three."

"Don't say hallelujah," her boss said.

There was silence around the table, and then laughter.

"We'll take you any way we can get you, Melissa," her boss told her. "The Cat People love you."

If they only knew.

Lunch had been heaven. They couldn't wait to get their clothes off. And this time they could lie there in bed afterward, eating, kissing, talking, laughing, reveling in the warmth, wrapped in the soft, thick terry-cloth hotel robes that slid open easily.

They had showered and dressed again. And had gone back to court.

Sitting here in the courtroom, Libby could still feel the pressure of Will's lips on hers.

The next witness called by the defense was Pascale Sabri, a guy about fifty or so, who had worked as the eleven-to-seven night concierge at 912 Park Avenue. According to Pascale, he was on duty in the early morning hours of Thursday, February 10, 1994, when the defendant came in at around two in the morning.

"And what condition was he in, Mr. Sabri?"

"High as a kite and drunk as a skunk," the concierge reported, provoking laughter around the courtroom.

"How did you know?"

"He walked into the wall by the elevator."

More laughter.

Geiggen good-naturedly shrugged. "And you say he came home around two in the morning?"

"Yes, sir."

"How can you be sure?"

"I looked at the clock."

"I see. And why was that?"

"Mr. Jim—that's what I call him, Mr. Jim—sometimes his family would call to see if he was staying in one of the apartments. So whenever he came in, I would check the clock."

"Why?"

"Mr. Layton—senior—he would pay me extra to keep track." He paused. "He was worried about Mr. Jim."

Before MacDonald began the cross-examination, he seemed to have some sort of an argument with Kathryn Schnagel. She kept shoving an index card in front of him and he kept shoving it back, muttering something with a frown.

"Mr. MacDonald?" Judge Williams said. "I said you may begin the cross-examination."

"Yes," MacDonald said, standing, obviously flustered over something. "Please, Your Honor, your patience for one moment." And then he rifled through his legal pad, had another muttering fit with his associate, and then finally began his cross, standing right there behind the table. "Mr. Sabri, you testified that the defendant came in around two in the morning?"

"Yes."

"If you looked at the clock, as you said you did, why didn't you see exactly what time it was?"

"I did."

"Well, then, what time was it?"

"Around two o'clock," the witness said.

"Are you saying, Mr. Sabri, that you don't remember the exact time?"

"I remember it was around two o'clock."

"Does that mean, Mr. Sabri, it could have been two-oh-five?"

"I don't know."

"Could it have been two-ten?"

"I don't know."

MacDonald scratched his head. "Mr. Sabri, how can you know what time the defendant came in when you don't know what time it was when the defendant came in?"

"Objection, Your Honor," Geiggen said. "The prosecutor is badgering the witness. He's already testified what time it was."

"Your Honor, the witness has *not* testified to what time it was. I am merely trying to help him refresh his memory."

"Objection overruled, but Mr. MacDonald, you will assist the witness, not browbeat him."

There was a little laughter. In the meantime, Kathryn had shoved her index card at MacDonald again.

"Okay, Mr. Sabri, let's get the facts straight, then. You saw the defendant come home in the early morning of February tenth, 1994?"

"Yes."

"You think it was somewhere around two o'clock, but you aren't sure of the exact time?"

"Yes."

"Objection, Your Honor," Geiggen said. "Prosecution is putting words into the witness's mouth."

"Your Honor." MacDonald made a show of frustration.

"Objection overruled."

"As I said, Mr. Sabri, you think the defendant came back to the apartment around two, but you aren't sure of the exact time."

Looking at Geiggen now, the witness appeared upset. "No."

"No?" MacDonald said. "You do remember the exact time?"

"No," the witness said again, looking confused now about what he was saying.

"Okay, so you don't remember . . ." MacDonald's voice trailed off as Kathryn frantically wrote something on his legal pad.

"Miss Schnagel," Judge Williams said, "what are you doing?"

"Making a note for counsel, Your Honor," she said.

"Do you think this is appropriate, to be interrupting the prosecutor during his cross-examination?"

"Perhaps we need a short recess," Kathryn suggested. The look of fury that MacDonald gave her provoked some laughter in the gallery.

"Yes, perhaps we do," Judge Williams said. And she dismissed the jury for ten minutes.

"What the hell is going on?" Rusty demanded, bursting in on the prosecution team, Jill following behind.

"Get out of here!" MacDonald directed.

"Whatever it is, I trust her a hell of a lot more than I do you. You've missed so many goddamn points, MacDonald, if you don't start listening to someone else, you're going to blow this case."

"Get out of here," MacDonald said.

Rusty looked to Kathryn. "*Make him* listen to you."

The Tompkinses backed out of the room and closed the door. "What do you think it's about?" Jill said.

"My guess is she's trying to stop his cross-examination. He's made his point, the concierge really didn't know what time it was—so he should stop. But he never does! He makes a point and then goes on until he either messes up or completely obscures the point. If he doesn't cut it out, all the jury's going to remember is what Geiggen says."

Court did not resume until close to four-thirty. Libby spent the delay pretending to read, but simply looking at the same line, thinking about what she and Will had done that day. It was like losing ballast, and finally lifting off this earth so at last she could see it. And feel the wind and the sun, and the gentle touch of what surely must belong to God.

"You look very pretty today, my dear," Mrs. Smythe-Daniels said to her.

"Thank you," Libby said, wishing she could be her mother instead of the one she had.

Once the jury was back in the courtroom, Judge Williams said MacDonald could continue with his cross-examination.

"Mr. Sabri, could you tell the jury, please, do you know the *exact* time the defendant arrived at nine twelve Park Avenue in the early morning of February tenth, 1994?"

"I looked at the—"

"Yes or no, Mr. Sabri. Do you know the exact time the defendant arrived?"

The defendant sighed. "No."

"Thank you," MacDonald said gently. "The people have no further questions of this witness, Your Honor." He sat down.

Geiggen looked vaguely surprised, but recovered quickly, said something to his assistants, and stood up to redirect. "Mr. Sabri, the apartment building you worked in, nine twelve Park Avenue, is located at what cross street?"

"Between Eightieth and Eighty-first."

"So, let's see, that would be about sixty-six blocks north of Fourteenth Street, and five blocks east of Eighth Avenue?"

"Yes."

"Do you think that in the condition Mr. Layton was in, he would have been capable of driving that distance?"

"No. He could barely walk."

"And how long do you think it would take, approximately, to get from Fourteenth Street and Seventh Avenue to nine twelve Park Avenue in a cab at two in the morning?"

He thought about it. "Oh, I would say, in a fast cab, twenty minutes."

"So if the time of the shooting was a little after two A.M. and the defendant had gone straight home, he still couldn't have reached nine twelve Park Avenue until at least twenty-five minutes after two."

"Yes."

"Did the defendant come in at two twenty-five?"

"No, it was around two."

"Thank you, Mr. Sabri. No further questions, Your Honor."

The witness was dismissed and the judge adjourned the trial until ten o'clock sharp on Monday morning. She told the jurors to have a good weekend, but to stay away from newspapers, newsmagazines, and radio and TV news. And, of course, they were not to discuss the case with anyone or amongst themselves.

Will, Libby, Mrs. Smythe-Daniels, Melissa, and Stephen left the jury room together, talking. In the elevator, Libby asked Stephen about his friend, Bill, and Stephen sighed and said things were not very good. It was nearing the end now. The doctor said he should think about transferring him to a hospice. With the periods of dementia Bill was experiencing, and his sight so badly deteriorated, home care was no longer possible.

They murmured their condolences. When they reached the lobby, Mrs. Smythe-Daniels whispered to Libby, "It is that young man's lover who's dying?" When Libby nodded, Mrs. Smythe-Daniels called out to Stephen. "There's a group I know," she said to him, "that might be of help to the friends and family of your friend."

The group just stood there, looking mildly astonished.

Mrs. Smythe-Daniels had taken out a card from her wallet and was handing it to Stephen. "My nephew died of AIDS," she said softly. "It was not an easy death. Not for him, not for our family. But these people helped me and my sister a great deal. It's the Manhattan Center for the Living. You may have heard of it."

"Will wonders never cease?" Will said when he and Libby parted ways with the others.

"It's funny," Libby said, "she reminds me so much of my mother. And yet with Mrs. Smythe-Daniels there is someone back there—behind the front, you know what I mean?"

"You shouldn't be too hard on your mother," he said, taking her hand.

"Why on earth not?"

"She brought us together," he said, giving her hand a squeeze.

Downstairs at the token booth, Libby and Will kissed briefly good-bye, reluctant to part even if only until the next day. Then Libby went to the uptown side and Will to the downtown. Libby tried to see him across the tracks so she could wave, but the platform was mobbed and she couldn't.

All he had to do, Will thought, was stop in at the office and then meet with Betsy at eight. If he could get through this meeting, he would be home free. At least, free to be with Libby.

Libby.

It was so extraordinary what had happened. *She* was so extraordinary, but what was really so unbelievable to him was that she had fallen for him as heavily as he had for her, and neither had really seen it coming.

He hopped onto the local and hopped back off at the Wall Street stop, fighting the rush-hour crowd coming down the stairs to get out. He took the indirect route to work, preferring the little side streets this time of night in order to avoid the worst of the Wall Street crush eager to get home. Although dark and usually full of potholes, the little streets offered some space and a sense of quiet. He cut down one street and turned down the wide alley leading to the back service entrance of Connors, Morganstern. The guard, Will knew, would let him in.

Any man who took the service elevator up to his floor so he could avoid most of the people he worked with, Will also knew, was a man who should be thinking about changing jobs. And he would. Now he would.

With Libby in his life, he felt sure he could pretty much do anything.

34

B Y NOON on Saturday Libby was worried. Will had not called. Okay, let's not freak out, she told herself. Let's go over the facts:

1. Will was meeting Betsy last night at his apartment.
2. Will was going to settle things once and for all.
3. Will promised to call her between ten and noon on Saturday.
4. Will had not called.
5. Will was back with Betsy and he didn't know what to say to her.

No! Stop it! You don't know that. Just call him at the office. He's probably working and forgot the time.

She called his office and got his voice mail. She left a message that she was home and to please call her when he got a chance.

She felt awful. And scared. And terribly alone. There were very real reasons people weren't supposed to jump into relationships. And yet, somehow, she thought it was the only way she and Will could have found each other, because once the trial was over, he would go his way and she would go hers, back to two separate worlds that would keep them from ever running into each other again.

So what had happened? Where was he? Oh, God, truly, she couldn't believe he would do this. Not now. Not after what they had done. And said.

"No, I understand," Melissa said, feeling her stomach sink with disappointment.

"His fever went up to a hundred and three last night—"

"Christine, really," Melissa said, "I do understand. I wouldn't want you to leave him."

Pause. "Do you like children?"

"Yes. Not too much in the old days, though. Children have a habit of wanting to laugh and giggle and play just when you're thinking of committing suicide. They're definitely not good for self-indulgent depression."

Christine laughed. "Well, listen, I was thinking, is there any possibility I could talk you into coming out here tonight and joining us for pizza and *The Greatest Stars of the NHL?*"

At five o'clock Libby thought to hell with it, it was better to know the worst than to know nothing at all, and she called information. Klein, William Seymour. Gramercy Park North. They gave her the number and she dialed.

"Hello?" a woman answered.

Oh, God, she was there. Still there. *Betsy.*

Libby hung up. And then, slowly, she sat down and held her face in her hands.

Renting a car in New York City was such a pain in the neck. Not only did the agencies here charge the highest rates in the nation, but they were normally insulted at the idea of renting a car for a single day of the weekend. However, it was Saturday already, and so Melissa was allowed to take an unrented car from the agency located down the street.

She missed having a car. A lot. Driving was to a Los Angelino what mass transit was to a New Yorker. Vital. A way of life. Freedom to go wherever you wanted to go.

She tried not to think too much about where she was going. In fact, she was trying to think about it as an errand of mercy, visiting a friend stuck at home. The notion that romance and a child could exist under one roof—to be interested in some child's *mother*—was . . . Was—

Well, grown up for a start.

Like she had to be fully aware of what she was doing.

And she was. Now she was. For sure.

She shot out the Holland Tunnel and was in Montclair within thirty minutes, the directions Christine had given her sitting in her lap. When she reached Valley Road, she wondered a bit at it. She didn't know why, but when she thought of New Jersey she thought of oil tanks and beaches, not steep wooded hills and wide, windy roads.

She slowed down. The landmarks were just as Christine had described. The stone entrance way at the end of the drive, the lanterns on top, the number on the wooden mailbox. Way up the hill, there was the blaze of lights of what looked to be a very big house. She drove up the driveway, heart pounding, asking herself yet again what she was doing.

Living my life for a change, she answered.

The house was not quite as large as it looked from the street, for it was built lengthwise, along the top of the ridge, and a great wraparound porch in front added to the illusion of depth. It was from around the 1920s, she guessed.

There was a separate three-car garage. Two doors of which were open. In one she could see the Lexus, in the other a Cherokee.

Christine was waving through the kitchen door as she parked. "You found us!" she called, opening the door.

"Your directions were excellent," Melissa said, walking toward the house. She stopped. And sniffed. The air smelled wonderful.

"It's the pine grove," Christine told her. "You should hear it when the wind's blowing. The kids used to think we were haunted."

Melissa went into the kitchen and recognized immediately that she was wrong again—if the kitchen was any indication, this house was tremendous. It was an old-fashioned kitchen with wood beams and a brick wall, a tremendous six-burner stove and a pantry off to the side.

Christine was wearing blue jeans and a pale blue cotton sweater. Melissa had never seen her like this. She liked it.

"Let me take your coat," Christine said, stepping forward to help her take it off. After she took it, Christine took her hand for a moment. "I'm so very glad you came."

"Me, too," Melissa assured her. "Nervous, though."

"Relax," Christine said. Then in a louder voice, she said, "Come on, I'll give you a tour. I told you Eric's here because he's sick, but Steve went on to his cousin's, so you'll have to meet him another time."

Christine walked her through the massive living room, full of chintz and early-American furniture and paintings of dogs and horses and landscapes, pausing only at the piano to point out pictures. Eric. Nine. Steve, six and half. Their house on the Cape. Her ex. Handsome, yes— maybe Melissa could give her some advice about how to get him into a rehab. The way he was she wouldn't let the boys be alone with him, for fear he might crash the car or burn down the house.

There was a small cozy den, a formal dining room, a big screened-in porch in back, the verandah out front, and then a playroom, where they found Eric. He was sitting in flannel pajamas, slippers, and robe, working on some kind of three-dimensional jigsaw puzzle. The TV set was on in the corner.

"Eric," Christine said, "I'd like you to meet my friend Melissa Grant."

Eric looked over. He was a cute kid, blond like his mother, but with large soft brown eyes. Melissa could tell he wasn't up to scratch; he had that slightly beaten air that children do when they're sick. "Hi," he said.

"Hi," Melissa said. She took a few steps over. "Empire State Building?"

"Yeah. It's pretty hard. Mom's been helping me."

"You did this part all by yourself," Christine said, pointing out part of the puzzle.

It was so strange to see her in this role. She looked so natural, so right with Eric, and yet Melissa found her alluring as ever. Maybe more so.

"We're going to eat very soon," Christine told Eric, touching his hair. "The Domino man is coming. Drink up your juice, will you? It really does help."

Eyes on his puzzle, Eric dutifully reached over for his glass and sipped orange juice through a straw.

They went upstairs for a brief tour. Christine's bedroom was a knock-out. It had huge windows looking out over the front and side of the house, and a king-sized bed, a chaise lounge, and overstuffed chairs, all covered in light, breezy colors and fabrics. There was a guest room with both a double bed and twin bed in it, and then there were the boys' rooms, full of the usual junk, a set of bunk beds in both. Then, up on the third floor, part of the attic had been finished as an office/studio for Christine, complete with a window looking south.

There she turned around to face Melissa. "How are you holding up?"

"Great," Melissa said.

"Come here," Christine murmured, holding open her arms. Melissa went to her and Christine held her, rubbing her back. They stood there like that until the doorbell rang. "The Domino man," Christine said, giving her a soft kiss on the mouth.

The rest of the evening was very relaxed and pleasant. They set up TV tables in the den and ate pizza and salad, and watched an ice hockey video. When Melissa let it slip that Wayne Gretzky of the Los Angeles Kings had done a charity benefit with her father's production company once, she had Eric's complete attention. And when she answered yes, she had gone to some of the Kings' games, and proved to Eric that she did indeed understand the basics of the game, he thereafter shared his observations about the video with her instead of his mother.

Later he went up to bed to read for a while, and Christine went up to make sure he took his medication. Melissa walked back into the living room, looking at the pictures, thinking how happy families always looked in pictures and how little one could tell about the problems haunting them behind the scenes.

"He likes you," a voice said from behind her.

She turned around. It was Christine, arms crossed, leaning against the archway. She pushed off to approach her. "He wanted to know if you're a work friend or a friend-friend."

"The difference?"

"He wants to know if I really like you or if I *have* to like you because Uncle Mark and Aunt Emily said it would be good for the family business."

Melissa smiled. "I liked him, too."

"Normally I can't get him to sit still. I guess there are advantages to a touch of the flu now and then."

They stood there, smiling at each other. Melissa thought she had never seen anyone so attractive in her life. Finally she spoke. "I've had such a nice evening, Christine."

"Are you going?"

"I think I should. Don't you?"

Christine stepped closer to her, taking her hands, inhaling deeply and then exhaling slowly. She nodded. "I keep telling myself to take this slowly."

"Me, too." Her own voice was so faint she barely heard it.

"I think you're wildly attractive, you know," Christine murmured.

"The feeling is mutual, I assure you," Melissa murmured back.

Christine kissed her softly, lingering a bit. And then she pulled back. "Okay, you better go." She smiled. "Oh! Before I forget . . ." She dropped Melissa's hands and walked over to the bookcase to take something down. "This isn't your friend Libby, is it? The one on jury duty?"

Melissa had to laugh. Christine was holding a copy of *When Smiles Meet*. "Yes, that's her."

"I like this woman," Christine declared, coming back with the book. "I feel like she's been my guardian angel, sending you to me."

Libby had finally managed to fall asleep when the in-house phone rang. For a minute, she thought she was still in her dream, at 912 Park Avenue, and it was the witness Pascale calling to find out what time the defendant had come home. She shook off her disorientation and got out of bed to go to the front hall. "Hello?"

"William Klein is here to see you," the night concierge announced.

Adrenaline immediately surged through her—relief, too. "He is? Great! Send him right up." She bolted for her robe, threw some water on her face (although nothing but nothing would help the swelling around her eyes, from crying herself to sleep), brushed her hair (but not too much, she didn't want to look too prepared), and there was a knock on the door. She opened it.

Alex.

Before she could react, he pushed his way in. He smelled of liquor. "Nice apartment." He bent over to hold his hand out to Sneakers. "Hi, Kitty."

Still holding the door open, Libby pulled her robe tighter. "What do you want, Alex?"

"Oh, I just wanted to say hi," he said, walking ahead into the living room and plopping himself down on the sofa. "I figured if I used the dweeb's name, you wouldn't be so nervous. You know a guy like that could never hurt you."

How wrong you are, she thought. "Is that why you're here, Alex? To hurt me?" Libby said, riveted to the door, grateful she had so many neighbors.

"Come on, Libby," he said, gesturing. "I'm just here to apologize and bury the hatchet. I was at the Outback Bar down the street and I just walked over."

"Okay, the hatchet's buried, Alex. And I think you should go home now. I was asleep."

He studied her expression for a moment and then he stood up. "I'm sorry, I guess I shouldn't have done this. I had a couple of beers, you know how it is."

"I think you better go home," she told him.

"Don't be mad, Lib." He came to stand in front of her. "All I want is for you not to be mad at me."

"I'm not, Alex, but I think you better go."

"Okay." But then he jerked the door away from her and closed it, pulled her to him, and forced his mouth on hers. She couldn't fight him, he was too strong—she didn't know what to do, so she just stood there, hard as a board. She thought he would stop. But he didn't. He shoved her against the closet and pulled open her robe, forcing his hands on her breasts. Now she really did panic because she couldn't get him off her. He laughed then, and she had the opportunity to scream, but she didn't. She should have. He clamped his hand over her mouth, shoved her into the wall again, and began grinding himself against her, hurting her.

With one great surge of adrenaline she shoved him backward and opened the door and screamed, "Get out of here! I'm calling security!"

When he reached for her again, she did scream and ran out into the hall, thinking this was crazy, this was ridiculous, she didn't go screaming rape in the hallways, she was from Greatfield, Ohio, these things didn't happen to her. By the time she reached the elevator, one of her neighbors had opened his door and she ran straight into his apartment, pulled him in and slammed and locked the door. Without explaining, she picked up his in-house phone and hit the desk button. "Get security up to twelve C! The guy you let up here attacked me! He's not who he said he was!"

"She's crazy, absolutely nuts!" Alex was yelling in the hall. "She's been fucking me for weeks and now all of a sudden she's mad at me and yells rape! She's crazy!"

They could hear the ding of the elevator and Libby wondered if it was security coming up or Alex going down. It was silent. Her neighbor opened the door a crack and looked out. And then opened it all the way. "He went down, I think."

In the next moment, another set of elevator doors opened and Nick came bounding out, clutching his walkie-talkie. "Libby? What's wrong?"

"This guy from jury duty just lied his way in here and attacked me!" she cried.

Nick's walkie-talkie squawked and the concierge's voice said, "Nick, the guy just ran past the camera in the garage."

"Let me go," Nick said, slapping the elevator button.

They didn't catch Alex and now, with Nick sitting here in her kitchen, Libby was faced with the choice of whether or not she wanted to call the police and file a complaint.

"I don't know," she said. "I mean, he was drinking, I don't think he really meant to do anything." Her face burned at the memory of his hands on her breasts.

"This guy's on the jury?" Nick said.

"I'm not scared of him, if that's what you mean," Libby said. "I mean, as long as he's not drunk. Actually, I'm more scared of taking action and then having him really go off the deep end."

"Libby, this is very serious," Nick said. And then he asked for some details about Alex, his name, where she thought he lived, and he said while she was making up her mind about filing an official complaint, he'd track this guy down. By Monday, Nick promised, he would have spoken to him and she could be sure Alex McCalley wouldn't dare go near her again.

Yes, but what about Monday? Libby wondered. Did she have to face him again? And what the hell had happened to Will? Where was he? Why wasn't he here with her?

35

ALEX WAS waiting for her outside the jury room on Monday. "Oh, Libby, I'm so sorry," he whispered, "I can't even begin to tell you. I was loaded, I didn't know what the hell I was doing."

"Alex, look, just leave me alone, all right?" she said. "Let's just get this damn trial over and forget it." She was scared that she would burst into tears, she felt so rattled. She hadn't heard from Will all day Sunday, either. Whoever had thought this up, facing both Alex and Will this morning, had a pretty sordid sense of humor. Thanks a lot, Big Guy in the Sky.

"But wait, listen, Libby," he urged. Sure now that she wasn't going to bolt, he looked sad. "Thank you. I mean it. I know you could have made it pretty bad for me. That cop guy Nick told me."

She looked at him. "And I still can, Alex."

"Believe me, I know how you feel. I just wanted to apologize—and thank you for giving me a chance. You won't regret it, I swear, I promise you."

Libby walked on into the jury room before she spit in his face. This guy was nuts. And she was going to have to deliberate a murder case with him? About another nut? No wonder people wondered about the legal system.

Will wasn't in the jury room yet. Thank God for small favors, she thought. She didn't know what she would do when she saw him. She hung up her coat and headed to the opposite end of the table from Alex to sit with Melissa. She, Libby noticed, looked radiant, but before they could talk, Chuck came in to take roll call.

Still no Will. On top of everything else, he was pulling a no-show here. But then, not for the first time since Saturday morning, Libby had a horrible plunge into anxiety. This simply was not like him. When

Chuck got to Will's name at last, he muttered something Libby couldn't catch.

"Did you try his office?" Libby asked. "He might have gotten hung up there."

"Don't you worry about him," Chuck said mysteriously.

"What do you mean?" Libby said. "Do you know where he is?"

"Oh, no," Basha said, putting her book down, "where are the obits?"

"That's not funny," Stephen told her.

"I know where he is," Chuck said, "and I told you, don't worry about it. When it's any of your business we'll tell you. Those are the judge's rules, not mine."

Now Libby felt truly frightened. The weekend had been a nightmare. She'd had hardly any sleep; she looked and felt like death warmed over, which, she supposed, was just perfect for this god-awful trial. "Please, Chuck," she whispered, going up to him, "is anything wrong?"

"He's all right," Chuck whispered back. "He's coming. Don't worry."

After waiting another ten minutes, Chuck came in to tell them there would be a further delay. Melissa offered to go downstairs for coffee. There were a lot of takers and she wrote down orders and when she got to Libby, Libby announced she was going with her.

She had to do something. Just sitting here was driving her crazy.

Going down in the elevator by themselves, Melissa finally said, "I don't want to pry, Libby, but you look so awful I have to ask if there's something I can do."

"Get me a new life," she said.

"Something go wrong with you and Will?"

"He vanished off the face of the earth, if you consider that a problem," said Libby sarcastically, and even to say it made her feel short of breath. So short had their time been, so deep and sharp the pain was. It was hard to believe.

They got the coffees and one tea at the cafeteria. As they crossed the hall to the elevators, Libby blurted out, "But it's not just Will," and despite her best intentions to forget the whole thing, she told Melissa what Alex had done Saturday night.

Melissa was horrified. "And he's still on the jury?"

"Oh, they don't know anything about it."

"Libby! The man sexually assaulted you. You have to tell them."

"No, Melissa, please, the trial's almost over. I just want out of here."

Everyone was still waiting around in the jury room. As they doled out the drinks, Dayton, smoking out the window as usual, suddenly let out a cry. All heads turned. "Look!"

It was starting to snow. Hard.

Slicked-Back Ronnie started humming "I'm Dreaming of a White Christmas," and Elena joined him.

The delay continued and the jurors couldn't figure out what the hold-up was about. When Libby asked Chuck about Will again, he said not to worry, he was here, just in another part of the courthouse.

"But why?" Melissa asked.

"When they let me tell you, I'll tell you," Chuck promised.

They speculated about what was going on. Mrs. Smythe-Daniels's theory was that Will had come up with a lulu of an excuse for being excused from the case. Libby felt her stomach lurch. That she had never even considered, that he might try to get off the jury just so he never had to face her again.

No, no, she couldn't believe it. No, she knew he cared. She knew he did. It had to be something else.

But what?

At a quarter past eleven, Chuck opened the door and there were audible gasps. Will limped in, dressed in blue jeans, a striped shirt, and blue blazer, head in bandages on one side, and half of his face swollen beyond recognition. He had the blackest eyes Libby had ever seen, and one eye, behind glasses Libby didn't recognize, was red with blood. Under his blazer on the left side, his arm hung in a sling. "He can't talk very well," Chuck said, "so I'll field questions."

Will's eyes were on Libby and she thought he tried to smile. She went up to help him immediately, leading him over to sit in her seat. Then she made Adelaide move so she could sit next to him. To hell with that g.d. Alex. She was near tears, whispering, "Oh, God, Will, I was so scared something had happened."

"He got mugged Friday night," Chuck said. "And we just picked him up from the hospital, so be gentle. He has a concussion, twenty-nine stitches in his head, and his mouth is wired on one side. No, they didn't catch the guy. He got walloped over the head a couple times with a blackjack, they think, and his wallet was taken. It didn't happen around the courthouse, but down on Wall Street outside his office building. He'll be okay, but he's very sore and very tired and he's here only because he's a hero. No kidding. Even Judge Williams is impressed, and nothing fazes her. So, since he volunteered, she's taking him up on it; the case goes on and he's still an alternate juror. I'll be back to bring you guys into court in a minute."

As soon as Chuck left the room, Dayton said, "Shit, Will, you'd do anything to get a little attention." People laughed.

"Thank God you're alive," Mrs. Smythe-Daniels said. "Our poor Will."

"You're going to be able to collect big-time from your company, you know," Ronnie told him.

"Thees ceety!" Elena cried. "Ah yi! Beasts out there. Beasts!"

"Were you in the hospital all this time?" Libby whispered.

"Uh-huh," he said, mouth wired. His eyes were on hers, though, and she could tell he was very glad to see her.

Thank God.

Thank God he was alive!

Gingerly he pulled out a pad and pen from his blazer pocket. He put the pad on the table and wrote, *Couldn't call. I was out of it.*

"Oh, God, don't worry about that," Libby whispered. "I just hate to think of you alone. I hope they called Betsy."

He shook his head slightly, causing him pain, she could tell. He wrote, *Called my parents. They came.*

"Well, thank heaven for that."

He scribbled again. *Mom's here.*

"Your mother's here? In the courthouse?"

He wrote, *Wants to meet you.*

Chuck came in to take them into court. Will's entrance into the courtroom caused a great stir. The court artist would be drawing him today, no doubt about it. A great story, a juror mugged after court, nearly killed, struggling now to make it in because it's toward the end of an important murder trial and he knows they might need him.

The judge pretended nothing was unusual in the least and instructed the defense to call their next witness.

"Defense calls James Bennett Layton, Jr., Your Honor."

Murmurs broke out through the gallery. Clearly this was not going to be a normal day.

James Layton was a lot shorter than he looked sitting down, Libby noticed immediately. The shoulders of his jacket were very well padded, hence the illusion. He didn't look like someone who could be violent. In fact, he looked completely out of place, and if he were to be sworn in as anything, an officer of a country club seemed the most likely bet. He was very nice-looking. He had a good head of hair; his eyes were blue and friendly looking; his mouth was nice, too. And right now all he looked was scared. And Libby didn't blame him. At best, he had an awful lot of family heartbreak to answer for. Yet again, she wondered if the wife was in the courtroom. If she was, Libby still hadn't a clue which woman she might be.

"Good morning, Jim," Geiggen said.

"Good morning." His voice was surprisingly soft, and a great deal higher than Libby had imagined. If she didn't know to the contrary, she might have thought he was an aging pretty-boy.

"I just want you to answer my questions, Jim, and to answer them truthfully."

Layton nodded.

"You don't have to be nervous. Just tell the jury the truth."

He nodded again, looking at them, eyes settling first on Mrs. Smythe-Daniels and then moving on to Libby—who averted her eyes.

Geiggen asked him about his background. He had been raised in Locust Valley, Long Island. Went to boarding school at fourteen. Went to the University of Colorado in Boulder. Graduated. Joined his father's company. Customer relations. Meeting with customers regularly and making sure they were being handled properly, and answering any questions they had. What was his father's business? He insured insurance companies. Geiggen had gotten up to the defendant's marriage to his high-school sweetheart when the judge said they would break for lunch.

As the jury filed out of the courtroom, a female guard met Will at the door to lead him away through a side door. Libby was in the jury room, putting on her coat to go out with Melissa, when another guard came in to ask for her. "Mrs. Klein would like to see you a minute," the guard said. "William Klein's mother? She says that she knows you."

Libby knew everyone was staring at her, but she didn't care. She simply nodded and followed the guard.

Will was lying on a couch in somebody's office. Mrs. Klein, a sweet-looking but still rather with-it-looking lady, about sixty, came over and hugged her. "A friendly face at last!"

Will, Mrs. Klein explained, had taken some Percocets for pain and had to rest, but he had insisted she bring Libby in and explain what had happened. Libby sat down and slipped off her coat. Evidently Will had been attacked right outside the back service entrance of the Connors, Morganstern building and was beaten several times over the head and shoulder with something the police thought might have been a blackjack. It happened very fast; no one saw the assailant; a worker had been leaving and opened the door and found William lying there in a pool of blood.

"Oh, and Libby! I don't mind telling you, when St. Vincent's Hospital called me at midnight to tell me my son had only briefly regained consciousness, long enough to give them our number—"

She stopped; her eyes welled up with tears. "I was beside myself. He had no identification on him. I didn't know who to call, not that awful Betsy, so William's father and I just got on the next plane to New York and went to the hospital." She looked at Will, sighing, and then began sniffling once more. "Once I knew he was going to be all right, sometime Saturday morning, I think, his father and I checked into a hotel."

Will was trying to say something.

"No," Mrs. Klein told him, "we're going home tonight to your apartment."

He tried to say something else.

"I've taken care of that," his mother assured him. "I had quite a chat with that Betsy and, not to worry, she's cleared out. For good." She smiled. "I have *all* the new keys to the apartment, William, is that proof enough?"

He made a sound of surprise.

"But what I don't understand is why you sent someone to change the locks on Thanksgiving. That's what set Betsy off, you know."

"Uh?" Will said.

"Betsy said when she and her parents came home to the apartment Thanksgiving night, they found the locksmith you sent to change the locks. They thought it was pretty dirty pool, considering she wasn't supposed to leave until Sunday."

"UH?" Will said, wide-eyed.

"Mr. Pratt asked the locksmith how much you were paying him, and he said three hundred, and Mr. Pratt told him he'd pay him three hundred more if he'd change the locks but give him the keys instead of you. And so the man came back the next morning and changed the locks and that's when Betsy decided to sue you, she was so angry."

Will was holding out his arms, obviously in pain, shaking his head, trying to talk.

"He's trying to say he didn't send any locksmith," Libby said.

Mrs. Klein insisted on staying with Will as he dozed and Libby returned to the jury room. Melissa was still there, waiting for her. "I got you a chef salad and a seltzer."

Libby was very grateful. And starving. She hadn't eaten anything yet today.

The snow was really coming down now. It was beautiful. Libby was cutting her salad with a plastic knife and fork when suddenly she felt dizzy and hot. She went into the bathroom and kneeled by the john, scared she might be sick. Melissa followed her in, closed the door, and matter-of-factly proceeded to wet paper towels and press them to Libby's forehead. "It's the shock," she said.

"It's my life," Libby said, starting to cry. It wasn't out of sadness, but out of emotional exhaustion. Melissa kneeled and held her for a minute, and then Libby tried to pull herself together.

Melissa sighed. "You know that you've got to tell them about Alex, don't you?"

"Tell who?" Libby said miserably.

"The judge and everybody."

"Oh, that, Melissa—God, why?"

"Because he might have had something to do with what happened to Will on Friday."

Libby froze. Then she thought a minute and felt dizzy all over again.

There was a knock on the door. "Just a minute!" Melissa said.

"Let me in, Melissa," they heard Mrs. Smythe-Daniels say.

Melissa looked at Libby, who said, "Go ahead."

As soon as the door was opened, Mrs. Smythe-Daniels made a beeline for Libby, bending over her. "I knew something was terribly wrong. Are you ill?"

"No, I'm okay."

"She's not okay, Mrs. Smythe-Daniels," Melissa whispered. "Alex attacked her this weekend. And he used Will's name to get into her building. I also think he might have had something to do with Will getting beaten up."

"Yes," Mrs. Smythe-Daniels said softly, "I was afraid of something like this. He's been quite wild-eyed and angry-looking, our Alex. And it was obvious it had something to do with you, Libby. Tell me, dear, were you involved with him? Is that why he's so upset?"

"No!" Libby nearly shouted. She was truly scared now. This couldn't be happening.

Mrs. Smythe-Daniels bundled Libby up with the intention of walking her around the block and making her eat something. A Danish, a cheese sandwich, something. When Libby protested, she became surprisingly stern. "Melissa is going to take care of things. You and I, young lady, are going out—and coming back to the jury room as if nothing's wrong. Understand?"

At exactly two o'clock, Mrs. Smythe-Daniels returned Libby to the jury room. Elena asked Libby if she was all right. "Just tired," she said, sliding into a chair. Alex was watching her.

"Did you eat anything?" Melissa whispered.

"McDonald's french fries and a Coke."

"Perfect. Listen, relax. Everything's taken care of."

Time ticked by.

It was now ten past two and Chuck had not yet come to get them. Finally, at a quarter after, he appeared. "Libby?"

She looked up, terror shooting through her.

"Your name's Cornelia Winslow, right?" Chuck asked, reading off his clipboard.

It was going to be all right. Chuck was playacting. "Yes," she said.

"So if you're Libby and you're Cornelia, who *is* Elizabeth Winslow?"

"That's my professional name, the one I write under."

"She's a very good writer, I tink," Debrilla offered, holding up Libby's novel.

"You're going to have to come with me a minute, Libby, Cornelia, Elizabeth, whatever the heck your name is," Chuck said. "They've got your name all screwed up in the computer."

"Now?"

"Now!" he directed.

She grabbed her purse and followed him out. Instead of turning right, Chuck turned left. Then he slowed to walk beside her and whisper, "Don't worry. We understand there's a problem with one of the jurors. The judge would like to talk to you."

"Okay."

Libby walked into a conference room. The judge, the prosecutor and Kathryn Schnagel, Geiggen and his defense assistants, and the stenographer and her machine were all in there.

"Sit down, Ms. Winslow," the judge said gently. "It has come to our attention that there is a problem with one of the jurors. And we'd like you to tell us about it."

"You have to understand, I'm not here because of what happened to me," Libby said quickly, "but because of the possibility he might somehow be connected with the attack on Will Klein Friday night."

She sat down and told them the whole story. About how she and Alex had been friendly since the first day in the central jury room, when they met, how she had sensed he was interested in her, but that she had allowed nothing to transpire romantically between them. He had never been to her apartment; he didn't know where she lived; and she hadn't given him her phone number, which was unlisted.

She had started to shake.

She continued about how Alex had been jealous of Will from the first day of the trial, how he kept calling him names, and then, after Thanksgiving, when he saw that Libby preferred to hang out with Will rather than him, he really said some nasty things. And then how, on Saturday night, he had come to her apartment building, drunk, and used Will's name with the concierge. And then, feeling shamed-faced, she told of his groping and her escape, his screaming in the hall and his escape, and her decision not to prosecute.

"Our security guy, who used to be an NYPD detective," she explained, "talked to Alex on Sunday. Scared him, I think. Anyway, Alex apologized to me this morning, and I thought I should just let it go. The trial was almost over. But then when Will came in this morning, all beaten up . . ." She let her voice trail off. She cleared her throat. "Will had a card with my address and phone number in his wallet. His wallet was taken Friday. And then Alex showed up on Saturday using Will's name with the concierge."

The judge and the lawyers were all looking at one another. Clearly this was not the standard jury problem.

"What are you going to do?" Libby asked the judge.

"Alexander McCalley will be dismissed from the jury immediately," the judge said. "The question is, do you think you can continue to serve?"

"Without him on it?"

"Yes."

"Oh, yes. I mean, at this point, I have to, don't I? There aren't alternates left." She noticed the meaningful glances around the table.

"Our focus is you, Ms. Winslow," Judge Williams said quietly.

"Well, yes, I can do it."

"What the judge means is—" Geiggen started to say.

"The judge will tell Ms. Winslow what she means herself, thank you, Mr. Geiggen," Judge Williams said.

"Sorry, Your Honor."

"I must ask you, Ms. Winslow, if you think the events that have just occurred could influence your verdict on this trial."

"How could it?" she asked. "Oh, I see what you mean. Because somebody got attacked? Or rejected? Oh, *Oh*," she said yet again, blinking rapidly. She got it now. "Gosh, I genuinely don't know. I mean, I don't think so. What's happened really has very little in common with the facts I've heard in this trial. But I guess it's up to you people to decide. Isn't it?"

The judge then allowed Geiggen and MacDonald to ask her a few questions, like "Do you think his motive was being rejected by you?" (Geiggen). "Yes," Libby said honestly. "You said he was drunk. Do you think that excuses his behavior?" (MacDonald). "No," Libby said, "but it helps to explain it."

The judge thanked her profusely and sent her back outside, where Chuck was waiting to take her back to the jury room. "Don't worry, McCalley's already been taken out." He patted her shoulder. "It's okay. You did the right thing. Don't worry. We'll take care of it."

Back in the jury room, Libby breathed a sigh of relief. Alex was gone. He had a computer screw-up, too, Dayton told her cheerfully from on top of the windowsill. With the wind that had picked up outside, the jurors now had a combination of smoke, snow, and hot and cold air wafting across the table. On the radiator someone was reheating a cup of coffee.

Twenty minutes later—not that the clock in the jury room showed anything but its eternal ten-forty—Chuck led them into the courtroom, sans Alex. Will was waiting to join them just inside the inner door. The defendant, James Bennett Layton, Jr., was back sitting at the defense table.

Judge Williams announced that the jury was being dismissed for the day and that the trial would resume promptly at ten the next morning. All counsel would remain in the courtroom.

When the phone rang, all Jill had to do was reach for the remote phone in her lap and turn it on. She'd been waiting for hours and was driving Rusty nuts. Rusty automatically pushed the mute button on the TV remote.

"Yes, yes," she was saying. "Yes. Well, thank you, Kathryn. I'll see you tomorrow morning." Jill slammed the antenna down and tossed the phone to the other end of the couch, as if she didn't want it near her.

"What did she say?"

"Defense moved for a mistrial."

"I knew it!"

"But they didn't get it. They're sticking with this jury." She sighed. "Kathryn says the motion was halfhearted, just to put it on the record so to have solid grounds for an appeal if it should come to that."

"We still have a chance, honey."

"Kathryn says Geiggen's confident he's going to win this one." She paused. "Layton's going to get off, Rusty, I just know it!"

"Jesus, Jill, I'm sorry—I don't know what to tell you."

"Tell me to believe in miracles," she said, getting up. She frowned and stepped back to peer into the front hall. "Peter?"

In a moment, Petey's small figure appeared in the doorway. "I woke up."

"It's okay, sweetie," Jill said, "I'll take you up and tuck you in again."

"Could I have some milk?"

"Sure, I'll get it."

When his mother was out of the room, Petey walked over to stand by his father's chair. "Daddy?"

"Yes?"

"If the man who killed Aunt Sissy doesn't go to jail, will you kill him?"

A glass fell and broke in the kitchen. "You okay, honey?" Rusty called.

"I think so." And then, "Yes. Go ahead." Seconds later Jill had moved into the dining room to watch as her husband took their son into his lap.

"Petey, the reason why we have courts is to see that justice is done," Rusty began.

"But Mommy says he's going to get off."

"No, Petey. She was just repeating what someone else said. We don't really believe that." He sighed, touching his son's hair. "The police and our courts enforce our laws. I would never go after someone. It's against the law, and it's also against God's law, too. We shouldn't hurt people."

Peter squinted slightly, looking up at his father. "So why did you sock that lawyer?"

Even Jill had to laugh at that. Oh, but these kids were smart nowadays.

36

WILL looked tremendously better Tuesday morning. His violet-black eyes were starting to streak green and a little yellow, his blood-soaked eye was open a bit more, and he could move his mouth a little better, although he still wasn't able to speak. Libby didn't care what anyone thought; when she arrived she walked straight over, gently touched his back, squeezed his hand, then sat down next to him.

Alex wasn't there, and there was so much whispering going on around the jury table that Libby told Melissa she was taking Will out in the hall so Melissa could finish filling in everybody about what has happened. Once outside, Libby kissed Will on the uninjured side of his face. In a minute they went back in and all was silent—and all eyes were on her.

Chuck came in to get them. In the courtroom, the defendant was in the witness box again. Once the jury had filed in and were seated, Judge Williams explained for the record that Juror #5, Alexander McCalley, had been excused from the trial for personal reasons, and that the remaining alternate juror, William Seymour Klein, would be moved in as Juror #5. Will moved down to sit in the front row between Mrs. Smythe-Daniels and Basha. If anyone in the gallery wished to comment on his battered appearance, no one dared.

The trial commenced as if nothing unusual had happened. Gradually Libby started to relax. She even felt grateful. It was safe here. The people on the jury were nice, trustworthy, helpful. At one point, Clay winked at her. She sat back in her uncomfortable chair, feeling protected.

Geiggen was leading the soft-spoken defendant through his version of events. They talked a lot about addictions and his use of cocaine, alco-

hol, and various tranquilizers in the Valium family, use which began
when he was around fifteen years old and in boarding school. By the
time he met Sissy Cook at the fund-raising luncheon, he had a four-
hundred-dollar-a-day cocaine habit and, at night, was taking forty to
seventy milligrams of Valium—or something similar—to sleep. He had
undergone two sinus operations; he had been hospitalized twice from
injuries in auto accidents; he had been taken to emergency rooms
countless times by friends and family who were terrified he had over-
dosed. When asked how this could possibly go on so long, he let out a
long, sad sigh and said, "Money. My family had a lot of it. It allowed me
to get out of a lot of scrapes."

The day he met Sissy Cook at the luncheon, he said, she had recognized he was a user.

"How did she do that?" Geiggen asked.

"She said, 'You can't con a con, you know.' "

Sissy Cook, according to the defendant, asked if he knew where she
could get some good cocaine. She was very beautiful, and seemed interested in more than just drugs, and they slipped out of the luncheon
early. They went to a bar where a dealer he did business with usually
hung out. He introduced them. Where was the dealer now? He was
dead. He was shot and killed sometime last year in a drug deal gone
wrong.

Anyway, he said Sissy Cook had done some business with the guy that
afternoon, and then they did a couple of lines and went out to party.
The next thing he knew, it was late and he thought he'd better call his
wife. But Sissy was really high and very excited—the jury needed to understand that cocaine did that to people—and so they went to one of his
parents' apartments, where they proceeded to have sex. Right after they
finished, she began to freak out, babbling about how she wasn't supposed to do drugs anymore, and that she didn't do one-night stands, and
she began sobbing and crying and hitting him like a crazy woman. But
Layton was used to that kind of behavior from drug addicts, hot one
minute and nuts the next. And so he had just gone into the dining room
to do a few more lines and she left, at which point he got in his car and
drove back to Locust Valley, where his sister was waiting with his wife,
wondering what had happened to him since the luncheon.

He had no contact with Sissy Cook for about six weeks, he said. Then
she called him for another cocaine source because the one he had led
her to, she said, had left town. It turned out he hadn't, but that Sissy

owed him ten thousand dollars and was ducking him. Layton had assured the dealer it had to be a mistake, Sissy had tons of money, and promised to look into it. But Sissy wouldn't take Layton's calls, and when he tried to see her at work, a bodyguard prevented him from doing so. He didn't know what Sissy had told people, but he did know he was persona non grata around the agency. The dealer was pressing Layton to cover Sissy Cook's debt for ten thousand dollars—because he had vouched for her—and threatened to cut him off if he didn't.

The night before the morning of the shooting, Wednesday, February 9, 1994, he had been on a pretty bad tear. He had coked up and was cruising around, drinking, and decided to stop in at Belle's. There he saw Sissy Cook on the dance floor and went straight for her, furious because this dealer was still on his case about the money she owed him. He didn't even get a chance to say what he wanted before she started screaming at him that he was impotent and all this crazy stuff, and then the men who were with her and the bouncer threw him out.

Yes, he had been very messed up. Yes, he had left absolutely enraged. Yes, he vaguely remembered shoving someone, but no, he had no idea what he might have said to him. What did he do next? He tried to find his car, but didn't know where he had left it, and then he thought it might have been stolen. He didn't have the keys on him; he remembered sitting on the steps of some church to think about this; the next thing he remembered was calling the police. He thought it had been from home, but obviously that wasn't the case. From where he called, he had no idea. He did get home eventually, and he poured himself a drink, he thought, and then he didn't remember anything until the police showed up to arrest him. That was it.

Since then he had been in extensive drug rehabilitation. When he was let on bail, he entered a hospital for six weeks. Then he returned home, where he was doing some volunteer work and fund-raising things for charities.

Then he started to cry.

This seemed to catch even Geiggen by surprise.

"Can you continue, Jim?"

"I just am so sorry for all I've put my family through!" he sobbed, holding his face in his hands. "I've hurt every good person in my life!"

Geiggen waited a moment before asking, "Did you have anything to do with the death of Sissy Cook?"

The defendant looked up, tears streaking down his face. "I swear I didn't." He looked at the jury. "I swear."

Since it was almost one-thirty at this point, Judge Williams adjourned the trial until two-thirty, and the jury was excused, filing past the defendant, who was still sobbing in his hands in the witness box.

All was quiet in the jury room as people got their coats. Will went next door to lie down for a bit, and Libby went downstairs to get him some yogurt and soup that he could sip through a straw. Back upstairs, she ate her own lunch and then read as he dozed. She returned to the jury room at twenty-five past two and, with the rest of the jurors, rendezvoused five minutes later with Will inside the door leading into court.

The defendant looked freshly scrubbed but a little red-eyed. And he was scared, it was obvious, as MacDonald rose to begin his cross-examination.

"Given your track record, as you so vividly described this morning for the jury, Mr. Layton," he began, "can you give us any reason why we should believe *any*thing you say?"

"Objection, Your Honor!" Geiggen yelled, jumping to his feet.

"Your Honor, the defendant's own sister has testified that he has lied about everything all of his life!"

"Your Honor, my client is no longer a drug addict. The lying in question had to do with his past, not the present, and certainly not in this trial!"

Judge Williams took a while on this one. Finally, she said, "Objection overruled."

Geiggen made a face of disgust and threw himself down.

"Thank you, Your Honor." MacDonald turned back to the defendant. "I repeat my question, is there any reason why we should believe anything you say?"

"Yes, there is."

"What reason could there possibly be?"

"Because I'm telling the truth. And as Mr. Geiggen said, I'm not on drugs anymore. And a key part of my recovery is vigorous honesty."

"So if you *were* responsible for killing Sissy Cook," MacDonald said, practically sneering, "you'd be glad to tell us all about it so we could send you to prison?"

"Objection, Your Honor! The prosecution is way out of line."

"Sustained."

MacDonald nodded, as if he had expected this. "Okay, let's start with this story of yours," and for the next two hours he hammered away at Layton, trying to find some inconsistency in his version of events.

"Mr. Layton," MacDonald said at one point, "how do you explain Sissy Cook's debt of ten thousand dollars when she had over seventy thousand dollars in the bank?"

"I'd say she was trying to dump the debt on me," the defendant said. "She knew if the dealer couldn't get to her he would come after me."

MacDonald stood there, looking at the defendant.

"A lot of drug addicts do that," Layton added.

"In other words, Mr. Layton, you're speculating based on your experience as a drug addict?"

"Well . . . Yes."

"But nobody has any proof of this or *any* transaction between Sissy Cook and the drug dealer, do they?"

"I don't know."

"There's no evidence that Sissy Cook had ever even met this drug dealer. As a matter of fact, there *is* no drug dealer, either, is there, because he's dead now, too, isn't he?"

"Objection, Your Honor!" Geiggen yelled.

"Overruled."

Geiggen reluctantly sat down.

The defendant took a breath and looked at MacDonald. "Yes, he's dead."

"So *you* say all these things happened, Mr. Layton, and there is absolutely no evidence that any of it *did* occur."

"If you had investigated better, you would have," the witness said.

MacDonald rushed on, but the defendant had scored a point, and he would not budge from any part of the story he had told. And although there was no physical evidence to collaborate the defendant's story, there was no way the prosecution could disprove it, either. Finally MacDonald retreated to the prosecution table and picked up a legal pad. He waltzed over near to the jury box, reading through some notes. Then he looked up at the defendant.

"It's very interesting, is it not, Mr. Layton, how the only two people who could substantiate your version of events—this drug dealer and Sissy Cook herself—were both shot dead in the streets of New York by a nine-millimeter gun?"

Geiggen was practically over the table screaming "Objection!" all through this, and Judge Williams agreed, chastising MacDonald.

MacDonald stood there, looking defiant. "I apologize to the *court*, Your Honor." Then he turned around and spotted a piece of paper on his side of the prosecution's table. He walked over, picked it up, nodded to himself, and put it down. "Mr. Layton," he said, turning around, "your sister testified that ever since you were arrested, you've led a . . . well, model life."

"I'm trying, sir," the defendant said, eyes glued to the prosecutor.

MacDonald turned to scan the faces of the jury. Then he turned back to the defendant. "And your wife has been supportive of you? In your quest to prove your innocence?"

"Yes. Very supportive," Layton answered.

"I see." MacDonald took a few steps back, toward the jury box, so the defendant was looking in their direction. "Mr. Layton, if your wife is so supportive, why is it that in all these weeks she has failed to come to court even once?"

"Objection, Your Honor!" Geiggen bellowed.

MacDonald held up his hand. "I withdraw the question, Your Honor. I'm sorry, Your Honor." Then he turned to the jury and said, with the utmost expression of contempt and disgust on his face, "The People are finished with this . . . *witness*." And then he sat down, sighing, shaking his head, as if he couldn't get over the ridiculous nature of this trial.

Geiggen rose to redirect. "Jim, is your wife living with you?"

"Yes."

"Are your children living with you?"

"Yes."

"Is your wife at home today, taking care of the children?"

"Yes."

"Fine. One last question." He paused. "Did you have anything to do with the shooting of Sissy Cook?"

"No," he said. "I swear to God, no."

Geiggen thanked him and sat down.

Judge Williams said this concluded the testimony of the trial and told the jury they would be getting the case tomorrow and that their guard would instruct them as to the procedure. They were dismissed until ten o'clock the next morning, at which time they would hear the summations of the prosecution and the defense.

In the jury room, Chuck explained that in the State of New York, on a murder case, the jury, by law, must be sequestered until a verdict is reached. And so they needed to bring an overnight bag tomorrow—packing for a two-night stay (groans), just in case—including all medications they might need. They also needed to notify people that they would be unreachable, although they could leave messages for members of the jury with Chuck at the following number. (They all wrote it down.) He stressed that they needed to arrange for child care for two nights, or parent care, and to have someone move their cars on alternate parking days.

When they were released, Mrs. Klein was in the hall to take Will home. As if they'd known each other forever, she gave Libby a kiss on the cheek and said she'd give her a call later about what care Will would need if they were sequestered.

"Model daughter-in-law," Melissa teased as Will and his mother headed into the elevator.

Libby made a face, but secretly couldn't have been more pleased.

37

OVERNIGHT bag in hand, Libby sailed out of her apartment building and up the sidewalk toward the Lexington Avenue subway. After a month of getting to court on time, this morning, the final time she was required to do so, she was of course running late. She dashed down the subway stairs, swiped her transit card through the turnstile, and pushed her way through. She was flying the corner to the stairs when she felt a hand take hold of her shoulder.

Then she felt an entire arm sliding around her shoulders, steering her away from the stairs. "Hello, Libby," Alex said, pulling her out of the stream of traffic.

To say she was totally flummoxed was putting it mildly. Like an idiot she heard herself say, "Oh, hi, Alex. How are you?"

"*Oh, hi, Alex, how are you?*" he mimicked, holding her close. His eyes narrowed and his mouth turned down. "How the fuck do you think I am, you fucking bitch?"

She was numb. "I have to go."

"Fine, go," he said, but he was still holding on to her, pressing her body against the wall. Libby looked over his shoulder for a transit cop. Or somebody. "I just wanted to warn you, it's not over, Libby. Unless you tell everyone it's over. If this thing goes on for me, it's going to go on for you."

"I'm not pressing charges, Alex, I told you that."

He gave her a little shake. "Then how the fuck did they find out about Saturday?"

"I don't know," she lied. "I guess Nick must have told someone."

For a moment, he looked nervous, and then he let go of her, but not before giving her a little shove in the direction of the stairs.

Dear God, he was big. And tough. How would she ever defend herself against him again if he came after her?

"Just remember," he told her, pointing, "if you end it, I'll end it." And then he was loping through the turnstile and up the stairs to the street.

"*Alex?!*" they all said in the jury room. "He was *waiting* for you?"

Will got to his feet and tried to say something.

"I'm coming with you," Melissa said, standing up. To Libby, "If you won't tell the judge, we will."

"No, please," Libby urged, "leave it. It'll just make it worse. I've already called Nick, our security guy, and he'll tell the cops. I swear, please, I just want to forget about it and get this trial over with."

"She has to get a gun," Elena said to Mrs. Smythe-Daniels. "Eet ees the only language guys like that understand. I had to shoot a guy once."

"You *shot* someone?" Mrs. Smythe-Daniels asked.

Clay's head swung in Elena's direction. "How the hell did you get on this jury if you shot somebody?"

"I deedn't keel him," Elena explained.

"Oh, I see," Clay muttered, "you only shot him."

"Eet was een Brazeel."

"Oh, well, I suppose that makes it all right, then," Mrs. Smythe-Daniels said, making a face of mock terror.

Young Slicked-Back Ronnie giggled, and it became contagious, laughter spreading around the table.

To all except Libby. This whole situation was so utterly bizarre. This was somebody else's life. It had to be. These things didn't happen to people from Greatfield.

Chuck came in to ask everybody what they wanted for lunch, because they would probably be given the case this morning and would then be sequestered.

"Who's paying?" Dayton asked.

"The State of New York," he replied with a small bow.

"Steak and lobster," Dayton said.

"Caviar!" Ronnie called.

"Lamb chops with mint jelly," Mrs. Smythe-Daniels said, getting into the swing of things.

"Lamp chops!" Adelaide cried, eyes wide in alarm. "*Lamb* chops!"

"Come on, people," Chuck said, "order something I can bring you. Take your basic coffee shop menu and choose."

"They theenk someone ees goeeng to try to poison us," Elena laughed to Adelaide.

"I don't think I want sit next to you anymore, Elena," Mrs. Smythe-Daniels commented. "You're positively dangerous."

"Vegetable soup, two poached eggs, whole-wheat toast, and choco-late ice cream for Will," Libby said, translating for him. "And for me a chef salad with vinaigrette dressing. And some kind of fruit juice."

"Those eggs could be pretty miserable by the time they get here," Chuck warned.

"We'll keep them on the radiator for a while," Dayton said. "I want a cheeseburger, rare, fries, and a chocolate shake."

"I would like sesame tofu, bean sprouts, seven-grain bread, and a car-ton of soy milk," Adelaide said.

"They're not going to understand that order," Chuck told her.

"Then make it tuna on white with lettuce and a Diet Coke."

"Tuna!" Mrs. Smythe-Daniels cried in mock alarm. "*Tuna!* Dolphin killer."

"Oh, shut up," Adelaide told her.

The courtroom was packed, as usual, but this morning it seemed partic-ularly stuffy. Or maybe Libby had just fantasized about being out of here soon and it seemed to be worse than it was.

Judge Williams announced that the defense and prosecution would present their summations to the jury and they would begin with the prosecution.

MacDonald stood, looking as deadly serious as they had ever seen him. And then he began his summation, slowly, deliberately, re-present-ing, point by point, the evidence against the defendant.

The defendant was an admitted drug addict. A pathological liar. A womanizer. And contrary to what the defense said, had a history of violent behavior. He simply had only been violent with *things* up until the time of the murder. The defendant was vindictive, mean, and prideful, and had been described as crazy.

As the jury knew, the defendant was a liar about everything. He had, in fact, made up this incredible story about Sissy Cook doing cocaine—while it had been testified to by everyone who knew her that she had not gone near any drugs for years. But how to disprove his wild story? About a drug dealer and Sissy Cook owing money? Conveniently for the defendant, the only two people who could possibly verify this story were dead. Both sh—

MacDonald evidently caught himself before saying something he wasn't supposed to. And then he went on.

The jury had heard the testimony of several witnesses about the truth of what had happened back when Sissy Cook and the defendant first met. That Sissy Cook had gone back to the corporate apartment with the defendant, presumably to have a sexual encounter, but changed her mind and the defendant, crazed on drugs and/or alcohol, became violent, and would have tried to rape her if he had been physically able.

But he hadn't been. And so he had merely gone into the dining room to snort more drugs. Sissy Cook took the opportunity to leave. The defendant couldn't leave it there, though. This was a womanizer; he wanted to prove to Sissy Cook what a man he was, convince her that she should have an affair with him. Forget the wife, the kids—heck, his sister would continue to take care of them while he played around in the city. But Sissy Cook didn't want any part of the defendant, and she told people about her bad experience with him, why she was scared of him.

And then, on the night of the murder, a little before midnight, he finally got to accost Sissy Cook face-to-face in Belle's. But she humiliated him, losing her temper and screaming for all the world to hear that he was impotent. He became so violent and crazed, he had to be thrown out of the club. Outside he pushed over a man, who testified here that he said, "That bitch will die before morning."

The defendant got into his car and drove through the Holland Tunnel and was seen by a New Jersey police officer speeding off the exit ramp of the Polaski Skyway, heading into Jersey City. This was at twenty minutes past midnight. As the jury also heard, the defendant was then seen and positively identified at the corner of Eighth and Byron in Jersey City. The eyewitness also testified that an unidentified black man, about six foot four, climbed into the Jaguar with the defendant and drove off. This was at ten minutes past one on Thursday morning.

At approximately 2 A.M., Sissy Cook came out of the club with her roommate, Marybeth Shaeffer. The Jaguar belonging to the defendant was headed toward them and both Sissy Cook and Marybeth Shaeffer recognized Jim Layton behind the wheel. The black man climbed out of the passenger side, Layton told him which woman he wanted killed, the one in red, and then the black man pushed Marybeth Shaeffer out of the way, fired point blank at Sissy Cook three times, and then finished the job by standing over her to blow off her face with a final fourth shot. The shooter ran back to the car and the Jaguar drove away.

After getting away from the scene of the murder, Layton got out of the car, and while the shooter drove the Jaguar away to ditch it at the waterfront, Layton called the police to report his car stolen. This was at 2:15 A.M. Then he either took a cab or shot up on the subway to his parents' apartment building, where the concierge saw him, but has conveniently forgotten the exact time even though he supposedly looked at the clock. Layton then went upstairs and dumped his stuff in one company apartment—

"Objection, Your Honor!" Geiggen screamed, glaring, enraged at MacDonald, although Libby didn't have a clue why. One company apartment?

"Sustained. Mr. MacDonald—"

"I'm sorry, Your Honor, I just—" He shook his head. "I'm sorry, Your Honor."

"You may continue."

MacDonald turned to the jury again and paused for a moment. "Mr. Layton then went upstairs and fixed himself a drink, took several milligrams of Librium, and went to bed. The police arrived an hour later to arrest him, at which time he called his lawyer."

He walked down the length of the jury box slowly, looking at each juror. "The defense has a wonderful version of the facts that sounds good—but there's one undeniable fact you have heard over and over and over in this trial. The defendant lies. He lies and he lies and he lies. About everything! Oh, yes, he got up there and told you how he has straightened out and what a family man and valued member of the community he has become while being out on bail. But ladies and gentlemen, I wish to point out that despite the defense's impressive series of witnesses, not one of them—not *one*—except Mr. Layton himself, has testified that he *has stopped lying* since he got off drugs."

He raised an eyebrow. "How could they?" He walked back the other way, across the jury box, eyes on the jury.

"The defendant had motive and opportunity—and he took it. We have the evidence and the eyewitnesses to prove it. The police may not have been able to find the shooter—*yet*—but we do have the man who hired him to kill Sissy Cook in such a brutal way. We have the man who drove the shooter to Sissy Cook. We have the man who pointed Sissy Cook out to the shooter. And after Sissy Cook lay dead, her face and chest blown all over the sidewalk, we have that man who helped the shooter get away.

"I beg of you, consider only the facts. Disregard the lies. See the truth. Justice depends on it. I thank you."

MacDonald walked back to the prosecution table and sat down.

Geiggen stood up. He looked almost handsome today, in an impeccable dark blue suit and black shiny shoes. His hair was neatly trimmed; his expression was earnest, kindly, and sincere.

He talked to the jury for over two hours, starting by explaining how the law worked, that it was the prosecution's duty to prove their case beyond a reasonable doubt. And that if they had failed to do this, then the jury had no choice but to find the defendant not guilty.

"Objection, Your Honor," MacDonald said. "It's not up to defense counsel to instruct the jury on the points of law."

"Overruled. It's his summation, Mr. MacDonald."

Geiggen thanked the judge and continued, citing the evidence that supported the true chain of events. That Sissy Cook had been a very beautiful woman with tens, if not hundreds, of unwanted admirers. That she had required bodyguards even at work. That the jury had heard even from the prosecution's own witnesses that the victim had been scared not only of whackos, but of men she had rejected romantically.

The jury had heard that the defendant was, at the time, a hopeless drug addict but that he was from a wealthy family who bailed him out of trouble and begged him to give up drugs. The irony was that it would only be this tragedy, being falsely accused of participation in a murder, that would finally bring the defendant to his knees.

In all his trials and tribulations as an addict, the defendant had no record of violence. His was merely a history of drugs, alcohol, and women. And when he met Sissy Cook, his addictions met hers, and they went to a bar he knew where she could score some drugs from his dealer. After doing some drugs, they went on to go dancing, and, finally, home to his parents' apartment to have sex. After they finished having intercourse, the victim went on an emotional tirade, the kind common to women on drugs. She then left the apartment.

The defendant heard from her six weeks later, when she was in search of a new source of cocaine. She told the defendant the dealer she had dealt with before had disappeared; this was not true. She had run up a ten-thousand-dollar debt with him and the dealer was holding the defendant responsible for making good on it. Sissy Cook didn't want to hear about it, and despite the defendant's many attempts to talk with or see her, he failed, for Sissy Cook had told everyone he was some sort of crazed stalker.

The defendant had given up on getting the money from Sissy Cook, but on the night of February 9, 1994, he walked into Belle's nightclub and saw her on the dance floor. He had been drinking heavily and doing drugs and was in such bad shape, he had merely left his car, unlocked, on Fourteenth Street, keys still in the ignition. He accosted Sissy Cook in the nightclub and was thrown out. Incoherent and staggering, he knocked into a bystander and staggered on. He couldn't find his car. Whether or not it was stolen at that point, we don't know for sure, but we do know he couldn't find it. Still in a stupor, he sat on the steps of a church, trying to pull himself together, but to no avail. He then took a cab home, staggered through the lobby at around two o'clock, went upstairs to his parents' apartment, poured himself a drink, and took some Librium to sleep. Sometime, somewhere, he had called the police station to report his car stolen, but he was too out of it to remember when—which, sadly, had often been the case with the defendant because of his drug abuse.

Meanwhile, Sissy Cook had been shot outside Belle's on Fourteenth Street by a black man who jumped out of the defendant's car. The defense does not deny that the car was there—or any other place after midnight. They only wanted the record straight that the defendant was not in it. Someone else was driving it. Someone who had either stolen the car or had seen a convenient moment to "borrow" it. After the shooting, the car was found down by the Hudson River at Morton

Street. After a witness told the police about the defendant's encounter with Sissy Cook at the club earlier in the night and they had the ID of his car, the police obtained a warrant for Jim Layton's arrest.

Now, at this point, Geiggen wanted them to understand, after the police arrested the son of a very prominent family in this country, the assistant DA requested that the detective in charge of the case, José Martinez, be taken off of it, and that another detective, Joseph Cleary, be put on. There was no apparent reason for doing so, except that Detective Cleary had worked with the assistant DA earlier in the year to successfully convict someone of murder.

This was where the question of the police reports came up. Did this mean that the reports of Detective Martinez, the first detective on the case, could then simply be *rewritten* by Detective Cleary to make a conviction more likely? Could that be why Detective Martinez was taken off the case? Because the DA's office didn't like the way he wrote his reports?

"Objection, Your Honor!" MacDonald cried. "Defense knows very well that those police reports are inadmissible."

"Sustained. Mr. Geiggen, I'll thank you if you'd watch yourself, please."

Geiggen gave a long, theatrical sigh. Then he scratched his head, dropped his hands to his side, and said to the jury, "A great deal has been made of the defendant's family in this case. Of their wealth, their influence. May I say, however, that no family's wealth or influence can manipulate the reports in a police department. Only within the police department itself—"

"Objection!" MacDonald cried.

"Sustained," Judge Williams said sternly.

Geiggen smiled at the judge—"Sorry"—and turned back to the jury.

"You have heard the testimony of the detective in charge—the detective who was in charge of the case until he was removed at the prosecutor's request. And you have heard the testimony of the detective reassigned to the case, Detective Cleary. Their accounts of the night of the murder do not exactly agree. I beg you to keep that in mind. For one of the detectives was actually there, shortly after the murder, and one, Detective Cleary, was not.

"You've also heard the testimony of Marybeth Shaeffer, the victim's roommate, who claims she saw the defendant driving the car. And then you heard the testimony of the nightclub bouncer, Kareem Johnson, who was standing right next to Miss Shaeffer, but who swears under oath it was impossible to see into the front seat of the Jaguar to see who was driving. Marybeth Shaeffer, as you will recall, spent time in a drug rehabilitation hospital, and although she said she no longer took drugs, she does readily admit that she continued drinking. And, on the night of the shooting, had imbibed at least three glasses of wine. She also wore contact lenses, which, as you learned in the testimony, often irritated her eyes if she wore them late at night. And last but not least, we know that the victim herself, Sissy Cook, *told* Marybeth Shaeffer it was Jim Layton's car.

"Okay, now we come to the fingerprints found on the steering wheel of the abandoned Jaguar. There were those of the defendant, naturally, since it was his car, but then there was a set of fingerprints belonging to someone else. Whose, we do not know. They may well belong to the person who stole the car.

"The defendant was arrested and booked for murder in the second degree. The police never caught the shooter—the man who actually killed Sissy Cook—and so the DA's office built a case against the defendant as the *most likely* suspect to hire a hit man. Well, ladies and gentlemen of the jury, that kind of convenient scapegoat justice just doesn't wash. At least it shouldn't. But we have, in this city, an unfortunate racial climate that the defense knows has put severe pressure on the DA's office to convict a white man for murder for once!"

"Objection, Your Honor!" MacDonald screamed. "Defense is just making up stories! This is ridiculous!"

"Defense is citing the reality of the political environment in New York City!" Geiggen protested.

"Objection overruled."

"Thank you, Your Honor," Geiggen said quietly. He turned back to the jury. "In recent years, as you know, our country has been divided over a number of court cases involving black suspects. And it is a well-known fact that most homicides in New York City are committed by black men. Well, ladies and gentlemen, in this case, everyone is in agreement that a black man brutally shot and killed Sissy Cook in cold blood, and yet the only person the police and the DA's office have managed to arrest and put on trial is the defendant, who, as you have heard time and time again in the testimony, *was physically incapable of driving*, much less masterminding this incredibly intricate plot to assassinate Sissy Cook right after publicly fighting with her."

He threw out his hands. "The DA's office has not only strung together an impressive amount of circumstantial evidence against the defendant, but has also succeeded, with the police department, in steering the focus away from the fact that they don't even have a suspect for the actual killing! This makes great copy, a trial like this, you see. 'Spoiled white rich boy plots murder of supermodel.' Forget the fact that, as you have heard testified in this trial by Rusty Tompkins, this supermodel, supposedly sweet, loving, and kind, was so sweet, loving, and kind as to attempt to seduce her own sister's husband!"

"Objection, Your Honor!"

"Overruled," Judge Williams said wearily.

"Forget the fact," Geiggen continued, "that the supermodel had rejected lovers left and right, to say nothing of an endless stream of kooks, cranks, and crazies she was scared might hurt her! And most of all, forget the murderer who actually shot her! And while we're at it, forget all the other suspects who had the motive and means to kill her!

"So the DA's office and the police department decided to forget all these facts and go after the poor little rich boy, the *white* rich boy, knowing how well they would come off in the press if they could get a conviction on James Bennett Layton, Jr. You see, ladies and gentlemen of the jury, this would prove they cared about all New Yorkers, regardless of color or creed, that justice will be done, even if you are white, rich, and male.

"Well, ladies and gentlemen, thanks to the DA's office and the police department, we'll never know who shot and killed Sissy Cook, will we? All we have is my client, served up as a public offering by the DA's office and the police department. They are desperate for you to find him guilty. Many careers depend on it. And all I wish to remind you is that they have to prove their case beyond a reasonable doubt, and obviously, they haven't.

"Ladies and gentlemen of the jury, from the bottom of my heart, I thank you for your time, your patience, and your attention. You are our only hope to see that our system works. For everybody."

Geiggen bowed slightly and returned to the defense table to sit down.

Judge Williams then spent some twenty minutes explaining the law to the jury: what evidence was and was not, how to weigh testimony, how to deliberate but refrain from speculation, the presumed innocence of the defendant, the prosecutor's case, and on and on. Finally, she explained that they had nothing to do with sentencing. They were merely to weigh the evidence, deliberate until they reached a unanimous verdict, and then return to the court to deliver it. Not guilty or guilty, of murder in the second degree.

The jury was now officially sequestered.

38

THERE was something very different about this trip to the jury room, namely that once they were all inside, Chuck locked them in. It gave Libby the willies—the fluorescent lights, the horrible color the walls were painted, the battered chairs, that damn clock set at ten-forty. The true time was near one-fifteen, and there was no lunch in sight.

Well, Libby thought, at least they had water.

On the table were some evidence request forms and some pencils. Adelaide, as Madame Foreman, cleared her throat and asked everyone what did they think, and deliberations began.

Very rapidly all the craziness of the outside world receded and the reality of the case loomed. A woman had been murdered, blown to bits on the street. The man who shot her had not been found. Another man had been charged with hiring the shooter to kill her and bringing him there to do it, and then helping him to escape. It was up to them, the jury, to determine whether the defendant would be found not guilty—and let him continue his new life with his wife and three children—or guilty, a verdict that would send him to prison, his life destroyed.

This was a complicated case with a lot of complicated and conflicting evidence, and, mercifully, Clay discreetly slid into the role of Madame Foreman's adviser.

"I think we should take a preliminary vote just to see where we are," Adelaide announced after Clay finished whispering in her ear. "Does anyone object to a show of hands?"

"There certainly isn't much point keeping our deliberations secret from each other," Mrs. Smythe-Daniels pointed out.

Clay whispered in Adelaide's ear.

"This is just to see which way people are leaning," Adelaide said, "so relax, everyone. Just vote which way you're *leaning*."

Still, Libby could feel her heart pounding. It was starting to snow outside again, the sky was dark, and the lights seemed to be growing more and more fluorescent.

It was so strange that Alex wasn't there anymore.

"All those who are leaning toward the defendant being guilty?"

Libby, Clay, Dayton, Stephen, and Melissa raised their hands.

"All those who are leaning toward not guilty?"

Mrs. Smythe-Daniels, Ronnie, Debrilla, Basha, and Elena raised their hands.

"Anyone undecided?"

Will raised his hand.

"What about you?" Libby asked Adelaide.

"Oh, me? I haven't the slightest idea!"

"I think that counts as undecided," Clay said, leaning over to write something on Adelaide's notepad. "Five guilty, five not guilty, two undecided. Split right down the middle." He looked up. "Okay, maybe we ought to start around the table, one at a time, sharing our thoughts about the case, the points we felt were most important."

"Okay, maybe we ought to start around the table," Adelaide repeated, "one at time, sharing our thoughts—"

"It's okay, Adelaide," Clay said, "they got it the first time."

Will raised his hand and tried to say something.

"Will's suggesting," Libby translated, "we each make a list." He was scribbling something now and she waited until he was finished. *List of points we thought important. As someone brings one up, can strike it off our list.* She looked up. "Adelaide, as we discuss each point, you can write it down on a master list, under 'Not Guilty' or 'Guilty.'"

"Huh?" Madame Foreman said, the little Dino Flintstone earrings dangling from her ears.

"I'll do it," Clay volunteered, taking the pad and pencil from her. "Who needs paper?"

There was a sharp knock on the door, the jangle of keys, and then Chuck's voice bellowed, "Jury, cease deliberations!" He poked his head in. "Lunch."

They ate for fifteen minutes and then started clearing the table, the jurors working on their lists. After another fifteen minutes or so Clay asked if everyone wanted to start and they all said yes. "Who'd like to go first?"

"I will," Dayton volunteered from down by the window. "He's guilty as hell."

Silence.

"And?" Clay said.

"What more do you need to know? He brought the hit man who killed her. Guilty."

"Okay," Clay said slowly. "I'll write down 'Identified as the driver who brought killer.' "

That was on several people's lists, that there was an eyewitness who had identified the defendant at the scene of the murder.

"Yeah, but later that witness picked a cop out of a lineup!" Ronnie said.

"That was ruled inadmissible," Melissa said. "You can't use that to form a decision, Ronnie. The only evidence was that Marybeth identified Layton as the driver of the car that brought the shooter and then drove him away."

"But the other eyewitness said it was impossible to see who was driving the car," Basha pointed out.

"But even the victim saw that it was him," Melissa said.

"No, the victim saw that it was the defendant's *car*," Mrs. Smythe-Daniels said.

Everyone started arguing at once. Adelaide pounded the table and turned to Clay. "Say something," she instructed.

"What? You want my list?"

"Yes."

"Okay." And so Clay listed the most important points in the case that made him think the defendant was guilty. One, he had motive. Two, he had opportunity. Three, drug addiction was not proof of anything except that if he had just coked up, he would have been thinking and driving just fine."

"Oh, that's ridiculous," Mrs. Smythe-Daniels said.

"I know what I'm talking about," Clay said.

"Oh, you know everything," Ronnie mumbled.

"I was an addict, cocaine and heroin, speedballing," Clay said softly. "It was fifteen years ago, but trust me, I know. If he was really a cocaine addict, taking it would have straightened him out, not made him incoherent."

"What about his drinking?" Melissa asked.

Clay looked at her. "In the testimony I heard, the only alcohol Layton had was one or two drinks at the apartment when it was all over."

"And some tranquilizers," Mrs. Smythe-Daniels added.

"But he only testified to taking those at the apartment," Melissa said. "He never said anything about before, when he was supposedly out of it. And if that's correct, that he hadn't even had a pill or a drink before, but only cocaine—"

And then everybody started arguing at once; Clay's points didn't prove anything, they were all beside the point, anyway, some said.

"I'm not finished!" Clay yelled.

Quiet.

"Okay, here are my points of evidence. One, he said he called the police station from his apartment. He lied. There is no record of it from the phone company."

"Yeah, but—" Ronnie began.

"Shhh!" Basha said.

"Two, we know without a doubt that it was his car that drove the hit man to the scene of the murder." Murmurs of agreement. "We know without a doubt that the defendant knew drug dealers in Jersey City. We know that the defendant's car went to Jersey City after the argument with Sissy Cook in the nightclub. We have an eyewitness who says the defendant was there standing next to his car in Jersey City about fifty minutes before the shooting, and that the defendant climbed into his car and drove off with a man who matches the description of the shooter."

"Yeah, but the witness cut a deal with the prosecution," Ronnie protested.

"Let him finish, Ronnie!" Libby said.

"As for the defendant's testimony, I have to discredit everything he says because if there was one fact proven in this case, it's that he's been a pathological liar since Day One."

"What does pathological mean?" Adelaide asked.

"That he lies so much he doesn't even know he's doing it, it's so natural to him," Melissa said.

Immediately everybody started arguing again, until Adelaide called on Mrs. Smythe-Daniels to read her list.

"Well, number one, the testimony of the eyewitness on the scene of the crime is highly unreliable, that girl with the drug and the alcohol problem who has trouble seeing." This provoked several minutes of discussion about contact lenses before Mrs. Smythe-Daniels could get back to her list.

"We are asked if we have any reasonable doubt," Mrs. Smythe-Daniels said, "and I have doubts about every aspect of the prosecution's case. It all seems too circumstantial."

"Two eyewitnesses?" Libby said. "One placing him in Jersey City and one at the shooting is circumstantial?"

Then everybody started arguing about the quality of the witnesses.

"Okay, okay, let's just move on," Clay said. "Libby, give us your list."

"Like Clay said, this guy had plenty of motive. We have all the evidence we need to know that he suffered from low self-esteem since he was a kid, that he'd do anything and say anything to get his hands on drugs, and that after he was on them, he was capable of almost anything. It makes perfect sense to me that if he felt publicly humiliated that, in the heat of the moment, he would have hired one of his drug gang buddies to blow her away. The value of human life isn't very high in those circles."

"But eet wasn't the heat of the moment!" Elena said. "Eet was two hours later!"

"So who do you think drove the defendant's car, hired one of the defendant's friends, drove him back to the city, pointed out the woman he hated, and then drove the shooter away?" Libby asked her.

"Someone else who wanted to see Sissy Cook dead," Ronnie said.

"Who just happened to be there? And found the car?" Libby said. "And knew the same people in Jersey City? Who looked exactly like the defendant?"

"It's not our job to find out who," Mrs. Smythe-Daniels said. "It is only our job to determine if there is reasonable doubt."

"No, Mrs. Smythe-Daniels," Stephen suddenly spoke up. "It is our job to come to a *verdict*. There's a big difference."

"Come on, people," Clay said, "let's get back to Libby's list."

People were still talking, but Libby went ahead and spoke loudly, forcing them to be quiet. "Like Clay, I have that we have eyewitnesses linking him to the murder."

"But the defendant said—"

"I think it's safe to dismiss everything the defendant said," Libby said.

"Then we ought to dismiss everything the eyewitnesses said!" Ronnie argued.

Libby pushed on. "I also have that every witness at the scene says the shooter asked the driver of the car which one was Sissy."

"That doesn't prove anything," Ronnie said.

"It proves the driver wanted to single Sissy Cook out," Libby said. "So we know whoever was driving the car wanted her dead, that it was no accidental drive-by shooting."

"So what?" Ronnie said. "Everyone knew lots of people wanted her dead."

"No, ve don't know that," Debrilla said, speaking for the first time. "There vas no testimony that anyvun had ever tried to kill Sissy Cook before. Or even threatened to kill her."

"They stalked her," Basha pointed out.

"But we don't know of anyone who wanted to kill her," Melissa said. "Except the defendant."

"I have just one more point," Libby announced. "That he lied about the phone call to the police."

"He probably thought he *had* made the phone call," Ronnie said. "But was too out of it."

"Oh, spare me!" Libby cried.

"Which brings us back to Clay's point that, according to the testimony," Melissa said, "he had only done cocaine that night before the murder, which we know would have made him superalert if anything, the exact opposite of what the defense claims."

"How the hell do you know so much about it?" Ronnie demanded.

"Well, as it happens," Melissa said, "I'm a recovering alcoholic who was not above using tranquilizers to function. Between Clay and myself, I'd say we know a lot."

"Ronnie, since you've got so much to say, read us your list," Clay said.

"Okay, one, this business about the detective in charge being taken off the case and being replaced with one the prosecutor liked."

"So what?" Melissa said.

"The question is, Why? So there's a lot of doubt there. And then there were those police reports—"

"None of that was admissible!" Libby cried. "Ronnie, you've got to get that stuff out of your head. This is the second time you've brought up points that rely on things we were instructed to forget." When Ronnie didn't say anything, she added, "That's why Geiggen tried to slip that stuff in. But the judge ruled against it, and you *can't* consider it evidence."

"But how are we not supposed to have reasonable doubt, then?" Ronnie asked. "If no one will tell us the whole story, that's all the reasonable doubt we need to find the guy not guilty."

"Just read your list, Ronnie, and let's get through this," Clay said.

"Okay, two—testimony proved the defendant was too incoherent and fucked up to drive, much less carry out this plot."

"Testimony by a paid expert," Melissa said, "and that flaky concierge who said he spied on the defendant for Layton Sr., which translates to me he got paid under the table."

"I'm writing this down, Ronnie," Clay promised. "That was an important point. Although, as you know, Melissa and I are experts of a more practical kind."

Libby laughed.

"Three," Ronnie said. "He had no history of physical violence toward anyone."

"What about pulling the phone out so his wife couldn't call for help?" Libby asked.

"That was ruled inadmissible," Melissa said.

"Whoops, right," Libby said.

"We do have evidence that he repeatedly *threatened* violence to people," Basha said.

"And then he was so screwed up he finally did it," Stephen said.

"Evidence that he had threatened people repeatedly, however," Basha said, "only bolsters the idea that his threat the night in question was empty—as always."

"My head hurts," Adelaide announced, clutching it.

"Okay, what other points?" Clay asked.

Will slid his paper over to Libby. It was divided neatly in two, *Guilty*, *Not Guilty*. "Under 'Guilty,' he has 'No hard evidence that he did not do it.' "

"Yeah, well, this is America, buddy," Ronnie snickered.

" 'Proven motive, means, and opportunity,' " Libby read. Murmurs around the table. " 'The racial element of the case implied by defense. Sounds like desperate move. Why bother bringing up if he's innocent?' "

"Because it explains why the prosecutor and the police conspired to convict him," Ronnie said.

"Conspired?" Basha said. "Do you honestly think the police and the prosecutor are going to conspire to do *anything* to the son of James Bennett Layton, Sr.?"

"Thank you, Basha, I couldn't have said it better myself," Libby said. "Anyway, on Will's 'Not Guilty' list, he has 'Whose fingerprints on the wheel of the car? Police said they were recent.' "

"Good point," Clay said, scribbling this down. "Although they could be the shooter's, like the prosecutor said in his summation."

"Maybe they vere the vino's," Debrilla said.

"Then they would have told us," Adelaide said.

Everyone paused to look at Adelaide in her sudden moment of clarity. She should have kept her mouth shut, though, because then she said, "I have on my list that the defendant just doesn't look like a murderer."

Everyone groaned.

This seemed to upset Adelaide, who looked accusingly across the table at Mrs. Smythe-Daniels. "The only reason you didn't write that down is because he looks like one of your sons, and you don't want the others to know that that's why you think he's innocent!"

"My dear, really," Mrs. Smythe-Daniels sniffed, touching her pearls.

"I theenk maybe she has a point," Elena said. "What mother could convict a man who looks like her own son?"

"I could," Basha announced, "and from this discussion, I must say I'm rapidly leaning toward guilty!"

They staggered on, nit-picking and arguing and rehashing the case. Then Ronnie asked them all why the courts would let James Bennett Layton, Jr., out of prison on bail if they really thought he was a murderer.

The room immediately escalated into chaos, everyone talking at once, most of the shouting about what rich guy *didn't* get out on bail anymore?

Inside Libby was groaning. This was not going to be easy. It was a very opinionated group. She was also worried about Will, who had moved his seat closer to the window and, every once in a while, rested his head against the wall and closed his eyes.

People were yelling again. Clay had fired up the group by telling Ronnie the only reason Ronnie thought the defendant was innocent was because he couldn't bring himself to believe that a rich white guy from the Long Island suburbs could do it.

"And this makes the situation better?" Mrs. Smythe-Daniels demanded of Clay. "That the defense introduced a race card one way, and now you're going to force it the other way? Well, I will not have it!"

Amazingly, Clay backed down immediately and said she was right.

Everyone started talking again, and Clay was trying to get them to speak one at time when Adelaide piped up and said that after hearing Mrs. Smythe-Daniels talk, she definitely thought the defendant was not guilty.

"Why?" Libby asked her.

"Probably doubt," Adelaide said.

"What the hell is probably doubt?" Stephen asked.

"I think she means probable cause," Clay said.

"Or reasonable doubt," Melissa said.

"No, I mean probably doubt," Adelaide insisted.

Ronnie groaned and dropped his head on the table. "With friends like this . . ."

"Maybe there ees a connection weeth the defendant's father," Elena said. "What do we know about him? Was he in the Mafia? Maybe he ees en the Mafia. Maybe he deed it."

They all looked at her.

"Where on earth did you get that from?" Melissa asked her.

"Why," Dayton said, "everybody knows a name like James Bennett Layton, Jr., is mafioso."

Everyone laughed and they all started talking at once again. It made Libby feel exhausted. She poured herself some water, and took a cup of it over to Will. He tried to smile.

"Leesten," Elena said, "I know he's not guilty, because eef he was guilty, he would have plea-bargained and not be seeteeng there, rotteeng in a steenkeeng preeson for two years, unless he was eennocent and wanted hees day en court!"

"But he hasn't been in prison!" Clay said, exasperated.

"He's been home sucking up to anybody whose testimony he can buy," Dayton said.

"On the other hand," Melissa said, "if he was guilty, wouldn't he have pleaded guilty by reason of insanity, because of his drug addiction?"

"Why plead guilty to anything if he can get off?" Libby wanted to know. She didn't know absolutely whether he was guilty, but she did know the defense had played havoc with jurors like Ronnie and Elena. They had heard but had not *listened* to everything, as the expression went.

Debrilla said she thought the defendant was not guilty. That he had intended only to scare Sissy Cook, not have the guy actually shoot her.

"But that's speculation," Clay said. "That's speculation on your part."

"Given how mixed up with drugs everyone in this case was," Basha said, "it's a wonder there's any case at all."

"But even on that score," Libby said, "we only have the word of the defendant that Sissy Cook used drugs. Everyone who knew her testified to exactly the opposite, including her roommate."

"Well, of course they would," Mrs. Smythe-Daniels said. "They loved her."

"Enough to try and hang an innocent man?" Libby asked her.

The words quieted the room.

"He'll only go to prison if he's guilty," Stephen said.

"And that makes it all right to send him there?" Mrs. Smythe-Daniels asked. "What if he's innocent?"

"He'll appeal and get another trial and another trial and another trial, I'm sure," Melissa said, "until he is found innocent. That you can bet on."

"But if he's found innocent, they can never retry him," Libby said.

"That doesn't prove anything except how desperate the police and the prosecutor are to nail somebody for the murder," Ronnie said.

"I must say, I tend to agree," Mrs. Smythe-Daniels echoed. "They do seem quite desperate. That little girl at the prosecution's table seemed very desperate to me."

"Little girl?" Libby nearly shrieked.

"I bet the defendant *does* look like her son," Adelaide said to Elena, looking at Mrs. Smythe-Daniels.

"Maybe she has a peecture of her sons," Elena said craftily. "So she can show us how wrong we are."

"Oh, pooh!" Mrs. Smythe-Daniels said, sticking her tongue out at Elena.

"We're allowed to apply our life experience to the case," Adelaide reminded everyone. "Does anyone have any life experience with this?"

"Life experience with murder?" Libby asked her.

"You shot some man in Brazil," Mrs. Smythe-Daniels pointed out to Elena.

Clay tapped the table with his pen. "Let's settle down, people, this is getting us nowhere. We have to take turns speaking or no one can hear anything." He turned to Adelaide. "Call on someone."

She looked around the table. Stephen, Melissa, and Ronnie were waving their hands at her. "Elena," she said, choosing her friend.

Elena frowned. "I deed not have my hand up. But as long as you called on me, I theenk he ees not guilty because he's too good to be that crazy over that girl. He knew he could get a better girlfriend."

"But it sounds like this was a case of obsession," Libby said. "And the guy was a druggie. I don't think he could have *thought* straight if he wanted to, even if he could drive straight."

"Shhh!" Adelaide admonished her.

"What's to argue?" Stephen said. "He hired a guy to kill her, drove him there, pointed her out, and drove him away. He's guilty as hell!"

"Shhh!" Adelaide told him, holding her finger to her mouth with great intensity.

"What I want to know is," Melissa said, since Adelaide would not call on her, "what happens if we believe he's guilty of something other than murder in the second degree?"

Silence.

"What do you mean?" Clay asked her.

"What if we reviewed the evidence and come to the conclusion that he didn't hire the hit man himself, but knows who did and is obstructing justice? What would happen then?"

"Then we'd have to find him not guilty as charged," Clay said.

"And he'd walk?"

"We can't find him guilty of something this case isn't about," Mrs. Smythe-Daniels said impatiently.

"And there's no way the police and the DA would have spent nineteen months preparing this case if they thought there was any chance he was anything but guilty," Libby said. "They've taken the time to build this case because they know he's guilty and refuse to let him off—no matter whose son he is."

"You seem awfully anxious to convict him, Libby," Mrs. Smythe-Daniels said.

"Yeah," Ronnie said, "I didn't want to say anything, but are you sure all that stuff with Alex hasn't made you a little overanxious to convict?"

The words stung. No one said anything. Finally, Libby looked up from her hands, which were folded in front of her on the table. "I swear to God, the only reason why I think the defendant is guilty is because the evidence indicates he arranged for a woman to be murdered and helped the murderer to carry it out."

"Beyond a shadow of a doubt?" Basha asked, clearly interested in Libby's response.

"We don't *have* to know beyond a shadow of a doubt," Libby said. "We only have to review the evidence and decide whether or not the prosecution has presented their case beyond a *reasonable* doubt." She cleared her throat. "Reasonable doubt—not any old doubt at all."

"Reasonable doubt," Adelaide echoed. She looked at Elena and whispered. "What's that again?"

They talked on and on until eight o'clock. Libby was getting worn down. It looked as though the verdict was going toward not guilty. Maybe they're right, she thought. Maybe Alex was coloring her thinking.

There was a knock on the door, the jangle of keys, and Chuck barked, "Jury, cease deliberations!" He then came in to take them into court.

Much to Libby's surprise, the courtroom was packed, everyone in place. Judge Williams announced that deliberations would cease for the day and that the jurors were not to discuss this case any further until they were returned to the jury room in the morning. They were not to speak to anyone not on the jury, except the guards who would take them to dinner and to a hotel for the night.

They filed out and Libby felt like she was on another planet. She was emotionally exhausted. And thirsty. They all were. Dehydrated. She could only imagine what poor Will must feel like, but he showed no signs of fading. In the jury room a female guard came in and handed out requests for telephone calls to be made for them. Libby filled one out, for the guards to call her neighbor to confirm he should feed Missy and Sneakers tonight and in the morning. Will wrote out a slip for the guard to call his mother and tell her he felt fine and would get a lot of rest tonight, not to worry.

They stood around then with their bags, waiting for the guards to come and get them. As time passed, one by one the jurors sat down again, and for some strange reason, Libby remembered when she was six or so, waiting for her first group swimming lesson at the county YMCA. There was that same kind of nervous chatter among them, and there was that same kind of hideous indoor lighting that only a swimming pool locker room could replicate. No smell of chlorine, though. There was only the smell of heat and wet wool, with drafts of cold cigarette smoke air from Dayton's activity out the window.

It was almost nine when Chuck and two other guards—one man and one woman—came to get them, and the long and bizarre day turned into a long and bizarre night as the guards led them across the desolate streets around the courthouse to a nearby restaurant, Forlini's, and Melissa made a crack that if Elena wanted to find her mafiosos, clearly this would be the place. They were led to the back room of the restaurant and each was handed a typewritten card that said JURY DUTY MENU, from which they could choose a salad, an entree, a dessert, and a beverage. Each juror could purchase up to two alcoholic beverages if they wished.

It was a very strange meal, with all twelve of them sitting together at a long table, as though it were some sort of weird family reunion of long-lost relatives who didn't know one another well. They talked. They laughed. They made jokes. They were, in other words, trying to make the best of the situation. Next to them, the guards ate dinner at their table, guns in their holsters.

When Libby had to use the ladies' room, she was accompanied by the female guard, who stood right outside the door.

When dinner was over, they were led outside to a small white bus that said JURY BUS on it. Libby imagined this had to be the same as a prison bus, and if it wasn't, it should be, because clearly punishment was the idea. They strapped themselves in their seats—which had no headrests—and the bus bumped and crashed and heaved and swayed across the Brooklyn Bridge at sixty-three miles an hour. It began to snow again. Will was seating next to Libby, by the window, and had fallen quickly into a dead sleep. Libby opened her bag to take out her flannel nightgown and robe, and ball them up against the window before he cracked his head open again. Once he was safely padded, Libby looked around. She could see Adelaide riding in the backseat, her feathers bouncing in silhouette against the swirling night lights of the streets, and she smiled when she saw Mrs. Smythe-Daniels and Dayton whispering between themselves.

The bus bounced and swayed and crashed over potholes from Brooklyn to Queens, and then over several surface streets to end up at the Ramada Inn across the Long Island Expressway from La Guardia Airport.

Thoroughly groggy, the jurors were led into the Ramada Inn lobby, where they were to wait by themselves in the corner while the guards checked them in. Libby and Stephen had helped Will off the bus and laid him out on one of the banquettes. Some evil-looking stuff had seeped out of one of his incisions and onto Libby's nightgown and robe during the bumpy ride. She went off to get some water and paper towels and came back to gently dab the remains off his face as he slept.

The poor guy. She took off his glasses.

"Give them to me," Stephen said. "I'll bunk with him and take a look at what's going on under those bandages."

"He's got changes of dressing," Libby said.

"Trust me, I've had a lot of experience in recent months with this kind of thing," Stephen said, and Libby, remembering about Stephen's lover, felt simultaneously relieved and awful. She handed him Will's glasses.

After about a half hour, hecklers from the hotel bar were calling across the lobby, making fun of them. "Yo, jurors! Hang 'em! Hang 'em!" the drunks called. "Whatever he did—hang 'em, fuckin' hang him!" Even Mrs. Smythe-Daniels was too tired to rise to the occasion, but sat on the banquette, put her head back, and closed her eyes.

Finally, near eleven, they were taken up to the sixth floor and told to pair off, girl with girl, boy with boy, no exceptions. Stephen had already taken Will and their bags into their room. Melissa and Libby paired up; Adelaide and Elena; Clay and Dayton; Debrilla and Basha . . .

"Well, let's see," Chuck said, "that leaves Mrs. Smythe-Daniels bunking with Ronald," and they all laughed, tired as they were, and keys were issued, Ronnie and Mrs. Smythe-Daniels each getting a private room. Libby walked down and knocked on Will and Stephen's door. Stephen let her in and she went over to where Will was sitting on the bed, and she very gently kissed him good night. When she walked away, he grabbed her arm and pulled her back with surprising strength. He stood up, looked into her eyes, and then kissed her gently on the lips.

By the time Libby was at the door to her room, jurors were yelling down the hall that their telephones and TVs didn't work, and Chuck yelled back what did they expect, they were sequestered!

Libby was so tired she could hardly care about anything. She merely rinsed out the worst of the stains from her nightgown and robe, washed her face, brushed her teeth, hung the nightgown and robe over a chair to dry, stripped off her clothes, and slipped under the covers of one of the two double beds. Silently she said the Lord's Prayer. She was vaguely aware of Melissa taking a shower and climbing into the other bed. She was telling Libby something about Christine. Christine wanted to meet her. Yes, that was it. And then Melissa said good night.

Libby's dreams were full of violence and faces from the trial. She awakened with a start around three o'clock. In one of those nighttime epiphanies she cherished as a writer, but as a juror did not welcome at all, she knew that if Geiggen had been the prosecutor, and MacDonald the defense attorney, they would have convicted the defendant yesterday, no question about it.

Regardless of what the truth had been.

39

AT SIX-fifteen on Thursday morning, December 7, Pearl Harbor Day, the guards knocked on the hotel room doors to awaken the jurors. Melissa bounded up, washed, and was dressed in a flash, and she went outside to talk to Chuck in the hall, leaving Libby the room to herself. She took a long hot shower, followed by a brief cold one, but she still felt as though someone had sandbagged her during the night. She couldn't imagine what Will must feel like. She dried her hair and then, hesitating only a moment to make sure she was still alone, slid to her knees by her bed and clasped her hands, just as she had been taught as a child.

"Dear God," she said quietly, "please help me to make the right decision. Please rid my head of all the noise—about Alex, about I don't know what—but please let me make a just and fair decision today. Please. Thank you. Amen."

She got up. Yes, she felt better. She finished drying her hair.

"I didn't want to say anything before," Melissa was saying quietly in the hallway to Chuck. He was sitting in a chair, gun in his holster, where, he said, he had been on guard since 3 A.M.

He smiled. "I didn't, either. But I saw you, you know. The first day, at One Police Plaza. I knew you were there. I figured you'd say something if you wanted me to say something out of the AA rooms."

"How long have you been in?" she asked him.

"Nine years next week."

"You're kidding!"

"Nope, came in right before Christmas. My mama said it was a miracle right up there with Jesus rising from the dead."

They both laughed. "What about you?"

"It'll be three years in March. Listen, Chuck, before this is over, may I get your number? I'd love for you to speak for me at a meeting someday. That is, if you want—because if it's too weird how we met—"

"No, it'll be great. I haven't spoken in a while. As for how we met—come on, girl, the outside world's weird, that's how we ended up where we did!"

Promptly at seven the jurors were rounded up and herded downstairs into the hotel restaurant. Breakfast was served buffet style and the jurors threw down their belongings in a corner where there were tables set off especially for them. As they approached the food, they were warned by one of the guards not to speak to any strangers. They—the strangers in question, another group of people set off at another group of tables, with their own gun-carrying guards—were also a sequestered jury.

Will looked surprisingly well this morning and Stephen reported that his incisions looked good. He also said everything had gone well overnight, except when Will tried to gargle with peroxide, as he was supposed to, and lost about half of it down his front, soaking his pajamas.

Libby smiled to herself. Will had been stripped half-naked with a gay man in his room and she had been stripped naked with a gay woman in hers. She wished Jesse Helms were here.

They sat down to breakfast, which actually tasted pretty good, and eavesdropped as one of the guards from the other jury came over to sass their guards. "Whoa!" he said. "It's the fancy schmanzies from Manhattan! What are you doin' slummin' out here in Queens?"

If the breakfast had perked them up, the drive back to Manhattan was deflating them. The bus was cold and uncomfortable and the traffic was unbelievably awful, partly because of the slush and salt mess that was all over the roads. What had been a thirty-minute ride the night before lasted an hour and forty-five minutes this morning, and it would have been longer had the driver not taken any piece of shoulder to squeeze through the traffic.

By the time they rolled into Manhattan, the jurors were morosely quiet, feeling exhausted already. Faced with going back into that court-house, Libby felt like crying. She was completely stressed out already.

The guards swept them through the courthouse crowds, and were careful to make sure they got past the newsstand without seeing the pa-pers. They were put on the elevator and others who tried to get on were escorted off. "These jurors are sequestered!" the guards bellowed. They counted heads. Twelve. As they rode up to the sixteenth floor, Will briefly held Libby's hand. She turned and smiled. His black eyes were turning seriously yellow with healing, and his face was half the size it had been. She was starting to remember what a nice-looking man he was.

The guards took them up to 16, escorted them into the jury room, took their orders for lunch, and locked them in.

Shortly thereafter, there was a knock, the jangle of keys, and the cry "Jury, cease deliberations!" It was Chuck. With a phone message for Stephen. His friend Bill was stable and doing okay.

"Oh, thank God," Melissa said, others echoing the sentiment.

After they settled down, Clay suggested they take a vote this morning to see where everyone stood, this time a written one. He handed out lit-tle slips of paper and asked everyone to write down "not guilty" or "guilty." Basha complained that she didn't know for sure anymore, and couldn't put down "not guilty" with any certainty, and so Clay said to write "neutral" and then, in parenthesis, which way she was leaning. Everyone wrote down their vote and folded their paper. Clay passed a brown paper bag around to collect the slips and gave the bag to Ade-laide.

She unfolded each paper, and read, "Guilty . . . not guilty . . . not guilty . . . don't know/not guilty . . . neutral (not guilty) . . . not guilty . . . guilty . . . undecided—not guilty . . . not guilty . . . not guilty . . . guilty . . . neutral (not guilty)."

Everyone looked around the table in amazement. They were a lot closer to arriving at a verdict than anyone had realized.

"Okay," Clay said, "that's three guilty, five not guilty, and four neutral leaning toward not guilty."

"I'm sure it won't come as any big surprise," Libby said, "but I voted guilty, and I frankly don't understand how so many people could have changed their minds since last night. I mean, based on the discussion we had yesterday."

"Yesterday Mrs. Smythe-Daniels and Ronnie agreed that you only thought he was guilty because of Alex," Basha reminded her. "Perhaps that swayed some people."

"No, that wasn't it," Dayton said, yawning and stretching. "There are too many doubts in this case. And if we push this along, we might get out of here tonight."

Immediately he was shouted down.

"I didn't say that's why I changed my vote!" he protested, climbing up on the windowsill.

"But you changed your vote, Dayton," Libby said. "Why?"

"Because there are too many holes in this case."

"I think we have to have the testimony read back to us about the eye-witnesses," Clay said to Libby. "I don't know how else to make these guys look at the facts."

"Why bother?" Melissa said, tired. "They don't care about the evidence. They just don't want to be responsible for sending the guy to prison."

"Well, aren't we high and mighty this morning?" Mrs. Smythe-Daniels sniffed. "I suppose you and Libby were up all night planning the defendant's execution."

"For your information, Mrs. Smythe-Daniels," Libby said in her severest schoolmarm voice, "Melissa and I barely spoke at all."

"Like you'd tell us if you did," Ronnie said with a smirk.

"I can't help it, Ronnie, if I have to take the evidence into consideration and all you think you have to do is base your decision on the acting skills of the defense lawyer!" Libby snapped. "This isn't a movie, you know."

"And what eef you're wrong?" Elena asked her.

Libby threw her hands up. "We haven't even asked for a formal vote yet! We're still discussing it. And that's what I want, a discussion separating the facts from lawyer tricks—a *discussion*, not potshots from the Sutton Place peanut gallery."

"Libby!" Melissa said, surprised, checking to see how offended Mrs. Smythe-Daniels might be.

"Oh, I'm sorry!" Libby wailed, nearly in tears. "But this is so frustrating! Don't you understand? This is exactly what Geiggen's performance in there was designed to do to us in here." She got up and went into the ladies' room to compose herself.

Oh, great, she was getting hysterical. From now on, she would just keep her mouth shut. And listen.

Clay was helping Adelaide to write out a request to the court. They wanted to hear the testimony read back of the eyewitnesses to the shooting, Marybeth Shaeffer and Kareem Johnson. They also wanted to hear the testimony of the officer who ID'd the defendant's car in Jersey City. And they wanted to hear the testimony of Jamal White, who identified not only the defendant's car in Jersey City, but the defendant himself.

"And tell them we want it read in chronological order," Clay told Adelaide. "First the cops, then Jamal, and then Marybeth Shaeffer and Kareem Johnson." When she was finished, he took the paper, went over to the door, and knocked on it.

There was the jangle of keys and then Chuck's voice: "Jurors, stop deliberations!" Chuck read the request and warned them that it could take some time for the stenographer to look all this up.

"Wait!" Mrs. Smythe-Daniels called. "I think we need to request—"

"Shhh!" Elena told her.

"Bring back that paper and go out and close the door," Mrs. Smythe-Daniels instructed Chuck. He did so. When the door was closed: "I think we should ask for all the photographs, the ground plan of the scene of the murder, and any police reports that *were* entered into evidence."

"And the picture of the car," Clay said. "I want to see that car up close."

"And make sure to get the photo ID card," Ronnie said. "I want to see if the other pictures even look anything like Layton."

They were in agreement and Adelaide filled this out and Chuck was summoned and dispatched with their revised request. In ten minutes he was back with all the physical pieces of evidence they had requested. It was strange seeing all of it up close now, particularly the photographs of the bloody scene of the shooting. It certainly quieted everyone down. After a while Libby couldn't look at them anymore.

"You know, this *is* at least a seventy-thousand-dollar car," Ronnie remarked, holding one of the photos.

"You vould tink they vould have sold it to pay back some of the money he stole," Debrilla said.

"He didn't own it," Dayton said. "It was a company car."

Mrs. Smythe-Daniels sighed heavily. "It does paint a rather sordid family picture, doesn't it?"

Something in her voice made Libby look at her.

"I cannot possibly imagine allowing one of my children to destroy the lives of so many people," Mrs. Smythe-Daniels continued, "particularly those of my grandchildren. I'd sooner shoot him first." She looked up to see the surprised faces around the table. "I mean it. It's one thing to destroy your own life, quite another to victimize poor helpless children."

"Will wants to know," Libby read from a piece of paper he had pushed in front of her, "how do you know he victimized his children?"

"Good God, even if he never came home, he was victimizing those children! The family was in financial jeopardy, their mother was worried sick—possibly abused—and their father was a constant source of shame and embarrassment and humiliation to them all! How could a father like that not leave scars? And if he pulled the phone out of the wall so his wife couldn't call out—"

"We don't know that," Clay said. "We don't know *why* he pulled it out."

"So ripped it out," Mrs. Smythe-Daniels said. She looked around the table. "How often has that happened in your home? That the one who is supposed to be working and supporting the family is at home ripping the telephone out of the wall?"

"But he has cleaned up hees act!" Elena argued. "Now he can be a good father."

Mrs. Smythe-Daniels turned so that she was looking at Elena out of the corner of her eye. "There's no guarantee of that, my dear. A bad seed—" She shook her head. "We're talking decades of lying and cheating and stealing."

"Show me a boy at seven and I'll show you the man he'll become," Stephen said softly.

"But that doesn't mean he killed Sissy Cook!" Ronnie cried.

"No one said he did," Melissa spoke up. "Only that he drove to Jersey City and got someone who would."

There was silence for a while, as they sifted through the evidence some more, passing it around, making quiet comments to one another.

"This lineup card is impressive," Stephen said, looking at the yellow card. On one side it had six photographs. "Every one of them looks like the defendant."

It was handed to Libby. Yes, they sure did. Each picture had a man with light hair, cut fairly short and preppylike, and with blue eyes and white skin. She turned the card over to where Marybeth Shaeffer and Jamal White had positively ID'd the defendant as the person they had seen that night.

Time continued to pass, their discussion rising and falling with spurts of leads, interest, and energy. Lunch arrived. They ate and continued talking, but were getting increasingly antsy about when they were going to hear the transcripts read back.

Lunch was now long over, and the jurors were taking turns getting up to refill the water pitcher about every fifteen minutes, they were all so dehydrated. They were dazed, too, but determined, Libby thought, if not vaguely obsessed. By this time she herself had apologized three times to the group for her outburst in the morning.

Finally, they were called into court. It was packed. The requested parts of the transcripts were read, one after the other. Their being read like that made a difference. The police were positive it was the defendant's car they had seen speeding off the Polaski Skyway ramp to Jersey City shortly after midnight. Jamal White was positive it was the defendant he saw in Jersey City at ten past one in the morning, talking to a tall black man, who then climbed into the car with him and drove off. Marybeth Shaeffer was positive it was the defendant driving the car at shortly after 2 A.M., when a black man got out of the defendant's car, asked the driver which one Sissy was, and then pushed Marybeth on the ground and repeatedly shot Sissy Cook until she was dead.

When they filed back into the jury room, it was very quiet. The transcripts had affected them all. Frankly, none of them looked very well now. Even Clay seemed blanched, worn, tired with responsibility.

The brutality of the murder had truly sunk in. And as if the testimony of Marybeth Shaeffer had not been enough, the bloody photos of the sidewalk, bits of carnage splashed everywhere, had been lying face up on the table when they came in.

"Will wants to know," Libby began, waiting for him to finish writing, "did anyone say anything in court about the records for the telephone in the Jaguar?"

They murmured, sharing the photos of the car, looking at the telephone that could be clearly seen inside.

No, they agreed, no one had said anything about it. Then Will wrote something else and Libby read, "Was there anything about testing the interior of the car for bloodstains? Gunpowder? The gun? Anything?"

No, they agreed, not a word had been said about the interior of the car, except that recent fingerprints had been found on the steering wheel that belonged to someone other than the defendant.

"You know, now that he mentions it," Mrs. Smythe-Daniels said, "isn't it odd that no mention was made in the trial about testing or searching or looking in the car?"

"Except for the fingerprints on the steering wheel," Adelaide added.

"They didn't say the cops fingerprinted the inside of the car?" Dayton asked.

"No," Ronnie said, looking baffled. "The cop just said fingerprints were found on the steering wheel that did not belong to the defendant."

"Who called that cop as a witness?" Stephen asked.

"The defense," Melissa said.

They were quiet a moment, thinking. And then Ronnie said, "You know, they never said anything about the gun, either."

"They said it was a nine-millimeter."

"No, I mean, they just said it hadn't been found. Wouldn't they normally tell us where they looked?"

"Not necessarily."

"Will wants to know," Libby said, "is this evidence of a sort? When something has obviously *not* been discussed in the trial?" She looked at him. "I don't understand." He wrote something more. She read it. "Was the phone in the car used on the night of the murder?"

"Obviously we're not allowed to know," Clay said.

"Maybe eet was broken," Elena said.

"But still they should have addressed it," Melissa said. "They tell us the defendant said he called the police from his parents' apartment to report the car stolen. Then they tell us no call was made out of the apartment until the defendant called his lawyer. And they also told us the defendant did call the police, but from where, they don't know."

"The car phone?" Dayton said.

"That's what I mean," Melissa said. "It's very odd the car phone would never be mentioned at all, when it's right there in the photographs."

"We can't speculate," Libby said. "We can't. But it does bring up a good point. Why was the picture of the phone in the car admissible, but any mention of the phone or if any calls were made from it wasn't?"

"I wonder what else was inadmissible in this trial," Clay said.

"We can't speculate," Libby repeated. "We can only go by the evidence that was presented in court. The testimony—"

"By known liars, drug addicts, thieves, and other psychopaths," Mrs. Smythe-Daniels snorted, sitting up a little straighter.

"Most of all, Layton," Clay pointed out.

"And the physical evidence," Libby continued.

"What physical evidence?" Ronnie said. "There's no gun, no shooter, no footprints, fingerprints, nothing."

"But there vere eyevitnesses," Debrilla said. She looked at Libby. "I must confess, I have changed my mind. I am vid Libby. I tink he's guilty."

"Why?" Ronnie said, surprised.

"Because that lawyer—Geiggen—he tried to fill our heads vid all kinds of tings he vas not supposed to say. And I tink ve all remembered them, anyway."

"I think what Debrilla's saying is valid," Stephen said. "Once you take away the cracks and innuendos of the defense, what are you left with but a very savvy cross-examination based on the best private investigation money can buy?"

"But we don't know that, either, about the investigators," Libby said. "All we can go by was what was presented to us in court."

"But *is* it evidence?" Melissa persisted. "That certain topics were not discussed at all in what otherwise was a very detailed trial? Remember when MacDonald entered the photos into evidence? How long it took? The questions over and over and over with the police and the doctor and the forensic guy—it seems hard to believe they just decided not to say a word about the investigation of physical evidence. We got hours and hours on the dead body, but nothing on the inside of the car."

Mrs. Smythe-Daniels slammed her hand down on the table. "If this is true, how do they expect us to come to a decision? If they won't give us all the facts?"

"But they *have* given us all the facts that the judge ruled admissible," Libby said. "Listen, you all know how I fccl, but that doesn't mean we can convict somebody on evidence that's missing from the trial. If anything, *that* would be reasonable doubt and even I'd have to go along with that and let him off."

"Find him not guilty?" Clay said, thunderstruck.

"If that was the way we were supposed to deliberate, yes," Libby said. "But it isn't! We are asked to weigh the evidence and come to a verdict. All I've been saying is, I'm a storyteller by profession—and so is Geiggen. I know all the tricks, I know all the dramatic moves; the fact that he does it in court and I do it on paper doesn't mean they're all that different. Firmly planting an idea in a person's mind, even if by innuendo, will affect every aspect of the story as they hear it from there on in." She looked at Ronnie. "That's why I got so upset this morning with you, Ronnie. Because, you see, you're just the kind of bright young person who has grown up with a certain kind of dramatic training from the media. That's what Geiggen takes his cues from, popular culture. You've literally been taught to respond to Geiggen in a certain way."

Everyone was looking confused.

"Tell me if I'm wrong, Ronnie," Libby said, "that everything you've been taught says you're supposed to find a loophole in a trial and free an innocent man."

"If he's innocent, yeah."

"But what if he's guilty? And the prosecutor isn't so hot, but is overworked and understaffed? And the millionaire defense lawyer has an unlimited budget to find evidence and witnesses that will appeal to the story he knows you know like the back of your hand? Ronnie, why do you think he wanted *you* on the jury?"

"How do you know?" Adelaide squealed.

"I don't know!" Libby said impatiently. "But I do know Ronnie's bought the defense's act hook, line, and sinker, to a point where I can only wonder if Geiggen reminds him of his father or something."

"Come, come," said Basha. "Now we have the defendant as Eleanor's son, the defendant as Libby's friend Alex, and Geiggen as Ronnie's father."

"All I can think of is Henry Fonda in *Twelve Angry Men*," Adelaide admitted.

Everybody laughed. Things were getting ridiculous and they knew it. But they were onto something here, some thread. At least, they were deliberating in an intelligent way. On the other hand, they were all tired, cold, and getting hungry again; it was getting dark outside, and the threat of another night at the Ramada Inn was hanging over them.

The discussion staggered on, the jurors going over and over the facts as they had heard them.

"If two eyewitnesses are in conflict, then that is reasonable doubt," Ronnie said.

"But they didn't disagree," Adelaide said. "Only one witness could see who was driving; the other one couldn't."

"They only agreed on the *car*," Ronnie said.

"The car another eyewitness saw the defendant get into in Jersey City fifty minutes before the shooting, at which time he drove away with a man who fit the description of the shooter who killed Sissy Cook," Clay said. "Man, Ronnie, what is with you?"

"The Jersey City eyewitness had a drug history," Ronnie argued.

"But at least he was clean at the time of the murder!" Melissa cried. "Which is saying a lot more than the defendant, for crying out loud."

"I'm with Libby and Clay now," Adelaide announced. "He's guilty."

"There's something else that needs to be mentioned," Libby said. All heads turned toward her. "Don't you find it odd that the sister was the only member of the family who testified on Layton's behalf?"

Silence.

"And why hasn't the wife been in court?"

"That question was withdrawn!" Ronnie said.

"You know, I noticed that all through the trial," Mrs. Smythe-Daniels said, "that there wasn't any woman in that courtroom besides the victim's sister who even remotely looked like she might be the wife."

Adelaide turned to Clay. "Why wouldn't his family come to support him?"

It was a question that did not need to be answered, and several looks were exchanged around the table.

"I'm almost embarrassed to say it," Dayton said, "but now I think he must be guilty, too. I know I changed my vote before, but . . ."

"But what?" Libby asked him.

"I don't know, it's kinda like you said. That stuff Geiggen kept slipping in. I think that's what had me on the fence before. Take that away, look at the evidence, and he's guilty."

"But how could he carry out that whole plan if he was on drugs?" Ronnie said.

"Well, we've got a former heroin and cocaine addict over there," Melissa said, pointing to Clay, "and you've got a sober alcoholic here. And I think both of us will tell you, again, it's when an addict *doesn't* have his drug of choice in his system that there's a big problem. And then there was absolutely no testimony about the defendant taking any tranquilizers or drinking anything before he got to his parents' apartment. The evidence indicates he only got incoherent—if he truly was— *after* he got there."

"What about the concierge?" Elena asked.

"Anybody can feign incoherence," Clay said, "particularly when it's convenient. Like when you want an alibi."

"But it seems like there ees some kind of conspiracy to get the defendant," Elena said. "I truly believe thees."

This time Will groaned, making everyone look at him. He scribbled a long note and slid it over to Libby to read. "Elena, you grew up in Brazil—you'll be seeing conspiracies for the rest of your life!"

There was laughter—from Elena, too. "Perhaps," she conceded.

"I do think they might have chosen a person of a less prominent family to conspire against, don't you?" Mrs. Smythe-Daniels said. She touched at her pearls and sighed. "I have to say, it was a brilliant summation by the defense." She paused. "He quoted Lincoln. I must admit, that influenced me. The prosecutor does not seem very well educated. I must admit, I think that influenced me, too."

Everyone was looking at her.

"I must also say," she continued, "that I didn't realize how uncomfortable I was with the responsibility of finding a man like that guilty." She looked around the table. "He does *not* remind me of my son"—a small smile—"but he does look as though he might have gone to boarding school with him."

Laughter.

"I have to say . . ." She sighed yet again, took a deep breath, and looked at Clay. "I think he's guilty."

Ronnie got up and went into the men's room. The rest of them sat there, thinking, no one looking at anyone else. Libby thought if she looked up at the broken clock on the wall one more time she would scream.

"The more I think about it," Basha said quietly, "the more I can't see any possibility that he didn't do it. Malarkey taken aside, it is a fairly straightforward case."

"I'm sure it was in the beginning," Stephen sighed.

"What's that?" Clay asked.

"I said I'm sure at the time of the shooting it was a straightforward case. They've had nineteen months to get it all fucked up." He looked up. "We all know how things work in New York."

Ronnie was standing by the partition. "You think if it had gone to trial right away, it would have made a difference?"

"Who knows?" Stephen shrugged. "We can only go on what we have here." He pushed one of the photographs of the blood-soaked sidewalk.

Interesting, Libby thought, she had grown immune to the sight now.

"We've got a spoiled-brat rich kid turned drug addict, liar, cheat, and thief," Stephen said in a depressed voice. "We've got the spoiled brat publicly humiliated and, high as a kite, storming out of the club vowing that Sissy Cook was going to die before morning. We've got an eyewitness who places the car in Jersey City, another eyewitness who places the defendant with the car and a man who fits the description of the shooter. We've got an eyewitness who said the defendant drove the shooter to Sissy Cook's murder and then drove him away. Ten minutes later the cops get a call that the Jaguar's been stolen, only the call, which the defendant said was made from his parents' apartment, wasn't, but we don't know where it was from."

"What about the bum?" Ronnie said. "What he said about the keys left in the Jaguar? Maybe someone did steal it."

"And disguised himself as the defendant and then made sure to drive past the cops so they could ID the car, and then make sure to get ID'd with the shooter and the car by someone only the defendant knew. Right," Libby said.

"You know, that's true," Basha said. "Who else in Layton's life would have known he knew those people in Jersey City?"

"Layton's twin brother, right, Ronnie?" Clay snickered.

"Come on, Clay, I already gave him a hard time," Libby murmured.

"No, it's okay," Ronnie said, coming back to sit down at the table. "Some of the stuff you said was true. But a lot of stuff I said was true, too."

"Whatever," Melissa said, yawning.

All fell quiet. "Well," Clay finally said, "I think we should take another vote and see where we are."

"Is this a real vote?" Adelaide said.

"A real vote," Clay confirmed, ripping up pieces of paper and handing them out.

"Ve are going to be here until Christmas, I know it," Debrilla sighed. "And my brother does not know how to make a proper plum pooding."

"Don't even mention food," Dayton said, folding his piece of paper and reaching for the brown paper bag to deposit it. "I'm starving."

"If we had brought a teakettle," Mrs. Smythe-Daniels said, yawning, "we could have made coffee and tea on the radiator."

The bag had made the rounds of the table and Adelaide withdrew the first piece of paper.

"Put 'Guilty' here, Adelaide, 'Not Guilty' here, and 'Undecided' here," Clay suggested, pointing to three areas in front of her.

"Guilty," Adelaide read, placing the paper in the first area.

"Guilty," she read, placing that on top of the first.

"Guilty."

Libby looked up.

"Guilty."

Clay sat up straight and looked at Adelaide.

"Guilty."

"My word," Mrs. Smythe-Daniels murmured.

"Guilty," Adelaide read from the next. Now they were all looking at Adelaide.

"Guilty," she said, dropping the paper and reaching in the bag for another.

"Guilty."

"Guilty."

"Guilty."

Basha took a loud intake of breath.

"Guilty," Adelaide read.

She reached in, took the last piece of paper out of the bag, and unfolded it. They were all staring, waiting.

"Guilty," she whispered, dropping the piece of paper on the pile.

The room was silent; they were all aghast. No one had any idea they would all vote this way, that they would all agree after all. Each had thought, okay, on this round I'll vote—I'll vote guilty and—

Libby found that Melissa was clutching her arm. She looked at her but Melissa looked away. She looked at Will. He couldn't meet her eyes, either.

Clay recounted the pieces of paper and murmured, "I think we've come to a verdict in a fair and thorough way."

Basha was crying and Mrs. Smythe-Daniels murmured something about God helping the defendant.

They were all sad. Devastated was more like it. But there was no argument, no one who wanted to contest the vote. The verdict was guilty and all twelve jurors were in agreement.

Adelaide got up and knocked on the door.

They were all scared. Libby could feel it, the fear gripping their collective body. They filed into the courtroom. It was nearly eight at night, but it was packed. Libby tried not to meet anyone's eye, most of all the eyes of the victim's sister, who was desperately scanning their faces for a sign.

Let her hear it when the defendant heard it.

They filed into the box; Mrs. Smythe-Daniels stumbled and Will caught her. They sat down. The courtroom was deadly silent. Libby could only look at the judge; she tried to keep the rest of the courtroom a blur. The judge read out the charges and asked if the jury had reached a verdict. Adelaide stood up, amazingly calm, and said in a clear, strong voice, "Yes, Your Honor, we have," and handed the guard the verdict sheet.

"And what is that verdict, Madame Foreman?"

"Guilty, Your Honor."

There was a shriek from the gallery and a cry escaped from the defendant as he grabbed Geiggen's jacket and buried his face in his lawyer's chest. Libby felt a tear fall on her right cheek. People were bolting out of the courtroom, people were talking, the judge was hammering with her gavel for the first time in the whole trial.

Dear, God, Libby prayed, please have we made the right decision.

Judge Williams asked if the verdict was unanimous, and Adelaide said it was. Geiggen then polled each member for their verdict, and each said "Guilty." The judge then thanked the jury for doing their duty and dismissed them.

Bam, it was over. They could leave.

They were all motionless in the jury box for a moment, wondering what to do next. They were numb, wasted. The defendant was sobbing, spectators were rumbling, the judge hammering again. Libby hazarded a look at the victim's sister, but couldn't find her in the crush.

Suddenly they were all filing out, hurrying out, saying nothing to one another, only wanting to get out of this place. Libby was terrified of having to talk to anyone about what had happened. *Oh, God, the press*, and she wondered how it could be that she felt both mugged and mugger, how she could feel so sordid and awful.

They were getting their things from the jury room when MacDonald came in. "Thank you, thank you," he said solemnly, but he was obviously elated, flushed with victory.

Clay snarled, "We just did our job—and just want to get the hell out of here."

"I'm here to answer any questions you may have," MacDonald said.

There was a silence, all of them frozen in position. Open your mouth, Libby thought, but she couldn't. She was too frightened. Of what she had done, of what they had done. They had destroyed a man's life. A family's life.

"Was 'air-suh-ing we 'eren't allowed to know?" Will struggled to say

"Was there something we weren't allowed to know?" Melissa translated.

The prosecutor beamed. "Damn straight there was. How about the jacket of the shooter that was found in one of the Layton apartments? With gunpowder burns on it that matched those on the victim?"

"Well, why on earth—" Mrs. Smythe-Daniels began.

"The Laytons had three corporate apartments," MacDonald said, "and the warrant the police had was for just one—the one where they arrested Layton. But when they learned from the staff that there were two other apartments, one of them vacant, right next door, they went in to look around. That's when they found the jacket."

"You mean there *vas* physical evidence that directly tied the defendant vith the shooting?" Debrilla said.

"Oh, yes," MacDonald said. "Layton had her killed, all right. But now you know why Detective Martinez had to be taken off the case. He completely messed up the search. Instead of calling for another warrant to search the second apartment, he went straight in. He had no right to take the jacket, and the judge in the preliminary hearing had no choice but to throw it out as evidence. As to the car, they had no search warrant at all, and everything but the fingerprints on the wheel was ruled inadmissable."

The jurors were looking at one another, a massive load being taken off their shoulders. Ronnie let out a loud breath of air and collapsed in a chair. "Holy shit," he said, putting his head down on the table.

Basha went over to pat Ronnie on the back. "We did the right thing, that's all that matters."

"So he did it?" Dayton asked, to be sure.

"He did it," MacDonald confirmed.

"What about the car phone?" Melissa asked. "Did anyone ever check the records on it? If any phone calls were made from it?"

MacDonald's smile broadened. "I can see we were very lucky to get such a smart jury. Yes. A call was made from the Jaguar to one of his parents' apartments, presumably to make sure no one was staying there. There wasn't; the answering machine picked up. The call was logged by the phone company at twelve forty-five A.M."

"After the car was supposedly stolen," Elena said.

"But why couldn't we know this? This is outrageous!" Mrs. Smythe-Daniels said. "Had we known he had been in the car at that time—"

"I would gladly agree with your indignation," MacDonald said. "But you must remember, our system of justice is based on the premise that the defendant is innocent until proven guilty. And after the defense team got through busting the NYPD on procedure, our open-and-shut case turned into anything but. In fact, the preliminary hearing was a nightmare. It rapidly became a case of the ever-diminishing evidence, to the point where our evidence was bordering on circumstantial." He gave a sigh of relief. "I'll tell you, if anything had happened to either one of our two eyewitnesses, if they had refused to testify, we would have been sunk."

"You can say that again," Clay said.

"Oh, thank God," Libby sighed, pulling out a chair and falling into it. She was crying now, with relief. And if she had any residual doubt about whether their verdict had been the right one, it vanished forever when Kathryn Schnagel led Jill Cook Tompkins and her husband into the jury room.

The sister just stood there, looking at them all, crying, smiling, unable to speak, but trying to express her gratitude.

It was Mrs. Smythe-Daniels who burst into tears first and ran to hug her.

40

O H, MY gosh," Libby said, staring at the photo in the newspaper. "I called my parents to tell them it was over last night, and then I unplugged my phone and went straight to bed. I got up this morning and came straight here." The next newspaper was equally interesting to her since her author photo was in that one, too.

"The 'Today' show," Will said. They were sitting with Mrs. Klein around his dining table, the nine-thirty sunshine streaming in.

Libby's eyebrows went up.

"Yes, it was on the 'Today' show news," Mrs. Klein confirmed. "And as you can see by that piece, the story's on the Associated Press wire."

Libby had to laugh. "This is unbelievable. Why should they care if I was on the jury?"

"Not many celebrities get through," Will said.

"I didn't dare tell Will that one of the papers broke the story right at the beginning of the trial that there was a famous writer on the jury," Mrs. Klein said. "I knew he wasn't supposed to talk about the trial. Anyway, your judge put a gag order on the press and there was to be no further mention of it. Until last night, obviously, when the trial was over. But when Will told me you were on the jury, Libby, I couldn't tell him that I wasn't surprised, that everyone in the country knew there was a novelist on the jury. It was just so nice that you were one I enjoyed reading!"

"I can't believe no one in my building said anything about it," Libby murmured. "Of course, I did scream at all of them not to talk to me." She stood up. "Would you mind if I used the phone?"

"Just don't stay on long, dear," Mrs. Klein said. "You two have to leave shortly."

Libby didn't stay on long. She came back to the table, dazed. "My publisher has ten thousand back orders for *When Smiles Meet* from today alone. They think one of my paperbacks might hit the list next week."

Will laughed and laughed and got up to hug her. He could do that now. And more, as she would later find out. A lot more.

"Haverhill wants me to go on tour and talk about the trial."

Will stepped back and held her at arm's length.

"I told them to go to hell," she told him. He hugged her again. "Except 'Oprah,' " she added. "I told them I'd do 'Oprah.' "

She could feel Will's back shake with laughter.

"So what are they doing?"

"Katie's putting Ken's clothes on Barbie and Petey was making people crazy with his Gameboy. I turned the sound off," Rusty reported, sitting down in the aisle seat next to Jill.

Having made their arrangements at the last moment, they hadn't been able to get four seats together, and were trying out how the kids would do on their own three rows behind them. So far, so good. Katie was always a good traveler; Peter was the one they had to keep an eye on.

"So what do you think we should do about her?" Jill asked him.

Rusty looked at her. "Why? Can't Barbie wear Ken's clothes?"

"No, silly, my mother."

"Oh. Well, I think we should go ahead and have a couple of days at Disneyland and then we'll call her and drive down and see her. We'll stay at that Sheraton in Fort Myers; it's got a great pool and tennis courts."

"It's not too expensive?"

"Not after what we've been through," Rusty assured her, taking her hand.

"Maybe we should do one of those interviews," Jill said. "The money could come in handy."

"There's no reason to think about that now, honey, just relax. Let's try and unwind a little, get our marbles back, remember who we are."

She nodded and looked out of the plane window. Then she whipped her head around. "He's going to get off, isn't he, Rusty?" she whimpered. "On the appeal?"

"Honey," he murmured, taking her hand again and squeezing it, "all I know is that James Bennett Layton, Jr., is behind bars on Rikers Island today. For the first time ever, the guy is exactly where he belongs."

She nodded, wishing she could calm down, that the surges of panic would go away. She had barely slept last night. Every time she nodded off, she had nightmares about Sissy and about how Layton had got off and was going to kill the children.

"I promise you, darling," Rusty whispered, "it will get better now. It's over. Now you just need time."

She nodded. And then she looked at him. "I told you how nice the jurors were, didn't I?"

He nodded.

Then she laughed to herself. "I'm losing my mind—you were there, for heaven's sake!" This time she squeezed his hand and gave it a little shake. She brought it up to kiss it and then lowered their hands to settle together on the armrest between them. "Yes, darling, you were there. Nothing else matters. Except that I love you."

"Excuse me," the flight attendant said, "sir? I'm sorry, but somehow your little boy pried open his compartment so that the oxygen mask came down, and I was wondering if you might—"

"Trade places with our daughter and keep an eye on him," Jill finished for her, laughing. "Of course." She kissed Rusty on the cheek. "Bye, darling. Send me Barbie the cross-dresser."

The reporter on the telephone was offering Melissa five thousand dollars for her version of what had gone on in the jury room.

"I got an offer three times that already," she told him. "How do you know who I am, anyway?"

"We have our ways."

"Well, I have mine—and you better watch your back!" Melissa slammed down the office phone. One good thing about sitting on a murder trial was that one learned how to get tough and talk out of the side of one's mouth. "Bonnie!"

"Yes?" her secretary asked timidly.

"If any normal people call or stop by, I'd love to chat, but if anyone even smells of wanting to ask me about the trial—boss included—I am not here. Understood?"

"Yes."

"And warn Roger or anyone else that if they try to talk to me about it, they're history. Monday they can ask me, but not today. Understood?"

"Yes."

"I *promise* I won't ask about the trial," a familiar voice said. Christine stepped out from behind Bonnie.

Melissa was thrilled to see her. "Hi. Come in."

"Would you like some coffee, Mrs. Harrington?" Bonnie asked her.

"No—no, thank you. I'm not staying, Melissa, I just stopped in because we're in the city today—at J. Walter Thompson, I'm afraid."

"I can't believe you have your cereals over there," Melissa teased, sitting down behind her desk, "and all we get is cat food."

Christine closed the door and came back to stand in front of Melissa's desk. "Since the trial's over . . ." She took something out of her pocket. An envelope. That said American Airlines on it. "I was hoping I could talk you into stopping by your apartment and picking up a suitcase and—well, going to the airport with me."

Melissa could only look at her.

"The boys are at my sister's for the weekend. These"—she gestured with the tickets—"are for the Bahamas. As soon as I heard the trial was over, I went over to the airport satellite office and got them." She smiled. "That means they're fifteen minutes old and we have two hours to get to the airport." Her eyebrows went up. "I'll have you back Sunday night." She didn't look very confident. "Was this a terrible idea?"

Melissa stood up. "It's the best idea I've ever heard of in my life. Let's get out of here!"

Detective Gregory was a tall, attractive black man, a bit tired-looking, but still very enthusiastic. After shaking hands and getting an extra chair so that Libby and Will could both sit by his desk, he explained that they would be taking official statements from each of them about their involvement with Alex McCalley. He would be taking Will's, a female officer would be taking Libby's. The evidence spoke for itself, but they wanted a file on the sequence of events that had led up to Alexander McCalley's arrest.

"Arrest?" Libby said. "For what? I haven't even filed a complaint yet."

Detective Gregory looked at the papers on his desk. "Let's see, we've got him on burglary—"

"Burglary!" Libby and Will both cried, looking at each other in confusion.

"Assault with a deadly weapon, assault with the attempt to rob, assault of a police officer, and resisting arrest—and that's just for starters." The detective squinted at them. "How much do you know about what's gone on the last couple of days?"

"Nothing!" Libby cried. "We've been sequestered on a murder trial from Wednesday until last night."

"Oh, well, then you're in for a few surprises." He chuckled. "Certainly we were." He sat back in his chair, smiling. "Mr. Klein," he said, "we haven't found your wallet yet, but we did find your blood on the blackjack used to beat you last Friday. It was in a toolbox belonging to Alexander McCalley. We found it at his girlfriend's apartment."

"Girlfriend?" Libby said.

Detective Gregory looked at her. "We've also found a slip of paper with your name and address and unlisted phone number, Ms. Winslow."

"I never gave him my number."

"Did you give it to Mr. Klein, perhaps?"

"You did," Will said. He turned to the detective. "It was in my wallet."

"We also have a pile of used cylinder locks, and we're pretty confident two of them will be found to have come from your apartment door, Mr. Klein."

"Wait, slow down, I'm confused," Libby pleaded.

And so Detective Gregory got them both a cup of coffee—and a straw for Will ("You see a lot of people come through here with a busted mouth," the detective explained, "that's why we've always got them")—and told them the story as the police had pieced it together thus far. Acting on the information they received from courthouse officials about McCalley, in combination with a chat Gregory had with Nick Albanese, the former NYPD detective who was Libby's security man in her building, Detective Gregory and another officer had gone to the address they had on McCalley to ask him a few questions.

They had buzzed the door of the brownstone, a woman answered, and they identified themselves. She said she was just out of the shower, could they wait a minute? Gregory sent his sergeant around to the back of the buildings, where he saw a man climbing over the brick wall that fenced in the little yard. The sergeant yelled for Gregory and gave chase and caught the man in another yard. The runner shoved him backward into a bird bath, though, dislocating the sergeant's shoulder, but by that time Gregory had a gun on the suspect, who finally submitted to arrest. It was Alexander McCalley.

They obtained a search warrant and hit the brownstone near midnight. They found all the tools every good burglar owns, some of which were illegal to possess unless you were a licensed locksmith. They also found the blackjack.

"He wasn't the one Betsy and her parents found at my apartment, was he?" Will asked. "On Thanksgiving?"

"Your friend Betsy Pratt's already picked him out of a lineup," the detective said.

Libby and Will stared at each other in awe. "He knew you'd be away on Thanksgiving," Libby murmured. "Remember? How we all said where we were going?"

"We think this guy is responsible for about seven burglaries we know of," Gregory continued. "With the exception of your place, Mr. Klein, they were all places where at some time he had worked construction."

"He owned a renovation company," Libby said.

Gregory shook his head. "That was only wishful thinking on his part. McCalley was a part-time handyman on nonunion construction crews—smaller jobs, you know."

"What about his brownstone?" Libby asked. "He told me he owned a half-interest in the brownstone."

"He doesn't even have an apartment," the detective said. "His girl-friend rented an apartment and he lived with her."

"And the cabin he said he owned?"

"That exists," Gregory confirmed, nodding. "Upstate. And that's where we've found all kinds of silver and watches and jewelry. Small stuff. Small, very pricey stuff. Presumably he'd stored it up there awhile before trying to get rid of it."

"This is just unbelievable," Libby said, shaking her head.

"What's McCalley have to say about any of this?" Will asked.

"The only thing he'll admit to is jumping you on Friday night. He said he did it because he was temporarily insane with jealousy." He looked at Libby. "He claims he was your lover, Ms. Winslow, and that you suddenly ditched him because Mr. Klein was rich."

"*Lover?*" Libby shrieked, making other heads in the precinct turn.

"He's very insistent on that point, I'm afraid," Gregory said, "that he was sleeping with you."

"That is absolutely untrue and completely outrageous!" Libby cried, furious.

"Hold on, hold on," Gregory ordered, holding up his hand.

"I'll press so many charges against this guy," Libby vowed, "he's going to still be reading them from Alcatraz when he's ninety years old!"

She glanced over at Will. He was laughing, and trying not to, and was hurting at the effort of both.

"Oh, be quiet," Libby told him, starting to smile. "It's not funny."

"That's not what I was thinking about," Will swore. "I was thinking about court."

"Court? Oh my God! I didn't even think of that," Libby said, turning to the detective. "We're not going to have to go to court over this, are we?"

"They're criminal charges," Will said, laughing. "We'll be right back at one hundred Centre Street."

Libby looked at the detective in abject horror. "No."

The detective was trying very hard to look sympathetic. "Well, look at

it this way, Ms. Winslow, after what's happened to you, it's highly unlikely you'll ever get chosen to serve on a jury again."

"Not to be disrespectful, Detective Gregory," Libby said, "but it was
supposed to have been next to impossible the last time."

V
JUSTICE

41

NOT TO hurt your feelings, Libby dear," Mrs. Smythe-Daniels said as she stood behind her, fussing with her veil, "but your mother is a first-class bitch."

"I tried to warn you," Libby said apologetically. Looking at herself in the mirror, fourteen months after the trial, it was hard to believe she wasn't more nervous. But how could she be? This was about the only thing in her life she had known for sure was right.

"What do you suppose she meant," Mrs. Smythe-Daniels continued, "who the hell did I think I was? What were you supposed to do? Have her arrange everything by mail from Ohio?"

"Oh, Eleanor," Libby said, reaching up to take her hand, "you do know how eternally grateful I am to you for helping me, don't you?"

"Yes, of course I do, dear."

Libby released her hand and reached up to straighten her veil, which Mrs. Smythe-Daniels had given a sharp yank to the side on the word *hell.* Then she stood up from the vanity table and moved to stand in front of the full-length mirror, into which she smiled at the older woman. "She loved the dress, though."

"What's not to like? Good heavens, this is as traditional and beautiful as it gets."

True. All white silk, embroidered top, flowing skirt, long veil, a four-foot train, a bouquet of spring flowers and nosegay. And they had found a pair of matching silk shoes that were not only comfortable but still gave Will a half-inch over her.

"She got her Presbyterian church, and the Union Club is perfect for the reception," Mrs. Smythe-Daniels continued, standing back to survey Libby.

There was a knock on the door and then the door burst open, startling them both.

"Good God!" Mrs. Smythe-Daniels said, clutching at the pearls on her chest.

"We came to weesh you luck!" Elena whispered, giggling, leading the way in from the vestry.

"You can't do this!" Mrs. Smythe-Daniels sputtered as the small crowd of people piled in. "It's bad luck!"

"Vhen you get married, der is no law dat you can't see a jury," Debrilla said, pushing past Mrs. Smythe-Daniels to look at Libby. She clutched her hands. "Bootiful, Libby, bootiful!"

Libby could only laugh, hoping she wouldn't ruin her makeup.

"Yo, babe," Dayton said, coming in all dressed up, "lookin' hot!"

"Don't touch her!" Mrs. Smythe-Daniels scolded, grabbing him. "You can kiss her afterward."

"Hi, Libby!" Adelaide called, standing obediently in the corner, waving. She was dressed in a long black dress with different-colored crayons all over it, and had matching green and purple crayons dangling from her ears.

"Shhh!" Mrs. Smythe-Daniels said. "They'll hear you in the church!"

"Nahw," Dayton said, "somebody's singin' 'Ava Maria' or something. They can't hear anything."

True. The music and voice of the soloist coming from the church was pretty loud.

"Oh, Libby, you look just darling," Basha told her, squeezing in past Mrs. Smythe-Daniels.

"Very sopheesteecated," Elena added, nodding in approval.

"Gorgeous," Clay said from the doorway. (Out in the vestry, Libby could see her cousin Freddie and his wife from Shaker Heights staring in at the scene.) "Libby, this is my wife, Alice," Clay added, bringing forward a pretty black woman by the hand.

"Hi, Libby!" Ronnie called from behind Clay, waving. She almost didn't recognize him. His hair wasn't slicked back anymore; it was fluffy and blond.

Another hand was waving from just outside the door and Libby strained to see who it was. "Stephen! Hi!"

She was touched to see him here. The last time she had seen Stephen was with Melissa and Will, at the memorial service for his lover.

"Oh, this is absolutely ridiculous!" Mrs. Smythe-Daniels finally declared. "You can all see her after the wedding."

"Yo, Ellie, sorry, but the Union Club's not exactly my scene, if you get my drift," Dayton said. "Besides," he added in a whisper, sidling next to her, "your old man's here, isn't he? What fun can we have with him around?"

"Oh, Dayton!" Mrs. Smythe-Daniels scolded, smiling, objecting not at all as he slid his arm around her waist and gave her a big kiss on the cheek.

The music in the church changed. Libby knew that the moment was approaching.

Someone was pushing through the crowd to get in, inspiring some ooh's and ahhh's along the way. It turned out to be Melissa, Libby's maid of honor, looking smashing in the long, silk, pale yellow dress. Dayton whistled.

"You guys," Melissa urged in a whisper, "come on! Out! It's almost time!" And she started shooing people out with her bouquet.

"Ellie, ya gotta promise us," Dayton said as he was hustled out, "we'll have a party for Libby and Will when they get back. So we can really celebrate."

"At that restaurant where we went when we were sequestered!" Ronnie suggested.

"Oh, God!" Mrs. Smythe-Daniels said.

"Goot luck!" Debrilla called.

"Break a leg, babee!" Elena whispered, blowing a kiss.

"Lib?" a voice said from the door. It was her dad. "Corny Girl, we're on soon."

"Dad, this is the jury!" she told him as they shuffled out past him, murmuring hellos.

Another face appeared at the door. Christine Harrington's. "Hate to break up the party . . ." she began.

"They're going," Melissa assured her, shooing Adelaide along, who was admiring herself in the mirror.

"We'll get them seated," Christine promised Mrs. Smythe-Daniels before disappearing. Melissa went out, too.

Now it was just Mrs. Smythe-Daniels and her father left in the room. "Good luck, dear," Mrs. Smythe-Daniels said, stepping forward to give Libby's hand a squeeze. "You look so very beautiful."

Libby mumbled some kind of thanks to her. The door closed and Libby looked to her father, who was standing there with tears in his eyes. "This may be the happiest moment I've had since the day you were born, Corny Girl."

"Daddy, if you start crying . . ." Libby began, blinking rapidly.

"No, baby," he murmured, holding his hand out. "It's your mother who's crying. She's very proud of you, you know."

"Yeah, right, Dad," Libby laughed, moving to the door. She took a deep breath and let it out slowly. Then she nodded and her father opened the door.

In the vestry, Christine was lining up the wedding party for final inspection. The nieces were adorable as flower girls (Christine stopped to fuss over one of them, making her spit out a piece of chewing gum into a tissue); the bridesmaids, Will's sister and Libby's sisters-in-law, looked lovely; and the ushers, her brothers Ted and Jimbo, and Will's cousin, looked very dapper. Melissa, last in line, was joined by Christine to look Libby over and assure her she was perfect.

The church organ opened with the call of the "Wedding March," bringing people to their feet inside. Christine moved over to stand just outside the door, holding each member of the procession until it was his or her time to start down the aisle. They all did amazingly well. And then Libby felt her father gently tug on her arm, signaling that it was time, and slowly they advanced into the church and down the aisle.

Her smile for everyone was genuine, for she was genuinely happy. Soon this would be over and she and Will would be left in peace. Oh, yes, there was still the appeal of James Bennett Layton, Jr., coming up in the fall, and heaven only knew what she and Will would do if Alex McCalley ever got out of jail, but for the moment, the only ordeal left was this one, doing their duty to their families and friends. And then, thank God, it would be just them.

Her smile expanded.

Will.

She could see him waiting for her.

Acknowledgments

My love and eternal thanks to my sister Susan Ault, and my brother, Bob Ault, and the rest of my family, for their unfailing support, now and always.

I am indebted to my gifted editors, Betty A. Prashker of Crown and Dianne Moggy of Mira, and my agent, Loretta Barrett; and owe grateful thanks to Gary Morris, F. Amoy Allen, Amy Moore, and Cressida Connolly.

I also wish to thank Annabel Davis-Goff and Seymour Wishman for their advice and expertise, and Tom Zito, James Spada, Ann Douglas, and Chris Robinson for being the extraordinary people they are.

And, finally, to the guiding inspiration behind this novel, Carolyn Katz, thank you for pushing me on to a whole new wonderful frontier.

About the Author

Laura Van Wormer grew up in Darien, Connecticut, and graduated from the S.I. Newhouse School of Public Communications at Syracuse University. Prior to becoming a novelist, she was an editor at a major publishing house.

Laura was writing her fifth novel when she was summoned to jury duty, where she ultimately found herself sequestered as a juror on a murder trial. *Jury Duty* thus became her fifth novel.

She lives in Manhattan and Quiogue, Long Island.